DOC SPEARS **JASON ANSPACH** **NICK COLE**

NO FAIL

DARK OPERATOR **BOOK 3**

GALAXY'S EDGE

Edited by Lauren Moore
Published by Galaxy's Edge Press

Cover Art: Tommaso Renieri
Cover Design and Formatting: Kevin G. Summers

Website: www.GalaxysEdge.us
Facebook: facebook.com/atgalaxysedge
Newsletter (get a free short story): www.InTheLegion.com

EXPLORE ALL PRODUCTS AT

GALAXYSEDGE.US

Failure is a hateful word to a legionnaire. For Dark Ops Sergeant Kel Turner, it's unthinkable. Until now. Kill teams are accustomed to achieving the impossible, and Kill Team Three has done the impossible more than any other. Tasked with mission after mission, against a never-ending list of enemies, Kel and Three brace themselves to rise to the occasion yet again.

Kel lived under no doubts about his kill team's ability to win against any odds, until an enemy thought long defeated reappears. From a dingy city locked in the center of a cold war to a nightmarish alien landscape, the one constant that defines their latest missions is that a kill team is always alone.

Living in the black world of covert operations, there are secrets, then there are *secrets*. The first might lead to his death. The second might lead to failure.

For this Dark Operator, in a galaxy filled with potentials, death is preferable to failure.

PART ONE

THE DIVIDED CITY

01

Breaking expensive things and killing bad guys, Kel mused as his men scouted the target site. *That's what it always comes down to when it's time to teach people the error of their ways.* Then, to his unseen enemies, he thought, *Now you're going to learn why you don't want the Legion after you.*

Through the trees, he spotted a maglev track. They'd have to get closer to be sure, but for now Kel saw nothing to make him change his plan. *No hint of a patrol. Not even a roving guard.* An even layer of clouds obscured the moonlight. There was a good chance of rain in the forecast. The darkness sharpened his hunter's instinct, filled him with electric anticipation. It was exactly the kind of weather he would have ordered if Cassell had a planetary weather grid.

He'd chosen the small depression above the slope as their objective rally point, and left the body of the force to take two of the Gs with him for his leader's recon. The ten members of his guerilla force left behind at the ORP would be anxious. It caused him some anxiety, too, depending on them to remain quiet and disciplined when they were amateurs. College kids. Little more than boys. Soon they'd find out for themselves if there was a warrior somewhere deep within.

The hills offered excellent concealment. The heavy woods thinned out at the bottom of the slope, and that caused Kel some trepidation. *When it comes time to move to the target in force*, he thought, *that last push to the objective could be a bloodbath if there's anyone waiting.* It was a lot of open ground.

This was the first real operation that they'd undertaken with their guerillas. Some of the targets—like the maglev track—were low risk. Others would have been best for his kill team to take alone. It wasn't to be. If they were going to disrupt as much of the infrastructure of Mercia as they could, this was how it had to be done.

Under less urgent circumstances, the maglev line was a perfect example of a confidence target. Low risk, high yield. The planet had a mix of energy sources and a large amount of their electrical energy was produced by burning anthracite. The dark, energy-rich stuff was transported by rail across the country to the power generating facilities that supplied the electrical grid of North and South Mercia. It was primitive, effective, and easily disrupted.

While not as vital as some of the other targets being hit tonight, it would still help create havoc for the invaders. At the core of his being, Kel lived for such opportunities. He laughed to himself. *If I was doing this in any other context, I'd be a criminal. Lucky for me, there's a Legion.*

The maglev track stretched for hundreds of miles. No security force could protect it all from sabotage, no matter how well prepared. It was impossible. After tonight, the Crudes would have to divert a large portion of their forces to guarding such targets. By then, it would be too late. After tonight, their pace of operations would only increase. By dawn, the city would be brought to a standstill.

It didn't pay to annoy the House of Reason. Above all, it didn't pay to annoy them to the point where they turned loose Dark Ops.

The Crudes were about to learn.

Kel froze. He saw movement ahead—a lone biped on the tracks. Even with his bucket's augmented night vision, it was difficult to tell what the human presence represented. His bucket layered more thermal to the image to compensate for the lack of infrared detail, but did nothing to improve the resolution. His carbine's optic was far more powerful. He brought up his K-17, then signaled to the two kids with him to hold up. They froze and remained silent. *Good boys.*

Five hundred meters away, walking along the track above the trestle, was a slowly moving figure. Kel could have illuminated the area with his shortwave infrared light to clarify the image, but there was a strong chance he'd be detected by anyone with a similar night vision capability. In that event, it would look like a white flood light and betray their presence like an igniting plasma flare. While the invaders didn't have peer-grade tech, they did have good tech. Good enough, anyway.

Watching the figure, Kel considered options. *Kill him. Don't kill him. Kill him later.* He chose to continue watching the figure as it crossed the trestle and moved out of sight, obscured by the trees. He hadn't identified a weapon on the dark outline. Was the figure part of a roving patrol? Was it some derelict, wandering in the night? A refugee, trying to escape the city? Rail lines were like roads in that they offered an easy walking path, especially in this rough and hilly terrain. The figure could simply be one of the unfortunate Mercians, trying to flee the madness that accompanied the brutal invasion.

Tens of thousands had fled the city when the Crudes made good on their threat and finally invaded.

Kel extended his arm toward the target, pointing with his index finger and thumb rotated like an upside-down pistol, as he nudged the G to his right. The kid brought up his specs and scanned the target site. After a moment, he nodded to Kel and shrugged as if to say, "What do you think?"

Kel held up his palm to indicate "Take no action." Kel could waste the guy if he reappeared. Whoever he was. The issue wasn't capability. The K-17 was a line of sight weapon. There was no range uncertainty. Braced against a tree to reduce his wobble zone, Kel could get a standing shot and burn the man down as he strolled down the track bed. The issue was an ethical one. He was not going to take the chance and murder some unfortunate refugee. There would be ample opportunity to discriminate soon enough if the man was a legitimate military target. He was confident that if there were guards on the maglev line that they would be able to overwhelm them as they rolled onto the objective.

Meanwhile the kids Kel had with him were inexperienced. Minimally trained before Kel's team arrived. No doubt they fancied themselves as badass urban fighters. They weren't. But at least they were realists. They'd all experienced the suffering the Crudes brought to their city. In Kel's opinion they were motivated by the best driving force of them all: they had hearts full of hate. They wanted to see the invaders not only repelled, but made to suffer in turn.

Kel loved working with such raw material. He could mold their venom into dreadful art. Tonight, he would deliver on the promise their kill team made to them.

We will teach you how to get your bloody revenge.

Rail lines of any sort were a good target. Difficult to defend, easy to destroy. Kel had chosen this part of the maglev line for many reasons. First, this section was curved, making it harder to repair or replace. Second, the curve limited visibility up and down the track. Anyone setting plasma charges on a straight track could be observed for an incredible distance in either direction. Any break in noise or light discipline would result in compromise. Thermal or infrared technology, not to mention quantum detection, could easily reveal their presence. Third, this spot was excellent because it combined two critical features. The curve around the bend was supported by a trestle.

The track was cut into a bluff where the curve hugged a craggy hill. The track needed support from below where it passed over a long run of loose shale. A tunnel would have made more sense on this part of the escarpment rather than building above a rocky slide. He was glad they hadn't. Blowing up a trestle would make for a much more spectacular disaster.

A few well-placed charges could bring the trestle down along with the rocky bluff. It would take every resource available to rebuild this portion of the track. If the Crudes used military engineers to do it, they in turn would also be a viable target and could be harassed by precision sniper fire at will. Kel had already picked out several sites for hides where he could conduct just such a mission. That would delay the rebuilding of the maglev track and tie up a brigade of Crude troops for months.

He was looking forward to it.

It was as good a site for sabotage as Kel could conceive. A critical, vulnerable site—therefore, good for some

7

form of defense. If the Crudes had their act together. Finding no sign of life, he made his decision. He nudged the Gs on either side of him. They would stay put with eyes on the target. He would bring the rest of the force back. Then, they would unleash hell.

As he moved silently back up the slope, he thought about the Gs in his patrol. Kel's guerillas had a crucial role, but because the maglev destruction was lower risk, they had purposely assigned the weaker of the group to his mission. Kel disliked himself for doubting the abilities of his patrol, but it was his honest assessment as the leader. *No matter*, he vowed. *The rest of Team Three and their Gs aren't going to fail tonight, and neither are we.*

If the Crudes thought that their surprise invasion across the wall into North Mercia would remain uncontested, they would soon know differently. After several decades of peace in the divided city—an oasis of freedom in the likewise divided Andalusian republic—the Kroedellian Union made their play to finally consolidate their holdings through their puppets in South Mercia. North Mercia had been a thumb in the Crudes' eye for decades, a free city in the middle of their workers' paradise. A paradise where you were free to labor or be legally starved to death for failure to relegate one's self to the will of the state.

The war for North Mercia was over before it began. Multiple generations' worth of policies, whose aim was to placate the aggressive Crudes in belief that their expansiveness would be contained by diplomacy, failed for the final time. No one came to the aid of North Mercia as it fell under the control of the totalitarian hordes that swept across the grimy, quaint, but vibrant city.

The team had conducted some targeting by drone, some by satellite, and much by direct surveillance. They formed an excellent picture of the critical infrastructure even before their infiltration into the city. It was difficult to disguise the physical plants and structures that provided life to the metropolis. It was as true here as it was anywhere in the galaxy. Power, water, transportation, storage facilities, centers of commerce—where there were humans trying to live in large numbers, the telltales of their civilization's infrastructure were always evident.

The plan was to deny any of the necessities of life to the invaders. Spoil their cowardly victory. By the time the sun rose the next morning, the inhabitants of North Mercia, along with their unwanted guests, would be cut off from power and water. Thousands had already abandoned the city. There had always been the potential for invasion, and it had seemed at hand many times in their past. It was miraculous that so many had escaped out of the city by maglev and repulsor sled at the first sign of the invasion. Those who chose to live in North Mercia lived with that very possibility every day, growing up with the knowledge that to survive they may have to someday abandon their city, long lusted after by the statist empire to their south.

North Andalusia was prepared to accept the refugees, but not to repel the invasion. Other nations on Planet Cassell protested, but their noise did nothing to frighten the Crudes off their conquest. North Mercia was a jewel to be stolen, a pearl to be hoarded. Now that they had it, the Crudes would not give it up without a fight. And if it came to a fight, the Crudes would be sure to destroy the city before they left. It was their pattern of behavior. Occupy by force, mutilate the institutions and culture, then rule.

So, the team's mission parameters had been simple. Make it costly for the Crudes. Make them uncomfortable. Make them pay for their aggression with blood.

The House of Reason would work to encourage a resolution by the Cassellians, but if one did not seem at hand, then perhaps the diplomatic intimation that the Republic would take the lead would be necessary. Right now, Kel wasn't interested in how the pols would flex their feeble muscles. First, Kill Team Three would kick off the action. They were divided to tackle as many strategic targets as possible.

Kel would destroy the main maglev line that allowed all anthracite to feed the two electrical power plants that supplied the metropolis.

Braley and his force were destroying the electrical grid more directly by demolishing key power substations and downing main lines that led into the city and even south across the wall into Kroedellian-held South Mercia. The paradise that was the Kroedellian Union barely produced enough power to allow their own cities to function. They had to purchase power from the enemy North. It was an insult the Crudes thought to avenge by their invasion. The whole team savored the idea that their sabotage would deny the Crudes the basic commodity they thought to acquire by theft.

Poul was leading his group to destroy the water reservoir and purification plant. It was the most dangerous of the missions. The reservoir and adjacent water treatment plant were guarded installations close to the city with many high-speed avenues of approach. If a quick reaction force responded, Poul and his crew could have a real fight on their hands.

Bigg was to have one of the most enjoyable of the night's sabotage tasks. The famous Azure River Bridge was a landmark distinguished by its beauty and architectural uniqueness. The multi-tiered bridge carried light-vehicle and maglev traffic across the river that ran through the center of the metropolis of North Mercia. It used long-span construction and repulsor-reinforced tech to give the effect the bridge virtually floated above the mineral blue waters of the river below. They had seen holos of the bridge in their target brief back on Victrix, and documentaries they'd all seen about Andalusia. It was a beautiful bridge unlike any other.

And if North Mercia regained its freedom... it could be rebuilt.

Sims's job was by no means easy but involved minimal danger. He and two guerillas would be entering the communications node facility and not only rendering it inoperable, but introducing an intrusive parasite into the network that would corrupt the entirety of the Kroedellian Union information net. The worm was designed by Republic intelligence. Sims spent a week locked in the Quantum Stasis Zone facility within the Intel Cell, being trained by RI techies on how to employ the weapon.

The QSZ was an intimidating place. No electromagnetic wave or particle could enter or escape the room. The secure space could be used for briefings, but was best used to guarantee the containment of any form of electromagnetic radiation or even biologically coded information. An individual's bio-signature had to be recognized by the containment field or discorporation of the entity occurred, be it just a tiny splotch of biomaterial or an entire person. Kel had been in the room himself. He found entering and leaving the QSZ to be an anxiety inducing event. You could be separated into isolated amino acids simply because the security system experienced a glitch. If the requirement was for the absolute containment of classified information, be it on a datalink, quantum chip, or encoded by proteins into a sequence, the QSZ was the only place where it could be guaranteed.

Even so, he preferred not to be in the place. Each day when Sims returned to the team room, he'd commented on how impressed he was with the parasite program. "I didn't know RI had a capability this awesome. It kinda restores my faith in the Republic," he joked. If it truly wiped out the Crudes' ability to communicate or access information, Kel would share Sims's enthusiasm for the Republic intelligence service. To date, his experiences with them had left him indifferent.

The complete surveillance state that the Crudes believed in meant that other than their L-comm, there was no way to have secure communication between the separate G-bands and even between the operators and their own G-patrols. Once the parasite began its disruption of the enemy network, the Crudes' ability to suppress and trace any comms should disappear, as well as their ability to communicate with each other.

Reaching the ORP and his Gs' tight perimeter, Kel took a knee and popped his lid off. He now made his way around the perimeter, crawling next to each man, whispering the information he'd gained on his recon and reviewing the plan forward.

"There's movement on the tracks. At least one individual. Can't tell who it is. We're going to move single file, just as we practiced. I'll lead. If I need to fire, no one else is to shoot unless I say to. If there is more than just a lone

Crude, I'll put us into a skirmish line and we'll assault through and onto the tracks. Mind the release point."

He repeated the same to each man, and gave extra instructions to members of the patrol with subordinate tasks. Before he buttoned back up, he paused to speak to his assistant patrol leader, Pieter, an older kid in his early twenties, whose studies at the polytechnic university had been interrupted by the Crude invasion. Pieter demonstrated an eagerness to lead. Tonight was a good chance for Kel to assess his abilities and determine whether he would be moving forward in that role. So far, he had not been impressed.

Working with irregular forces like the urban guerillas meant that a certain amount of informality was necessary. They were not a military unit. They were civilians who had stepped up to resist the impending invasion of their home. There were a lot of personalities involved, along with family connections and friendships that defined who was trusted to be a member of the resistance. Pieter had the trust of the G commander. Therefore, Kel couldn't choose someone else until he had cause to do so.

"Pieter, bring up the rear and make sure we have a good head count. When we peel out of here, everyone must pass back through the release point so we have another good count. We won't have time to play find the lost lamb," Kel explained. Most importantly, they couldn't leave someone behind to get captured.

They'd practiced the patrol and actions on the objective as best they could in the countryside and in the abandoned subterranean levels of the city's public works. They'd only been on the ground a month before the Crudes finally acted on their threat and invaded. They'd had a few weeks to gain the trust of the G chief and his budding resistance force and start training them before they no longer had any freedom of movement.

Post-invasion, it was too late to practice patrols overland. Their environment was entirely hostile now. No more practices. If only the team had been in Mercia sooner, months before the full invasion, they could have trained the G force properly. Instead, they'd done the best they could. He hoped it would be enough.

"Yes, Kel. Can do." It was the least number of words the kid had ever spoken to Kel. Normally full of brash bravado, Pieter was demonstrating that he had some sense of the situation. In training, Pieter had always had a retort to any of Kel's recommendations or suggestions, always answering like a petulant adolescent with, "I know." Now he was hyper-alert and shrunken in his movements, crouched over with shoulders sloped. Pieter was not alone. While it was a common human response to danger, it was a physically exhausting way to move, especially when many kilometers needed to be covered. In their short time together, Kel had tried to convince them otherwise, but to the Gs, walking bent over was somehow "stealthy."

Kel had surveyed his force early for experience in the woods or hunting. Zero. Not one hand raised to admit to even the smallest amount of experience outside their duracrete world.

You go to war with the army you have, not the army you wish you had, he thought, not for the first time in his Legion career.

"If we need to assault the track, it's going to be chaotic. Don't let it be. Just concentrate on your job and get your demo team working quickly. I'll take care of everything else. If we do have resistance waiting on the objective, push everyone on line before you start shooting. People lose their heads in their first fight. Literally. Get everyone doing their work. Killing. Do that, and we'll be fine."

Pieter nodded vigorously. Kel put his bucket back on. They had drilled every contingency and practiced every part of the movement. The Gs had so far proven that they understood the basic concepts of a stealthy patrol and were putting into practice what he'd taught them. If they got through tonight, their confidence and abilities would rise dramatically. They'd need the boost. Because the Crudes were sure to respond.

Everyone was on their feet, pack slung, weapon in both hands. Kel started downhill slowly, carefully testing each foot on the ground before shifting all his weight on to it. They had maybe a few hundred meters to descend to reach the end of the forested cover.

His bucket magnified every tread and to Kel, they sounded like a herd of rindar. He fought the bubbling feeling of dread, focusing his attention ahead rather than on the noise behind him. Soon he spotted the hot images of the two men he'd left to observe their target. They each gave him a thumbs up.

Down the slope they went. An open area lay before the short rise to the plateau of the maglev track. They'd come out exactly where Kel intended, concealed from observation in either direction by the rock bluff. The trestle would be just around the curve to their right. It was the perfect spot from which to ascend to their target.

He set the two men facing opposite directions, looking both ways up and down the track. Their release point would remain to provide security until their task was completed. He'd known generally how he wanted to make the final move onto the objective and now that he had eyes on the terrain, one good option stood above the others. He led the patrol up to the human gate he'd created and gestured to the next two men.

He pointed at each of the two men and then pointed down the tracks to their left. They knew from rehearsal that their job would be to ascend the tracks, then make their way forward to where they could put eyes past the curvature, ready to alert the main body of any approaching threat. They'd all been instructed that their movements had to be slow and purposeful. Once on the track bed, they'd crawl past the curve to get eyes ahead. If they did as he taught them, they could probably evade even remote sensing from any distance the Crudes might have technological eyes on them.

The two men nodded. Kel was about to tap them on the back and send them out when he heard it. Footsteps on loose rock, coming from above. It was almost deafening in his bucket, and Kel knew it could only be the same unknown figure walking the rail bed. Kel didn't hesitate. He brought his K-17 up as he turned, registered the outline of the walking man, and fired. A silent, low-powered discharge from his carbine issued forth when his dot settled on the figure's chest. Even at reduced power to maintain silence, the particle beam drilled through the man at the fifty-meter distance. What followed was a brief report, the sharp collision of the body and the shot rock bordering the edge of the track.

Kel held his left fist up, hoping that the patrol would be able to see it. He heard a voice behind him say, "What was that?" He held his rebuke for breaking noise discipline, hoping there wouldn't be another violator.

He waited and watched. No one else appeared.

He tapped the two men kneeling beside him, sending them up the slope.

He watched them disappear, and waited.

Nothing.

He led the rest of the patrol up the embankment and onto the tracks. He motioned the G behind him to get on line. It was a natural human response to want to follow behind someone during a time of potential danger, especially in the dark. Natural, but flawed. It was a response whose basis was fear. Whenever feasible, it was vital to have as many guns possible forward in the fight. To his credit, though he had faltered at first, the man fell in next to Kel and stayed with him as they moved along the rail bed toward the trestle.

This is the hardest classroom in the universe, he thought. It took time to build the confidence and innate aggressiveness necessary to be an effective warrior. *Time we don't have.*

They moved in a column of twos, Kel focused to see as far ahead as his bucket allowed. He'd been watching the spot where he'd dropped the Crude, anticipating that the man might resurrect. It was unlikely that the blast from his K-17 had failed to turn the man's heart and great vessels into pulp, but that didn't mean the man was necessarily dead. Yet. Kel had seen men reanimate after being fatally shot. After lying on the ground, a well-shot man's blood pressure often rose as an autotransfusion from the legs brought back consciousness, allowing a brief period of combativeness to recommence.

Years ago, he'd learned, *it's the dead ones that'll kill you.* He didn't remember who'd first taught him that aphorism, but it came into his head whenever he shot someone. As he got closer to the body he was certain the man was dead, and more so, felt relief. Now he knew he was right to have killed him. It was a Crude sentry. The long, calf-length coat that had concealed his outline was Crude standard issue. His rifle lay between his legs, and a large hole punctured his chest. DRT. *Dead Right There.* This one wasn't coming back.

Knowing there was a sentry meant that there would be more, if not already on site, then moving this way soon. At any moment, a grav sled full of troops could appear around the bend, ready to drop off the dead man's relief.

"Drag him over there," Kel said, pointing to a small depression in the cliff. He snagged a nano-inquisitor drone and tossed it overhand straight up. A drone feed window popped open in his bucket, and the small disc disappeared into the night.

"Let's move," he whispered.

They reached the sharpest part of the curve, the trestle now visible just beyond. Halting the column he slid himself slowly right. He trusted the drone but knew that barreling into the danger area was unwise. He cast his vision far. Nothing moved. Nothing was hot on thermal. Only cold maglev track and the trestle underneath.

"Pieter," he said to the assistant patrol leader. "Get your team up. Go." He pointed at the two nearest Gs. "Helmut. Rolf. You two with me. We're going to block from the far side."

On the drone feed, all was still past the trestle. But it would take time to set the charges. They needed someone on the far side of the trestle to guard around the blind curve at its far end. If, at any moment, the drone showed approaching activity, it would be too late to send a blocking force. The demo team was working under Pieter's supervision. Kel had the heaviest firepower; it had to be him. It had to be now.

Kel trotted forward and paused before hearing the footfalls of the men behind him. He had to divert some of his attention to the placement of his feet as the bed underneath him opened significantly between the widely spaced duracrete ties. A narrow shelf for the grav rails ran at each side. He chose to move left, away from the precipice, and was soon able to pick up his pace to a run. That he lost the sound of the men following caused him no concern. He knew their own pace would be a fraction of his. Kel practiced navigating such obstacles frequently; with mindfulness but never with thoughtfulness. Knowing you could fall was important. Focusing on it led to fear and a self-fulfilling prophesy.

If one of those kids does fall to his death trying to keep up with me, I hope they have the patriotism to do so silently.

He slowed as he reached the end of the trestle and checked the drone feed. The bed was solid again on the far side. He waited for his trailing companions, but kept his attention in front of him. The drone feed fortunately still showed no movement beyond. He cautiously slid right.

Nothing but clear track ahead.

Past the curve the track disappeared into the distance, descending the hills and the rock bluffs for the lowlands of the city. Normally, light pollution painted the landscape of buildings and towers. Instead, there was little to indicate a terrified city sat obscured in the murk.

He frowned when he checked on his companions' progress. Only one kid was still moving toward him, and he was only a few meters past where the demolition team was hopefully planting their charges. *Did they stop altogether? They should be here by now. I didn't run that fast.* He wanted to yell at them to hurry. It would be a relief when the comm node was disabled so they could use even simple wave-propagated devices to communicate with his Gs.

Then he caught their figures—men spread out against the cliff face, placing charges where abutments tied the tracks to the wall and the trestle below. Pieter and Max had both been engineering students. They'd demonstrated a keen interest in demolition early on. Their team sergeant, master breacher, and all-around demo-god, Bigg, had been pleased to take them under his wing for instruction in the fine art of destruction. Kel hoped they'd learned well. The charges would absolutely go off. Their priming and ignition were redundant and reliable. Placement was the key. Nonetheless, when Bigg calculated the net explosive weights needed for the task, he used a favorite mathematical formula, "P for Plenty."

What is that?

The small drone feed window caught his attention and he snapped around to look down the tracks. Lights pierced the darkness, aimed like lasers up the track in their direction.

Of course. This has been too easy. Time to get in the game!

He increased the magnification of his bucket by jutting his jaw to the right and clicking his teeth repeatedly; his field of view narrowed and the images at the center enlarged. It was not a train. Smaller. It was about two kilometers away and as it slowed to a stop, Kel saw hot figures exchanging positions on and off the vehicle. It was as Kel had feared. A grav sled was delivering sentries to roving outposts along the rail line, probably interspersed every couple of kilometers.

Behind him a panting voice spoke. It was Helmut.

"Sorry, Kel, Rolf couldn't do it. I got here as fast as I—"

"It's okay, Helmut. Listen. This is important. We're about to have company. There's a Crude patrol coming up the tracks. Get back and tell Pieter to finish up, no matter what. He's got to get the charges set. I'm staying here to delay the Crudes. Don't wait for me. Blow the charges when you are back at the ORP, got me?"

"But—"

"Hurry, Helmut. Do your best. Tell him, 'no matter what.' *Go.*"

To his credit, Helmut turned and started running.

Pieter knows what to do. Kel checked the drone feed again. They'd gone over their contingency plans dozens of times. If they were compromised on the objective, the demo team was to complete the placement of the charges at all costs. If the force got separated at any point, individuals would make their way back to their last rally point, the ORP. If they could not do that, they would evade capture and if not pursued, were to go to one of the designated safe houses and wait for pick up by members of the auxiliary.

The final contingency was the easiest to remember. If they were caught on the objective with no way to escape, they would detonate the charges in place. If Kel couldn't stop the advancing grav sled and troops, it was just the sort of condition that would force that worst contingency.

Kel picked his spot. He moved toward the wall and leaned against it. He dropped a plasma grenade into the launcher tube beneath the barrel of his K-17. He took out another one and in turn prepped it, but placed it in the small open pouch on his left lower chest where his load-ing hand could get to it quickly. He swiped the fire control on his carbine, powering the weapon to full, and checked the charge pack. *100%* the indicator showed. He felt and confirmed a second charge pack was still in its chest pouch, with a third beside it.

I'm about out of patience anyway. He smiled. *Time to start a fight.*

02

Ambush is murder and murder is fun.

Kel kept the chant up as he picked the spot. He knew just where to start the killing. There was a stretch of track ideal for his first ballistic intersection. Where the concavity of the track curved against the rock cut. The bank below was composed of more of the shale scree that necessitated the trestle behind him. It was steep enough that anyone who survived his initial assault could do nothing to escape the kill zone but tumble down the bank. And it was a long way down.

His most casualty producing weapon was the plasma grenade launcher of his K-17. He forced out a deep breath, and brought the carbine up while his bucket's visor collimated with the optic on his weapon. Kel confirmed the range to the curve. *109 meters.* The reticle changed to a grid. He was linked to the weapon through his bucket, and confirmed that the grenade was set for a focused charge. That would give him the best chance of disabling the vehicle with his first shot.

The grav sled headlights grew brighter, casting black shadows into the wall's crevices and crags. The lift carried a dozen troops with a small raised compartment up front housing the driver. Underneath that compartment lay the repulsor cell. Kel started his track just in front of the intersection of the driver compartment and the subtle swell of the body below it. As the sled slowed into the curve Kel placed a 2.5 mil lead on the reticle, tracked, and fired. He could've waited the extra second for the targeting software to determine his lead for him. It would've been a redundancy.

He was already loading another grenade as the first detonated. A beautiful purple discharge lit up his view as he centered his reticle on the passenger compartment. The vehicle nosed into the rock bluff. He pressed the trigger and stayed with the sight picture just long enough to ensure a perfect follow-through, then returned the weapon to particle beam mode and scanned to acquire more targets.

The second grenade detonated exactly where intended. His reward was the involuntary chaos of the bodies. The universal reaction to white hot pain. The screams died quickly. Now only the flames moved, the only noise the crackle of arcing energy. Concussion sheared neurons. Plasma seared skin. The grenades caused a high order effect, igniting the guards' own charge packs. Uniformed bodies burned as he searched for more targets.

He observed the scene for another minute until satisfied, then scanned the surrounding kill zone for movement.

Nothing.

He glanced down the track for more headlights coming their way, but all was dark and silent.

Time to go.

The trestle was empty. The Gs had vacated during the fight. *Good boys. They followed my instructions.*

Now he had another decision to make. Run through the zone of the impending detonation, hoping that Pieter had not made it back to the ORP just yet, or go down the embankment to find another way out? Peering over the side he considered the route. He could slide down the loose rock to the bottom to find another way around the gully and back up into the hills, but couldn't make it to the ORP from here before the patrol left. It would take too long. Plus, soon and very soon, Crudes would be swarming the place.

Decision made.

He ran. Once again, he chose the rock wall side of the track and ran along the rail, ignoring the wide spaces between the ties a half a meter to his left. It took him no time to reach the far side of the trestle and the safety of the solid maglev bed. He slid down the shallow bank toward the release point.

Two conflicting thoughts came to him. *Thank Oba they haven't set off the charges.* Then, *why haven't they blown the charges?*

He pushed himself up the hill at the hardest pace possible. Glancing over his shoulder, he scanned for any lights headed up the tracks.

No quick reaction force responding. Yet, he thought as he slowed at the last rise before the ORP.

A shot rang out in his direction. He knew it wasn't the Crudes.

"*Knock that off. Coming in.*" His rebuke was louder than he intended. Friendly fire put him in a bad mood. Someone was panicking. Kel checked his temper as he crested the rise to find the patrol standing around.

He kept his voice low. "Who shot and why?"

Silence.

"Never mind. Pieter, blow the charges."

The young man held his datapad, frozen.

"We were waiting to see if you'd come. I was going to give it another five minutes unless we saw more Crudes moving in. What happened?"

"Later. Blow the charges." Kel could have done so from his own link, but wanted to let the Gs have the experience. It was important to let them feel this was their mission.

"Here goes."

Everyone turned in the direction of the maglev line lying through the trees and darkness.

Nothing happened.

"Pieter, hit it," Kel encouraged. "Now."

The datapad screen's faint blue glow illuminated Pieter's face. "Nothing's happening. I'm transmitting. There's a problem."

Kel knew the most likely cause. "The Crudes are jamming everything. The RF signal isn't strong enough. I need a line of sight and I can push the detonation signal by microwave. Stay here." Without waiting for a response, Kel took off down the hillside. From the site where he'd done his leader's recon, he'd be on line with the trestle and should be able to trigger the detonation sequence from his own datalink. He'd be a half-klick away from the blast. Closer than he'd like, but far enough. *Farther than when I was running for my life across that trestle.* If everything went right, this was going to be a very large explosion.

Running so fast he nearly fell, dodging trees and boulders as he went, he reached the spot. The depression was familiar and through the trees he recognized the horizontal line that was the maglev bed.

He heard the voices before he saw any movement. *There. Crudes!*

On both sides of the trestle were troops, weapons postured, searching. *Had they come from the other direc-*

tion? *No matter.* Kel brought his forearm in front of him and keyed a code to the datalink displaying the detonation commands.

He pressed *Transmit*.

The creation of the universe. From nothing, everything. He flopped to the ground, faster than gravity alone should have allowed.

Five hundred meters was not a great amount of standoff distance. The matter concentrating cores of the charges generated about four gigajoules of energy each. They had placed five charges around the trestle where buttresses tied spans of the trestle to the rock bluff. The ground underneath him lifted. His bucket muted to silence, but still he felt the long rumble through his armor, deep into his chest and bones. Rock and debris spewed onto the hillside. Boulders rained, fracturing trees. If one of those were to land on him, he'd be crushed. *Nothing I can do about it*, he thought. *But what a stupid way to die.*

The rumble quelled. Kel stood. Grit tinked off his armor. Dusty rain filtered through the trees. It was like trying to see through grease smudging a lens. A battle damage assessment was impossible. Whatever destruction they'd wrought would have to suffice. It was time to go. He trotted back up the slope, feeling for the first time the strain deep in his knees and ankles from the pounding they'd taken on the slopes tonight. *How must Bigg feel, as old as he is? Or am I just whining?*

He crested the rise yet again, fairly certain this time no one would take a shot at him. The Gs remained in their loose perimeter, somewhat more organized than before.

Moving into the center of the circle, he took a knee and removed his bucket. He unconsciously scratched his head as he spoke. "We've done what we could and we can't stay for a damage assessment. I've left the drone grounded. Maybe we can get some kind of damage readings out of it later.

"They're going to start hunting for us. The rest of the targets are being hit as we speak. That may keep some heat off us. The Crudes are going to be very busy if everyone completes their mission."

The kids watched him with wide-eyed solemnity. Everyone understood the danger that faced them was no longer theoretical. It was real as the explosion. Real as the dust they coughed. They'd just kicked off a war against the Crudes.

"We can't be sloppy. Maintain noise and light discipline. I'll lead us out. Same order of march." Kel would have been happiest if there was an option for a different route out of the short mountainous range. There wasn't. They'd have to take the same route out they had followed in. Which meant that if someone had tracked them in, they could be walking into an ambush. Yet another reason why Kel would be leading the patrol from the front.

"Pieter, what's the count?"

Pieter was silent.

Kel expected this. Pieter and his crew had hurriedly placed the charges, then ran for their lives off the objective and back to the ORP as the echoes from Kel's one-sided combat chased them. A count of their team was probably as far away from their minds as this planet was from the Core.

"Get in formation and send the count up from the rear," Kel whispered. He put his bucket back on and moved forward up the slope, letting the Gs fall in behind him. After some milling about, one man after another whispered the head count to the man in front of him.

The man behind Kel leaned toward him.

"Eleven."

His heart skipped a beat. Kel would make thirteen in the patrol. The count made him twelve.

"Stay put," he said to the man as he moved down the line, placing a hand on each man's shoulder as he counted. He started the count with himself and when reaching Pieter at the end said, "Twelve," and touched the man's shoulder.

"Pieter. Who're we missing? Inspect the line with me. Let's go." Although when Kel thought about the night's events, he had a guess.

They got to the front of the column again, the silence around them eerie.

"Helmut is m-missing," Pieter said, a quiver in his voice.

"Where's Rolf? Get him and bring him here."

Pieter returned quickly with the other man.

"Where's Helmut?" Kel asked quietly. He pointed to Rolf. "You were with us when we set off across the trestle, but I never saw you reach the other side. I made contact with the Crudes and sent Helmut back to tell Pieter to finish the job. Did he make it back to give the message?"

Pieter shook his head. "I never saw Helmut. I didn't get your message. I just followed the plan and got off the maglev bed when I heard the commotion ahead."

Rolf shook his head as well. "I never saw him again when he left with you, Kel. I couldn't cross the trestle. Sorry. I stayed to help with the charges."

Kel sighed. "He fell. He had to have fallen off the trestle when I sent him back to tell you to hurry up." Helmut had been brave. He'd been scared, but he'd crossed the trestle anyway. Kel sent him back for another urgent trip across the height. Then he'd fallen to his death without making a sound.

Pieter's voice cracked. "We need to look for him."

Kel considered it. "No. If he fell, then there's nothing left to look for. He'll be buried under the trestle and about a million tons of rock. When you got everyone through the release point and took count, didn't you notice anyone was missing then?"

Pieter flustered. "I... I.., I just..."

Kel sighed. "It's not your fault. By that time, he'd probably already fallen to his death. Nothing you could've done. Get back in formation and send the count up again. When I get it, we'll move out. We can't stay here any longer."

When the man behind him leaned forward toward Kel and softly said, "Eleven," Kel thought, *Twelve*.

There just hadn't been enough time.

Kel recon'd the factory from the edge of the wood line by himself. It was still dark outside. The exterior lights were extinguished. He moved through the woods to see around as much as possible of the dilapidated building. A dim interior light glowed through the windowed rear entrance; the far-recognition signal that the safe house was secure.

He continued around to find the second-story office window he was told to expect. The drapes were open, and a small square of infrared tape was stuck in the lower pane. The near-recognition signal. An older couple who lived nearby maintained the safe house. The factory was full of unused parts-printing machines and huge piles of crystalized silica.

The grounds were overgrown and unkempt, unlike the lovely cottage at the front of the property. The older gentleman should be in the factory awaiting them, his wife in the cottage, alert for any unwanted visitors approaching from the road.

Kel moved back to the waiting patrol and gave them the news. "Time to move up. Pieter will go in and make contact. When he comes back to give the safe signal, one at a time I'll bump you through into the building. I'll be the last in. Questions? Let's go."

Kel patted Pieter on the shoulder and sent him off as the rest took a knee and formed another perimeter. Kel did not have to tell them. After an interminably long time that was likely less than five minutes, the door opened and Pieter appeared in its threshold, raising both arms over his head twice to indicate it was safe to start passing men through.

Kel patted a G and pointed to the door. He sent one at a time until he was alone. After a last sweep of where they'd been holding, he made the slow walk into the building.

He activated the infrared flood on his bucket to pierce the blackness through the threshold before stepping in. The Gs were spread between rows of commercial machinery, stacked barrels, and waste from the manufacturing processes. The door closed behind him and he watched Pieter and an old man brace a solid looking bar across the door.

"This is our friend, Zed," Pieter said quietly as he introduced their benefactor. It was a pseudonym. They all knew the location of the safe house, but if any of them were captured and interrogated, they couldn't give up a name.

"Thank you for what you are doing," the old man said. "Come, we have a place to hide all of you that is more comfortable."

Cool blue lights illuminated a stairwell. Zed led them down through a door into another large industrial space, and around an open elevator shaft to a utility room. He paused in front of a large control panel with power relays covering the wall. A small lever was lost in a jumble of other electrical contrivances, and Zed pulled it. As he did, the entire panel gave way just enough to allow a man to slip through.

Kel followed Zed in. More of the light blue illumination emanated from the lower wall to light the floor, and a gentle white light spread to fill the room from above. The space was no more than ten by twelve meters, but large enough for everyone to lay down at the same time.

"This room has been used many times over the years, but not since the last war," Zed said, referring to the war thirty years ago that led to the split between North and South Andalusia. "You'll be safe here until our friends come tonight after dark to move you again."

There was a small adjoining fresher as well as a sink and table. Sleeping mats lay stacked in one corner next to boxes of military rations. Whoever had planned the hidden space all those years before knew what they were doing.

Kel checked his chronometer. The sun would rise soon and the rest of the team and their Gs should be moving to their own safe houses. Their scheduled commo check would be at 0815 hours. Kel removed his bucket.

"Pieter, pick two men for the first watch and then we'll accompany Zed to find a good spot on the top floor—"

"No! You mustn't leave the room," Zed insisted. "It's too risky." He was about to continue when Kel cut him off.

"Sorry, Zed. We can't fight our way out of this room if we're surprised. It's an excellent hiding place, but if it's known to the Crudes—"

"It's not!" Zed protested. "It was never discovered during the war and it's been unused for a generation."

"I'm afraid that this is nonnegotiable, Zed. Pieter, pick your men and let's get set," Kel told him. The youngster frowned and said nothing. Kel continued, "Zed, wait outside for us. We'll be right there, thank you."

With one last glance at Pieter, the old man left.

"How well do your people know Zed?" Kel asked so low only Pieter could hear.

Pieter shrugged. "I don't know him personally. Adam gave me the contact and codes including the recognition signals—you were there. The Underground coordinated the safe house. You know we don't all know each other for security reasons."

Adam Hargest was the head of the armed resistance, the G-Chief. Members of the auxiliary support for the guerilla movement were managed by the underground. Only Adam and a few of his lieutenants would know who their underground contacts were, and even then, would only know them by pseudonyms. They would primarily communicate with them through dead drop messaging. If anyone was captured, interrogated, and turned, it would be virtually impossible to give up the whole resistance network.

But Pieter seemed resistant to his instruction. *There's a time to be an authoritarian, and there's a time to be a big brother.* Pieter was young and inexperienced. Kel was conscious that what he did next would set an example for the developing leader. He thought about how Bigg would handle the situation.

"I'm sure Zed is a patriot," he said, taking as gentle a tone as he could muster. "I'm sure his family has a long history of supporting the underground, even when it went dormant after the war. But Zed's not in charge of our security. We are. Hiding down here without any early warning in place is unacceptable. Praying that this location is completely hidden and unknown is not a safe strategy. Understand? We're as good as dead if the Crudes get in here. So, let's find a good spot for two men on the top floor where they can keep an eye out. I'll give them my link and if they spot something suspicious, we'll have an early warning. Got it?"

Pieter nodded.

Kel did not completely trust the organization of the Mercian underground and its auxiliary support network. It had supposedly existed for generations. To Kel, that simply meant there were generations of loose lips and even informers ready to give up family secrets either out of foolishness or malice. It was a given that the Crudes' intelligence apparatus knew who the families were that formed the core of the Mercian underground. The Crudes had already been picking up individuals for interrogation during their short time in North Mercia. Any number of people in the underground and its auxiliary could be compromised.

"I know you want to expel the Crudes and make them pay. I know you have confidence in your organization, and that you're a patriot. But that doesn't mean everyone in your organization is necessarily trustworthy. The only way to stay alive is to never place your security entirely in someone else's hands. Because, when I'm on the other side, working to extinguish an organization like yours, that's how we do it. We exploit laziness and trust, and when we get one person to talk, it's the beginning of the end for them."

The political arm of their movement, the underground, was organized in cells—small groups of a few individuals who then each recruited more members known only to them. Communication to lower echelon cell was from only a single individual within a higher-level cell, and from each individual to the respective cells underneath each of them. The arrangement had guaranteed secrecy since the first conspiracy was organized by dissident amoeba.

Auxiliary members were identified and recruited from those known by the underground to be sympathetic to the cause. Those that had the resources to provide sustainment, transportation, and refuge to the members of the movement were ideal candidates. They generally did not participate directly in revolutionary violence, but gave material support to those that did.

When the underground decided that it was time to form a military arm, then an army was raised and trained—the guerillas. An underground might maintain a small military arm for generations, ready for the circumstances that would kick off their armed resistance. In the Mercian emergency, the G-force expanded quickly. The Kroedellian buildup in South Mercia was the signal of the impending invasion anticipated for decades.

"Zed and his wife could have a family member held hostage by the Crudes. Giving us up might be the only way to get their loved out of a firing squad, or worse. Betrayal can kill us all. You know this. That's why can't rely on Zed. So, let's go set up some observation positions and set a watch. I'll spend most of my time with the watch, but I have to get some rest, too. Back at the G-base, we can rest. Sound good?"

The young man winced. "You're... right. Learning how to think... tactically, is a new thing for me, Kel."

Maybe the kid isn't the brat I took him to be, Kel thought. This was another case where Bigg's advice paid off. *Treat someone how you would like to be treated; teach them what you wished someone had taught you at their stage. When that doesn't work, throat punch 'em.* The last was his own corollary.

He showed Pieter the way to set up a concealed observation position from a window on the top level and from a ventilation panel in one of the eaves, then set the first watch. He sent Pieter down to get some rest and found a quiet place to start his own work. He went to the unused office and found a chair and pushed it away from the dusty desk, moving it back against a wall from where he could see the door. Staying buttoned up in his lid he sat, and took a deep breath. He'd get out of his bucket and try for an hour's sleep as soon as he could. He first checked on the dormant drone at the maglev trestle. The link was good.

He activated the small drone and was immediately relieved to see the feed come through clearly. He nudged the drone to pan around and show him the entire scene. In a tree across from the gulley, it overlooking their target site. Or what was left of it.

The bottom of the gulch was filled with loose shale liberated from the rock bluff, with spans of the trestle mixed in. Somewhere in that grave lay their comrade, Helmut.

There was no Crude activity yet around the area. Kel risked launching the drone to a higher elevation for an overview of the region. To the east were the remnants of the grav sled he'd ambushed, with an empty grav sled behind it. The troops who were on the trestle when they'd set off the charges must've come in the other sled. They must have killed them all in the explosion or the other grav sled would not still be there. But why wasn't there a reaction force now scouring the site for forensic information? Where were the troops with the sniffer bots looking for the trail of the saboteurs? Where were the engineers evaluating how to get the maglev bed reconstructed?

Kel thought he knew. *Sims must have done it! The parasite crashed the Crudes' comm network!*

The Kroedellian military structure was like that of most statist regimes. Central control was the norm. The military existed as much to repress the population as it did for external defense. The security of the state required that individual action or initiative be suppressed. Subordinate leaders excelled in carrying out orders from superiors, not in exercising judgement and adapting to a fluid situation as was common in combat. Complete control of information was a necessity.

The rest of the team had probably been as successful as Kel in accomplishing their missions, and the Crudes were paralyzed trying to regain order and respond. He turned the drone west and checked. There was no activity on the tracks as far as he could see. He let the AI select a location to go dormant for later reactivation.

He checked the time. His L-comm was active. They'd stayed off it the entire night. With the team separated performing independent tasks, it served only as a distraction. He had a few minutes until Braley or Bigg initiated the team check. If they failed to do so, it would fall to Kel to start the process. He wanted to pace with nervous excitement, but stayed seated to conserve energy. After a few minutes he was relieved to hear a familiar voice in his ear.

"Three, this is Bigg, how do you copy? Sound off by roster."

Their team captain's voice came next. "Yost up."

Kel sounded off.

Poul came next. "Radd up."

Sims answered last. "Simons up."

Kel let a long breath escape. Now that he knew the team was safe, his anxiety turned into excitement. Had they all been successful?

"All right," Bigg said. "Listen up. We'll do a full debrief later tonight. Me and Sims are already back at the G-base. We were both successful. Captain, what's your status?"

"Mission complete. In our safe house. Ready to come in when it's quiet."

"Turner, you next," Bigg said.

"Mission complete. In our safe house. Secure," Kel answered.

"And you, Poul?"

"Mission complete. In our alternate hide. Our safe house was compromised. We haven't made contact with any auxiliary. Secure."

Kel remembered that one of Poul's alternate hide selections was an abandoned warehouse several kilometers deep into the old industrial section. If their planned safe house was compromised, then Poul and his Gs had to navigate through the relatively barren area surrounding the water treatment plant into the urban landscape of the old factories. The Gs were experts at navigating around the city scape, as opposed to Kel's group that was unaccustomed to rural operations. Kel imagined the Gs of Poul's patrol were ducks in a pond. If Kel hadn't been here, his Gs might not have made it to their safe house, much less even found the target site on time.

"All right. We took the Crudes by surprise. The city's in chaos. I'm going to bounce each of you separately and we'll review your next movement for link-up. The only one with a change in plan coming is Kel. Stand by, Kel, I'll be with you shortly."

"Roger, Bigg," Kel replied as Bigg switched to a sub-channel. Bigg and Braley discussed the current situation and reviewed the plan for Braley's return to the G-base. Kel knew that the rest of the team was listening in, as they would be when it was Kel's turn for instructions from Bigg.

What's the change in plan for how we're getting back?

03

A collection of petty thugs, the Kroedellian Union controlled the Southern Andalusian continent. Only the fecklessness of the other Cassellian nations permitted their expansion. The Kroedellians were temperamental—almost—in their dealings with the rest of Planet Cassell as well as with the Galactic Republic. But their tantrums worked.

The other nations often rewarded the Crudes' bad behavior with appeasement. Who wants to be responsible for starting yet another bloody war? Still, delaying the inevitable only kicked the can down the road for another generation to deal with. Meanwhile the Crudes kept expanding. The more brutish their tactics, the more the rest of Cassell wrung their hands, but did nothing. At some point, they would have to be confronted.

Even the House of Reason knew this.

Listening to Bigg on the sub-channel, Kel got a good picture of the damage the team had wreaked overnight. It was a start. The big event was still to come.

"Kel, you up?" came Bigg's voice on the main.

"Yeah, Bigg. Tell it to me."

"Some special assistance became available so we won't be depending on the Auxiliary for your pickup." Bigg went on with specifics. Recognition procedures would be simplified since his contact had L-comm. It would be relatively easy, especially in comparison to their movement out of the G-base and into the countryside for their mission.

The movement his Gs took to assemble for the mag-lev strike had been protracted. It took several days for the Auxiliary to transport all of his Gs to the way station before taking their long walk to the maglev track. Kel was the last to join Pieter and the rest of the patrol at the farm that had been their jumping-off point. Their buildup at the farm was easily concealed from overhead observation by the number of rindar and other domesticated animals that roamed the grassy fields and pens. To get there, some of the men had been concealed in repulsor wagons that took enriched feed from the city's railhead up to the farm country. Some had gone concealed in the hidden spaces of empty bullitar transports returning from their delivery to the slaughterhouses in North Mercia.

A similar scheme in reverse was to have been used to smuggle the men back into the city and to the G-base hidden in the subterranean part of the old city works. Now, they would be returning as one group, ready to assume the next mission almost immediately.

Back in the basement, Pieter was on watch with an-other one of the men. With the door secured behind him, Kel removed his bucket. "Do you want to wake the men up to see the results of our work?"

Everyone's head lifted from their mat.

"Really? How?" Pieter asked.

"I'll show you." Kel aimed the datalink emitter on his forearm to the center of the room. "I left a drone dormant. We can see the site live."

When the holo sprang up, a dozen men exclaimed like excited children.

"Look! Not a column left standing."

"Do you see that! I don't believe it."

"I knew that was a helluva explosion!"

"Helmut would be proud," one man said, and everyone grew quiet.

Kel let them have a moment.   "No Crudes have responded because it seems that the rest of the strikes went as planned. The comm node is destroyed and the Crudes are acting like worms pulled apart in the middle."

"That's good news," a fuzzy faced G said. "But what's next? We're still knee-deep in the swine! What's our next mission?"

"First things first. I'm in contact with the G-base. There's a plan to get us out of here earlier than we'd anticipated." Kel explained the concept of operation for the movement to their G-base. "Pieter, let's keep rotating the watch. I've already briefed the guys upstairs. We're going to keep Zed in the dark about this until we move out."

Pieter nodded. "You don't think it'll cause a problem?"

"We'll come out when I've gotten the signal and in time to alert old Zed and prevent him from stroking out when he sees our transport arrive. I'm going to catch a few winks." He moved to a clear spot on the floor. "My comm with the link upstairs will come through on my bucket speaker. If they have anything to alert us to, we'll all hear it."

Kel found a mat and stretched out, his carbine beside him. Restless men whispered and squirmed. Kel closed his eyes. There would be time for more killing later.

"Kel, you got me?" the voice came from his bucket beside him. He opened his eyes and spoke into his link.

"Yeah, give me a sec." He sat up and put his bucket on to have a private conversation. He noted the time. He'd slept for a little over four hours. He'd stirred at the last watch change, but quickly fell asleep again. It felt like a full night's sleep.

After the conversation, he woke up his Gs.

"We're good to go." Kel stayed in his bucket, transmitting his voice on low volume to the men around him. "I'm in commo with our recovery team. Pick up will be just after sunset, about two hours. Let's start taking turns in the fresher, getting a ration down us, and packing up and sanitizing the space. Leave nothing. Also, it's going to be a long ride and there won't be any stops unless we've gotta fight our way out of a situation. Everybody, keep an empty ration pack handy while we're traveling."

The ration packs were pretty standard. Once opened, the container could be resealed repeatedly and the contents kept for days if need be. That was Kel's preference. Open one and eat a little out of it so as not to get stuffed or sluggish, just enough to stave off hunger. One ration could last him more than a day when on a sustained operation.

When empty, the container served another purpose. It could be used to store bodily waste so as not to leave any trace for dogs or a snooper to find. While he had not made the group carry all their waste on this patrol, they were going to be hidden in the back of a vehicle for several hours or more. Someone would need to relieve themselves during that time, and there'd be no stops to the ladies' room along the way.

Soon enough, Kel checked his chrono and gave Pieter the go-ahead to start the movement out of the hide. They called down their upstairs watch as they exited the small room for the last time, Kel securing the large panel behind him and confirming the head count. Pieter led as the group made their way up the blue-lit stairs to the main factory floor, and waited at the exit nearest the tree line.

"Ten-minute warning," Kel said.

Pieter nodded and made for the narrow gravel road leading to the cottage. Just a hundred meters farther lay the paved road that could bring a motorized Crude battalion down on them in an instant. Pieter would warn Zed and his wife that they were about to have visitors and that their guests would be departing immediately.

Kel waited for several minutes, then moved to the front of the group. "Spread out, keep your intervals, and move in a wedge directly into the wood line. We'll set up a perimeter and wait for contact with Pieter, got it? Let's go."

He led off. The sky held the last hint of light to his west, but the dense forest around them made everything dark enough to obscure their presence to an unaided eye. Kel dialed up his night vision to watch the factory road. A vehicle's headlights pierced the dense woods.

"Kel, it's me. We're here. I'm going dark. Is your guide coming forward to lead us in?"

"Yes. You should see him near the cottage."

"Okay. I got him now. He's giving me the recognition signal."

Kel turned to face the Gs. "Vehicle is being led in. I'll come back for you and send you in by twos. Wait here until I make contact with our recovery team."

Pieter walked ahead of the heavy grav sled bearing the markings of the Kroedellian Revolutionary Forces. The sled halted and lowered. The driver and a tall passenger dismounted and spoke with Pieter.

"At your nine," Kel said into his bucket and moved out of the woods.

The large man, made even larger by the greatcoat he wore, pushed back his hood to reveal a Legion bucket.

"Thanks for the lift, brother," Kel said.

Meadows gestured magnanimously. "No sweat. Glad it worked out. I've had a wish list that I've been looking forward to filling, and this morning has been the best shopping day of the year," he said and nodded at the grav sled. "Let's get everyone loaded and make for the city. My spoofed creds are working well. The Crudes are paralyzed without the ability to confirm every little thing with central command. I've been able to scare anyone below captain into accepting my orders without even needing to show them anything. It's been kind of fun, actually."

Where the average thief would find anxiety, Meadows found exhilaration and amusement.

Meadows's driver stepped down out of the control compartment and opened a side panel to reveal the interior bed. A dim light shone from the compartment and tall grav-container stacks blocked the rear doors. Another stack sat near the front of the bed, ready to be moved into place to block the entrance that he now peered through.

"Once everybody's in and those grav-containers are stacked and locked in place, casual inspection of the bed contents will satisfy anyone not specifically looking for us. Otherwise, well, it'll be time for things to get sporty," Meadows said. "Let's do it and be on our way."

Kel directed Pieter to stay by the portal and to get a head count as he returned to the patrol and sent the men forward in pairs to load up.

"We up?" he asked Pieter as he returned to the sled for the final time.

"And you make twelve," Pieter told him.

Kel smiled. "And me makes twelve. Zed seem surprised?"

"Yes. He protested briefly, but I was able to calm him. He is not the most flexible member of the Auxiliary,

I think. Perhaps we will not recommend that site's use again, yes?"

"Agreed," Kel said as he followed Pieter up into the compartment. They may have not been compromised, but if there were any undetected eyes on them now, their presence would have blown the safe house for future use.

Meadows's assistant helped them move the grav containers. They held something heavy—Kel didn't know what—but with the repulsors powered, they stacked effortlessly. He keyed the controls, locking the crates into place.

"Set. Let's beat feet," Kel said through his L-comm.

"Rog. Hang loose back there," Meadows responded.

Kel sat with his back to the grav containers. Everyone else found space and did the same with legs stretched in front of them, weapons at their sides. Kel felt the familiar floating sensation of movement, and the dim light extinguished in the compartment. The rocking motion smoothed as the truck turned and they floated onto the hardball road. They would be traveling out of the rural hill country, down to the city.

The closer they got, the more dangerous it would be. Kel knew it was time to rest and recommended the same. "Nothing we can do now, men. They'll give us ample warning if we need to get spun-up. Rest."

They had a couple of hours until things had the potential to "get sporty," as Meadows would say. He hoped it was going to be the most boring trip of his life.

Kel chatted with Meadows over L-comm. Meadows was in his armor, but would soon take off his bucket to be able to pass any cursory inspection at checkpoints nearer the city. Dressed as he was in the garb of a Revolutionary Forces major, the officer's greatcoat concealed his armor decently when buttoned up, but a bucket would be tough to explain. They'd still be able to communicate through Meadows's link, but their conversation wouldn't be private from Meadows's man in the cab once his bucket was off.

"It was hard to find a Crude big enough to make it worthwhile stealing his clothes, but my guys did okay. Same for snagging this grav sled. I've had my eye on a couple of them, but before today the only way I could have nabbed one would've been by ambush. Whacking officers for their getups and stealing trucks in shoot-outs—not a good way to stay covert. Nah, now that their central net is down, I've pretty much spent the morning just taking what I want. Their army is pretty worthless. Flashing party creds and central committee authorizations with these boards on my shoulders has resulted in a lot of salutes and instantaneous cooperation. One thing these guys do pretty well is follow orders," Meadows laughed.

"Yeah, well, I guess you would too if there was a very definite risk of getting shot for individualism and disloyalty to the party."

Meadows sounded in good spirits. Aggressive. Confident. It was good to see the old Meadows again. They'd gotten to spend a little time together in North Mercia when they'd first infiltrated into the city, shortly before the Crudes made their play and finally invaded.

His friend Meadows was the only survivor of Kill Team Seven, murdered by their own alien troops. That was two missions ago for Kel. Kel's team had been on that planet as part of a Planetary Security mission leading another battalion of the same native troops when, in a quasi-religious fervor, they revolted against the humans.

Kel's team escaped the deteriorating situation with the fanatical aliens without casualties. Meadows's team had not been so lucky. He remembered the momentary elation Meadows had expressed when they landed in the Talon to recover him. He'd made his own escape from the camp, and was expecting his team to join him to continue their evasion back to the capital. Telling Meadows his team wasn't coming was one of the worst things Kel had ever had to do.

Meadows continued the fight without a misstep, but he was changed. When they'd eventually returned to Victrix and Dark Ops Headquarters, Kel went with him to Seven's team room the first time so he wouldn't be alone. It had hit Kel just as hard, seeing everyone's gear cages and desks, knowing that their friends would not be coming back. Every kill team had lost someone at some point in their history. Combat losses were part of the package being in the Legion, and especially so in Dark Ops. To lose an entire kill team in one incident was unheard of. It hit the whole unit hard. Kel tried not to think about the memorial service. It had been draining.

Meadows came to Team Three for a while as Team Seven was being rebuilt, but it was only a month or so before Meadows was called to the planning cell with an opportunity. Meadows had been cleared to talk about generalities of his proposed assignment with Kel and their team sergeant, Bigg, as they had the most experience performing the type of mission he was being offered. It was a project working for Republic Intelligence on Cassell in the sequestered city of North Mercia.

The separated condition of the Andalusian continent into a "free" north and a virtual prison colony in the south had made it the center of much espionage and intrigue during Kel's lifetime. Republic Intelligence had a presence in Andalusia for centuries. Keeping the Kroedellian

Empire in check, though they were a minor galactic irritant, was part of the Republic's ex-planetary policy. The Crudes' totalitarian-statist philosophy combined with their imperialism made them a faction the Senate and House of Reason wanted to contain. It would not do to allow the dangerous ideology to spread anywhere else in the galaxy, regardless of the Republic's stated policies regarding self-determination.

In Kel's estimation, Republic Intelligence was a peculiar agency. He'd had many firsthand experiences working with the spy masters. Few had been positive. The prospect always left him uneasy when RI requested help from outside their own closed service. Entertainment might portray RI as a group capable of performing dangerous clandestine activities but in Kel's experience when they needed something done that involved personal danger, they used proxies to carry out those acts. For the most part, RI intelligence officers were of the political class. While they undoubtedly thought of themselves as patriots, they were civil servants. Their careers were what mattered, and getting killed or maimed was not part of their career advancement plan.

No, when it came to dirty work, RI let others hold the shovels and do the digging.

Republic Intelligence's clandestine presence in North Mercia was for purposes of intelligence collection across the disruptor wall that divided the city. It also allowed an on-the-ground assessment of the North Andalusian response to the constant threat at their southern border. As it became more and more apparent, and correctly so, that the Crudes were finally going to follow through on two decades of threats to invade, RI anticipated that they would need help. The kind of help that was generally provided by operators from DO.

This was the opportunity now being offered to Meadows. While neither Kel nor Bigg knew the particulars of the mission offered their friend (or that they would later be the beneficiaries of their friend's presence in the city) they knew the type of mission and what it would entail.

"My experience running that program was good," Bigg told him. "The RI case officer I worked for was a real pro. It was a great opportunity for me to use all the tools I had learned in Operations and Intelligence school. I recruited and ran my own agent network, did a lot of target development, and ran my own ops with the guys I recruited.

"But it was clear what my role was. The guy was good, but information only went up; it never came back down. The only constraints were when my agents or investigations came too close to something he felt would jeopardize another activity. He never would tell me who his people were, just that I had to alter what I was doing so as not to interfere with his net. So, no big deal.

"They have endless monetary resources, you know? When it came to incentivizing intel collection, paying bounties—stuff like that—I had all the tools in the toolbox I needed to be effective.

"But my job was to do the dirty work and take the risks. He lived in the capital in a villa with private security and had a nuke-proof safe room he retreated into whenever the situation got a little crazy. I stayed in the field for nine months and never came in. I'd see him once or twice a week when he'd come out in an unmarked Talon and visit for a couple of hours, then he was off again. At least the guy wasn't breathing down my neck all the time.

"I made him look good, and advanced his career, and he never got in my way. So, overall, it was a good experience."

At the time, Kel knew Meadows needed something like this. Clearly he was distressed. Meadows would one day find his way back to the happy warrior he was before the tragedy on Qulingat't, but it'd take time.

Not wanting to dump his negative feelings about RI on Meadows, Kel gave him the truncated version of his experiences.

"If you take the job, it's going to be a fantastic opportunity to use all your skills. You just have to remember that to those guys, they see in color while you see in black and white.

"They're of the political class and they truly believe that everyone else is of inferior intellect and abilities. They went to the right school on Liberinthine, were in the right club, know the right people. They are of a class that confuses education with intelligence and ascribes status with ability. Whatever your experience and knowledge may be, no matter if you are right, they will always see their judgement as being superior and naturally correct. Always. Because they are a better, more worthy person than you.

"As long as you don't buy into that, stay strong, and never surrender your judgement to them, you'll be fine. Plus, if you end up working with folks who truly are professionals and value your contribution and abilities, you'll have an amazing experience."

Kel didn't want to be sanctimonious. He knew RI only wanted DO for their ability to do the dirty work, but wasn't that why they were in DO? He just hated to be used or mistreated due to a lack of basic respect. No one in the galaxy could do what he and his brothers could do, certainly not RI.

Meadows thought about it for a moment. "I'm going to take the mission. I need a new challenge and to tell you the truth, unless Team Three had a spot for me, I'm just not up to building a bond with a new team. Not yet."

That had been almost seven months ago. Kel and Team Three had completed another mission since then. He'd wondered how Meadows was making out on his venture with the spy masters. They were in mission planning in the underground isolation facility on Victrix when they'd learned that Meadows was going to be one of their assets on the ground. The whole team had felt relieved. Having one of their own supporting their intelligence needs instead of an RI asset was comforting.

Now, it was simply great that Meadows seemed himself again. Not to say through all this he'd ever lost his edge. He'd always been the leej Kel thought of when someone used the term "violence of action." His ability to supply death on demand was never in question.

"Hey buddy, I'm going to ditch my bucket. I don't think we'll come across any checkpoints for another ninety minutes or so. We didn't run into any on the way out, but I don't want to be fiddling around at the last minute either if I'm surprised. The Crudes are disorganized, but not totally disrupted. I've got my datalink active if you need me. I'll keep you appraised as we get closer to your drop point."

"Thanks, Meadows." He was about to break the link when he said, "Hey man, great job. Seems like this unconventional warfare thing suits you."

"Pfft. We wrap this thing up, I'm coming home and never leaving a team again. We'll talk, but it's like you tried to tell me. These guys think they float above the rest of us.

The reality is, they do what they do pretty well. What they don't know or can't do, they don't even know they don't know. They just know they don't want to do it."

Kel laughed. "Oh man, you're killing me. I'm stealing that."

"All yours, brother. Free of charge."

Kel spread the word to the Gs that they should be traveling undisturbed for a while and to relax. He was going to try to do the same.

Kel didn't sleep, but listened through his bucket to Meadows's open link in the cab. Meadows and his driver didn't talk much. Kel had seen the man once before. He'd accompanied Meadows as they led Kel and Poul on a target assessment several weeks ago. Meadows told him that the man was a Crude defector who'd made it through the disruptor barrier north to freedom. The man had been a policeman and had also served his mandatory time in the Revolutionary Forces Army. He was a good find. The man hated the Crudes.

He listened as they commented on the growing traffic as they neared the edge of the city and the industrial area concealing the guerilla base. Nearing a checkpoint, Kel alerted the Gs. They waited in the compartment, frozen, ready to uncoil and fight if needed. The momentary halt passed as Meadows's credentials and officer's uniform cowed the guards. Soon they floated away, farther into the old city.

After another long stretch skirting the built-up areas, they started the swerving path into the labyrinth of industrial divisions surrounding North Mercia. Kel followed their route on his own map projection, keeping track of their progress. An abandoned garage would be their drop point.

"Kel, we're getting close. Get ready to unload. I don't have to tell you we want to make this efficient. Best if we're not in the garage for more than a few minutes. I've got a drone overhead. There's no activity, but that doesn't mean that there aren't eyes on us."

"Rog." It had become fully dark during the trip from the countryside. The Crudes did not have an abundance of tech, but that didn't mean they had none. Most likely, it would be a sniper team observing for suspicious activity, and that type of element would certainly have enhanced night observation tech. Kel would be doing exactly that if he were acting as the counter-insurgent.

Disrupting patterns—or better yet, not establishing any pattern—was the key to avoiding detection. The garage they'd be using as a drop-off point was one they'd used several times to access the network of tunnels and caves, but always in small numbers and on foot. This was the first time they'd access one of the entrances to the G-base by vehicle. They would not do so again unless it was absolutely unavoidable.

"Get ready," Kel told the group. "As soon as they pop the door, we head underground. Pieter, be the last man and make sure the compartment is sterile." The vehicle stopped; the side door slid open. Kel was in front of the forward compartment hatch, releasing the grav container locks.

Meadows was there beckoning everyone out. His assistant stood over the concrete pit in front of them, shining a dim handheld light into the space below. The pit was used for maintenance of the repulsor arrays when a vehicle was grounded, and frequent maintenance required draining coolants and other fluids from the units. Kel jumped down and found the grate at its bottom. On the other side was a narrow passage. Kel held the grate with one arm as he motioned those behind him to start their descent.

He counted as men passed him until Pieter was the last in line. "You're eleven and I make twelve," Kel said to him as Pieter ducked below the duracrete lip and passed out of sight into the darkness. Meadows came behind Kel to hold the grate.

"Take off, brother. See you soon."

Kel gave him a thumbs up. "Thanks for the lift. Be safe, man."

"Always. KTF."

Kel turned sideways to fit through the passage in his armor. He turned on his infrared flood and immediately had a bright view ahead of the line of bobbing heads dodging the maze of plumbing. They entered a small chamber where many more intertwined pipes and wires took off at crazy angles. Pieter had a small white light in his hand as did another G, and they searched one of the walls behind the most intricate collection of plumbing. Oily, green liquids dripped from bends in the pipes into caustic pools.

With a grinding noise the two men pushed a section of the wall aside, revealing yet another passage. Kel stayed behind as everyone passed into this next hidden passage, before looking to make sure no one was left behind, then followed. The wall rotated back into place with a clunk.

"I think we're safe now," Pieter said.

"We need to be ready for contact with the outer security. Are the guys set with the far recognition signal?"

"Yes, but I'll move forward and double-check."

The first thing the outer perimeter security would be looking for would be the backward caps everyone wore and the light-colored panels sewn into their outer coats, displayed by wearing the garments reversed. The Gs all wore clothing common to their fellow Mercians. If they were evading capture in the urban scape, they could dispose of any weapons and try to blend in with the populace.

The underground complex beneath the city was like that of population centers everywhere in the galaxy. As the city grew and the infrastructure increased, aged works were abandoned, subterranean spaces beneath buildings became disused. The city grew up and out, leaving behind forgotten a meshwork of tunnels and sewage pipes.

Much of subterranean Mercia had been anthracite and salt mines. Beneath the old industrial area of North Mercia kilometers of abandoned mines stored toxic waste or archaic machinery, while others held archives of records, long sealed and forgotten. Kel was told that the true extent of the subterranean network was largely unknown. The Mercian Underground had utilized the complex for generations to prepare for the day when they would wage war against an invader. That day had come.

In the past, Mercians escaped from the south through complex ratlines to reach freedom in the north. Just as defectors had escaped to the north, infiltrators and agents also traveled south. The intelligence apparatus of the Kroedellian Union most certainly knew of the presence of the underground tunnels. They were so extensive though that it would be difficult for them to know the full extent and location of the ones currently used. The Underground kept those locations a closely guarded secret. Now that the crisis had come, those spaces were being utilized for the first time in recent history.

Within this maze operated the guerilla force, about a hundred Mercian freedom fighters and five legionnaires. Carelessness would lead to their puny number being discovered within the maze. Or bad luck. To Kel's way of thinking, there was no safe place.

The only safe place was in your mind.

They followed the roughhewn tunnels for several kilometers. At intersections with other routes, a jumble of markings covered the cavern walls. Some were old symbols and notations from the days of mining, letters and numbers of peeling paint naming the different shafts. Some were laser carved. The cacophony of information would be indecipherable to any who did not know what to look for. Kel projected a 3D map in his bucket to direct him while Pieter read the cipher of hidden symbols to lead them in.

Through an intersection of three wide tunnels and into a narrow passage they followed an upward grade until a high-pitched voice cried out, "Who is that?" Kel was content to let the Mercians lead the way. He'd already been shot at once by his own excited troops. He was not ready to repeat the experience.

"Karl, I know that's you!" Pieter yelled ahead. "Give the correct challenge, you dolt."

Voices echoed from ahead. A rapid discussion was happening.

"Five."

"Eight," Pieter answered. The challenge and reply when summed had to total thirteen. It was a simple system that required little memory.

"Advance to be recognized," came the reply. Kel knew that there would be many guns on them. There were also explosive charges in the tunnel walls, ready to seal the entrance permanently if there was a compromise.

Two men stood in front of the reinforced steel door behind a deceptively sloppy array of unremarkable looking mining sleds, turned on their side but reinforced out of view by stacks of sandbags. The disarray of the exterior security layer would deceive most observers as to its true purpose. Kel remained at the back of the column as they approached a security door flanked by firing ports.

Pieter was in the lead and raised his hands to give full view of his white-paneled coat and turned his head so his fellow guerillas could recognize his cap.

"Pieter, thank goodness!" Karl sprinted out from behind cover and grabbed Pieter by the shoulders. "Everyone's back. We did it! We're going to bludgeon the Crudes into submission." The man was younger than Pieter, making the student seem old and wise by comparison.

"Let's worry about that later, Karl. Pass us through and remain alert. There's always the chance we were followed."

Pieter stood to one side as he counted his men through the passage until Kel approached. "Last man, Pieter. Good job for your first patrol. Next time you'll be patrol leader." The security door closed behind them as new men moved into the firing ports.

Pieter blushed. "Thank you, Kel, but I learned I still have a lot to learn. We succeeded because of you. I'm proud to have been a part of the operation, but not even I am brash enough to think I could do what you did."

Kel pulled his bucket off and scratched his head as he always did when removing his lid, whether his head itched or not. "Don't sell yourself short. You did fine. Believe me, no one ever goes out as a patrol leader and feels like he's ready to take on the mantle of command the first time out. If you did, you'd be a danger to everyone."

"Pieter," a man interrupted them walking into the antechamber. "Good to see you. Adam is waiting for you in the command bunker. Let's go."

Pieter turned to Kel. "I have to report to Adam. I'm sure he'll want a report from you as well."

"Go. I'll dismiss the patrol. See you later." He didn't work for Adam. He popped his bucket on again.

"Bigg, you miss me? Me and my Gs are through the security checkpoint. All good?"

Bigg responded. "All good. You're the last in. See you in a few. We'll debrief when you get here. Don't expect a break. We've stirred the fire. Now we have to put some more wood on it."

Kel expected nothing less.

04

It took him a half hour to get the Gs ready again. They were good kids. There hadn't been a single grumble. Weapon maintenance always came before rest. They all understood that the Crudes could find the G-base and the fight for their lives could start at any moment. They had matured in the last few weeks, especially the last few days. If not yet very experienced, they were at least acting like professionals. Kel was pleased.

Killing enemies and losing friends does that to you, he thought.

After he dismissed them, he made his way to the team's quarters. Deeper in the complex, the tunnels and adjoining rooms grew larger before leading to the main chambers. This part of the underground complex had been dug generations before. Thick black veins of anthracite still ran in the rough walls.

Following the map in his bucket he entered one of the largest chambers. Recognizing a few of the key landmarks let him ignore the projection in his left eye. The ceiling vaulted up several stories. Two tank-wide shafts fed the chamber from different directions, one tunnel grading up, the other down. Interstellar freight containers sat around the periphery, and a dozen light civilian repulsor trucks were parked at one end. The trucks were modified with light armor and had mounts for heavy weapons in their beds. When the time to fight came, the Boars—as they called the highly mobile platforms—would be helpful. That would only happen if the Andalusians decided to repel the Crudes with a full-scale military response. Kel wasn't holding his breath. His impression of the Andalusian national character so far was a combination of malaise and timidity.

Gs moved about, working and organizing for the next phase of their operations. Many nodded or waved to Kel. Most of them stood straighter, as he pounded a shoulder in passing.

"You look like warriors." Kel knew what a few words of encouragement from a leader could mean. They moved with purpose and had smiles on their faces. Their morale was high after succeeding in their first military operations against the Crudes. It was the best position they could be in. He hoped it would last.

It took him another twenty minutes of brisk marching through several tunnel sections to reach a smaller chamber with its own checkpoint where the guerilla chief quartered and the team had a small room to themselves. As he walked through the deep arch of the door Bigg and Braley at their makeshift desks looked up from a holo. Several smaller screens held drone feeds from around the city. Poul and Sims were sorting through grav containers, pulling out items and tossing them on their cots. Everyone had their buckets off.

"'Bout time, laggard." Sims plopped onto his cot, datapad in hand. He flashed Kel a grin. "Have fun? I know I did."

"Don't let him kid you, I only just got back," Poul said. "It was a little tricky, but nowhere near as far a return as you had."

"Get something to eat if you need it, Kel, and let's gather round and debrief," Braley said.

Kel dropped his bucket and K-17 on his cot and grabbed a compact ration from a stack beneath it. He just now noticed how hungry he was. He hoped there would be a chance for a real meal soon.

The Mercians liked their food fresh and the Gs balked at eating rations of any kind unless absolutely necessary. They had a kitchen in a lower level, staffed by several older ladies who cooked a hot meal twice a day for the freedom fighters. There were huge stockpiles of food stuffs in stasis around the base, enough to last for months.

Kel usually skipped lunch, but had gotten used to eating it cold with his men. It had become an unspoken part of their routine in the underground base that at noon, no matter if Kel was in the middle of teaching or leading an exercise, Pieter would detail two men to retrieve the midday repast. Thick slices of sausage and cheese eaten with fresh bread were washed down with a bottle of the golden beer the Mercians preferred. His first time invited to share a "field lunch" with the newly minted Gs, he'd thought about resisting. He'd accepted the offer out of courtesy, as a way of building rapport. Now, he found himself each midday thinking about the marbled sausage and cheese and how the sweet beer enhanced their flavor.

As he pulled up a small crate to sit on, forming a circle with the rest of the team around Bigg and Captain Yost, he looked at the ration in his hand. It was not a Republic military ration, but a generic ration that, if one traced the source, led to an unimpressive commercial supplier of the same meals intended for the spacefaring industry. The label said "Protein and Carbohydrate Balance Number Six." He opened it and felt it warm in his hand. It smelled as plain and unremarkable as he knew it was flavorless. He wished he'd had some of the sweet red peppers and olives that accompanied so many of the meals from another of his favorite planets, a place where he'd learned that he'd suppressed a gourmet appetite his whole life.

Am I the only one who thinks that edge planets have better food than the core? he wondered briefly. He never thought the day would come when he'd be particular about the food he ate, other than that most essential variable: quantity.

Maybe I am getting old and soft? he mused.

"Alright, let's keep this short," Braley began. "I've got a meet with Adam in about an hour unless he calls for me sooner. He's getting briefed on all the ops now. Get me up to speed on each of your hits before I have to tackle any unknowns from our G-Chief. I'll start off.

"The hit on the power substations and towers went smoothly. I divided our force to hit the six inner-city substations simultaneously. Everyone nailed their substation without a fight. By the time I took my squad to drop the relay towers, Sims had already knocked out the net. Surprised the tower guards easily. With major power already down and their comms dead as cold vacuum, they didn't slow us down at all."

Kel envied the op to kill the power substations. Sabotage was the grandest form of vandalism in the universe. Braley's hit was a teenage boy's dream.

The infrastructure of the entire planet of Cassell was a mix of ancient and modern equipment. The huge substation transformers and power lines were secured by a mere perimeter fence. Its single-beam energy disruptor on top was enough to keep kids from scaling the fence and frying themselves, but provided little barrier to a determined saboteur.

Destroying the substations was ridiculously simple. The North Mercian ones still used physical power lines that led to other power distribution stations around the inner city. The energy transfer only became wireless in the newer parts of the city. Virtually any large gauge wire laid across the primary power lines would induce an electrical short that fused breakers and buses and melted the transformers into slag.

They chose kids with good throwing arms. Polymerized graphene wire tied to a rock could be tossed high over the power lines. The wire was as thin as a hair and as strong as impervisteel cable many times its diameter. It was also an excellent electrical conductor. The material encouraged the transition of the flowing energy into a plasma phase, creating arcs of high conductivity between the different nodes. They used the wire for many things. That the wire worked so well in this application was its one-plus-a-thousand use.

He wished he'd been there to see the sparks fly. What he really wished he could've seen in person were the towers coming down.

Where centralized electrical generation and subdivided transmission still existed, wireless relays were used. Even older fusion reactors that powered individual homes or buildings made that infrastructure unnecessary. Cassell was even more stunted in tech than most, and it worked to their advantage. The wireless transmission towers were a more modern part of the local power grid. The two hundred-meter tall towers were visibly interspersed around the expanded, newer parts of the city. Except for one site where a large collection of them grouped together to form the relay that sent power south across the wall to the Crudes' territory.

"Then we knocked down the entire array on this side of the border wall. The det-initiators worked like a charm," Braley said.

Bigg gave a pursed-lip smile at the compliment for his construction of the demolitions.

Braley continued unabated. "One of the Gs laid a charge on the wrong side of a tower and I thought that bad boy was coming down right on top of us. Those things are twargin' behemoths when you see one falling toward you. Other than that brief excitement—where I ran the fastest hundred meters of my life—it was smooth. All my elements made it back here separately and without incident."

The Crudes hadn't completely shut down traffic in the city, but would be coming.

"Poul, you go next," Braley said as he sat back down. Kel could tell Braley felt proud of what he'd achieved. Disrupting the physical power grid would be a huge part of their plan to deny North Mercia to the Crudes.

"Roger." Poul leaned forward with his elbows on his knees. Kel had been anxious for his friend's role in last night's sabotage. The reservoir and water treatment plant were one of the few places in the city that were heavily guarded. It had to have been the most dangerous of all their missions, but Poul looked as relaxed as always.

"The plan to sneak us into the compound worked perfectly. The Auxiliary members who work at the plant lived up to their rep. Once we made contact at the garage, me, Lothar, and two of the Gs got smuggled into the compound by one of the engineering supervisors in his maintenance van. I was ready to slot the guards at the main gate, but it wasn't necessary. I staged the rest of the Gs at the chemical warehouse up the road inside a commercial cargo sled with markings from the same warehouse. They could have been there in minutes if we'd needed them.

"They got us into the main pumphouse of the waste-water plant and we placed fusion charges into the housings of every pump in the place. Then we got back in the truck and took a leisurely ride to the back side of the compound where the main reservoir sits. Those pumphouses weren't guarded either—it's inside the compound, you know? So, we one-at-a-time visited them and placed our charges again. The pumps are enormous and the housings cover a maze of pipes and controllers, so concealing the fusion charges was easy. If you didn't know what you were looking at, you could look right at one and wouldn't think it was out of place.

"I placed one shaped charge in the spillway control center. I honestly don't know if damaging the mechanism will keep the floodgates closed, or force them all open once the charge goes off. The engineer thought that with the height of the water column, they'll probably open, but he wasn't sure either. If we'd had a chance to pick his brain before the op, we might have been able to come up with a better plan. I put him on the spot to help me choose the most critical placement. We should know in about..." Poul checked his chrono on the link of his armor's forearm, "... ninety-three minutes."

Not even Bigg had an informed opinion about where to best attack the gates that controlled the reservoir spill-way. The central gear room seemed the most logical place, other than attacking the individual gates themselves. They all agreed that working around the individual floodgates would have been too risky with too much potential exposure and for little added benefit.

Poul yawned. "Anyway, then we just got back in the truck, passed back out the main gate, and I made link-up with the rest of the Gs. We got an early warning to bypass our original safe house, and hit the secondary lay-up site. No sweat. Then we made the trip to the rail-yard and through the tunnels back here. It was pretty dull, really. The guys were disappointed they didn't get to use their needlers and suppressed weapons. I told them, 'next time.'"

Kel didn't believe the act that Poul had found the mission boring, but admired his friend's attempt at stoicism. If Poul had ended up having to make an assault into or out of the compound, it could've been a meat grinder.

"What about the engineer and his crew?" Bigg asked.

Poul nodded. "Cool as ice. Must be real patriots because no one else would take that kind of risk. Their work shift ended at sunup and everyone who came on shift this morning knows to be in parts of the compound away from the charges. The whole plant is staffed by members of the Auxiliary. If the Crudes go back and review security feeds from last night, even the Crudes will notice the activity of the maintenance van around all the sites we targeted."

The Crudes ran a complete surveillance state over their own citizens. If they were competent at anything, it would be in their thorough investigation of the water plant sabotage. And there would be ample evidence to find.

"Lothar assured me that last night's crew were placed there with approval of the Underground. All young men without families, except the engineer. The Underground moved them out this morning while we were working to get back here. They should be well hidden by now. The engineer and his family will be funneled through a ratline northward as soon as possible. I'm sure the rest of the workers will be rounded up and interrogated if they're foolish enough to stick around after..." he checked his chrono again. "After another ninety minutes or so. I dropped a nano-drone and posted it on one of the water towers."

The fusion charges would heat to over five thousand degrees Celsius and sustain a reaction for minutes in a radius of a meter. The pumps and associated piping were constructed out of old-fashioned cast iron. There would be nothing left of the pumps or their fixtures; even the duracrete would be vaporized. As long as no one was within the confines of the pump houses to be injured by the heat or the fumes, there should be no friendly casualties.

Without sewage or clean water, however, the city would be a disaster zone within days.

"Great job, Poul," Braley said, giving a thumbs up to the man. "We're all relieved you had a quiet time of it. Bigg, you left the most obvious telltale that the resistance is active. Tell the rest of the team about it."

"I prefer to let the images speak for themselves." Bigg punched a datapad, prepared for just this moment, and a holo projected into their midst. The most obvious thing about the scene of the river and its banks was the absence of the huge multi-tiered bridge that should be spanning it. The famous bridge had been considered a marvel of architecture throughout the galaxy, both for its beauty as well as for its functionality. Only remnants of the superstructure could be seen protruding from the calm waters below.

"Amazing," Sims said in a reverent voice. "Just amazing."

"Bigg," Poul said like a small child pleading for a story, "is that the biggest thing you've ever brought down?"

Bigg stroked his chin. "Mmm, no. The orbital station over Takkas Four that I dropped on the planet was probably the biggest. This was the most *famous* thing I've ever destroyed, though."

Kel laughed. Only Bigg would have a target in his repertoire that was bigger than this monumental act of destruction. "How'd it run, Bigg?" he asked.

"Smooth. It wasn't hard. The implementation didn't change much from what we concocted back in isolation. It would've been very difficult without the swimmers. If we'd had to lay charges on the long spans, it would've taken the whole force to make it happen. Taking the bridge at both ends, then trying to get out alive—it would've been tough. Glad we had another option."

They'd all worked together for a week just on the target planning for the bridge. Everyone had been assigned multiple target packages to assess, and Bigg had overseen everyone's ops plans. It turned out that they each led one of the missions that they'd planned for the first strike, like Kel's to destroy the rail system. Bigg had taken the Azure River Bridge for himself. Sims had tried to claim it but Bigg immediately interceded. "Sorry, youngster. This requires a little more, shall we say, finesse than you have been known to use in the past."

Sims pouted. "Now, that's just plain hurtful, Bigg. I maintain my innocence. I set that plasma charge for low, concentrated discharge. I don't know how it ended up on high, dispersed."

The idea had been to remove the door in an efficient manner. Instead, the façade of the target building had vaporized in front of them. The inadvertent error had actually speeded their acquisition of the high-value target. The surprised man gaped at them as they serviced him where he sat from outside the building, which had been a plus.

In addition to helping everyone with their targets, each night after everyone else had knocked off, Bigg mulled over how best to destroy the Azure River Bridge, Cassell's glittering architectural gem.

It was one of the longest single-span bridges ever constructed. The repulsor sponsons that were part of the architecture of the spans operated on self-contained fusion plants. The redundancy and independent power source of each repulsor meant that to collapse the bridge more than half of the repulsors would need to be destroyed to drop it.

The multitiered spans were perfectly flat and the bridge had no mechanical suspension or arches. The only piers under the two-kilometer run of the bridge sat under the spiral towers at each end that served as the path onto and off of the different levels. The lowest span served the maglev rail line. The top tier was for those who wanted to enjoy the view. The middle tiers fed directly to other high-speed routes around the rest of the city.

Bigg had let them all in on his plan at the same time during their brief-back of the operation, including the DO commander Colonel Hartenstein and his staff. It was an ingenious plan and approval immediately followed.

Smuggling in the logistics to take down such a target was an issue. If they'd had to rely on material obtained once in North Mercia, it would not have been possible. Fortunately, they'd had an easy infiltration into the threatened city. Tensions were high and getting higher when they'd arrived in the divided city, but the Crudes' invasion across the wall hadn't yet happened.

They'd had no limit on what they could bring into the country and had brought enough gear to support every contingency. North Mercia was an oasis, surrounded on all sides and separated from the rest of North Andalusia by the Kroedellian Empire. Travel into and out of the city was by a single rail line and a single highway, each thoroughfare lined with energy fences and minefields to prevent uncontrolled access into South Mercian territory.

From the spacefield in North Andalusia, they'd loaded a train car with grav container after grav container camouflaged as typical cargo and protected by interference and deception tech. They'd planned for redundancy, and had divided duplicate loads between multiple rail shipments. It had proven unnecessary. Even in the heightened state of security, not one of their packages had been detected by the Crude inspectors.

The team made their entrance into the city under false identities and spoofed biometrics arranged by Republic Intelligence. After making contact with Meadows and the Auxiliary, they staged equipment and weapons at safehouses within the city and in the underground complex. One of the first things Bigg confirmed as they sorted through their gear was the safe arrival of the grav container containing his swimmers—AI-driven submersible drones that could deliver a variety of payloads, including explosives.

"Since any portal into the river is guarded, we knew we'd have to eliminate any sentries to get the swimmers deployed. Up till the last minute, I held out hope of the Auxiliary scoring us access to one of the anthracite barges that still traffic the river, but no dice. I've played with the swimmers before, and the AI is just stupid enough to get confused over a long infil, so I knew I would have to manually guide their placement onto the piers.

"The water access with the best concealment was guarded by four Crudes. Anders did a good job. It was slick. We drove the sled right down to the top of the boat launch, and he got out and distracted the guards while I serviced them." Kel knew what Bigg meant. He had dispatched the guards efficiently and silently.

"Luckily, they were all together and pacing about, trying to stay warm. Anders drew them in and they barely had time to raise their weapons by the time I finished with the last one."

Everyone was listening with rapt attention to Bigg's description, imagining how the scene had played out. They'd all seen what a machine their team sergeant was with any weapon system.

"Anders didn't flinch. Played it cool. He was still talking to them a hundred klicks an hour before they even noticed me come around the other side of the sled. He's a good man.

"Some of the Gs took the Crudes' topcoats and hats, stashed the corpses and took the sentries' place while we moved the sled to the bottom of the ramp and got the swimmers deployed. It was pretty humdrum from there. Things got a little hinky as the swimmers got closer to the piers, as I knew they would be. Driving them into final position took about an hour. The rest... well, I had the finest view I've ever had for one of my shots." Bigg swiped across the datapad to the feed he'd recorded from one of his drones.

The holo showed the beautiful bridge, lit in the typical manner known from the well-advertised tourist displays. Multicolored lights highlighted the sprawling architectural wonder and illuminated the unnaturally blue water of the Azure River underneath. It was one of the few notable attractions on the world of Cassell. Even the Crudes must have admired it in some fashion, as they had not interfered with the bridge operation in any way except to close it to civilian traffic during the hours of darkness.

"Watch this guy," Bigg said, pointing at a Crude heavy sled making its way across one of the middle tiers of the bridge. "He's about to be the luckiest guy in all of Mercia."

Kel watched intently with the rest of his team as the vehicle finished its traverse across the bridge and into the spirals of the tower, routing onto one of the exit ramps and off onto one of the highways leading north. No sooner had the sled towing its three trailers made it off the tower span than the waters around each of the piers erupted. The huge towers collapsed on themselves, billowing equally huge plumes of water into the air. Their lights continued to blaze over the river, spotlights on a stage, the final act of the catastrophe played out under their glow.

The spans seemed to float for another few seconds before the higher spans, no longer tied to the towers, torqued and rotated, finally collapsing on top of each other before plummeting into the river. Tsunami-like waves swelled as the team hooted and clapped.

Bigg smiled, stood, bowed to them, and took his seat again. "Thank you. It was my pleasure."

"Is that your first time using the neutronium charges?" Sims asked once they'd all settled down.

"Yup. I have to say, they worked as advertised."

Kel had been briefed on the new tech. He was not ashamed to admit that even being within ten grids of the stuff made him nervous. The material was supposedly dense as a star's core. The minute amount of neutronium, technically several micrograms of pentaneutrons held together by its containment field, was contained in a device that weighed several hundred kilos. When the containment field was released and the material instantly decayed into mononeutrons, the explosive force it produced was incredible, just as they had witnessed. The thought of the stuff detonating prematurely because of a containment system failure worried him the entire trip.

"I'm looking forward to using it again." Bigg grinned.

Kel was sure he meant it.

"You next, Kel," Braley prompted. Kel gave them a rundown of his op, and showed them the drone recording from the aftermath. It was a paltry demolition compared to Bigg's, but he felt proud of what his Gs had done. Poor Helmut was the only casualty any of the teams had taken.

"Getting the drop on that guard change was a great move, brother. Nothing else you could have done," Poul said.

"For such a basic confidence target for the Gs, you ended up seeing the most blaster play of any of us. Way to KTF!" Sims added.

"Thanks," Kel said. There was something about the sequence of events on the objective and losing a man that still bothered him, but he couldn't put a name to what it was.

"Yes. Well done, Kel," Braley said. "All right, Sims, take us home. Run us through it."

Sims had been rocking back on the two rear legs of the ancient wood chair during their debriefs. Now he leaned forward and assumed a sitting-at-attention posture, as though he was about to be interrogated. Sims was a great operator and fit well into Team Three's family dynamic, but was still the newest member of the team. At some level, he knew Sims felt that he had not been completely accepted though he had been, many times over.

"The hit on the communications node facility went smoothly. There were no obstacles that we had not anticipated or prepared for and so far, I believe the results are exactly what we had hoped for. By all measures I can find no evidence that any portion of the Crudes communication or information network is functioning. The parasite has achieved a total kill."

The silencing of the comm node had been without a doubt the most critical mission objective of them all.

It almost failed before it even began.

05

The galaxy had a sense of humor. But only frustration, failure, and death brought the laughs it liked best. It didn't care if you found the joke funny. They were old friends that way. Kel knew how it all worked. How nothing ever went smoothly. He should've known that the most important of the missions was primed to be the butt of the universe's next attempt at comedy. Legionnaires were the favorite target for its routines. He'd held out hope it would be different this time. Every so often, the galaxy took a day off from trying to kill you.

But the galaxy never passed on opportunities like this.

Two incidents nearly snuffed the entire operation. Kel was there for them both, and mused on the debacles they nearly were as Sims reviewed the specifics of his subsequent coup disrupting the crucial comm network.

One happened their second day in country. The next occurred just days before the Crudes' invasion. The first was the stuff of clenched teeth and red rage and cemented for Kel an old prejudice against a favorite target for distrust.

After arriving in the city, the team focused on establishing their relationship with the guerillas while covertly assessing their potential targets. They knew they were on the clock, and that it was very likely that they were going to run out of time to train the G-force properly. They weren't wrong.

The team transitioned to local civilian garb on arrival in North Andalusia. Everyone wore their nanotubule ballistic undergarments. The skins, as they called them, were effective in defeating a variety of ballistic, kinetic, and edged weapons, but were not the protection their armor was. They surrendered all their weapons to the grav containers for transport into the city, and everyone was as anxious as Kel to retrieve blasters once in their new hunting grounds.

Once in the city, they would divide and conquer. Bigg and Braley were going to cement the relationship between the Gs and Area Command and try to expedite the buildup and training phase with the guerrilla force. Kel and the others would work on caching their gear around the city and reconnoitering targets.

North Mercia was a city of contrasts. Everywhere you looked, the old and new coexisted. Modern architecture sat next to ancient stone buildings. During the day, older Mercians peddled goods from shops while young students milled about, ensconced in discussions and studies outside the many street side cafés. The Auxiliary had arranged to quarter them in the densest population center within the old city where nightclubs, drug dens, and other illicit activities flourished. It was excellent cover. Nightlife in the old city attracted tourists from all parts. In a galaxy where slavery could still be found, and any titillation, peccadillo, or misdemeanor could be catered to for the right price, it was noteworthy that North Mercia was renowned for its open tolerance of debauchery.

The first place they were to be quartered was an open loft above one of the most famous sex clubs in the city. The club was in an abandoned power plant not a block off the scenic river walkway. Dens of iniquity lined the streets, offering every sort of intoxicant and distraction known to man. Meadows had delivered them from the train station to their temporary base of operations on a midweek night. Kel was in the back of the windowless vehicle with the rest of the team, Bigg sitting in the front row with Braley, conversing with Meadows as he drove them into the old quarter of the city. Kel couldn't see but through a narrow portion of the front windscreen. As they neared their destination, they could all feel the primal beats of music in their bones as they drove slowly through parting crowds of partiers moving from one club to another.

"Meadows, where the hell are you taking us? To a parade?" Bigg protested.

"I know, I know. Trust me. Our people have this locked down solid. It's probably the safest location in North Mercia. The police don't even patrol here. I've gotten to know some of the club owners the Auxiliary uses for arranging safehouses. These people are a lot of things, but one thing they are not are fans of the Kroedellian Empire. Adam tells me his people here are some of the oldest and most ardent supporters of the Underground. You'll see. No one's going to notice our comings and goings. Trust me."

Meadows pulled into an alley, and quickly let them out of the side compartment door. What Kel saw first was a group of overly muscular men gathered together near a trash receptacle by the alley entrance to their safehouse. They were dressed, if you could call it dressed, in a variety of costumes that concealed nothing and seemed to serve no purpose other than to act as anchor points for various spikes and rivets, or animal tails and ears. They passed some handheld device between them, taking turns waving it in front of their eyes as it emitted a harsh, greenish light. After each took a turn blinding themselves, the user burst into uncontrollable laughter, and the next player took charge of the thing and proceeded to do the same. Kel thought he had seen a lot in his life. Not this.

"Come on, let's get inside." Meadows led them into the alley entrance and through a kitchen that was filled with as many partiers as it had workers preparing food. The music from the club floor beyond deafened them as the sliding door from the kitchen opened and a waiter slid past, the explosion of lights, noise, and feathered dancers magnified. They held in their astonishment while climbing the two flights to their new home.

Braley was the first to question Meadows's sanity.

"Meadows, have you lost it, man? I thought all this time with RI would've made you *more* adept at covert operations, not *less.*"

Kel had to agree.

"Captain, believe me, I know what you're thinking," he said, palms up in surrender. "You're not going to be here for long before your next move, and it will be the perfect site to stage from for your target assessments. No one will notice any of your night activities and during the day, you can work and sleep here in peace. It's going to work out brilliantly."

Everyone took a moment to look around the loft. Multiple beds were arranged around the open floor with a fresher on either end, each with its own raised tub.

"What do they use this space..." Kel started.

"Best not to think about it," Meadows interrupted. "Hey, did I tell you how great the food is downstairs? Anyone hungry?"

Meadows ended the night with a brief on the next day's activities. Their essential gear, especially their weapons containers and armor, had made it up to the flat. The many other containers Meadows had in one of his secured warehouses. Tomorrow they'd recover the rest of the gear and start the process of putting some of the extra weapons and demolition gear in caches around the city, then getting the rest to the proposed G-base. In the morning Braley and Bigg would meet for the first time with the G-Chief, Adam. It was another crucial threshold for the operation. Failure to attain rapport early with the man could jeopardize everything they had been sent to do. Almost everything.

"We haven't been completely successful locating the main comm node," Meadows revealed. "We think we have the location of the new node almost nailed down, but we're not confident enough to want you to hit it without better intel."

The comm system had undergone a gradual upgrade recently. It had been done by the North Mercian government in conjunction with the Andalusian intelligence service and great care had been taken to hide its location.

Their target package had lacked detail about the location, but its existence as a legitimate government information and comms hub was not in doubt. RI's ability to track the movement of the high-tech equipment into the area over the last year proved it. The Mercian government had good reasons to treat the node's location as a secret. It was as much to protect it from sabotage or infiltration by the Crudes as to protect the valuable equipment from espionage by rival information corporations trying to compete with the state-run entity.

Using the node as the entry portal for the parasite was hyper-critical. Post-invasion, once the Crudes channeled their own information network through the powerful hub, the upgraded pathways would allow the package to make its insidious intrusion nearly instantly. It would cripple the Crude response to their upcoming war against them.

"The other item that makes things difficult is the possibility that the Crudes already have control of the hub."

"*What*?" Bigg yelled from the other side of the room. He walked over. "What makes that a possibility?"

Meadows sighed. "My case officer agrees with me that Crude advance agents are everywhere in the city. Every time we go out, there's evidence of more activity by the Kookies. He's advised RI to up the threat level for an invasion to 'Imminent.'" Kookies was their nickname for the Kroedellians' intelligence service, the KOCI. "Their goons are showing up everywhere. Everywhere but the red-light district, that is."

"Okay," Sims said. "What's the plan?"

"We've got two RI tech geeks in the city to help us. We've outfitted them in a commercial delivery vehicle. The plan is to do a technical reconnaissance on suspected sites and try to nail down an exact location for you. I want you and Kel with us. You," he pointed at Sims, "because you're going to need time with the geeks and to get eyes on your hit. Both of you, because if we attract attention, we may get in a fight."

Meadows looked at Kel. "I've been with these RI guys for quite a while now. If I've ever needed another leej to back me up, it's going to be for this. These guys aren't up to the task if we have to get wet."

Kel and Sims looked at each other. It was a no-brainer. "Let's do it."

That night was the beginning of the combat phase of the operation.

This was a city brought to life by darkness rather than subdued. Meadows swung by the safe house to find Kel and Sims suited up and ready to roll. They'd talked through the different options for tonight's outing and decided to remain in civilian garb with their skins underneath as the only source of protection. If they got into a fight and ended up splitting up and traveling on foot, running around North Mercia in Legion armor would tip their hand. Even the indulgent bon vivants of the red-light district would notice.

Meadows drove them to one of his mission sites, a large garage where the surveillance van waited. Kel and Sims walked around the van and inspected their ride. Multiple fading colors where layers of older coatings showed through the top coat by its dents and dings made it like the city it drove through. There were no windows on the sides or back, but as Kel scanned the body, he found the telltale dull shimmer of micro sensors arrayed near the seams of the portals, hidden in natural areas of the fading and contrasting paint colors. From inside they would have 360-degree awareness of their surroundings.

Meadows slid the main portal back and gestured the men in. Kel placed a hand to his side to control the K-17 that he and Sims each carried slung underneath their calf-length coats as he stepped up into the rear compartment. They carried their blaster pistols and had filled their pockets with ener-grenades. The season and fashion that made the large overcoats unremarkable was a blessing from Oba. Had it been warm weather, concealing their armaments would have been problematic.

In the middle of the compartment were two young men attentively arranging stacks of components. Holos broadcast in 2-D the feed from the external sensors. Meadows got into the driver compartment and one of the young men stepped forward to take the passenger seat.

"Kel and Sims, meet Ted and Fred." Kel suppressed a chuckle. He knew the names were covers, but having two names that rhymed struck him as funny.

"Ready," the man in the front said. Kel arbitrarily made him the "Ted" of the pair. Ted held a datapad on his lap and started a quiet discussion with Fred in the rear, moving from one stack of components to another, making small adjustments to each as they drove.

Meadows kept a roaming commentary on their location and his intended route to locate the node as he drove around the city. Traffic was congested and slow on most of the main thoroughfares and Kel felt at ease, certain that they were unremarkable to their fellow travelers. Meadows informed them when they were a few minutes out from their first possible for the node center. Kel sat on the deck with his back against the compartment. He'd removed his coat and folded it underneath him for a cushion and kept his K-17 slung and between his legs. Sims did the same from the opposite side. They each had a projection to watch, monitoring the external environment around the vehicle.

The vehicle slowed as they rolled past a nondescript, unmarked building with a façade that screamed "Official Government Business." The two techs started conversing with each other in a language that sounded like Standard, but was so filled with acronyms and jargon that Kel stopped trying to translate it in his head.

"The PPK is coming through. Any QMD or QMP?" Ted asked.

"It could be QMD, but I need to reduce the background EMF to be sure," Fred answered.

Kel looked at Sims, who just shrugged. Sims was quite the techie himself, so if the chatter was nonsense to him, Kel knew he wasn't the only one out of his element.

After their slow pass by the building, Ted told Meadows, "Nope. Next possible."

"Come on, grandma, move that donkey cart," Meadows said aloud as he tried to veer around a vehicle stopped in front of them. A vehicle behind them paused to let them detour into their lane and they were rolling again to the next site.

"It'll take about thirty minutes," Meadows said over his shoulder. "Rest up."

Kel couldn't but instead observed the pedestrians and drivers around them. No one seemed flustered or hurried. None of the drivers acted agitated or aggressive. Despite the general sense of impending danger fostered by the local news feed, no one seemed to be letting it change the patterns of their daily life.

They made the same kind of pass by two more possible sites and listened as Ted and Fred spoke their secret babble back and forth, trying to determine if the necessary trace of invisible electromagnetic waves and particles fit the parameters they searched for. Twice again they heard, "Nope. Next."

Kel was getting restless. His legs started to fall asleep, and he'd lost interest in the Mercians around him. His thoughts turned to his mission to knock out the maglev rail. Perhaps he could make a trip out to the country to see the site for himself soon...

"Next site coming up," Meadows said. Their vehicle slowed.

The entrance to the building sat in a small courtyard behind a large impervisteel fence. Standing in the courtyard was a wide-shouldered man wearing a long coat like his own. The man's face had a single large eyebrow over a pronounced ridge. His nose looked like it had been broken more than once. Kel spotted the subtle stiffness under the man's coat, something long enough to be a carbine.

"Sims, look at my monitor. Check that guy out." Sims scooted into the center of the compartment and looked up behind him at the monitor.

"Thug. No question. He looks just like the guy across the street."

Kel glanced at the monitor. Tucked back into an alley was the twin to Kel's thug in the courtyard. Fred and Ted exchanged furtive words.

"Follow the peak—the peak, not the trough."

"No kidding, genius. Let the program do what it's supposed to."

"We're missing it, we're missing it."

They rolled past the building in question and turned onto a major thoroughfare and picked up speed.

"What?" Meadows asked. "Talk to me, you two."

Fred started. "We got some really whacky stuff back there. It may not be a comm node, though. I can't say. We need to do another pass-by."

Kel interrupted. "Meadows, we saw two thugs outside. One in the courtyard, one across the street. No question they were secret police types. If you think the node has been infiltrated already, then I'm betting that was it. Why else would they have goons on it? Let's check any other potential spots before we call it a night and save this one for a second look another time soon."

"*No,*" Ted said. "We might not get another night. Besides, we're getting out of North Mercia soon. We *have* to find the node tonight."

"Ted," Kel responded, not sure if he was actually Ted or not, "I am with you one hundred percent. It is critical we locate the node. What I'm saying is, if we roll past again, those guys are going to make us. Those goons are secret police. I'm sure of it. They may look like dumb muscle, but I'm telling you their job is spotting people and patterns. We roll past them again, they'll blow us and we'll have given up any advantage we might have. Meadows, don't do it."

After pulling off to the side of the road Meadows, turned to face them. "What do you need for a confirmation?"

The young man in back said, "I think I can get it with another pass. I have the signature cleaned up for comparison. If I can get another hit on it, we can call it a confirmation."

Meadows thought. He looked at the datapad next to him. "There's not another street on any side where we can get near enough to make a close pass. It has to be close, doesn't it?"

Fred nodded. "We need the origin point as clean as we can get to be sure. Got to be within fifty meters or closer. The detectors are sensitive, but there're so many other sources that could produce a similar trace."

This much Kel understood. The comm node did not produce a high output signal. That happened offsite at the relays. The signals generated at the node were transmitted by hard line to the relays. At the node, the signal they needed to confirm would be difficult to detect.

"Kel, Sims, what do you say?" Meadows asked.

"Whatever you think, brother," Sims told Kel quietly. "I'll back your play."

Kel thought. "If you have to do another, let's do it. If they do make us, it's unlikely we'll end up in a gunfight. But if they do burn us, we'll never get another chance to get near them again."

"Okay. I'm going to take the long way around. Relax. I'll give everyone plenty of warning. It'll be at least thirty minutes."

Kel closed his eyes and tried to relax. It was going to be a long thirty minutes.

He was surprised when he heard Meadows give the five-minute warning, and then alert them again as they made the turn unto the side street. Kel and Sims shifted toward the center of the compartment so they could spot both monitors together. The thugs were present. Meadows kept at the same rolling pace, smooth and steady. The thug in the courtyard appeared to take interest in their vehicle and walked toward the fence to follow them past.

"We're made," Kel said. "Thug number one has his eyes glued to us. First pass, he registered us but scanned to other things. Now we have his undivided attention. You can bet the kookies have the street observed under sensors."

Fred stopped his conversation with Ted. "No. Not to worry. We have an active interrupter signal on."

"What?" Kel said louder than he intended. "You're actively fuzzing any scans of us? That means they now have *two* different sensor signal interruptions associated with *this vehicle*. Meadows, get us the hell out of here. We're going to take a long drive around the city and see if we've picked up any trailers before we head in. Not good, guys."

"Agreed," Meadows said. "We'll play it cool, but we are definitely getting out of here. Good work, gents. You got the confirmation, right?"

In the back, Fred was silent. Then, "I've got bad news. I don't think I have it. We need another pass."

Kel grunted. "Have it or not, that's not happening. We are out of here."

"Hey, man," Ted said to him as the youth turned around to face him. "You aren't in charge here. *We* don't work for *you*," he shouted, flailing his arms. "It's the other way around. How come all you operators get cold feet when—"

Kel didn't let him continue. He pointed at the man in the front seat. Fingers and thumb extended and joined in a perfect knife hand. A soft voice commanded attention, like the tiny red light that read "danger."

"Turn around and face forward. Do it now. Stop drawing attention. Remain calm. Every driver or pedestrian who just saw your display knows there must be passengers in the rear and that you're agitated at them. Don't do that again."

Ted turned forward and was silent a long moment. "Okay. You're right about that. Sorry. Look, we need to verify the signal. It's as simple as that."

Kel thought he knew the score, but didn't want to aggravate the situation by voicing it. Ted and Fred were support personnel and they wanted out of North Mercia before the invasion went down. They also wanted to complete their mission. The problem being that doing so with a third drive-by would compromise Team Three's ability to complete their own mission. That was not their concern. They could go back, tell their boss about their daring exploits in the field, submit a self-aggrandizing report detailing how they'd found the comm node, and never give it another thought. Never mind that they'd alerted the Crudes along the way, turning the site into an impregnable fortress once the invasion occurred. That potential meant nothing to them.

"You both did a good job," Kel offered. "Do you agree that this site has been the most likely match so far?"

Ted looked over his shoulder at Fred. Fred nodded.

"Yes. We have to do some review of what we got. It'll clean up a little I'm sure, but, yeah. I'm betting it's a high seventy percent chance that's the node."

Seventy percent was pretty good. Especially since the other sites had been ruled out.

"Good," Kel said as brightly as he could. "Great. We'll have other ways of confirming the target before we hit it. Nice job, guys. Thanks."

The two techies nodded in satisfaction. They stayed quiet the rest of the night as Meadows performed repetition after repetition of simple maneuvers to try to flush out any vehicles that might be trailing them. Kel and Sims watched the rear sensor monitors for any indication of a tail.

Finally, after two hours of loops all over the city, he performed one last maneuver. Meadows set it up perfectly. He was at the lead of several vehicles on a two-lane road. As they approached the traffic drone hovering above a four-way stop, Meadows stopped at the green light. He paused just long enough for the light to turn yellow, then accelerated through the intersection. No vehicle behind tried to run through the red light, though one of them honked. No vehicle had passengers exit the vehicle to follow on foot. Meadows turned at the next street, and sped away.

Back at the garage they sanitized their ride. They said goodbye to the young techies and Kel drove the van, following Meadows and Sims to a lot several miles away where Kel parked the van and abandoned it. He hopped in with his friends and rode back to the red-light district as the sun rose.

"Now that we have a site narrowed down, if we get that information to the Underground, do you think they can get a better confirmation for us?" Kel asked Meadows.

"I'm betting they can. Hey, that was a nice way you handled those kids back there. You deescalated that little snot's temper tantrum. Sket, I think he even felt complimented by the time you were done with him. I sit at the feet of the master."

Kel laughed. "Complimenting him wasn't what I wanted to do to him."

The second incident became the stuff of legend.

Weeks later they'd been with the Gs full-time and making good progress. Meadows's contact in the Underground used the information, and word came back there was high probability that the site was in fact the new comm node. The situation was also not as bad as it had initially seemed. The Crudes were not in control of the node, but had a presence there. One of the civilian directors was suspected of being a Crude agent. He had brought in several "security consultants" on his own. The consultants were definitely Kroedellian secret police. Kookies.

Once the Underground knew where to look, their own operatives were able to make contact with sympathetic sources within the information technology branch of the city government, until after enough layers of questioning, a low level-employee at the node was identified whose cousin was a member of the Underground. Cautious questioning of his cousin yielded a wealth of information previously unknown about the node site and the composition of its staff. The director was acting odd and the recent appearance of the muscled thugs seemed out of place to the workers. That was enough to complete the picture for them all.

Still, they needed more information about entry points into the node building. It was getting closer and closer to the seemingly inevitable invasion. They'd considered launching a nano-drone to get them the information they needed, but quickly discounted the idea. If the Crudes did have adequate countermeasure detection and the drone's snooping was revealed, it would be another red flag that the site was being evaluated by someone for a tactical purpose.

Sometimes, the mark-one, mod-one eyeball was the best intelligence gathering tool of them all.

"I know you guys are secretly loving this," Poul said. "Don't pretend you aren't, not for our benefit." They were now in their quarters in the underground G-base, getting ready for their foray into the city. Poul was in armor, and had delayed his departure to train Gs to hang around long enough to witness the preparation Kel and Sims were going through for their close reconnaissance of the comm node. "You should take those outfits back with you. You'll both be very popular."

Kel didn't respond. He wasn't going to take the bait. Sims wasn't in the mood either, which was unusual for him. He normally enjoyed banter. Not tonight.

The Gs helped them acquire the fashions they now donned, probably from some of their personal wardrobes, if Kel had to guess. While the red-light district where such dress was normal was some distance away from the comm node facility, it was common to see groups of young people moving about the city dressed for a night out as they made their way to public transport hubs for the trip into the old quarter.

A few of the younger Gs fussed over making their costumes perfect. It was common for Mercian youths to dress as he and Sims now were, but it did nothing to ease his anxiety about appearing so flamboyant. It was the opposite of what a lifetime of mental conditioning as to what constituted "low-key" had prepared him to accept.

They kept their military-style boots. Their thick, loose-fitting trousers had been replaced with skin-tight stretch leggings. They wore their black nano-tubule skins underneath everything, much to their fashion consultants' dismay.

"You'll stand out more if you cover up your skin like that—your real skin, I mean," one had said.

"We've got plenty of body paint to keep you from getting cold," another insisted.

Kel let them know that wearing their skins was non-negotiable.

"Suit yourselves. But you'll stand out less if you don't look like prudes."

The multi-colored vests and metallic hair enhance-ments concealed sensors that would record vital details about the gate and main entrance—data they'd need to make a breaching plan. The gaudy wraparound visors concealed their gaze and also captured images. They would make a leisurely pass down the street in front of the target to collect as much information about the build-ing and surrounding structures as possible.

They hadn't much time before their window of op-portunity closed. Crude troops were massed across the southern barrier, waiting for the signal to invade. Many residents had evacuated the city for the safety of North Andalusia. Most had remained and were carrying on with their normal routines, hoping for the best. It was a pat-tern that had repeated in the past without the final step of a military invasion occurring. "Perhaps the current crisis will resolve itself," seemed to be the prevailing attitude.

Lastly, they put on thigh-length outercoats adorned with colorful feathers and baubles. Kel looked at Sims, hoping that he did not look as ridiculous, but knew that he did. They were dressed almost identically. Kel stole a glance at himself in the mirror. He wished he hadn't.

"Let's get this ball rolling," he said as he picked up his pistol and placed it at his rear waist, and felt the attractive grab of the retention device magically secure the pistol to his side. He preferred to carry the weapon near his ap-pendix for the fastest and most natural access when in civilian attire, but his current fashion did not permit him to conceal the weapon properly in that position. He had two mono-molecular edged blades, one on his left fore-arm, one on his right side. Sims grabbed a pair of stun grenades off the table and tossed one to Kel. Kel put it in his left coat pocket.

"The sooner we go, the sooner we can get out of this getup," Sims said.

Poul wished them luck as he put his bucket on. "I think you look *fabulous*."

Their ride dropped them off at a public transport hub not far from the node facility. They slipped into the crowd filled with workers journeying home and students just making their appearance on the streets after a long day of idleness. It was early for the partiers to be out, but not so early as to draw attention to their costumes.

They started their route, moving deeper into the labyrinth of streets between tall buildings to where their target awaited. They were going to make a single pass in front of the node, then box the streets leading around and behind the target building. Their visors would record a multitude of visual and spectral parameters. The sensors would give them excellent holos and stills of whatever they recorded, and would penetrate the façades of most of the buildings to reveal basic details about floor plans and concentrations of human occupants.

They came to the T-intersection of the two-lane street in front of the target building. Kel paused and while continuing to look ahead, darted his eyes right to peer down the street. A good amount of pedestrian traffic passed in both directions along the walks.

"This is our chance. Plenty of pedestrian cover. Let's go for it," he whispered to Sims.

He grunted in agreement and took Kel's arm. Once across the street, they joined the walk leading to the same side of the street as the node building. On the building side, Kel divided his attention by gazing hard left with head straight. Several times he had to turn sideways to avoid collisions with pedestrians traveling upstream. He knew Sims would be watching the right side of the street while maintaining the same forward attitude.

As he reached the hard corner at the start of the fenced courtyard, one of the thugs at the top of the small rise of duracrete stairs looked their way. The vertical fence had separations wide enough to allow a good visualization of the courtyard, but barely an arm could slip through the gap. He sensed the large man watch them as they traveled past. As they neared the entrance gate, Kel stole a glance at the coded lock, knowing the sensors would capture perfect images of the mechanism. He raised his head again, mentally willing the sensors to capture details about the front entrance and its closure and security mechanisms.

In less than a minute they were done, and continued silently down the block until they turned the corner.

"I felt like we got a good pass. I absolutely got us good captures of the breachpoint and the gate. My thug was in the courtyard by the stairs. How about you?"

"Yup," said Sims. "There's still a guy posted in the alley across from the entrance. He didn't pay us any mind. Pretty smooth."

Kel agreed. "All right, the hard part's done. Let's keep to our route and box back around the next block and make our way out of here."

"I'm with you," Sims said cheerfully as he unlinked from Kel's arm. The rest was just an easy walk. It was good to get out of the G-base, even as ridiculous as Kel felt to be dressed as they were. The walk was unremarkable. By the end of their last turn, the pedestrian traffic had thinned considerably. They took a new heading and angled toward the public transport hub. Sims steered them into a wide alley that separated several bars and clubs. About halfway down the block, three figures stepped out from a dark alcove to block their way.

"Hey pretty boys, looking to score?" a voice snarled in poor Standard.

Kel froze. In between two dark humans stood a zhee, his long face partially concealed by the high collar of the flowing robes that draped his large frame.

"Human boys want the jade lotus, yes?" the zhee said again in accented Standard. He snorted and made the wheezing noise that passed for laughter among their race.

Drugs. Kurkmen. Zhee.

The dark-haired, olive-skinned humans were not the same stock as Mercians. They were Kurkmen. Kel had run-ins with them on other worlds. They had a well-earned reputation for involvement in illegal activity, especially the narcotics trade, wherever they settled in their clannish groups. The donks, well, Kel knew them as well as he ever needed to. There was nothing about them he wanted to know more about. He'd made up his mind about them long ago.

Kel and Sims stepped backward and raised their hands.

"Sorry. Don't want any trouble. No thanks," Sims said for them both.

The two Kurks stepped to either side, trying to prevent their retreat. They were a little more than a block away from the node facility. Blaster fire would echo down the stone streets like a siren's call to any who knew the distinctive sound. Kookies and cops alike. It was the type of situation they'd hoped to avoid.

Kel acted.

He was in control, but from the moment he made the decision to act, all he saw was red. Kel closed. Cowering or fleeing is what the beast expected. Never this. Prey would never fight. He stepped forward at the precise moment the zhee raised his head. Still confident. Still expecting a victim. Its wheezing laugh fueled Kel's hate. The cackle's crescendo ceased as his strike landed.

Kel was a student of anatomy. As a medic, it helped him save lives. As a killer, it helped him take them. There was no better way to break something than to know how it was put together. He'd examined many zhee corpses over the years. How the shallow concavity of the occipital condyles of donk skulls allowed them to rotate their heads. It was a weak point. The connection between their craniums and spines was very strong in the frontal plane. A donk could headbutt a plasteen wall and the wall would lose. In the plane of rotation, however...

Kel's motion was a result of a gestalt created by years of reflection and training. His power came from the ground as he rotated on the ball of his rear foot and hip, and drove his open hand punch into the Donk's long snout. The plane he had selected for his strike rotated the head where it wasn't meant to go. Kel drove through the surface of his punch and into the reaches of the universe beyond. The creature's head followed the rotation of its long, ridiculous chin and Kel heard as much as felt the unnatural sound of tissues reaching their elastic and bony limits.

The massive beast dropped to the alley floor in a heap. Not a twitch remained to show the beast had ever lived. Off like a light. DRT. Like yesterday's fish.

Kel turned to see the stunned looks of the two Kurks. Without a word exchanged, they fled down the alley, disappearing faster than a wobanki in a rainstorm. Sims stood, pistol in hand, mouth agape, staring at the pile that was the dead zhee.

Kel looked for witnesses, then nudged Sims. "Let's get going." Sims put his pistol away and followed as they stepped over the dead zhee, through the alley and onto the next street, proceeding on another route towards their waiting transportation.

They said nothing as they walked away, adrenaline still coursing. Kel used his vigilance to search for new threats. For the first few minutes, every passerby seemed a potential enemy, ready to impede their way and challenge him. After a few minutes, the feeling faded. He forced deep, calming breaths through his lungs as he strode.

Their transport waited ahead. The two similarly dressed Gs stood outside the older model sled, sharing a stim stick. They acknowledged the two operators as Kel and Sims slid into the back seat and the vehicle lurched away. After several minutes of silence, Kel felt the seat shaking. Sims was biting his bottom lip, suppressing a laugh. Soon he could hold it in no longer.

"Bwahaha, Oba help me! Hahaha, hooo, oh mother!" He slapped Kel on the shoulder. "That was *the greatest thing* I've ever seen in my life! Bwahaha!"

Kel looked around, panicked. Sims's manic laughter was deafening within the confines of the small vehicle. Any observer would assume he was under the influence of some substance. Maybe their cover was a good idea after all?

"Oh, my friend, thank you. Thank you. I can't remember the last time I was truly gobsmacked." The vehicle shook as Sims's convulsion continued before he took in a deep breath. "Ooh! Ooh! I just thought of something—I got it all on sensor! Wait till we get back and pull the feed. I can show the whole team! This is going to be awesome!" Sims's laughter rang, but Kel couldn't manage more than a grin as he thought about the incident.

Kel wasn't a small man, but he was by no means the largest or strongest leej in Dark Ops. He had perfected the biomechanics of his strikes through years of training and discipline. Both Poul and Sims outweighed Kel by a dozen kilos, but neither could generate as much force as Kel could with his strikes.

The gymnasium back at the DO facility on Victrix had every amenity known to the galaxy. It was Kel's favorite place. He could be found there anytime he was off duty, climbing the different rock walls and simulated building surfaces, working out, or just striking the many bags and dummies gathered in small stations around the huge open space.

A force transducer that measured striking power had been installed on one of the training stations. During a team combatives session, everyone took turns seeing how much force they could generate on the strike plate, the newest gadget placed there for their elite training. Of course, Kel was eventually cajoled to try. He had a reputation for having one of the strongest punches in DO. Kel succumbed to his teammates' pressure and after a few warmup strikes, put his all into it. His third strong-hand cross registered over 6,000 Newtons. His fourth punch broke the strike plate. Everyone was amazed. Kel's registered punch was twenty percent stronger than his next closest teammate's.

A week later Kel was in the gym and noticed that the force transducer had been replaced. He was by himself and after a warmup, was curious about the device and

why it had broken. Kel again started with a series of esca-
lating overhand rights, and was rewarded with higher and
higher forces reported for each contact until, with his best
strike yet, the system sparked and smoked. Kel looked
around to make sure he was unobserved and quickly
left the area.

The next day after morning PT, Kel sat in the team
room. His link pinged with a message. His heart skipped
a beat when he saw that it was sent from Sergeant
Major Nail.

It said only:

-*Please stop breaking the gym equipment.*
-*The other children are complaining.*

06

"Okay, that's a wrap," Braley said as Sims finished the last of the debriefs. "I have to go brief Adam and the area command. Let's get packed and ready for the next phase."

They were running a security field in the room to prevent any unwanted scrutiny of their conversation. Even so, Bigg said in a low voice, "When do we tell Adam and the underground that they're on their own?"

Braley shrugged. "Soon. Let's get through this and get an idea what's developing outside and we'll talk about it after. Meadows is due to give us an update over L-comm soon. We'll make our decision then."

As Kel sorted his gear, he thought about the long walk ahead. For what they were going to do, they'd be traveling light.

After about an hour, Poul interrupted everyone's private reverie as they worked. "I'm pulling up the feed from the reservoir now. Want to see?"

They all moved to where Poul stood as he activated the holo. The elevated view showed chaos below. Smoke and flames poured from several flat roofed buildings. In the distance, white froth billowed from the reservoir as a torrent gushed down the spillway.

Just then, everyone's link pinged at the same time. It was Braley.

-*Come to the operations center. Adam is calling a meeting.*

They made it into the large dim room to find Braley sitting across from Adam. The older guerilla commander sat in the middle of several other Mercians whom Kel knew were members of the Area Command. He'd never met any of them before, and knew there would be no introductions. Pieter sat beside Braley. None of the other guerilla lieutenants were present. The back of Kel's neck tingled.

Adam gestured for the team to sit across from him at the large table. Kel took the seat next to Pieter. Once seated, Adam said, "Kel, I wanted to hear more about the operation you led with Pieter. We've been discussing it with Captain Yost, Pieter, and the joint area command. I would like to ask you a few questions."

Kel saw the flash of his grenades as the sled careened off the tracks. Adam spoke. "We are all very impressed with our combined successes. That is due in no small part to your efforts, gentlemen."

The men stoically accepted the chief's praise.

"Certainly, it was miraculous that we did not fail a single objective or engage in any combat where we were not the decisive victors. Your operation was the only one where a casualty was sustained. We have some unanswered questions about that."

Kel nodded, waiting to be prompted for more.

One of the men across from him, an elderly, intellectual-appearing gentleman said, "We understand what took place from Pieter's perspective. It's still unclear to us the events that led to Helmut's death. Please tell us what you remember."

"Certainly." Kel launched into a review of the events on the maglev trestle. "I didn't have time to pay attention to the men with me. I had to get to the far side of the trestle.

Almost immediately I saw the Crude patrol approaching. Helmut made it across shortly after and told me that Rolf hadn't been able to keep up. At that point I had to focus on stopping the advance of the patrol and sent Helmut back to inform Pieter. It wasn't until we were off the objective and were re-forming the patrol that we realized Helmut wasn't with us."

One of the other men asked, "Pieter, did Rolf find you to help with placing the charges?"

Pieter straightened in his chair. "No. At least, I didn't see him. It was completely dark and he could have been with one of the other demolition crews. We were quite busy placing the charges. Then, when the explosions from Kel's ambush made it evident we were about to be caught, we raced off the tracks. It was a hectic few minutes."

His questioner nodded. "We can all appreciate that, I'm sure."

Another man spoke. "Did Helmut find you to tell you of the approaching danger?"

"No."

"Did any other patrol member tell you that Helmut had given them Kel's message to expedite your actions?"

Pieter thought before answering. "No."

The older men all looked to Adam, who said, "Captain, thank you for your time. We need to have a short private meeting, but I am gathering the entire force for a briefing outside. Will your team join us as I address the men? We won't be but a few minutes."

Adam stood, silently indicating for the team to take their leave.

"Of course. We'll be with the men." Braley led the team out and down the short incline to the large chamber outside the operations room. The floor was already filled with the entirety of the G force, gathering outside during the team's meeting with the Area Command. Men milled about, some laughing and reliving the moments of their exploits a short time ago, sharing their adventures with the men from the other missions. Sims, Poul, and Braley split up and moved off to join familiar faces from their respective patrols. Kel nudged Bigg and moved over to Pieter as they both pulled him aside.

"What's up?" Kel asked the young man.

Pieter looked worried. "I'm not sure."

"Are we in danger?" Bigg asked him.

Pieter looked perplexed. "No. I mean... no. Why would you be in danger? Do you think they blame Kel for Helmut's death?"

"I'm not sure. There's something we don't know," Bigg said to them both. "I'm going to talk to the captain." Bigg moved off through the crowd to find Braley.

Kel turned back to Pieter. "What do you think?"

"I don't know. I'm uneasy. I can't imagine about what, though. We did nothing wrong."

Kel agreed. They were just going to have to be patient and wait. They didn't have to wait long as Adam's voice surprised them.

"Attention. Attention." He stood above them on the wide ledge outside the operations room. The men of the Area Command stood in a line behind him.

"Brothers. Patriots. I stand before you in awe of your accomplishments punishing the Kroedellian invaders. An important blow for the freedom of our homeland has been struck."

They cheered at that until Adam raised his hands for silence.

"There is much still to be done. Before we can continue, we have an important task before us. We must have a trial to determine the fate of a traitor in our midst."

A man set a wooden chair in front of Adam.

Kel looked about to see where his teammates were located. Movement at the edge of the chamber drew his attention. The crowd parted, and two men walked up dragging a bound man between them, bruises on his face, supported to remain upright as he was encouraged forward.

It was Rolf.

They sat Rolf in the chair, and he wept as an older man stepped forward.

"This man is accused of collaborating with the enemy." The man produced a datapad and swiped it, sending a holo projection over the gathering. The feed showed Rolf sitting on a park bench, conversing with an unknown man. There was no audio. The feed continued for another moment until the frame froze and an enlargement of the unknown man's face filled the view.

The older man from the Area Command continued, "This man is a known Kroedellian agent in North Mercia."

The room remained silent.

"He's my cousin! I told you that. He just wanted to see me, that's all," Rolf protested through split lips. "I didn't tell him anything."

"This holo was taken two weeks ago, while we were focused on our buildup for combat operations," Adam said, no emotion in his stentorian voice. "There is no record of you being released and no permission logged from any of the checkpoints for your return to the city at any time. There can only be one explanation for this—that you are engaged in activities against the movement."

"I sneaked out to check on my mother! I told you that. I asked my cousin to meet me to beg him to tend to her, that's all," Rolf protested.

"Silence!" Adam yelled.

The room was so quiet Kel heard Pieter gulp.

Pacing, Adam told the Gs, "We have interrogated this man thoroughly. His story does not convince us. He was the last man to see Helmut alive. He intercepted Helmut on his return trip to tell Pieter of the impending Crude compromise. He was engaged to halt the demolition of the maglev trestle by murder and subterfuge. We believe that his intention after pushing his comrade Helmut to his death was to murder Kel, his leader, and to allow the approaching Crude patrol to halt the operation. His own cowardice in crossing the open trestle in a timely manner prevented that. He was unable to carry out his plan to sneak up on Kel and murder our Republic comrade who so bravely faced off against the Crude patrol all by himself, saving the entire mission."

"I told you, it's not true! I would never do that," Rolf pleaded and burst into sobs. "It's not true, it's not true," he wept.

Adam looked to his audience. "We don't know the full extent of what this man has told our enemies or what further plans he had for our destruction. We have given this man a fair trial and the command has decided. Rolf, for your treachery and betrayal, you are sentenced to death."

Rolf closed his eyes, dropping his head to his chest as he continued to sob. Kel knew what was coming next.

The guerilla leader took a step behind the seated man, produced a pistol from his waistband, pointed it at the back of Rolf's head, and pulled the trigger. The older ballistic weapon discharged with a deafening blast. Echoes reverberated away down the stone hallways, racing to tell Rolf's fate.

Rolf slumped off the chair to the floor, dead.

Adam returned the pistol to his waistband and stepped over the body to address the men below him. "This is the only penalty for traitors." Two men stepped onto the platform and retrieved the body, dragging it down the ramp and off into one of the tunnels.

Tears gleamed in Pieter's eyes. "Do you think it's true?" he whispered to Kel.

"We'll never know."

Kel joined his team and waited for someone to say something. Around him, men stood in similar clusters. The room buzzed with whispered conversations.

"Guys," Poul said, "Adam's moving toward us." The man approached, his face filled with urgency.

"Captain, I would like you and your team sergeant to join us. We have new information awaiting us and I'd like you to be present."

Does Adam need to confer with Braley before dispensing more G justice? Kel wondered. His fears were partially allayed when Meadows entered the chamber. Two of his agents strode with him, looking grim. Meadows caught their eyes as he moved past them and frowned.

"We'll be right there, Adam," Braley answered, waiting for Adam to depart before speaking again. "Bigg and I will go find out what's up. Get back to the dungeon and keep working. We'll punch you if we need you." Braley and Bigg turned to follow Adam.

"What do you suppose Meadows is doing here?" Poul wondered. "We were supposed to have an L-comm link-up later. What would make him risk coming in person?"

"We'll find out soon enough. Let's go," Sims said, leading the way through the crowd back to their operations room.

I'm pretty certain our professional paranoia is baseless. For now, Kel thought. *But something else is in motion.*

They had been back in their room about an hour when they got a bounce from Bigg.

-Headed your way.

Shortly after, the door opened and Bigg, Braley, and Meadows walked through. Meadows gestured to his two men to wait outside. He closed the door and moved to a chair Bigg offered. Everyone pulled up something to sit on as Braley started to fill them in on the new developments.

"All right. Meadows has brought us news about what's developing around the city. You tell it," he said, jutting his chin toward their friend.

"The Crudes are in chaos. They aren't yet organized and their centralized command is having great difficulty forming an effective military response to last night's events. So instead, they're reverting to what they know best. The Crudes are rounding up civilians and taking them to interrogation centers around the city. They've concentrated most into the North Mercian Police Headquarters where the largest detention facility is. The KOCI have already rounded up the family of anyone suspected of being part of the resistance movement, including family members of the area command. One of the victims is Adam's wife.

"My case officer is burning up the links getting the word out to his people in the North, and to the Republic ambassador. As we speak, the diplomatic mission is encouraging the Andalusians to start a military intervention with the Republic's support. We all know that's not going to result in any rapid action on their part."

Sims sipped his kaff. None of Kel's teammates looked surprised by what they heard.

Meadows continued. "RI is approving a request by the Underground to assist in stopping the detentions and interrogations. You are being tasked to assist this effort."

Everyone was silent for a moment as they processed the implications, some of which Meadows would not be aware of. Neither would the Republic Intelligence case officer Meadows worked for. Kill Team Three was tasked with a mission apart from organizing the guerillas. The RI station chief in Andalusia would not have been read into their next mission, either. Kel looked to Braley. There would be some difficult choices to make in the next few minutes. He didn't envy his team leader.

Braley looked to Bigg as he communicated his concern, swiping down over his face with his palm, then nodded once. Braley had clearly made his decision. Bigg moved to his desk where he activated the security field. "Meadows, I have to read you into something we couldn't inform you of earlier. We were just getting ready to pull out to perform a detached mission on our own in South Andalusia."

Meadows took this in. "Okay."

"Meadows, we have an Astral Plane target to hit," Bigg said.

Meadows raised his eyebrows. "Wow. Well. I have to say, that makes sense."

"RI hasn't been read into it," Braley said. "They have encoded instructions that won't reveal until the signal is sent post-event. The ambassador will only get read in on a need-to-know basis. It's supposed to look like an error by the Crudes—provided it goes down as planned."

"Oh boy," was all Meadows could say. "Wish I was going with you. But not really, if you know what I mean."

"Actually," Bigg drawled, "we were going to read you in soon anyway because we think you can help with the infil. You and the Underground, that is. You seem to have developed some connections with them."

"All right. Let's table that discussion for later," Braley said. "I've been thinking about this and I want to discuss it amongst ourselves." This was pure Braley. In the Legion, a commander's word was law. A Legion captain would normally be in command of a two hundred leej company and responsible for millions of credits worth of equipment. In Dark Ops, an officer's authority and power were no different than in the regular Legion. In practice though, the team commander was the first among equals on a kill team. Braley always made them feel that way with his style of command. Instead of commanding dozens of subordinate leaders and a couple hundred troops, Braley was the leader of a kill team of five men including himself. It was an entirely different dynamic than in the regular Legion. Of course they'd abide by any decision he made. But he always looked to the team for options and consensus on any critical issue they faced.

"These are our choices. We can ditch and go on our way and get the mission moving. Ignoring the RI tasking is no big deal to us. We have priority from the House of Reason to proceed as planned.

"Or, we take the additional tasking. The question before us as a kill team: is it feasible for us to delay by another day or more and hit the jail to help the Gs free the civilian prisoners?"

Bigg spoke up. "Yes, it's feasible. The Crudes are still flailing. Their comms and command and control are nil, at least for now. If we're going to do something, it's best to move on it immediately before they get their act together. Unless they have a regiment parked around the police headquarters, I'm thinking we have a good shot to get in and make a jail break happen. We could at least assess the target and decide from there."

Poul followed. "Documenting a human rights abuse like this would be big. The underground gets concrete evidence to the media, maybe it spurs the Andalusians into action."

"I'd like to do the rescue mission if we can pull it off. I hate these Crude punks," Sims said. "Let's bring these creeps some leej justice."

Kel grinned. *Leave it to Sims to take the nuanced view.*

"Kel?" Braley asked. He was the only one who hadn't spoken.

"All right. I'll play the role of the naysayer, just as an exercise in decision-making."

Everyone leaned forward to hear him.

"Say enough of us bite it on this extracurricular job, enough that we can't complete the other thing afterwards," Kel said in vague reference to their other mission. "What then? We better hope no one survives, because whoever does is going to be living in a hole on a prison planet for the remainder of their short, tortured lives."

Everyone's eyes widened as they considered this.

Braley chuckled once. "Yup. Thought about that. That was my first inclination. Our priority is the Astral Plane hit. No doubt about it. It would be taking a big risk."

Kel shrugged. "But on the other hand, dead is dead. I'd like to punish some Crude secret police thugs and rescue some civilians along the way. Screw it. Let's at least get some intel and start working on a plan."

Everyone laughed, relieved. It was unanimous.

A metallic knock came from their entrance. Bigg got up to open it. Adam stood on the other side. The large gray man looked distressed.

"Friends, I need to ask for your help."

Everyone was already on their feet.

Braley answered for them. "That's why we're here, Adam. To help."

07

They moved to the G operations center to start the planning. Adam gathered his senior lieutenants to brief them all together. Braley stood at the head of the long table next to Adam. The Area Command members were still present. Kel and the rest of the team crowded into the room as well. The lighting was brighter than their last visit. Kel could see the faces of the Area Command members much better. They were all quite a bit older than Adam, and decades older than the average G in the force.

Adam spoke, the shock of the recent execution still evident on everyone else's face, their manners subdued. "A critical situation has developed. As a result of our refusal to be conquered and our actions to restore the dignity and peace of our homeland, the Crudes have responded in a fashion unspeakably barbaric and cruel."

Adam was a giant of a man, an imposing figure in any setting. Physical size was not a prerequisite for leadership, but it struck Kel that it often was a factor. How the man chose his words, combined with his deep voice, made an impression whenever he chose to speak. Kel thought about the show the man had just orchestrated, culminating in the execution of one of their own. Although Kel might not approve of his methods, he had to admit the man knew how to motivate people.

The Gs had been prepared early on that after their sabotage around the city, the Crudes would respond harshly, the populace viable targets. The Kroedellian Empire was a prison; their need for complete subjugation of the individual to the state was evident in their every act. Harsh, punitive treatment of their own citizens was the norm. That they would treat the North Mercians several measures worse than their own beaten subjects was foreseen. If such a thing were possible.

"In response to our declaration of war against the Kroedellian invasion, they have retaliated against the only target at their disposal, our families. The KOCI have rounded up men, women, even children from around the city. Mass executions of young men suspected of participation in the movement has already occurred. The burgermeister of Westphalia has been subjected to... well, I'd best let Daniel tell you."

Westphalia was a small borough in the western part of the city. It was unremarkable in that it contained neither industry nor great commerce. It was an idyllic part of the old city known for its classic stone architecture and peaceful neighborhoods.

Kel looked at Bigg, whose expression told him that he also knew nothing.

The same man who had produced the damning evidence against the traitor Rolf stood and manipulated a holo into existence. "This came to us an hour ago."

The story it told needed no narration. No explanation. No commentary. It had been recorded from a vantage looking down on the courtyard of a quadrangular block of apartments. Long-coated thugs with rifles manhandled a family into the courtyard. The dim early morning light revealed civilians dressed in bedclothes. The oldest male was forced into a kneeling position, held down on either side by a thug. Kel assumed the kneeling subject was the burgermeister. A Crude officer, denoted by his large-billed hat, stood in front of the man. A one-sided exchange occurred. The lack of sound only made the scene bleaker, placing a gray pall over everything.

One at a time, a member of the man's family was guided in front of him. Presented, like an unveiling. The Crude directing the show seemed to say, "Is this yours?" Then the noiseless recoil. Three women, two men, and a child were murdered, one at a time. The Crude officer continued his questioning. Finally, when there was no one left to kill, the officer made a sweeping gesture and the burgermeister was dragged out of the courtyard, followed by the rest of the uniformed goons. Only the bodies of the victims remained. The holo ceased.

The room was silent. Kel was sickened, but not surprised. Rage, fear, anguish flickered across the faces of the men around him. Kel understood. He'd seen much cruelty in his life. Many alien cultures meted out such barbarism. He'd never witnessed humans do anything as evil. Maybe not even the Savages.

"Brothers. We have a choice. Our countrymen in the north continue to pursue a diplomatic solution, pleading for intervention by the northern nations. We all know that our salvation by the Andalusians and their coalition of weaklings is not at hand.

"As we speak, the jails are full of our wives, daughters, sons, fathers, mothers—rounded up and awaiting torture and murder as retribution for our refusal to submit. If we remain hidden, we may live to strike at them again, and again. If we answer these atrocities, this provocation, and enter overt combat against our foe, we are likely playing into their hands.

"I have already decided my course. I ask of us all what I know you already ask of yourselves. We must act to free our people today. Even if it means our deaths, the movement will continue without us. The yoke of oppression will raise a new army to fight the Kroedellian devils. If we die as martyrs, we die knowing the world will know of our cause—the cause of freedom."

Kel was torn between feeling moved, and suppressing his cynical instincts. The man was good. Kel didn't doubt the correctness of his decision-making, or his call to action. What bothered him was how the man manipulated his people's emotions through his speech, instead of giving them the facts of the situation as a military planner would've done.

They're a political faction acting as a military organization, Kel reminded himself. *They're not an army. They're guerillas. Adam is motivating them like a politician would.*

Kel decided that he was ready for the team to separate from the guerillas as soon as possible. They would rescue the captive civilians and make their way to their next objective. He'd think no more about his distaste for the G chief and concentrate on his next task.

Adam surrendered the floor to Braley.

"We're going to move quickly. Planning is underway for what will be a hostage rescue to recover all detained civilians. Tonight. My team," Braley gestured at the legionnaires, "will conduct the hostage rescue at the jail. The guerilla force will be supporting the operation and will provide distractions around the city at essential locations, assaulting and harassing Crude units to prevent significant reinforcements from reaching the jail during our rescue attempt.

"We will utilize every resource at our disposal, including arming your sections with the advanced armaments we brought. We will not be saving them. It does not appear that the Andalusian coalition will be coming to our rescue any time soon. Combined operations that would occur during the consolidation phase remain hypothetical. So, we'll use the weapons now."

The team had brought with them some heavy blasters and crew-served ener-grenade launchers. These advanced capability weapons were beyond anything even the Crude military possessed. They'd drilled crews in their use, but hadn't planned on deploying the devastating weapons yet. The plan was to use them to prepare the way for the conventional military forces when the invasion commenced to free North Mercia. Now they could no longer be held in reserve.

Adam resumed. "I'm releasing you to see to your sections and begin preparations. We will have an operations order as soon as possible. Tonight, we pay the Crudes back the price of their arrogance in blood."

The lieutenants were dismissed, Pieter catching Kel's eye before he left. Kel gave the young man a nod. Braley remained up front speaking to Adam and the other elders. He was soon surrounded by his teammates. They huddled together in a corner of the room and spoke in whispers.

"Man, that Adam is some kind of G-chief, huh?" Sims began. "He's effective, but at times I think he's planning for a future political career."

"I wouldn't go so far as to call him a demagogue, but he is a politically-minded individual for sure," Bigg said.

"Well, maybe so, but did you notice what he didn't say?" Poul asked. They stayed silent, waiting for Poul to answer his own question. "He never mentioned to the men that *his own wife* was captured by the Crudes."

Kel hadn't considered that. Surely if the man had wanted to manipulate his followers' emotions, he would have played that card.

"All right. I'll cut the guy some slack," Kel said. "Anyway, we need to get the heavies out, get crews mounting them on the Boars, and review some basics while we can. These guys are going to have to keep the Crudes off our backs to give us a chance of pulling this off."

"Agreed," Bigg said. "You guys get on that. I'm going to check in and start synthesizing as much of the intel as I can get from all sources. And, we need a little real-time intel of our own."

Bigg grinned.

The team minus Braley edged forward to look down from the office building's window. Seen from this vantage, the headquarters was a complex, the three-story jail surrounded by smaller single-story administrative buildings like spokes on a wheel. The police headquarters occupied a corner of the block, the main entrance nearest the intersection. It was close to midnight. Though the lights in all buildings were out, they stood back from the large panes to avoid revealing themselves.

"I need another minute for the nanos to finish," Bigg said, staring off into space. Everyone knew he was watching a dozen small screens projected inside his bucket, following the feed from the nearly invisible insect-like drones. He'd launched a handful of them before entering the office building, their autonomous programming guiding them to their targets.

The jail was dimly lit on three sides, the walk from the front parking lot to the main entrance being well illuminated. Crude official vehicles mixed with municipal police sleds in the front lot. The rear of the property sloped downward, creating a sub-basement that opened to a walk-out level to the rear street where large garage doors provided secure access for official vehicles and prisoner transfers. There was only the token presence of a few stationary guards outside the main entrance. An armored grav sled sat parked in the intersection in front of the entrance with more long-coated Crudes aimlessly circling the vehicle. The heavy blaster on its rear deck was currently unmanned.

Bigg had laid down the law early during Braley's operation order for the rescue back at the base. "Sorry, boss, you have to stay off the objective. Going into the jail for the rescue is a bad idea. It's going to be a shooting gallery." Before Braley could protest, he added, "Our next job is too important. One of us needs to be there."

Braley nodded. "I was afraid that you were going to pull that on me, Bigg." Braley sighed. "But I'm not staying here, Master Sergeant Biggetti, and that's final."

Chuckles went all around.

"Of course not, Captain Yost," Bigg said. "I just figured staying with the Gs on containment and supervising the barricade work from outside would be a little less sporty than what we're doing inside. We'll need to smoke a lot of thugs and, most of them being kookies, they'll probably be a little more accustomed to self-initiated violence than the average Crude."

Adam, his lieutenants, and the team had worked quickly to put together a hasty operations order for the mission. About half of the G force would be helping to contain the site around the detention center to prevent Crude reinforcements from interfering with the jail break. The rest would be hitting Crude emplacements around the city to keep them occupied while they were inside the jail. The team had worked efficiently to craft their portion of the mission, the hostage rescue.

"No argument, Top," Braley said, reverting back to his favorite moniker for the team sergeant. "I'll be plenty busy."

"Now I'm trusting you to not screw this up. I've never let anyone else take responsibility for the barricade charges before." Bigg smiled as he said it. He was only partially kidding. While everyone was well-qualified as explosive breachers, Bigg never really trusted anyone but himself for certain tasks. The breach would be one of those.

"I can do it, Dad," Braley said, chagrined. "More importantly, I'll make sure the Gs don't screw it up."

Bigg snorted. "Of course, sir, that's what I had actually meant to say—make sure the Gs don't screw it up."

Their plan for rescuing the Mercian hostages from the KOCI secret police was predicated on their ability to maintain surprise as well as their combat momentum once the shooting started. A numerically inferior force attacking a well-defended objective, like the jail, left them few options. They could not achieve numerical superiority. The G force, no matter how well motivated, were not trained to do a hostage rescue and would be a liability accompanying the team into the jail. They all agreed they'd come up with the best plan. And that it was the most difficult way to do it. Lastly, that it could fail epically. But there wasn't a better way.

Bigg checked his chrono. "We should start our ascent before the fireworks start, which should be in about fifteen minutes." They followed him down to the ground floor. Kel looked at the body of the Crude sentry he had dispatched to gain entry to the building. Several Gs stood looking at the body of the young man, the base of the skull nearly severed from the neck. He'd spotted the sentry standing at the corner of the building. Kel had stalked closer by moving slowly along the wall that cast the most shadow from the overhead moon, stepping out at the last moment to close.

The man continued to draw on his stim-stick as Kel pulled him into the alley by his hair, simultaneously driving his vibroblade through the spine and into the base of his brain. Kel never paused to assess his effect. He continued the action, controlling the man's fall by grasping him around his chest and dragging him into the alley and out of sight. Seeing this, the rest of the team and their guides moved forward and gained access into the building's alleyway entrance. It took only a few minutes for them to ascend and make their visual recon of the target.

"Hey, let's get moving," Kel said, snapping the young men out of their contemplation of death. He knew the Gs had likely not yet seen the results of combat in such an up close and personal manner. *It doesn't get any closer than that, kids,* Kel wanted to say. Instead, he let Bigg continue the prompting, placing a gauntleted hand on the shoulder on one of the young men sporting a thin beard.

"Kinder, lead off. Get us through the sub-basement. Let's go."

Shaking off his discomposure, the young man regained his composure and moved to guide them through cubicles and tables to where another G stood blocking open a door. Beyond that were narrow stairs leading to a basement level. Brick-walled subterranean rooms gave way to rock hewn walls leading under the street to buildings adjacent the jail complex.

The intent was to approach unobserved through the tunnels to arrive at the street level near the rear entrance of the jail and its walk-out level. Removing any sentries along the way, they would be able to ascend the flat roof of the garage to reach the main jail building, and make an exterior ascent up the three stories to the top of the jail. The plan was to fight top-down, clearing the entire building and freeing hostages as they went.

Plans were like fantasies. They rarely became reality. They needed as much luck as will to be realized. And even then, more often than not, became little more than badly remembered dreams.

Braley was watching the complex from another vantage with his Gs. Once the team was ready to make entry from the roof of the jail, Braley's Gs would get to work. One element would remove the street sentries and the men on the heavy vehicle, others would split up to seal the entire structure with weld-charges at all the exits. All, save one. The rats needed a place to run. As Kel, Bigg, Poul, and Sims worked through the jail, discriminating Crude from non-Crude, Braley and his Gs would rain death from the roofs onto any escaping KOCI. It would be the easiest killing the Gs would ever do.

Elsewhere in the city, Adam and his forces would hit Crude checkpoints and troops with the Boars. The heavy blasters mounted on the vehicles combined with their speed and maneuverability would allow the Gs to create chaos around the city for the Crudes. The complete disruption of the information network continued, for now, leaving the separate Crude units to act on their own. In Kel's estimation that meant: badly, indecisively, and predictably. It would be a mistake to underestimate the Crudes, or any enemy for that matter, but without their central command to identify the real target of the night's activities and marshal troops to counter the jail break, Kel felt they had an almost unfair advantage.

Later, it was almost funny to Kel how as with all military operations, that he knew in retrospect where they'd made their errors.

Bigg's drone intel was priceless. While still at the G base, he'd piloted a larger recon drone into the city and over the jail complex once it had gotten dark. Everyone agreed the risk of detection was not outweighed by the benefits. They'd need all the information they could get to plan such a complex operation. Combined with their Gs' firsthand knowledge of the area, they'd been able to plan a perfect route into the city to stage. Other than Kel having to remove the one sentry, they'd not been close to having their operation discovered.

The nano-inquisitor drones had gotten close enough to interrogate all the external cameras and sensors around the jail complex. It was now almost twenty-four hours since Sims's destructive intrusion into the information network, and everything more complex than an analog propagated radio wave was still dead.

"Get to high ground and if anyone moves up our backside, you know what to do," Bigg told the three young guerillas. The men moved up the stairs to find a window from which to watch the avenues of approach to the rear of the jail. Kel couldn't help but notice how the three kids wouldn't meet his eyes after seeing how he'd dispatched the sentry.

If they're going to be scared of me, it better be because of what I'll do to them if they don't do their jobs. He didn't mind. The Gs weren't professional troops. No matter their political motivations, a few months ago they'd just been students. He remembered the old adage, *not everyone has the mean gene.* They'd have to toughen up. Their war was just starting.

They'd all activated their armor's mimetic camo. When moving, the camouflage did not conceal the first target indicator that was motion, but when combined with darkness, would confuse the eye of anyone not looking directly at the wearer. It ate some power, but was worth the expenditure in this instance. As they made their way down the street to the last cover and concealment that was the corner of the building, Kel glanced at Poul ahead of him and noted the gray, textured appearance of the armor that mimicked the brick wall they now glided past. Bigg paused as he looked around the corner toward the rear entrance and closed garage doors beneath the complex.

They were on L-comm, but Bigg softly said, "I don't know why they don't have sentries out, but let's not wait until they do." He stepped off, Kel and the others moving with him. Kel instinctively moved on line with the rest of the team, orienting toward the low building. If there were a surprise appearance by any Crude through the row of garage doors, they would be met by blaster fire from all four legionnaires. They did not run. A slow purposeful walk soon brought them to their first obstacle.

"Make the way, Kel," Bigg said. Kel had already been moving to perform the task. He slung his K-17 as the others faced in different directions. The wall ascent to the flat roof was a scant four meters. Kel took out a few mag-assist ledges and placed them at intervals as he climbed up the wall. Gripping the ledge above him, he pulled himself over, unslung his carbine, and looked down at his teammates.

"Set," he said.

From his new vantage point, Kel scanned the duracrete complex. Streetlights cast dark shadows, photonic barriers their buckets penetrated with ease, allowing nothing to hide from them in the shadows. In the span of a few breaths, they'd all made the first leg of their climb.

Kel crept across the flat roof to the back of the jail to make the long, multi-story ascent to the roof of the jail. Their climb could not be observed from either street, and it was even dimmer on this side. Only the dark office buildings stood behind him. Hopefully, Gs had made their way into some of those windows to watch their backs. Looking up he found a strip of wall running skyward between windows. It was a long, long way up.

This ascent would require a more significant anchor than the mag-assist ledges could provide. Kel knelt at the wall as Sims did the same beside him. Studying the wall, they made small adjustments to the packages at their feet. Finally, when they were satisfied, they activated their boxes. Thin, black carbon nano-tubes crept up the wall in two parallel, unnaturally straight lines. Kel couldn't help but step back as he tried to follow the deployments of the climbers all the way to the top of the jail. Even through his bucket, he couldn't see the ends of the deploying lines, but after a long minute received a message in his bucket: *Locked.*

At intervals of ten centimeters, small projections lowered from the nano-tubes, providing enough purchase for toes and fingers to grasp. Another message appeared: *Holds deployed. Ready.* It was not quite a ladder but much better than trying a free ascent.

"Alright, guys, we're good," Kel told them. "Time to work."

This would burn. Kel hadn't worked out strenuously, much less climbed, in weeks. Even with the assist from their armor, this would be painful.

"Climbing order—Kel, Sims, Poul, then me," said Bigg. "Hit it."

Kel made sure his carbine was tight to his chest and his small pack was secured to his back as he looked up one last time before starting his ascent. He needed to move safely, but rapidly. He'd have three people behind him as soon as there was room. The ladder was strong enough for four people at a time, but left them completely exposed and unable to fight. He'd need to be fast.

"Braley," Bigg said. "We're on ascent. Stand by for my next comm to begin assault."

Kel's heart started to pound in his ears.

It wouldn't be long now.

08

Kel was more nervous about the climb than he was about the assault. He did a lot of climbing in his own training and with the team. Climbing was a regular necessity in his life. But that didn't mean he liked it. He'd never admitted to anyone that he had a fear of falling. He simply supposed everyone did. His way of dealing with that fear was by ignoring it. A two-story fall wouldn't kill a fit man like him. A three-story fall might kill him. A four-story fall would kill him. That this was only a three-story ascent gave him some small comfort.

Even then, he thought as his fingers found the first hold, *it's not even the thought of falling that really bothers me*. He loved freefall. It was the thought of failure more than the pain of breaking his body that he dreaded.

He pushed those thoughts from his mind the higher he climbed until soon, he reached the parapet and found himself over it. He turned to see a large gap behind him until Sims finally reached the ledge. He helped the large man up and over as they both turned to do the same for the rest of the team.

On a sub-channel Sims said, "I thought I could keep up with you, but you ran up that damned thing. Guess I need to train with you more. I thought I was a good climber before I came to Three."

Is that why the team always picks me to climb? Because they think I'm good at it? That I like it? Kel wondered. *If I'm giving that impression, maybe I need to re-think always volunteering to be first climb.*

No sooner had Bigg gotten his feet on the flat roof than he searched for their breach point. Deep in concentration, he moved directly to a square hatch at the opposite corner of the roof and was removing a plasma cutter off his armor as he knelt to examine the coaming around it. It would be physically locked from the inside, and as he determined where the hinges were, he placed himself on the opposite side to slice through the opening.

Bigg looked up at them. "Ready, boys?" Everyone nodded their assent. "Braley, commencing roof entry now."

They waited.

Braley command his Gs to begin their movement toward the jail. Rapid cracks of shooting echoed up to them from the streets. The purple glow of Bigg's plasma torch focused Kel's attention back to the roof hatch. They knew from generalities that the access would lead down a ladder to a maintenance room, and from there, the top floor of the building would be theirs.

Poul and Sims peeled back the hatch and Bigg was the first down the ladder. Kel followed, descending only a few rungs before he jumped. He continued his momentum away to make room. Conduits ran from control boards along the walls. The only door sat at the corner. Bigg had already moved to the door and his non-firing hand came off his weapon to grasp the old-fashioned lever.

Kel paused, waiting for the rest of the team. When he saw the three men stack with him, he said, "Like bacon through a goose, boys."

Bigg pulled the door open, took a brief look and Kel moved with him through the threshold.

Kel could remember a time in his life when how one fought inside a structure was very different from how he had evolved to think about it. There was an artistry to the methods. But more than that, a science. The angles. How to use them, how to avoid them, how to exploit them. He was first trained in close quarters battle as part of a Legion squad. Urban operations for infantry were very different. Primitive to him as he looked back. Then, the goal was getting as many leejes into a space as quickly as possible without shooting each other. There were tactics and procedures, but they depended on very tight control of the shooters and much continual guidance by the fire-team leaders to ensure mission success. Sometimes what they did was little more than run into a room, shooting everyone who was not a legionnaire.

Those tactics resembled nothing of what he came to appreciate as the incredible beauty and artistry of room clearing. What they did as a kill team was otherworldly. The Dark Ops method of building heuristic pathways—wherein they could read a room and carry out their precisely violent performance unconsciously—was as close to a feeling of perfection as anything Kel had ever felt in his short life.

With four men, a kill team could enter any room and end any threat in seconds, a building, in a matter of minutes. And do so with impunity. What four men could *not* do was take prisoners or hold a room indefinitely. To perform a hostage rescue required securing a structure, moving surreptitiously to a crisis site, killing the hostage taker, and separating hostages from any remaining wolves among the sheep. Controlling and processing suspects took time and manpower. Dozens of operators could manage it. Four men could not.

What four men could do was move efficiently through a confined space and ruthlessly kill any who resisted. That's what Kill Team Three's mission now was. Liberate the prisoners taken by the Crudes. Only there was nothing more complex in the universe.

When faced with the complex, it was best to keep things simple.

Their rules of engagement matched their mission. They would be killing anyone not a hostage. Anyone armed would be killed. Anyone in a Crude uniform would be killed. Anyone resisting would be killed. This was war.

The exterior G teams under Braley's command quickly sealed off all exits save the front entrance, eliminating any chance for escaped KOCI to form a counterassault and reenter the structure. Any KOCI exiting the structure would be slaughtered by the waiting Gs. With relish.

Braley spoke over L-comm. "We hold the intersection. Exterior sealed. Overwatch set. Good luck."

They moved down the hall. A set of doors partially cracked open beckoned. Light shone into the dim hall. Staggered opposite was an open latrine and showers. This was a barracks floor, then. The sound of men scurrying to dress penetrated into the hallway. A man came out of the latrine. Bigg shot him. Bigg and Poul moved into the latrine as Kel and Sims flowed past and to the double doors. They'd already made their decision on the way there and each said only one word: "TBs."

They swiped the small thermobaric grenades as they moved to the door. Kel sprung the door with one hand as he and Sims tossed their grenades into the room, and continued moving down the hall. If there was any doubt below that the detention center was under attack, it would be gone now.

Two explosions joined to form a sustained roar. Even through his armor, Kel felt the deep pulses push through his spine. Kel stepped back and had a brief look in to see bodies and flames in the bunk room. No one still living would be functional as TBs ripped all oxygen from the room. In their armor, the leejes were only mildly discomforted as they continued to move away from the blast site.

At the end of the hallway was a stairwell leading down. Kel and Sims pushed ahead and held guns down the stairs as the last man through, Bigg, ran a weld across the striker side of the door. If anyone left alive tried to descend behind them, they would be deterred.

Below them, a door banged open and men shouted. Without thinking Kel tossed a stunner onto the landing just as two faces peered up through the narrows between the rises. Kel and Sims took a half step back as the arcs of purple flashes expanded up into the channeled column of the plasteen stairwell. The arcs rode the metal handrail, then stopped. Kel and Sims had already started their descent, guns forward, insulated in their armor from the lingering effects of the stunner. Without hesitation they shot the two men sprawled on the landing, another laying across the threshold, conveniently blocking open the door.

"With me," Bigg said to Poul as he passed Kel and Sims on the landing. Kel knew to hold up and wait. Bigg and Poul ran down another flight to the first floor landing to spot-weld the door closed. In a minute, the four were together again on the second-floor landing. Kel and Sims had penetrated past the threshold, standing on the body of the man underneath them. Each was pushed into the hallway just far enough to get their weapon around the hard corner and deliver fire in their respective directions.

Kel was on the left facing a hallway that held only a single door at its end.

"I'm short this way with one door," he told his partner.

"Long hallway, multiple opposing doors," Sims replied.

He felt the presence behind him of his other two teammates, and glanced right to see Sims push into the hall as Poul fell in on line to his side. Kel immediately pushed across the hallway to the lone door opposite him, Bigg following. Kel didn't stop moving his feet until he was directly in front of the door, raising his K-17 to point just above the old-fashioned strike plate and pressed the trigger, his muzzle oriented toward the jamb. With a bright flash from the superheated metal Kel pushed the door open, Bigg's muzzle rising with his. Stacks of containers and loose bundles of old paper files filled the room. A central passage of a few meters between the piles left no room for any hiding space.

"Short," Kel said as they both turned out of the room and moved to where Poul and Sims faced down the long corridor. Kel saw several bodies down the hall in front of open doors. The pair had eliminated the three KOCI without a word while Kel and Bigg had been working. Their blasters made little noise on discharging and it was difficult to be aware of any shots fired by another operator from even a meter away.

"Three kookies down ahead," Sims said, orienting Kel and Bigg.

"Hold," Bigg said as he stepped to pull the body out of the threshold and into the hallway. The stairwell door closed and Bigg used his plasma torch to seal it.

"Up. On you," Bigg said only a few seconds later, indicating he was finished and ready to move.

A dozen pairs of doors lined the long hall. Muffled, panicked shouts and hasty orders were coming from behind some of them.

"Hold. Stunners going out," Kel said. He had a pouch at his left side that he had stuffed with as many of the small spherical balls as he could fit. There were at least twenty of them. Instead, he reached to Poul's back and removed two from his partner's armor, prepped them, and tossed one deep to the end of the hallway, followed by another midway. The second landed as the first one detonated, and before the arcs stopped, their train was rolling.

A door on the right was open, a body in front of it. On the right Sims and Bigg moved to it as Poul with Kel behind him moved to the closed door on the left. Sims tossed a stunner through the open door and as the arcs faded, pushed into the room with Bigg on his heels.

Empty. *Look for work*, an old voice echoed in his head.

They flowed out and to the next door. Poul blasted the striker and pushed the door open with his muzzle as Kel tossed another stunner. The fading purple arcs illuminated all. Uniformed men lay among the desks and tables, one frozen on his knees, pistol in hand. Kel shot him. They fired until every uniformed men had charred holes smoking through their chests.

Kel found himself in the lead on the left and knew it was Sims with him on his right as they moved to the next set of doors. Both were closed. They flowed together into position, the four men moving without pause—neither fast nor slow but simply constant—pausing only the two seconds required to allow the stunners to dissipate their charges before moving in.

Kel cleared the next empty room, but as he stepped back through the doorway, an armed and uniformed man staggered into the hallway. He snapped up his carbine; a bolt fired from his right. Sims. The man dropped, arms flailing. Kel fired another bolt into the man's head where he lay on the ground.

They continued down the hall, hitting each room as they went. Finally they came to the last door, the one that last kookie had run out of. Inside they found a weary, beaten man chained to a chair. One eye was swollen shut and blood covered his white undershirt. The man studied them with his one good eye.

"We're here to rescue you. Where are the others?" Poul got out his torch and sliced through the cables and chains securing the man, leaving the manacles on his wrists but severing their connections.

"The main holding cells in the basement. Some of us they took but never brought back. Have you seen my wife? They arrested her too."

Kel pulled a pain patch from his med kit as Poul spoke to him. He applied it to the man's spine between his shoulder blades. "We're going to get you out of here, but you have to stay put for now. We're going to free the rest of the prisoners. Don't pick up a weapon. We don't want to shoot you by accident. Stay here so you don't get hurt." The man nodded, dazed and silent.

"Hide until we come for you," was the last thing Poul said to the man as they left and pulled the door closed behind them. "Got our first hostage, Bigg. Rest of the prisoners are in the downstairs holding cells."

"Rog. Let's move," Bigg acknowledged as the four men turned to work back through the hallway, turning attention and weapons into each room as they passed, ensuring no threat had been missed. At the stairwell door Sims produced his own torch and simply sliced into the door, turning his wrist to carve a large crescent around the lock where it had been welded shut. Sims pushed on the door with the muzzle of his weapon and followed its opening into the landing, clearing up the stairs as Bigg moved with him, clearing the downward path.

"Braley, we're rolling to the ground floor now. Bulk of the prisoners are in the basement holding cells. What's the situation outside?" Bigg asked.

"Good news. The Crudes are channeled straight into our kill zone. About a dozen came out the front. I estimate at least that many still on the ground floor."

"Rog. It's going to get noisy in here, stand by."

Bigg set the pace as they eased down the stairs and halted at the next landing. "Blasters on the door, then I'm bouncing a grenade in."

"Ready," replied Sims and Poul. Weapons on target, they fired at the door together. A chunk of door flew off its hinges while more melted in place, a wide hole glowing around the threshold. Bodies scrambled on the other side as Bigg fired his grenade launcher. The round skipped off into the foyer and detonated. Dust filled the air as the kill team barreled through the opening.

They shot on the move. Kel's blaster came up and took out one man at his twelve o'clock, then another standing down the hall, firing a sub-machine blaster in their direction for an ineffective burst before Kel's shots dropped the man.

Bigg's grenade wrecked the room. Furniture was turned over, doors blown off their hinges, glass shards covered the floor. Ahead was a short hall. An open office lay to their left, where desks were aligned in rows behind a tall counter. To their right, the foyer led to a breezeway and the main entrance. KOCI bodies littered the floor.

"Braley, we have the first-floor entry cleared. We're moving downstairs to the cells. Get in here and finish the ground floor. Don't come downstairs till we call you up."

"Moving," Braley replied over L-comm.

Bigg led the way, past the counter and through the section of desks. They cleared as they went, hastily but efficiently. Two large security doors lay behind another counter surrounded by security glass, a control checkpoint to the cells below.

Kel and Poul watched their rear as Bigg and Sims set a plasma charge on the security door.

"Fire in the hole," Bigg said.

The charge's electric energy sizzled. There was no blast or concussion with the ignition. It superheated anything it contacted, turning the metal into poisonous vapor. Kel turned to see Bigg with his torch finish a small section at the top of the door that had not completely separated, and moved out of the way as the heavy door fell out into the room. *Boom.*

"Stunners first," Bigg said. Another set of security doors lay ahead and along the right wall of the corridor Kel saw a series of what could only be firing ports.

"Hold!" Kel shouted. The team froze. Kel forced his way between Bigg and Sims and brought his muzzle up, aiming at the slits. He fired off two shots before his teammates joined him. The metal port fell into the hall, leaving a large gap in the wall. With grenade in hand Kel took the risk of reaching into the hole to release the device before stepping back. The detonation rocked the surrounding walls and more dust billowed. If there was anyone behind the firing ports, they weren't happy.

"Go!" Kel said. Bigg and Sims repeated the breaching routine at the interior doors. Kel turned back as the light dissipated to see the door laying at an angle in the threshold. Sims quickly kneeled and grabbed a corner with both hands to walk backward with it, prying it out of the way.

A set of wide stairs led down. The space was well lit, not to Kel's liking. They would have a distinct advantage if the lights were out. He wished they'd fried the control panels back in the roof access room. The stairs were wide enough to allow the four to move shoulder-to-shoulder and they did so, weapons leading.

"Toss," Bigg said and chucked a stunner. It bounced ahead into the large space. They all did the same, sending the devices into as many different directions as possible as they took the last steps to the floor below.

A reception area spread out before them with halls going in three directions. A security station sat at its center with several Crudes flopped over the counter stunned, placed there by their superiors to die in place. They ensured they did. Behind the station was a wide passage with cells lining either side. The passages to their flanks were shorter—perhaps for interrogation rooms.

"Braley, we have a strongpoint into the jail. We need some help down here," Bigg said over L-comm.

"Moving to you," Braley replied.

How far up the mountain you climbed doesn't matter, Kel thought. *It's only smelling the sweet air at the top that counts.* The easy part was over.

09

"Cover those halls." Bigg moved next to Kel. "Wait for Braley. Kel and I will take this short side ourselves."

"Wait one," Sims said. "Maybe I can access the locks from the security station."

Bigg shrugged. "Fine. Move." They gave cover to Sims who had his wrist link sitting on the security console. Dulled yells and pleas came from the direction of the holding cells.

"No good," Sims said moments later. "It's all analog and mechanical, nothing's iso-linear or even digital. I can't control it."

Bigg pushed the large leej aside. Just then Braley's voice came over L-comm as well as through their externals. "Coming in at the stairs. Coming in at the stairs."

Kel being closest to the stairwell keyed his speaker to yell, "Come in!" Braley led the way down the stairs with a trail of Gs behind him. As he neared, Kel said, "Send guys up to the second floor. There's one prisoner in the last room at the end of the hall. First floor secure?"

"Yes, " Braley said. "We know some took another stairwell to reach the basement garage. Adam is leading a section to clear it. They tried to drive a sled out through the garage doors we sealed, but an exterior team cut them down on the spot. There could still be a good number of kookies trapped in there now."

"You kids crack me up sometimes," Bigg said over the team channel. "This is just a simple control system. The cells are all numbered by wing and there's a switch to lock and unlock each cell. Sims, come over here and see."

Sims walked over to where Bigg stood, pointing at the console. The large man looked shrunken at the realization of the simplicity before him. A voice boomed down the stairwell.

"I would like some KOCI prisoners if you can manage it, Captain."

Adam had arrived.

"No promises, but we'll try," Braley answered. "Do it, Bigg. We're losing time."

"Braley, take Poul and go down that hall," Bigg said, pointing. "Kel and I will take this one. Sims, pop the doors in order and we'll clear as we go. Let's move."

The mechanical lock clanked and Kel pulled it open. He and Bigg snapped their guns up, their weapon mounted lights filling the space. It was a morgue. Shelves filled with stacked body bags.

"Next. Let's go," Bigg said as they moved to the next door. On the other side was a small room with a desk, a chair, and a stripped and bound corpse on the floor. They would have to confirm its condition later. They left the door open as they pushed on to the next. Here, the occupant was alert, crying, and frightened.

"Stay put," Kel said as they moved to the next door, and the next.

After the sixth and last door, they returned to the security station to see Braley and Poul had finished as well. Adam had descended and now stood at the security station.

Braley spoke first. "Adam, get your people in here and start evacuating the victims. Most will need to be carried. We have the main cell block to liberate."

Adam issued orders and Gs rushed down the two short halls to retrieve their countrymen.

"There's two large holding cells on each side," Sims said. "Let's pop them one at a time and sort as we go."

"Got it," Bigg said as he led the way down the wide hall.

The holding cells were barred and paneled with a transparent barrier; holes peppered through the clear wall at head level. Dozens of people were crammed into each cell. Kel scanned faces, looking critically at the occupants. He was looking for something that stood out among the occupants. He didn't see what he was looking for among the group.

"Open it," Bigg ordered.

A throng crowded the cell door. As the door opened, prisoners tried to press out en masse, pushing in the panic to be freed. Kel and Bigg yelled at the civilians to remain calm and to stop pushing as they gave each a cursory search before sending them one along to the security station. Gs were receiving the prisoners and herding them up the stairs as fast as they came out.

"YOU. DON'T MOVE. GRENADE!"

Behind Kel was the same pandemonium. Civilians pushed to get out of the cell. In the center, a large man. Kel instantly recognized him as a Crude thug, one of the KOCI strongmen. He wore a white sleeveless T-shirt and his uniform pants. He had shed his uniform top, attempting to hide among the prisoners. In his right hand was a grenade, held at head height.

"I'm walking out of here or I'll kill everyone!" His left arm was around the throat of a middle-aged woman. Her arms were at her sides. She seemed resigned to her fate. Almost serene. Cowed prisoners stood around the man, blank-faced and shocked that their rescue was being thwarted at the last moment.

Kel moved quickly across the hall to the security glass and produced his own torch. He cut a large circle into the transparent barrier. As he completed the last pass, he pulled out the piece and rested his muzzle on the edge of his hastily cut port. He now had the thug in his optic. Poul and Braley stood inside the cell, their own muzzles raised toward the hostage-taker.

"We'll all die for the glory of the empire and the Imperial Father, you sleeping dogs of the Republic. Our glorious leader will—"

He never finished his sentence. The man nearest him, a thick balding older man, reached up and placed both hands around the thug's raised fist, pinning the grenade in place. Kel pressed the trigger, sending a single burst of coherent energy at the thug's head. A neat, smoking hole appeared, and the thug sunk. The older man followed the collapsing mass down, locking his hands around the grenade still in the thug's hand.

Poul was already there. "Good job. Good job. Now, relax and let me take it from you. Ease back. Ease back," he coaxed the man.

Kel relaxed with his gun.

Then Poul yelled, "Get everyone out of here. This ancient thing can't be deactivated. I've got it. Go!"

Kel rushed to the next set of cells to find Bigg with him. He prayed there would not be a repeat of the same problem as he scanned the crowd jammed against the bars. Braley and Sims removed prisoners from the last cell as he and Bigg did the same. Finally, the last prisoner ran to the security station where a line of Gs continued to push civilians up the stairs.

Poul stood alone in the middle of the holding cell. He looked up. "Damn, thing is a relic. I'm holding the detonator. It's spring-loaded. What an artifact. Keep going and I'll ditch it in place once everyone's clear. Get going."

To think someone would use that trash! Kel thought.

The Crudes were predictable. He marveled at their society's psychological conditioning. It betrayed the delusional nature of their empire. Propaganda holovids of the Crude army marching underneath a flowing banner morphed into the same forces riding giant steeds, wearing ancient metal armor breastplates and carrying long spears, swords, and shields. It was a reference to an imagined glory from their history. They saw themselves as warriors and conquerors, as the holo tying their history to their present illustrated.

The Crudes were a theatrical army with sheet-metal spears and soft wrought-iron swords. Their equipment was mass produced, low-tech junk, just like the grenade Poul now held. It was a device that could be used by an imbecile and could not be deactivated. It was a deadly analogy of their entire culture.

"I'll stay with him. Go," Kel told the others. If Poul needed medical assistance, it would be Kel's job to render it.

"See you up top," Braley said.

Bigg was the last man up the stairwell. He gave Kel a thumbs-up as he turned to go.

"All right, Poul, let's do this and get out of here."

Kel stepped away from the cell door as Poul moved toward the exit.

"Good idea. I'm going to ditch it in the room and let's make for the short hall on our left."

"Ready when you are."

Poul tossed the device and ran. Poul met him around the corner as—*Kra-BOOM*—dust sprinkled from the ceiling.

Poul sighed. "Been fun. But let's not do anything like this again soon."

"No kidding, brother."

"Was it you who cut that port and shot that thug? Nice work." They hurried past the security station and up the stairs.

"Me? That was nothing. The coolest thing I ever saw was you taking charge of that crappy grenade."

"Nah. The old man who pinned the grenade in that kookie's hand—he saved the day. Dude deserves a medal."

They made it to the top of the stairs and back into the main foyer to see Meadows and several of his men swimming upstream against the civilians still being herded out the front entrance.

"Hey, what's up, shouldn't you be going the other way?" Kel said as he passed them.

"Got work to do. Come on," Meadows said as he kept walking.

Poul cocked his head. "What the—"

"I'll go with him. You get outside." Kel slapped his shoulder, then followed Meadows. "Hey, what are we doing?"

Meadows barreled ahead without responding. Meadows's men were paused ahead at a large wood trimmed doorframe, the door already blown out of the threshold by their previous explosive entry into the main floor. Seeing Meadows, the men took that as permission and entered, Meadows following, Kel in tow. In the back was a bookcase that one of Meadows's men shoved aside to reveal a wall safe.

"Torch that open for me, if you'd be so kind," Meadows said as his three-man crew left the room for other destinations in the building.

Kel sighed. "We don't have time for this. We've been here too long. We've gotta get these civilians out of here. Intel gathering isn't mission critical right now."

"Hey," Meadows yelled. "I'm doing this for you dummies. I've got a plan. Hurry up."

Kel thought the quickest way to get them moving was to comply, and surrendered to Meadows's wishes. He went to work on the wall safe as Meadows leaned over the large desk, datapad in hand, running a program that copied information from the devices pulled out of drawers and from the pockets of the two uniformed bodies on the floor.

Kel had the safe open in seconds.

"Grab all that and toss it in here," Meadows said, holding open a small bag. Kel shoved in stacks of files and datacards. "Let's move."

They stepped outside to see the civilians loading into large grav sleds, a convoy of them lined up.

"Meadows, you bring it?" Bigg asked over L-comm.

"Coming now," Meadows replied. Two of Meadows's men pulled a grav container from the back of a Crude truck and trotted toward the front door. Kel knew what it was.

"Coming through," Bigg said as he moved past Kel. He pointed at the two men making their way over with the grav container. "You two with me. Hurry." The container carried a 4-gigajoule plasma charge. Their plan was to place it at the sub-level and set it for a one-hour delay. When Bigg set it and sealed the container again, any attempt by the Crudes to move or access it would detonate the device.

If the Crudes even recognize it for what it is, Kel chuckled to himself. The eruption would bring the better part of the block down and anything on it. The Underground had evacuated the area of all civilians before their raid began. The resulting blast would be a terrific blow to the Crudes.

Braley's voice came over L-comm. "Adam says there's a Crude mechanized battalion moving through the city. Want to bet they're coming here? We gotta go. Now."

Sims spoke. "Crudes must have some microwave or radio wave commo up and running. It was bound to happen."

"If that mech battalion does converge here, they're in for a big surprise," Braley said wryly. "First, let's get off the objective. Find out what the holdup is, Kel. I'm collecting up all the perimeter teams."

"On it," he said, as he trotted down the stairs toward the head of the column of trucks. He spotted Adam, holding a woman he recognized. It was the hostage he'd shot past to kill the grenade-holding thug. The G Chief's wife.

"Adam, we have to move. Now." Adam broke his embrace as Kel spoke to him.

"Yes. We are moving now. Kel—" he said to him as Kel had turned to resume his run.

"Yes, Adam?"

"Thank you."

Kel made a big nodding motion to make sure the man saw it through Kel's armored head, then ran. Several Boars flanked the column, energized young Gs atop them manning the heavy blasters. They no longer looked like boys. The high of combat aged them during their hit-and-run adventures. He'd hear about it later.

At the intersection sat a Crude armored sled and atop it behind the heavy blaster was Pieter. The young man saw Kel and waved. "Kel, what do you think? We'll be taking this one with us! It's been a great day!"

Kel was about to admonish the man for his premature enthusiasm when a bolt crashed into the back of the sled and Pieter disappeared.

More bolts spat from the top floor of the jail onto the street. Kel planted his feet and raised his own weapon. The source of the incoming fire was a single window. Kel swiped the side of his K-17, boosting it to maximum, and unleashed. He sent three full-powered blasts into the window. Without hesitating he clicked his teeth and brought up the targeting reticle for the grenade launcher.

Foosh. The ion trail of the grenade passed into the opening and an explosion filled the top floor. Glass rained onto the street.

Sims ran over. "That the only one?"

Kel shrugged. "Beats me. I don't want to send one into the second floor. Meadows and his men are somewhere in there still. Hope they weren't on the third floor."

Kel ran around the Crude sled to find Pieter. Two Gs stood staring. There was little left of the young man he'd heralded into the ways of the warrior.

"Get going, you two. He's dead. You'll be too if you don't start moving. Meadows," Kel said over L-comm. "Where you at?" Just then Kel saw Meadows and his men run out the front door carrying large sacks over their shoulders.

"Okay, okay, we're hurrying. Man. Believe me, we get it. Time to go. Oba!"

The column of trucks mercifully began their forward glide, a Boar in the lead.

"Team Three, the column is moving out," Kel said. "How copy?"

"Making my way to you," Braley responded.

Everyone else responded in kind. Kel heard some sub-channel traffic between Meadows and Braley but couldn't decipher what they were talking about. Kel hurried over to the last waiting truck. Two Boars pulled to its rear to provide security for the column. The truck was empty and Kel looked for the rest of the team before jumping in.

"Team Three, meet in the front parking lot," Braley said over L-comm. "The column is going on without us."

Kel wondered what Braley meant, but double-timed to the front parking lot where he found Sims and Poul waiting. Meadows and his men slid into two of the Crude armored vehicles sitting in the front lot.

"We're taking some new rides with us," Meadows said. "Hop in." Kel turned to see Braley and Bigg catch up and move to the back of one of the sleds. Kel joined Poul and Sims as they hopped into the one Meadows had ascended to pilot.

"Give me the count," Meadows said.

The whole team sounded off by roster order as their sled lurched forward. Kel crouched to stabilize his walk, placing a hand on the roof as he moved forward to see Meadows behind the controls, one of his men seated beside him. Meadows pulled his bucket off and slapped on the large brimmed hat of a KOCI officer.

Kel pulled his own bucket off. "Meadows, what gives?"

Meadows chuckled. "Nice work back there."

The column of the rescued civilians headed north, but Meadows led their vehicles on a different route east. "Thanks. What's up?"

Meadows chuckled. "I gave your team leader a brief. The plan is changed. I figured out the infil into South Mercia for your Astral Plane. And I'm coming with you."

Kel found himself speechless.

Meadows looked back over his shoulder as he piloted. He winked. "You're welcome."

Kel had been to this location before. It was one of Meadows's many clandestine sites around the city outskirts. They pulled into the warehouse as waiting men closed and sealed the doors behind them. On the trip they conferenced on L-comm about the change in plans, the accelerated timetable, and about the operation they had just completed.

Their team leader led the discussion as they swayed in the backs of the vehicles. "Meadows is right. The Crudes are going to have their act together soon. Penetrating into South Mercia was already a difficult task. But Meadows has capitalized on the situation and come up with an acceptable plan for the infiltration."

Since he learned of the team's assignment, Meadows had been brainstorming. The timing of the rescue operation at the KOCI station had merely been the icing on the cake for his plan. They would infiltrate south past the barrier by spoofing the Crudes. They would pose as an escort for a senior KOCI officer heading south to Zhukovkia, the capital.

"This may be a case where the adage, 'The more audacious the plan, the more likely it is to succeed,' applies," Poul said.

Kel had to agree. It was an audacious plan. Meadows had queried his sources in the Underground about routes into South Mercia. What few networks and ratlines they'd run to smuggle people across the closed geo-political border to the south were now belly up. There was no reliable way to use the Underground to get south. That left two options. One, exfiltrating north back to better support to organize an orbital freefall insertion— a complex task that it was unlikely the North Andalusians had the capability to help with—or to try a different land infiltration method. Meadows chose the latter.

"Once we get in to his mission support site, he thinks it won't take him long to find what we need among the material we exploited from the hit. Even so, we have the KOCI marked vehicles and enough uniforms and equipment to spoof the Crudes with just that," Braley said. "We'll make a final decision by late afternoon. Once we're at the MSS, first priority is to recover what we need from any caches around the city. Is there anything mission critical that we left at the G base?"

Kel thought. Like all of them, they'd left small items at their quarters in the base, but nothing critical. The datapads everyone had left behind would be useless without their biometrics to unlock, and they'd soon send the L-comm signal to scrub the pads. There were spare enerpacks and grenades as well as some other crated munitions in their dungeon quarters, but nothing that they didn't have amply duplicated in other caches. Kel had become partial to some items of local clothing he'd used when moving about the city, especially a certain narrow-brimmed hat. He intended to take it home as a souvenir.

"Nothing here," Kel said, sounding off with the rest of the team.

"Good. I want to be heading out by evening. We'll see if we can't coordinate some more distractions around the city when we make our move to the barrier gate. We'll spend the morning recovering caches and the package, then get some rest before we move out. Anything to add, Bigg?" Braley asked the team sergeant.

"After action on the rescue. I'll lead." Bigg had been the action-leader for the operation, so it was appropriate for him to start the review. "It was as perfect an operation as it could have been, given the constraints. I have nothing to say to you all except it was an amazing piece of work. Captain, Poul needs to be recognized for his actions in the jail. If I don't make it, I want it known that I am formally recommending him for the Order of the Centurion."

"GET STUFFED," Poul said, too loudly. "If you do it, Bigg, I'll never forgive you. No thanks."

Braley spoke softly. "Sergeant Radd, what you did was..."

Poul finished his sentence for him. "Nothing you guys haven't all done a dozen times in different ways. No thanks. I appreciate what you're saying, I really do, but please don't ruin my life. I don't want anything to change, and *that* little piece of metal and cloth will change everything."

"All right," Bigg finally said. "I respect that. But..."

"Why don't I go on with my part of the AAR?" Poul said, derailing the discussion. "What we could've improved was our control of the structure. We missed a perfect opportunity to crash their internals when we failed to take out the power control panels."

Kel was ready for that. "True, but if we had, getting those cells open in the basement would've slowed us down quite a bit. It might've been an even bigger nightmare."

Sims chimed in. "Agreed. The lights on didn't compromise our effectiveness, as I see it." They continued the discussion until they felt the vehicle slow. They'd reached the mission support site.

Kel saved his big one for last. "My only regret is that we didn't hit the barracks room harder. The urgency to get to the hostages compromised our thoroughness, and we obviously left someone combat capable on the third floor. It got poor Pieter killed."

Sims shook his head. "You always know what you should've done the day after."

With the team assembled outside the vehicle, Meadows walked up.

"What's our final destination, by the way?" he asked. "Time to read me in, I think."

Everyone pulled off their buckets as they formed a circle. Morning light peeked through rusted holes in the metal siding of the industrial building. It was as good a place as any. Braley was the one to tell him.

"Polislava. We're nuking the spaceport."

10

Kel rode in the back of the KOCI sled with Meadows driving. One of his men, a burly former planetary police officer named Joachim, now wore the uniform of a KOCI major and Meadows was dressed as a low-level foot soldier. Joachim would do all the talking if they were stopped at any checkpoints. In a society where there were only two punishments, assignment to a work camp for a slow death at hard labor versus instant execution, most people avoided the dreaded KOCI secret police and reflexively obeyed them.

Braley accompanied Kel in the back. They both were also dressed as KOCI thugs, wearing their armor underneath the large coats, buckets at their sides on the benches. Their blasters lay on the deck and they now carried Crude blasters. Kel looked down at the weapon. He was worried. If he fired the thing, would it melt? What he'd seen of Crude equipment did not fill him with confidence.

They weren't stopped at the solitary checkpoint on their way to the cache site, merely waved through. They'd anticipated the detonation of the plasma crater charge planted in the sub-level of the jail, Bigg giving them updates on the countdown until the last minute. It rumbled like an earthquake even twenty klicks away. That brought a huge smile to their faces, imagining the Crude mechanized battalion's demise as their officers searched the jail for clues as to what had happened. Any evidence of their presence and the missing KOCI vehicles was now lost.

Meadows pulled into a narrow alley between tall buildings and stopped. This is where they had cached the package and a few other duplicated essentials. The package had been out of their direct control for only a few weeks. It was best not to have it at the G base or anywhere nearby in case their guerilla force was compromised at its source. Kel had helped build this cache and had performed many mental rehearsals of how he was to recover the items. They moved quickly into the building and up the stairs to the second floor, through rooms stacked with useless collections of junk, dust piled on detritus someone had once thought valuable.

They came to a dingy bedroom, long unused. Meadows shoved the bed aside. The paint behind the pictures was dirty, but not aged quite as much as the rest of the walls. He stooped and began a vertical cut, remembering the landmarks he had set for himself when he helped construct the hiding place. Extinguishing the torch, he motioned the others over to help him pry the wall away.

The grav container was the size of a coffin. Braley knelt to activate it. He swiped the panel several times. "Damn grav container is dead. We don't have time. I'm going to active it and let it walk itself. Let's get it out."

Kel and Meadows knelt and pulled at the handles of the container as together the three men slid the container into the room.

"What a time for a dead cell. Thing weighs every bit of three-hundred kilograms," Braley strained to say as he bent over, setting his link on the container's receiver plate. The container unlocked and within lay a large rectangular shape a meter-and-a-half long. He put his link on another receiver plate set into the curved gray surface, then scanned his palm over a biometric reader.

A soft voice from the device said, "Active."

The three stood back as the cuboid raised itself on eight legs and stepped out of the container. "Command query," it said without moving.

"Follow at close interval," Braley commanded. Kel and Meadows stayed out of the way as Braley led the DOGR out of the room. The AI of the deployed operational ground robot would follow many simple and some complex commands. Unlike some AIs, it was not programmed with a personality or advanced conversational interface. Its job was to pilot the MkIV Area Denial Nuclear Payload to its destination. It could do so autonomously on order, but was designed to also be directed by a human voice. It could never be expected to independently cover the hundreds of kilometers to its ultimate destination without fail.

They followed as Braley hopped into the back of the sled, and the DOGR leaped in behind him. As Braley sat, the DOGR waited at his feet until Braley commanded it to lie down. Kel loaded the smaller grav containers he recovered from another room and closed the doors behind him. Once Meadows was in, they pulled away.

"Good dogger," Braley said. "Try not to prematurely detonate and I'll give you a treat."

Their convoy was convincing. One of Meadows's men, Christopher Shaw, had defected from South Mercia two decades before. He'd been involved in operations for the Underground to move agents back and forth across the barrier for years. Meadows assured them that the man understood the Crudes. "He was a local cop and worked under the KOCI in Koenighorst. His whole family was sentenced to death once he escaped north."

Shaw inspected them all and pronounced them as passable thugs. "No one will look closely at the underlings. Everyone knows thugs are more likely to smash a face or crush a windpipe than they are to answer to anyone scrutinizing them," Shaw assured them.

Their convoy consisted of an armored sled with a remote-operated heavy blaster mounted on its top deck, the team on the KOCI sled in the middle, and another armored sled to trail.

"This is how the departmental level and higher KOCI officers travel, even in Kroedellia," Shaw told them. "Everyone gets out of their way. You never know who they're coming after. It could be you."

Meadows told them he'd hit the interstellar lottery with the information and credentials he lifted out of the material exploited from the jail. "The head KOCI was a Major Divanomich. He's just high enough in the kookies to be above the orders of any higher ranking Kroedellian Army officer, but not so high as to draw attention that he's missing, not with the network disruption still in place. His creds will get us through the barrier without question. In another day or so, their wave-propagation communication network should be developed enough that they'll be able to start piecing things together. It's now or never, I think."

"That it is," Braley agreed. "Let's move out."

Their planned route wound through the region of Polislava. A direct route would be faster, but the potential exposure along the main military supply route going south was too great. The mountain range west of the spaceport would be their destination.

They would not have to infiltrate the ground facility of the spaceport to place the MkIV. That would have been nearly impossible. Their employment of the Area Denial Nuke would have to be more sophisticated than walking it in to its final destination. Their route would take them through several backwater towns along rural routes to reach their drop point. Then the team would proceed on foot to the deployment site.

It would take two days of continuous travel to reach the site. A lot could go wrong on the way. Unspoken was the knowledge that if they were compromised, Braley and Bigg would have a decision to make whether to detonate the device prematurely. Meanwhile, Meadows had chosen to be with them on this potentially one-way mission. Why anyone would want to be on a team that specialized in the Astral Plane mission, Kel couldn't understand.

"When was the last time a team even pushed the button on a Mark-Four?" Poul asked. "Late Savage Wars? This is going to be one for the history books." Few teams were kept current in the Astral Plane doctrine. At one time, the Legion maintained tactical nukes at the company level. That had been at the height of the Savage Wars. Now, only DO maintained them and even then, it had shrunk in doctrinal importance. Kel was told that two decades ago, every section in DO had one team assigned full-time to perform the Astral Plane mission. Now, Team Three was one of only a handful that maintained proficiency in its use.

One of the persistent rumors about Astral Plane was that when armed, the MkIV device would not accept a delay command but would instantaneously detonate. It was supposedly a fail-safe to ensure that no one could change their mind once determined to unleash the devastation of the device. Everyone had heard the rumor and discounted it. The stuff of team room banter. Prison planets. Classified projects. Savage tech. Still, the thought of being vaporized standing next to the device was not comforting.

"It would be historic, except no one will ever know it was us," Bigg reminded them. "The signature of the device will mock a Crude nuke. The whole galaxy will hear the SNN reports blaming a faulty Crude nuke that detonated at the spaceport. All too believable given the quality of Crude tech. The Kroedellians will be blamed for bringing nukes into the theater to intimidate North Andalusia and their allies. No one will ever know it was us false-flagging their so-called empire."

Poul shrugged. "We'll know. That's enough. Is it true that Rex walked one of these in by himself to block for a retreating Repub Army division? The balls!"

Bigg grunted. "You'll have to ask Sergeant Major Nail about that. Him and the old man were the only ones I know who knew him personally." Colonel Hartenstein and the sergeant major had been in Dark Ops since the beginning, when General Tyrus Rex had created the covert action force within the Legion. Like so much about a covert unit, even parts of its own history were unknown to its members. Don't ask, don't tell was a way of life.

Meadows's voice filled the rear compartment. "Approaching the barrier checkpoint now."

Kel tensed as their glide slowed. Electricity hummed in the air as the rest of the team braced themselves. Part of him wished he could see the barrier as they passed through. The barrier itself was a double row of energy panels separating North from South with the famous Zone of Demarcation about 100 meters wide in between. Normally, North Mercian police manned the northern wall with Crude army troops along their side, acting as mirrors.

Holos from when the barrier was first erected decades before were still burned into his memory. Images of escaping Mercians being gunned down by Crude soldiers in the open space of the demarcation zone. It had driven him early in life to be a person who sought justice for the oppressed, a virtue his parents encouraged.

The sled halted and Shaw, now a KOCI major, dismounted to address the troops at the checkpoint. Soon they heard yelling. Kel grabbed his K-17, ready to dismount, just as Shaw got back in the cab and gruffly motioned his subordinate Meadows forward. The sled began its glide again. They all remained silent until after their convoy entered a high-speed lane and picked up velocity.

"The army captain at the checkpoint was concerned for our safety and offered to detach a platoon to escort us through South Mercia. Apparently, more attacks by the guerilla force are developing across the city, some even in the south. Seems the Underground has activated cells in South Mercia and they are engaged in sabotage on their own. It is chaos for the Crudes. I told the captain the KOCI will order the army, as pitiful as it is, to serve its needs when necessary, and to not be so presumptuous on behalf of the state. The guy was shaking in his boots."

Meadows grunted. "Great. Now we have to worry about being ambushed by our own Gs in South Mercia. Sooner we get out of the city, the better."

Their route headed west and eventually south. They took turns sleeping and when passing through long stretches of countryside, stopped and exited the vehicles to refresh themselves. There was little military activity on the roads. At one stop they watched children working in a sparse field, harvesting vegetables and carrying them in sacks. Kel waved but received no return recognition. Humans laboring by hand was the kind of thing Kel only saw on holos.

The mountain range peeking above the horizon told them they were well into South Andalusia. It had been almost thirty hours since they'd crossed the barrier. It wouldn't be far to their departure point.

They passed through a small village on the switchback up the mountain foothills and stopped in the town center.

"Wait here," Shaw said. "I'm going to take Joachim with me and do some scouting. I won't be long. There are only a few local constables here. It's safe for you to get out and stretch."

Meadows started to open his door. "I better go with you."

Shaw balked. "No, boss. Best not. These country folk will pick you out as a foreigner the first time you open your mouth. They speak the old language around here. Please wait."

Meadows shrugged.

Kel and the others got out of the sled and looked around. The sun was beginning to dip below the mountain peaks ahead. The stone-paved street and a small town square lay in front of them. The few people around averted their eyes and hurried past as Kel and the team looked about. The village was spotless and orderly. The poverty they had seen in the low areas was not apparent here. Planters filled with colorful flowers and trees lined the narrow streets. Kel thought it was beautiful.

It had been almost a half hour since the two men departed. Just as they began to wonder what was keeping them, Shaw and Joachim returned carrying baskets in each hand. They were woven straw baskets like ones Kel's mother had for decoration in their living room. Hers were filled with dried flowers. As the two men approached, Kel could see they carried bottles and loaves of dark bread.

Shaw lifted the baskets to show them their contents. "I found a few treats. I don't know where you are going, but I know it will be hard. You must eat well for whatever you have ahead of you. Come." Kel looked at Bigg, who in turn looked to Braley for guidance. Shaw saw their hesitation and continued. "I found the town constable. He gave me a full report. There are no troops nearby. I tried to act less convincing than usual so not to terrify the man, but I was unsuccessful. We will not be bothered. This is not an unusual thing, for troops to break for a meal while in convoy. Come." Shaw again gestured and Joachim led the way across the street to the green space of the small square. It was empty.

Joachim passed out bottles and bread to the men standing around the armored sleds. Bigg nodded his approval and followed, as did Kel and the team, Meadows coming last. Shaw set bottles at places around a long chiseled stone table, then moved to the head where he broke apart the loaves and produced a knife to sliced up thick pieces of sausage and cheese that he passed around as they found space on the benches.

Poul sat next to Kel. "Last meal for dying men, huh?" he whispered.

Kel nodded. "Just so."

Shaw passed around the food. "This was how life was where I grew up. After weekly worship, our town square was filled with families picnicking and playing games. *Er vin vuvariba*," he said. "Truly wonderful." Shaw took a swing from his own bottle. "I hope you will remember this place."

Joachim nodded as he chewed. "The Crudes took it all away. We may extinguish our lives in this war, and those of many more of our people. These monsters will not rule here for all time."

"To happier times, my friends," Shaw said as he raised his beer. "Oba be with you until the upper spark."

Kel took a swig and tore into the dark bread and thick sausage. He felt a lump in his throat as he looked at his hosts and the beauty around him.

If this package does go off when we arm it, I'll be thinking about this last good meal in that moment.

They dismounted at a wide spot in the road, a pass between the peaks to their south. It was fully dark and the moon had not yet risen. The stars were bright with no light from the village behind them to pollute the sky. The Mercians stood around them. The team had shed their KOCI overcoats and clothing, and held their buckets at their sides as they shook hands with the men who had gotten them this far.

"We'll make west for the coast and try to return north to rejoin the fight. Who knows? We may be more effective remaining behind if we can contact the local resistance," Shaw said.

Braley looked at the Mercians. "The mountain range will protect you, but try your best to be as far away as possible by daylight."

"We will, friends, but what about you?" Joachim asked. "Are you sure you don't want us to wait? We are not afraid." They had discussed it many times. The team had a plan for exfiltration when if everything worked out would be their best option to return to safety.

"We'll be fine. Safe travels." Braley slipped his bucket on.

"Oba be with you until the upper spark," Shaw said again. It was a saying Kel didn't recognize, but knew it came from the man's heart.

Kel secured his own bucket and was soon back in his most familiar environment. Night became day as his visor came to life. He fell in as Sims led the way up a narrow path, Bigg behind him, the DOGR in the middle trotting behind Braley, then Meadows and Poul. Kel brought up the rear. He turned to watch the three-vehicle convoy disappear down the winding road.

The wait was almost over.

Kel didn't think about much as he marched. The L-comm stayed quiet, save Sims conferring with Bigg as they discussed navigation through the pass to reach the other side of the mountain range. He paid attention to the route and their progress in his visor, and made frequent scans of the rear and the slopes around them to detect any sign of biologic activity.

Bigg sent a drone ahead at low level to further map the route, and then risked an aerial penetration to look for activity on the face ahead. "We're clear. Nothing hot for kilometers around. I think we should up the pace, sir," Bigg suggested.

"Agreed. We won't be sacrificing security for a little speed. Set the pace, Sims," Braley ordered.

"Moving," Sims said.

Kel started to step out as he perceived the men ahead of him increase their velocity. The route was easy. They followed a well-worn animal trail that was almost as wide as a man. Like many such routes, it had probably been used for eons by different quadrupeds and bipeds.

Kel enjoyed feeling his pulse and breathing quicken. It was good to feel his body work. If this was to be his last day among the living, it was good to feel the strength of his body and its abilities a last time. After several hours of varying the pace as they ascended and descended through the pass, a narrow channel of starlight between two peaks filled the view ahead.

Bigg broke their silence. "We're not far from the deployment point. Let's move carefully."

Sims slowed the pace as they moved through an open glade between the thick, straight trees, and started a descent onto what his visor indicated was the forward slope of the range. The forest was dense. Through breaks Kel could see faint lights in the distance. He let the map in his visor go to a larger scale and noted their position relative to their target. He didn't bother to maneuver cursors, but estimated by grids that they were thirty kilometers from the spaceport's center. He oriented the map and let it tilt to a ground-topo view. The city of Polislava lay another thirty kilometers farther to the west of the spaceport, the sky above it filled with light.

A break in the trees in front of a rocky outcrop gave them a view of the entire valley below. Kel walked a few meters to join the others, where they now knelt.

"We've got line of sight. Better than we need," Braley said, the DOGR kneeling by his side.

"Look," Poul said, pointing at the sky. A light descended toward the spaceport. Kel increased the mag in his visor and the stabilized image soon resolved into the shape of a boxy cargo transport. Above, Kel could see other craft in a holding pattern at higher orbit.

"I see three heavy ships on the ground, too," Sims said. "I bet the Kroedellian Empire is moving in with some heavy support for their beleaguered satellite."

"Bigg, I think this is the time and the place," Braley said.

"Rog," Bigg replied. "Poul, shoot us a plot to the target for confirmation."

Bigg sank next to Braley and the two worked. There wasn't much for Kel to do. He turned back in their direction of travel and continued making sweeps. From the distance came the faint whine of huge repulsors as the ship neared its landing pad. The ADN's robotic voice responded to Braley's inputs, each command authorized by Bigg a second time.

"Confirmed. Authorized," the ADN responded at each input.

"Guys," Braley said, "it's almost time. Get back around the pass, and Bigg and I will join you when we're done."

Meadows was the first to speak. "I've had a lot of time to think about this. No thanks, sir. Always wanted to see a Mark-Four go off. We're at a good distance. I've eaten more radiation than this will give off. I'd prefer to stay."

Poul was next. "Yeah. If this thing cooks off right here, being a little farther away won't help."

"All right, all right, I get it." Braley said, annoyed. "We still have to move to a safe distance from the jump engine's field. Find us a scenic viewpoint farther down the slope and stay out of our way, because we'll be beating feet once we get our last confirm."

To his left Kel saw another animal trail leading through the trees into a small clearing. He trotted down the path without speaking. The jump engines within the ADN would produce a twenty-meter distortion field around the device. The spot he'd chosen for them was easily twice that distance.

Once he reached the spot, he turned to see his teammates close behind him. Kel took a knee and looked toward Braley and Bigg beyond. Poul made no pretense of tactical mannerism and sat cross-legged with his back against a small tree, facing the valley below. He had a front row seat. Meadows and Sims got prone and put their weapons in front of them, facing into the valley. They saw Poul in his position, thought better of their own decision, and both flopped onto their backs, propped up on their elbows. Kel chuckled at their appearance. It was almost comical. They looked like children watching a holovid.

In his bucket Kel heard the last commands from Braley. "Commence jump sequence."

The cold voice responded, "Confirmed. Authorized. Move to safe distance."

Braley and Bigg trotted down the trail to where the rest of them waited. Everyone looked back toward the ADN.

"Shouldn't be much to see," Bigg said. "Once the drive kicks on, the shift to the target will be..."

A cold blue glow grew around the ADN and then disappeared. The DOGR jumped. A white light in the distance expanded over the valley floor.

Kel's bucket dimmed the flash too much at first, blinding him in complete darkness, but soon adjusted and brought back enough contrast to let him see the blast over the valley floor. It was breathtaking. The holos didn't do it justice. The white plume burned red as it rose high into the atmosphere. Layers of expanding clouds formed at different altitudes and pushed out and up until they billowed into that familiar mushroom shape. A pressure wave swept outward, crushing everything in its path. Kel dropped prone and counted until the front reached them on the mountainside, whipping the bending trees away. Kel covered his head as the flurry buffeted him, rocks and grit pelting the back of his armor.

The gale eased. He raised up to see his teammates doing the same. While the wind was still strong, it didn't stop Kel from rising to his feet, straining to see the target area.

"That was worth the price of admission," Meadows said over L-comm.

Bigg whistled. "I saw a live one once, but that was thirty years ago."

"Amazing," Sims agreed. "Never in my wildest dreams did I think I'd actually ever see this."

"Look." Poul pointed over the spaceport. The descending ship was nowhere to be seen. One of the ships in low orbit was on an erratic course, bobbing until it lost power and crashed over the horizon.

Everyone remained silent. Kel thought about the city far beyond the spaceport. The nuke was as clean as one could be made. They were told the ADN would spoof the signature of a Crude tactical nuclear device but that its radiation would rapidly decay to a level safe for human occupancy in a few weeks. Supposedly, outside of the five-kilometer blast radius, there would be little physical damage to reinforced structures. Any person at least ten kilometers away and shielded from the blast by at least six centimeters of plasteen or stone would receive almost no ionizing radiation.

Within the blast zone, Kel knew there would be devastation. The Crudes would be permanently denied the spaceport. Any military material or personnel there were already obliterated into charred ruins.

"Well, we can stand here all night or we can get moving. I vote we start walking," Braley said.

"I for one am just glad to be alive," Poul said. "Turns out the rumors are false."

"Everyone knows the rumors were nonsense anyway," Sims said. "What would be the point of having a line of sight jump drive if the ADN was meant to detonate on activation? The damn thing wouldn't be over the intended target. It never made sense to me."

"Yeah," Poul retorted. "But what *if*."

"Then we'd all be blown to atoms, Poul," Bigg said with a sigh. "Did I actually say I was putting you in for the Order of the Centurion? I retract my nomination. You're either too stupid or not stupid enough to be an OC holder. Actually, I take that back!" Bigg waved away his words. "Every living OC holder I ever met was just as moronic as they were brave. That's you. I'm putting you back in for the big one, no argument. 'What if,' indeed. Oba's beard!"

Kel's bucket was filled with laughter and Poul's continued protests. He looked back, a last glance before they passed into the darkness of the treeline. Somewhere out there in the valley, civilians had been killed, people like those from the village they had just visited. He prayed not.

Sometimes he didn't like his job.

"Able Quasar, Able Quasar, do you copy?" the voice came over L-comm. They had been descending through the mountain pass, heading northwest to keep the mountain range to their backs as they skirted to lower elevations along the easiest route available.

Braley studied the sky. "This is Able Quasar," he said, using their designation for the mission. "Good copy. Do you have traffic for me?"

The voice on the other end said, "Roger. We got your signal. Very subtle. Are you ready to mark a pickup location?"

An hour later the six men sat in the pax compartment of a stealthed Talon dropship, watching the external feed from the holo on the front bulkhead of the large passenger bay. As they reached orbit and closed with the Republic carrier *Stalwart,* dozens of heavy and troop-sized drop-ships marshaled around the huge capital ship. Much had happened in the last few days. Their Legion recovery liaison brought them up to speed as they lifted.

"The Republic committed two Army divisions to the fight, the Guard's Armored and the Light Coldwater Divisions. Two companies of the Legion will be leading the assault into South Andalusia to hit Zhukovkia, followed by the Army," Captain Humphries from Lightning Company told them. He was due to join his unit once Team Three was recovered. He was cool and unhurried but keen to re-join his unit before the invasion.

"There're representatives from Legion and Army Intelligence, as well as from RI waiting to debrief you on the boat. The North Andalusians have a coalition formed with another dozen countries across Cassell, and will be making a full push into North Mercia and then south to meet the Republic forces. The Kroedellian Empire is going to have a tough time reinforcing the Crudes in South Andalusia anytime soon."

Kel listened to Captain Humphries, but couldn't take his eyes off the holo. It was a beautiful sight. The Pachyderm heavy dropships carried the armored division. The Pachyderms could land with impunity anywhere that had a footprint large enough to accommodate them, not needing the duracrete surface of a spaceport to accept their mass. Built for planetary assaults, each was able to disgorge two Magnus IX heavy gravtanks. Each of the behemoth tanks were crewed by ten troops plus a commander and sported five tank-class heavy blasters and high-angle energy canons. The next largest weapons in existence were only found in the inventory of the Republic Navy.

The Magnus IXs were simply massive hulks of floating death that could not be stopped. A single platoon of four Magnus IX tanks would be a match for the entire armored defense of South Andalusia. It would be wonderful to witness the Republic Army rolling across the plains of Andalusia. He hoped that the North Andalusian coalition could retake Mercia before the retreating Crudes leveled it on their way back south. His only regret was that he was going to miss witnessing the defeat of the Kroedellians and their captive cronies.

"Meadows." Kel got his friend's attention away from the holo. He was just as absorbed by the massing of the dropships as the rest of them were. "Are your RI handlers going to be torqued out that you took an extracurricular excursion with us?"

Meadows laughed. "Who cares? I wouldn't have missed this for anything. I'll use my mission priority to take a drop back into North Andalusia and link up with the invasion into Mercia. Gotta try to get my network together to pass off to RI before I come home. Like I said, it was a good experience, but I'm done being away from a kill team. Time to build a new family."

Kel smiled. He'd seen his friend up and down over the past several years. It was good to have the old Meadows back. It warmed his heart to see his friend ready to come home to DO for good. Where he belonged. Where they all belonged.

After a full day of debriefs, Team Three minus Meadows found themselves the sole passengers on the Republic corvette *Pride of Fornax* and returning to Victrix. It had not been a lengthy mission. While the past week had been practically nonstop combat action for them, the weeks preceding had been all preparation. The team had a large section of the ship to themselves with plenty of time to finish reports, get back to physical training, and rest. There was little gear and weapon maintenance to perform as they brought back only what they had carried with them on the last patrol for the Astral Plane. What had been left behind at the G base and what caches remained would be found and used by the Mercian Underground, if not now, in future wars. From what Kel had learned of their history, victories over the Crudes were temporary. The Mercian Underground would continue to pass on their secrets to the next generation for as long as they had breath to fight and Kroedellian stooges to kill.

They stayed segregated from the rest of the ship's crew and after a three-day jump, were alerted that they'd enter Victrix's orbit within four standard hours. Kel was relieved. He had reached the limit of his imagination for what physical training he could do in the compartment with and without his teammates. Kel did not get bored easily, but found himself looking forward to being in his own quarters for some solitude. Bigg had an innate ability to nap silently on combat operations, but when in garrison snored so loudly that the rest of the team found it necessary to put their buckets on to sleep. Kel was ready for a break.

They made small talk as they sterilized the compartment that had been their home the last few days, when a communication came across the console in their room.

"Commander of Legion contingent, this is ship's communication center. Please hold for an escort to bring you to the intel center, acknowledge."

Everyone looked to Braley as he spoke into the air. "Acknowledged." He looked just as puzzled as the rest of the team. Braley and Bigg checked their forearm links. Bigg spoke first.

"Hmm. Stand fast, men. We just got a bounce from Sergeant Major Nail. He's on his way up to personally escort us off the *Pride*."

Kel's first thought whenever a Dark Ops command staff member appeared unexpectedly was, *What have we done wrong? Are we going to jail?* Kel knew that for all the times he'd experienced such dread, criminal charges never followed. Nonetheless, a personal escort by the Dark Ops sergeant major? That did not sound good.

The compartment chimed; Braley opened the hatch to see a lieutenant with several other Marines outside.

"Sir," the smart-looking lieutenant said, "we're to escort the commander to the secure room in the intel center. Please follow us."

As he stepped out of their quarters, Braley said over his shoulder, "I'll comm you as soon as I can. Relax and try not to get spun up about anything."

The hatch sealed behind him.

It was good advice. *Useless*, Kel thought, *but still good advice.*

Everyone resisted the urge to ask the same pointless question—what was happening? Poul plopped down on his bunk. Sims did the same. Kel looked to Bigg who winked at him in reassurance, then looked at his wrist.

"Going under, guys. Message from Nail," Bigg said as he put his bucket on. After a minute, Bigg said, "Buckets on, guys." Bigg had something to say under the security of L-comm.

"We're going directly to the ISOFAC. Nail is a few minutes out. That's all he could tell me. Braley is receiving a more detailed set of instructions, but that's the gist of it."

The isolation facility at Battery Pratt under Mount Fronius was where DO did all mission prep and planning in an environment of maximum-security. Even though they were the covert action force of the Legion, they didn't spend a lot of time there. Many of their missions were sensitive and did not require complete deniability by the Republic. In those instances, their planning was carried out in the secure room of the intel cell at DO command, and the team were still allowed access to their quarters and the rest of the base. For missions that required the highest level of security, internment in the isolation facility was doctrine.

The compartment panel chimed again and the hatch opened to reveal another group of Marines. This time a sergeant headed the small detail. "Gentlemen, I'm to escort you to flight deck Gamma. If you're ready?"

They each grabbed the few items Braley had left behind as Bigg L-comm'd their commander.

Bigg talked as they moved. "Braley, we're headed to the flight deck to meet Nail. We've got your stuff. See you there."

"Rog. Moving now. I'm in receipt of orders from Hartenstein. I can confirm what Nail told you, we're headed directly to the ISOFAC. We won't know anything else till we get there. See you in a minute."

Everyone was curious, but they all kept off comms. Kel walked silently. He was looking forward to getting off the cramped corvette. The ISOFAC had few comforts but was at least roomier than the little ship. They soon broke out onto the expansive flight deck to see a black Talon with its ramp lowered, the familiar figure of Sergeant Major Nail at its side by a crew chief. Nail's armor was distinctive. All black with only a hand blaster breaking up its outline. Even on an operation Nail rarely used the active camouflage, preferring the black nonreflective surface. Except in space, black was not a color found in nature. Kel never thought to question it. *Nail can be in any color or pattern he likes. He's earned it. He's Nail.*

Bigg paused to shake Nail's hand. Moving up the ramp, the sergeant major patted each of them on the shoulder, even Captain Braley. They stayed buttoned up in the pax area, everyone sitting against the fuselage on the soft jump seats. The crew chief continued to work at the ramp before closing it and moved forward and past them to the crew compartment without comment. He had worked with DO before and was not going to bother the operators by checking their harnesses before giving the pilots the ready to lift signal.

Nail made small talk with them, asking how each of them was before finally steering the conversation toward their present circumstances. "The colonel and I are very sorry to have to do this to you, Team Three. You deserve a break and some team time before we tap you for another mission."

Thank Oba, Kel thought. The relief of being assigned another mission immediately was comforting; it meant they weren't in trouble.

"Anything you can tell us before we get into isolation, Dave?" Bigg asked on behalf of the whole team.

The wait made Kel's skin tingle.

"Savages."

PART TWO

FOE OF FOES

11

The ride down was quiet. The whole team needed to process that one word, *Savages*.

The Savage Wars had raged for centuries before General Rex finally maneuvered—and won—a final confrontation. In Kel's lifetime the word had gone from the idle threat he had heard as a child to a part of Legion history. "Be good and go to bed or the Savages will get you." His mother teased him as a little boy with the admonition every time he argued to stay up past his bedtime or to play outside after dark. In his ten-plus years in the Legion, rare encounters with Savage worlds occurred—places that had once been colonies and were in turn colonized by Savages seeking to install their own galactic order. Those Savages were primitive remnants of humans, presenting no danger to life elsewhere. The real deal—those who had supposedly left the fabled earth in their lighthuggers and developed fantastic tech—Kel only knew about them from the oral history transmitted by elder legionnaires like Bigg.

The legend goes that the first wave of Earthers trying to escape into the unknown reaches of the galaxy did so on generation ships known as lighthuggers. The planet's best and brightest propelled themselves at a fraction of light speed across the hostile expanses of space. Their plan was to breed for generations as they made their crawling journey toward the stars and a new home.

History had recorded no successful contact with any of the explorers until centuries later, years after faster than light travel had finally been developed.

The hyperdrive's advent led to an age of rapid human expansion across the galaxy. Many early lighthugger colony ships had been deemed lost. But in a galaxy that teemed with an untold number of worlds, who really knew?

Kel's public school education taught him the accepted dogma of what had happened to those early explorers. The lighthuggers had been populated by scientists and the intelligentsia of the home planet from all its cultures and subgroups. A supposed "brain drain" of the best of Earth had left a dying world, escaping toward an unknown future. He'd been taught that the evolution of the isolated societies had been one guided by dark social experiments attempting to shape the colonies within the generation ships into something... more. Societies developed that had been warped not only by social engineering but twisted attempts to evolve their members through technologic experimentation. The results were catastrophic.

All this was told somewhat tongue-in-cheek. Not the realities of the Savages and the war, but the almost mythical origins. Of earth and all that went with that supposedly real but now missing planet. There was always a look by those teaching those lessons that made Kel think they didn't quite believe it. Not really.

But the Savages themselves, whether impossibly ancient relics from a mythical planet or just colonies that went mad and were unable to replicate the hyperdrive tech that populated their planet of origin... no one ever had any doubts about them being real. Too many had died. Too many remembered the suffering of the war that brought about the Republic itself.

In the Legion, Kel had been taught a history more graphic and detailed regarding the planet-seeding of the surviving lighthugger communities across the galaxy. The war against the Savages challenged humanity's very survival. The Legion had been formed to fight that threat. The United Worlds had first attempted to counter the threat of the Savage Alliance. What came to be called the First Battle of New Vega was the impetus for the Legion's existence. That fifteen-hundred-year-long war dominated the galaxy. It was more than pride alone that justified Kel's belief the Legion saved humanity. They had fought to the last leej to cut down waves of Savage marines countless times.

And so what did this meeting now mean for the galaxy? It appeared that time had now come again for the Legion. Kel could think of no other possibility.

Mount Fronius occupied one side of the Victrix Spacefield. A corner of the field was occupied by the Navy, a small wing of corvettes and a single frigate dedicated to supporting Dark Ops. Commercial traffic dominated the rest of the spaceport. Underneath the mountain range sat Battery Pratt, a remnant of the Savage Wars at its height. It was a planetary defense station set deep within the mountains, virtually impervious to orbital attack. Its invulnerability had never been tested in battle, its huge particle beam weapons never fired in anger. The guns sat sealed and entombed within the underground complex. The layers of underground chambers and rooms were now occupied by Dark Ops for their sole use. It was one of the most secure places in existence.

They rode to the ISOFAC entrance by autonomous sled. A civilian contract police force provided security to the facility, and Kel saw the familiar gates and energy barrier perimeter leading down to the underground entrance. A pair of armed guards awaited at the covered entrance to the world beneath the mountainside. A signal was given, and the massive gate rolled to one side, revealing the artificial lights within the cavernous world below. The gate behind them slid closed again, shutting out the last rays of daylight.

The sled came to a halt. Sergeant Major Nail was the first to exit. Standing at the only entrance within the huge lot was a security station. As the guards scanned them in, Kel saw another figure awaiting on the other side. Joe Crane. The short stocky operator was dressed in silks and smiled as he saw Kel. Kel extended his hand to his friend.

"Eight's out and about. I'll be your isolation support coordinator. Hope you weren't expecting someone else."

"Heck no, Joe. Great to see you. How's the arm?" Kel asked.

"Like new. Just finished regen last week. The rest of the team is deployed. I'll be with them again next month." Joe had lost most of his right arm in a raid on a zhee compound several months before. An explosive device worn by a zhee fanatic had escaped detection as they were processing detainees. Joe took the brunt of the explosion and saved the rest of his team from injury. He was another man deserving an Order of the Centurion, but had begged off the award to remain anonymous in Dark Ops.

The medicos had thought a regen was possible instead of replacing his injured arm with a bioprosthetic. Joe had thought carefully about having the limb amputated and replaced to decrease his recovery time and readiness to rejoin Kill Team Eight.

"It looks good, man."

"Feels good. Can't really tell a difference. This one doesn't ache at the elbow. I'd taken a beating on the old one, your joint locks being no small reason for that, buddy." Kel and Joe worked out together when both were on Victrix. Built like a mini-gravtank, Joe was a master of grappling and all combatives. While Kel could keep the man at a distance with his longer reach, when Joe was within grasping range, he was nearly unbeatable. He'd choked Kel into unconsciousness many times. It taught him not to let Joe get a hold on him.

"Let's make our way to the team module," Bigg said after the team had stopped to shake Joe's new hand. "First we need to get working on a list of needed personal items, then we'll get essential gear lists for you to recover from the team room cages after we get our warning order."

Joe would serve as Team Three's access to the outside world during their mission preparation within the ISOFAC. Kel had a stash of Hiberian chocolate wafers in his kitchen that he wanted Joe to snag for him. He was dying for something sweet to savor after his next meal, which he hoped would be soon. He checked his chrono. Ship's time had been nearing lunch when they'd departed the *Stalwart*. Here on base, it was closer to just after breakfast. He usually skipped lunch but his stomach now rumbled in protest against this habit.

They followed Joe deeper into the complex and entered what would be their new home for the next... Kel didn't know how long. In his experience they could be here as short as a few days, or much longer. The longest he had ever spent in the ISOFAC had been two weeks. Political circumstances had been in flux, and they had waited on the order to go for another week after their mission had been planned and approved. He hoped they were not in for a repeat of that experience.

The module was not unlike the space provided for DO on some of the Navy's capital ships, but was much larger. A large central area that contained a long table and chairs was surrounded along the walls by workstations next to individual sleep cubicles. It made for a perfect mission planning space. Kel often found himself waking in the middle of the night, unable to sleep after thinking about a problem or a mission need, and would immediately rise and return to work. His teammates did the same.

A common sitting area and kitchen were at the rear of the main room. They would be taking all their meals within the module. They would train hard daily in the facility gym. If they were here long enough, they would even get to go on breaks to the courtyard above to get some fresh air. But escorted. Always. No one went anywhere alone. Security and preservation of mission integrity was paramount.

Sergeant Major Nail spoke. "I'll leave you to it. Your first briefing will be at 1300 hours. Get settled and get Sergeant Crane working on your first list and we'll see you in the conference room. Anything I can do for you right now?" They all looked at each other and to Bigg to see if there were any requests. No one spoke.

"Fine. See you then," and the man in black turned and left.

"I don't know about anyone else, but how about getting the mess to send us a meal while we get settled?" Braley said.

Thank Oba. I thought I was the only one, Kel thought, but didn't say so out loud, not wanting to show any perceived weakness to his teammates. He was well known for his avoidance of the midday meal.

"Except for you, Kel, right?" Joe asked.

"No. I think I could eat a little something," Kel answered as aloofly as he could. "Last op may have given me a new appreciation for lunch."

"No kidding, hero," Sims said. "I can hear your stomach growling through your armor. Nice to know you're human too, tough guy."

They wore silks to the conference room. They would not be speaking to each other over L-comm during the briefing and Kel was glad for the comfort. Though armor was a second skin, he found the older he got, the more he looked forward to times out of his shell. But that lasted for only a day or so before he felt naked and needed to don his protective layer with all its abilities.

"The commander," they heard as they all snapped to stand at attention, facing the podium at the front of the room. Colonel Hartenstein strode into the room, trailed by his staff, including the sergeant major. As the colonel took the podium and his staff moved to stand before the front row of seats, Kel took a moment to assess their commander.

Hartenstein stood over two meters tall. His shoulders were so wide that he could barely fit through most doors. He was gray at the temples and kept his hair buzzed short. He usually seemed grim but never projected an aura of anger or hostility. Kel had seen the unflappable colonel KTF many times. He guessed the man was in his sixties by Standard years' reckoning. He'd been at the helm of Dark Ops for years, only its second commander. Sergeant Major Nail alone had more time in DO. Kel knew he was not unique in his awe for the man.

"Please be seated, gentlemen." As everyone sat, Kel caught the colonel's eye. He thought he detected a slight smile as the man met his gaze. "Welcome home, Team Three. I've read the debrief from your mission on Cassell. Well done doesn't suffice. It's shameful we're rewarding your hard work with another mission so abruptly. Sergeant Biggetti," the colonel looked at Bigg. "I made a personal visit to your quarters to let your wife know that you were perfectly safe and to apologize for having to send you out again before she could see you. She is an amazing woman. You chose well."

Bigg blushed slightly. "That was very kind, sir. Thank you." Bigg was a confidant of the colonel's and Kel knew they had a close relationship. Bigg's opinion was often solicited by members of the command staff and the colonel himself, as well as virtually every member of Dark Ops. He was Kel's hero.

"I'm sorry to say that the next few days are going to be short on tangibles, gentleman. The mission you are tasked with is in response to the discovery of an isolated world that is suspicious for a Savage culture. We are still awaiting the arrival of a representative from the Senate Planetary Security Council as well as key members of

Republic Intelligence. They have special instructions to deliver that the command staff is not yet informed of.

"As a result, it makes specifics for mission planning almost impossible. It does leave you with at least a few days to train as a team and get some rest. Captain Yost, unless you and Sergeant Biggetti have other priorities, we have the shoot house locked down for your team's exclusive use tomorrow. The following day we have a drop planned for you into Area Doxy."

An orbital freefall would be a good skill to refresh, Kel thought, as the team had not jumped for months, much less had an orbital drop.

"What I do have for you now," the colonel continued, "is the planet and as much as is currently known about the target."

A major handed each of them a packet of physically printed pages. Most everything they would be given to read here in the ISOFAC would be printed, micro-encoded material that could not be scanned or duplicated.

Kel flipped his open and thumbed through the contents as he listened to the major talk about security protocols for handling classified material in the ISOFAC. Many of the staff officers had been promoted from the ranks of Dark Ops and after reaching grades above captain, had to leave a kill team. Some remained in DO on one of the staff cells. This man Kel had never seen before. He was most likely a Legion intelligence officer who had been posted to the DO staff and not a legionnaire who had any time as an operator. Kel was willing to let the man have the benefit of the doubt as to his pedigree and usefulness. He was still a legionnaire.

Kel quickly flipped through the packet and its contents. A nameless planetary moon with the designation

Proteus Four-Three was pictured. Kel had never heard of the Proteus system. The fourth planet was a gas giant with a ring system and several large moons. Moon number three had a type-M atmosphere. A holo on the next page showed a two-dimensional image of the planetary body. Kel spread the image to magnify and saw several active volcanic peaks on the dark surface. A further magnification showed evidence of sentient activity on part of the surface with multiple population hubs connected to each other by long tendrils. Roads? Canals? The image would magnify no further.

The Intel Cell major continued to review security protocols that Kel had exercised dozens of times before. Kel tried to give the man some of his attention, but failed as his words turned to white noise in the background. Kel's focus was fixed on the pages. The information mentioned a Legion reconnaissance of the planet nearly forty years ago. The full report was included in the packet. Kel flipped past the rest of the material detailing the other planets in the system to find the appendix mentioned. He found a heavily redacted document. It was in the format of a Legion after-action report by Legion Reconnaissance, Kel's old unit.

He flipped through it to see the list of contributors and froze. The third name on the report was one Sergeant A. R. Hartenstein. Kel looked up to see the colonel meet his eyes again.

"I'll be giving you the brief on Proteus system, Planet IV, satellite three. I'm the only living legionnaire who has been there. Maybe the only person still alive ever to have left there."

Everyone stared at the colonel in shocked silence. For the first time Kel could recall, the colonel appeared weary and old.

"I ask your forgiveness for having to send you out there. If we hadn't failed then, you wouldn't be going to that hell now."

They sat around the module—the team, the colonel, Nail, and the division chiefs from the intel and planning cells. The colonel had recommended the change in venue from the conference room and dismissed the rest of his staff. The colonel sat in one of the loungers while they sipped their hydration pouches. In the team room, it would've been natural to share brews on an occasion like this. Intoxicants were not allowed in the ISOFAC.

"I was younger than Sergeant Turner by the time I'd already seen three Savage actions." The colonel had regained the steel in his bearing. "Even before I went to Recon. Three times I saw what the Savages were."

Everyone listened intently. Firsthand Savage Wars stories were becoming a rarity as the participants aged into retirement or senescence and death. The men who told them were legends to the legionnaires of Kel's generation.

"My first Savage battle really wasn't much. That's because the Savages were a tribal collection of psychopathic mongoloids, any trace of humanity long extinguished. It was quickly decided we weren't needed. They pulled us out and quarantined the planet.

"The next was a colony of pirates, hijacking ships in the travel lanes and abducting spacers. That was a pursuit mission. We found their nest. Slaughtered them. They were still human. Human-like, I suppose. Tribal. Crude. They relied on stolen tech. I was on the rescue force to secure the surviving abductees. There weren't many. Only the women, penned like animals. Breeding stock. When there were no humans left to rescue, we backed off and the Navy bombed them into the Stone Age. We went down for a damage assessment afterward. Nothing survived.

"The last... the last was the most memorable of the three. Trexel Two had been attacked and devastated. The colony eradicated. Another group of raiders. We tracked them. Our planetary assault was textbook.

"These were a different kind of Savage. This time we found a highly advanced civilization. The colony's infrastructure was the work of hundreds of generations—hundreds of generations of clones. There were three primary lines. Workers, warriors, and leaders. The workers had low IQs and did not resist in any way, but went about their various tasks. The warriors were aggressive and had augmented strength. We slaughtered wave after wave of them. No matter how relentlessly we cut them down, they sent more.

"Finally, we punched through the inner walls of the capital where the leader class ruled. All clones from the genotype of a single individual. When I shot the first one, the clones nearest it shrieked and collapsed. It was a psychic injury. Our scientists later determined that the clones were linked telepathically. I never learned if it was technology that linked them through some device, or whether they had true telepathic abilities. I've often wondered."

Kel tried to imagine. It would be unbelievable coming from anyone other than the colonel.

"Anyway, in each case I observed that the Savage cultures were outwardly different, but at their core the same. Barbaric. Inhuman. Vicious. So, after my experiences on three Savage planets, I felt that I was a good selection for the mission to Proteus Four's moon to evaluate it for a Savage presence.

"A merchant vessel on a miscalculated jump discovered the system by accident. They surveyed the system, hoping for discoverer status of any habitable planets. They found the moon all right. From orbit it was evident they weren't the first. After no comm signal response they landed. It was a miracle they escaped.

"Within weeks my Legion Reconnaissance platoon was heading toward Proteus. A Legion battalion and a Repub Army Brigade were on standby just out of system. Though the Savage Alliance had mostly consolidated— we knew where they were—the investigation of a *new* Savage planet was taken very seriously in those days.

"We had no doubts about what we found. They were Savages. We spent weeks on the moon. The original colonist lighthugger occupied a place of reverence in one of the cities, as if everything had grown out from it. We scouted several of the outlying settlements. We transmitted images and made reports and dug into a hide and waited. And we waited. Finally, we were told to exfiltrate and made it out on a stealth ship, undetected.

"I expected after our debrief that the invasion would commence immediately. Instead, our platoon was sequestered and confined. We were visited by men in suits who ordered us to forget everything we'd seen. We were told we were mistaken. We protested. We damn near revolted! 'Why don't you believe us?' we asked. 'What wasn't clear about the intelligence we produced? Those are Savages,' we told them."

The colonel looked down, lost in the memory. "They told us that what we found was a colony that had perhaps sprouted from a Savage lighthugger or maybe one that survived the invasion and was coming along on their own just fine. We were not to interfere with their development."

Kel wondered if the others were fighting the same urge to exchange looks. This was crazy. Who in their right minds would have let a Savage colony go on undetected. Certainly not General Rex, nor any of those in the Senate or House of Liberty as it was called back then.

"My platoon leader was a good officer," said the colonel.

The room was rapt, waiting to see what would develop from the apparent non-sequitur.

"Recon only has first lieutenants for platoon leaders. I wanted to be the kind of leader he was. Lieutenant Thomas promised us he wouldn't stop until he had gone up the chain of command to make sure this wasn't buried. These were Savages. He made us NCOs promise to take care of the men and leave the problem to him. He was escorted out of the confinement area. We never saw him again. I never learned what happened to him."

"Sir?" Kel said, breaking the melancholy silence that followed his tale. "What happened to your platoon leader?"

"I have my suspicions, Sergeant Turner. But perhaps it's best to... No. Given the circumstances I think it's a fair question. Sergeant, my suspicion is that they sent him far away where he couldn't tell his tale. Probably sent to an ice planet to supervise a one-man weather detachment. Not to sound dramatic, or at least any more dramatic than the situation demands. I don't think he was 'disappeared' for knowing too much or anything like that. That's the stuff of holodramas."

Kel and some of the others chuckled.

"Sir, what are we looking for?" Poul asked. "What did you see on the moon?"

The answer made their flesh crawl.

"What you always saw with them... insanity."

Kel lay in his bunk after sorting through the gear Joe had recovered and brought to the ISOFAC. He had what he needed to get him through the next two days of training and most importantly, his favorite snacks. He popped one in his mouth and chewed slowly. There wasn't more to be done tonight. After the colonel and his staff departed, they'd had a brief team meeting then agreed to take a break and workout. They were the only team in the ISOFAC and could call for a gym break as desired without scheduling concerns.

After dinner they sat around the module with the intel packets in hand. They'd each taken a section and after an hour for review, each man gave a summary of the material assigned. For the most part the information was pretty dry stuff—nearest systems, star type, orbital distances, gravitational acceleration constants, anticipated climate and weather data for the moon. All information potentially helpful for mission planning and contingencies, but hardly more than what open source material could provide. Then there was the highly redacted report from Sergeant Hartenstein's Recon platoon.

Kel lay in bed pondering the man—now a colonel's—story. It did sound insane.

"It's been a long time, but I still remember my first look on the ground," the colonel told them after more prompting from the team. "The moon was truly barren. Half ice, half desert. If you removed your bucket, the sulfur stench made you put it back on, quick. The people were barely recognizable as human. They had misshapen, rotund, hairless craniums and elongated limbs and torsos. Some of it a result of the low-gravity environment, some of it from genetic manipulation, if I had to guess. They wore loose, pale robes that hung off their cadaverous bodies.

"But their level of tech was advanced. Their cities were orderly, almost institutional in design, and without variance or personality. Every population center had some large complex reserved for manufacturing where almost everyone seemed to toil. They grew crops in underground tunnels. Their actions seemed highly coordinated and intelligent. Each person was engaged in some purpose, moving toward a common goal. Not everyone was a willing participant, though.

"We observed them manufacturing and delivering item after item of undecipherable tech to the population center closest to the northern pole. An enslaved class did the heavy labor. If one of the slaves seemed to err or become fatigued, he was taken away by uniformed Savages. We found one of their slave pens. Useless slaves were rendered into biomass and turned into fertilizer or used for some other purpose.

"The cities were connected to each other by a surface transit network and in the northernmost city, the object of their labor sat. It was a mass rivaling one of the distant volcanic peaks. A Savage-constructed mountain. What its purpose was, we never were able to guess. Our job was to gather and transmit the raw intelligence, not to interpret it. But it seemed clear enough to us; it was some grand project directed by their central authority. The whole civilization was orchestrated around its completion."

The colonel painted a picture much more detailed than anything they had received so far. It seemed therapeutic for the colonel to share the tale of his mission as a young Legion Recon sergeant. "We performed our mission flawlessly. We infiltrated and observed, sometimes at close distances, and were never compromised. Lieutenant Thomas was the most competent leader I had ever known. He would have been a natural for DO. I regret I never fought to take our concerns to Command. Every. Day.

"When the LT never came back, we were all shocked. Eventually we were sent back to Recon. Most of the younger guys were sent down to the Legion. I was selected for officer candidate training soon after. I was never asked for an after-action report by anyone in the command group.

"I made a decision to follow orders, even if I wasn't sure who gave those orders. Someone at higher levels wanted my silence. The more I thought about it, the more it seemed that for me to be a good legionnaire, in this instance, I had to accept being silent was what was required. It's only now that I have to send you men to do the job my era's Legion should have completed, that I know I was wrong to remain so."

Kel didn't feel it was his place to correct the colonel, and was relieved when Bigg spoke up. "Colonel, no man leads a blameless life. But if there were ever someone to hold blameless, it would be Sergeant Hartenstein."

12

Kel awoke the next morning thinking about the last thing Colonel Hartenstein told them.

"Out of everything we saw, there was one thing that stood out. Tech I still can't explain to this day. It was one of the only times I felt... scared." The word left a hole in Kel's image of the colonel. Scared? Like a mortal man. Impossible.

"We didn't have Inquisitor-sized drones back then, so we did most of our observation through the quantum optic multipliers, so no sound. Wouldn't have mattered. The translator programs had no reference to extrapolate from.

"The incident where we observed the tech I'm speaking of, it was used by a class of Savages distinct from the rest. Chieftains? Commanders? We took to calling them priests. They dressed in crimson. One of them was inspecting a gathering of laborers loading items onto a transit.

"A supervisor—he was dressed differently than the laborers—had evidently failed in some way. The crimson priest raised his hand toward the offender, and the Savage boiled and evaporated. Just... disappeared. At first, it wasn't clear anything had happened. When we reviewed the holovid, we all agreed. By the reaction of the laborers around him, what happened to him had not been a good thing.

"We didn't see any weapon or instrument in the priest's hand. We didn't record any flash or indication of energy discharge. One second, he was there. The priest raised his hand, and the man was gone. It had the desired effect. The slaves all double-timed back to work.

"We saw another priest work the same magic. Transported? Reduced to atoms? Whatever happened, it didn't seem benign. We made every effort to remain undetected, especially when we saw a crimson robe in the crowd."

Kel considered the colonel's description. The whole thing did sound insane.

He put his feet on the floor. It would be a busy two days. Two days to train. To shake out equipment. To push themselves. It would give them all the opportunity to not fester over what the colonel had told them.

After dinner Kel found the team lounging around the module. He tossed the intel packet down. None of it held his interest anymore. It was an exercise in re-reading the same information for the umpteenth time, no new comprehension coinciding with the effort. It was bread with no meat. He wanted something he could tear into to plan this mission with.

Poul and Sims had surrendered as well, engaged in a game of twelve-star, playing the roles of the athletes in the holo, each working against the clock and avoiding the other players' tackles to get their discs on the twelve-pointed star first. It was mildly entertaining to watch. Kel preferred real world activities to holo-gaming. The door chimed and opened, revealing Nail's weathered face.

"Hey Three, how did the day go?"

Bigg answered for them. "It was a good day, Sergeant Major. A good shakedown. It's what we would have done after a mission even if we hadn't been in the ISOFAC. It put us all in a good mood while we're waiting for some golden bead of knowledge to drip onto us from the brow of the cognoscenti above us."

"You and me both," Nail grunted. "Listen, I dropped in to see if there was anything I could do for you, but wanted to let you know that tomorrow's drop on Area Doxy is a go. Zero-seven-hundred lift time. We'll be here to help start your load out to the airfield at zero-five-hundred."

"We've talked about it," Braley said. "While we're still in the dark without specifics, it only makes sense to test for the heaviest drop we might need to make. We're assuming we'll have only minimal orbital support, probably only a single stealth bird nearby. If we think we're going to be assessing targets for a strike, we're going to be taking everything with us for the duration. So, we go heavy. We'll be shaking out two 'saff-sucks' on the drop as well as jumping additional individual weapons containers."

"Saff-sucks," or SFSCs were slaved, freefall support containers. They were semi-autonomous AI-driven robots similar to the eight-legged DOGR that had carried the MkIV nuclear package. Mission essential gear necessary to sustain the mission above what the operators could carry on their bodies would be contained within the SFSCs. In addition to extra charge packs and munitions, water would be one of the important items. Procuring and treating water on the moon would be a resort of last option. With the mission-specific upgrade, their armor could recycle and purify some of their liquid waste into drinkable water, but it didn't give a one-to-one output. Much of their bodies water loss was insensible and was sweated by the armor through exhaust ports, unable to be recovered. On the desert portion of the moon they would sweat a lot, even in their armor.

They would each jump their individual K-17s exposed and secured to their armor for immediate access on landing, a rucksack, and an extra weapons container. Kel and Poul would jump their N-22 sniper rifles in attached containers, the others would jump heavy blasters that could be mounted on the DOGRs once on the ground.

"That's a plan I approve of, but I had an additional thought," the sergeant major said. Poul and Sims had stopped their game and gathered with the group formed by Nail, Bigg, and Braley. "Have you thought about adding tandem rigs?"

Kel, Bigg, and Sims were all rated for orbital freefall with a tandem jumper. For a mission that required insertion of a non-free fall qualified specialist, the team could take someone with them, literally attaching the passenger to the primary jumper by a harness. It made for difficult flight control in thin atmosphere. Did Nail have some information about their mission he wasn't yet sharing? Bigg beat Kel to the punch to ask.

"What gives, Smaj?" Bigg said, using the familiar form of sergeant major in his address.

Nail put his hands up. "I don't know anything concrete. I just know how the system works. Within the next two days, the ISOFAC is going to be crawling with outside visitors from various agencies of the Republic. My intuition tells me that when something as big as this comes along, no matter how classified it is, there's always someone else who wants to grab some glory. I just think it's best to be prepared."

Nail was right. If there was a way to take something difficult and make it even more so, politicians would find it.

The jump had been one of the most difficult Kel could re-member. He, Bigg, and Sims each wore a simulated tan-dem jumper on their chests—a hundred-kilogram dum-my. Even with the gravity decking turned off in the back of the Talon, the weight was excruciating. Combined with the exposed weapons, the extra weapons bags, and a full carryall between their legs, they waddled to the edge of the ramp bearing an extra 150 kilos, not including their chutes. Ignoring the weight, the bulk alone was absurd.

The jump was smooth, and no one had any major stability issues during the freefall. The canopies had no problem with the extra mass, but were rated for very lit-tle more than what they were carrying. The moon over Proteus Four had a much lower constant for the acceler-ation of gravity, so it would give them an extra margin of safety on the actual infiltration jump.

Kel sweated the landing. He wasn't alone. "If I miss my chance to hit a Savage planet because I screw myself up on this jump, I'll drink enough to kill me," Poul said un-der a full canopy. A broken ankle would sit you out of this mission just as sure as if you were dead.

"If you get off L-comm and pay attention to what you're doing, maybe you won't have that problem. Now shut up," Bigg said. The ground rushed and Kel flared his canopy. The strain on his knees relieved as he crumpled onto the dummy secured to his chest harness, prostrating forward ungracefully as he released his canopy.

They all landed within visual distance of each other. Kel was the first to dump his silent passenger and stand to see the rest of the team. They were not in as tight a formation as they would usually have maintained, but were on the ground safely. The two DOGRs pranced toward them, their eight-legged frames dancing across the desert in a caricature of ease.

"I never want to jump that much weight again. That's got to be a record, at least for me," Sims said.

Poul was laughing. "I'm thinking about a career change. I swear I heard my back make noises it's never made before."

Bigg grunted. "Maybe we need to rethink this and risk taking a stealth delivery craft to the surface. Whose idea was this?"

Braley, never one to complain or admit adversity as the team's commander, said, "I'm ordering a day of rest after we get back. I'm not ashamed to admit that I for one need it. Are there cryo tanks in the ISOFAC? Gonna cocoon myself for a week."

"I'll check everyone when we get back and dole out the ligament regen tabs," Kel said. He'd take a couple, too. His knees popped as he walked.

"Blackbird, we're down and secure," Bigg said to the pilots. "Come take us home."

There wasn't a cryo tank in the ISOFAC, but there were plenty of cold packs to wrap around their knees. Kel applied combined field stimulator units to everyone's back to help with the cellular regeneration as they flopped in the module. They'd be back to fighting shape by morning. There still hadn't been any word on when they'd receive an actual mission warning order. They been in the ISOFAC almost three days with a "warning to receive a warning order" hanging over their heads. At the rate this mission was proceeding, Kel thought he might be heading for a new record for being locked up in the underground sanctuary.

The door chimed and Joe Crane appeared.

"Heard you had a fun time. Nice job, Three." He plopped himself next to Kel. "Looks like everyone survived. Barely."

Sims had a cold pack on the back of his neck where he was slumped on the couch, both legs elevated on a table with pillows underneath his knees. "You got that right. Any word?"

"Not that I've been told, but there's a lot of activity in the ISOFAC since you got back. I've seen no less than a dozen suits. Looks like the whole command group and all the staff cells are set up in every room in the place. I think you're getting nearer to hearing something soon." That was good news.

"Well, hopefully they can wait until tomorrow to share their grand vision with us," Sims replied with a sigh. "Think I'm going to sleep right here."

The room comm chimed and Nail's voice filled the module. "Team Three, there will be a warning order delivered at 0900 hours tomorrow morning in the conference room. Get some rest and look sharp. Eyes on you."

So. There would be high-level attendees at the meeting. Three's real work had just begun. Joe stood. "I've got some special chow ordered for you guys and I even smuggled in some brews. I think you're going to need it."

They gathered in the conference room early. The second row of seats was always reserved for the team receiving the mission. The various briefers would sit in the front row and any visitors would be seated farther in the back. They chatted as staff members entered, exchanged greetings, and waited for Colonel Hartenstein to start the brief. At 0859 the sergeant major announced, "The commander."

The room came to attention as the commander strode to the podium.

"Please take your seats. Team Three, this is the warning order for your mission."

Kel stole a glance behind him as a dozen civilians who had filed in behind the colonel and the sergeant major took their seats. It was as Joe had described, a bunch of suits. Kel knew they would not be introduced. If they shook your hand, they wouldn't offer their name. Some were most certainly from Republic Intelligence.

Two caught Kel's attention. One was a young woman, the only one in the group. She appeared to be in her thirties and didn't look like any RI case officer he'd ever seen. Her blonde hair was tied back in an unkempt ponytail, her movements clumsy, almost tripping as she moved between the rows of chairs to find a seat. She kept her eyes on the ground, even as she sat. Next to her was a thin man in a non-descript dark gray suit. He scowled at Kel as he followed the woman to the seat beside her. His hair was red and thinning on top, though he appeared young. He continued to stare at Kel until he turned forward to give attention to the colonel.

"This briefing is classified Ultra," the colonel said. "I will turn the lectern over to Major Kendall." The planning cell officer moved to the lectern and began speaking as a holo appeared over his shoulder. Major Kendall came from the teams. He'd put on weight since going to the puzzle palace. All muscle. Not even Meadows could keep up with him in the gravrack.

"Please hold all questions. Situation. System Proteus, Planet Four, Satellite Three is a large moon bearing an M-Type atmosphere and human compatible biosphere that has been previously catalogued by the Republic." Behind the major, a holo of the moon appeared. The multi-colored rings around the large gas giant that was the fourth planet filled the background. "No Republic or independently settled worlds exist within its galactic arm by a radius of seven light years. Inhabitants of the moon have been identified as potentially hostile to the Republic and all Republic civilizations and fit the known archetype of Savages.

"Mission. Kill Team Three and assigned elements will perform a covert infiltration of the planet for purposes of intelligence collection and assessment of conditions on the ground for determination of targets for planetary denial." Planetary denial was another way of saying termination of all life on its surface. "This will commence at the earliest opportunity based on critical factors." In other words, as soon as the team had a viable plan, they would brief it and with approval, carry out the mission. "Proteus four-dash-three has been designated a Savage world of non-primitive capability, and as such is identified for potential planetary denial by Senate order seven-point-five of the Republic Galactic Security Doctrine."

Insane, Kel thought. They'd officially been given the mission to destroy a Savage community. *I never thought I'd hear those words.*

"Execution. Tentative concept of operation. The operational element will travel by frigate to the system and will transfer to a stealth vehicle for orbital freefall insertion onto Proteus Four Three. Other methods may be considered by the operational element..."

Kel only half listened to the briefer as he considered what he'd need for the jump. As the jumpmaster, he would be sitting down with the pilots and the intel cell to get as much information beforehand with which to make his calculations. He refocused on the briefer.

"... subordinate tasks and elements. Exploitation team will accompany operational element under direction of the exploitation team leader..." Kel couldn't maintain his rigidity. He leaned forward to gauge Braley and Bigg's reaction. Even Braley's forehead was wrinkled. They'd heard what he'd heard.

Exploitation team. Someone they did not yet know was going to be going along for the ride. Kel looked over his shoulder at the row of suits seated behind him. The young woman met his eyes. He'd seen panic before. She had it. The skinny guy next to her frowned at Kel.

I think I've just identified our straphangers.

"What do you make of that, Braley?" Bigg asked once the briefing ended. The team stood in a closed circle, crowded into a corner of the conference room.

"Sounds like we're going to be using those tandem rigs."

Everyone nodded.

Exploitation meant one thing. Their subordinate element would be acquiring additional intelligence while on the ground. Intel meant RI. With DO as the muscle. These two didn't strike Kel as RI.

"Captain Braley, Sergeant Biggetti." Colonel Hartenstein came over. "I'd like the team to accompany us to the intel cell annex for introductions."

Sims chuffed in a whisper. "I can't wait."

It was usually Poul who got the one-eyebrow-raised death stare from Bigg. Poul took the hint and remained silent as they followed the gaggle of civilians.

The colonel sat at the head. The rest of the seats were filled with suits. A single seat at the opposite head was reserved for Braley. The colonel gestured to their captain. They crowded behind him and stood.

"Gentlemen, this is Captain Yost and Kill Team Three. You've read the summary we've supplied about their backgrounds and previous mission profiles." The colonel gestured toward their end of the table. Kel disliked that the unknown civilians had information about him and that he had not received the same courtesy about them. "Team Three, we'd like to introduce you to the civilian specialists who will be joining your mission."

A slick-haired older man in a brown suit said, "This is Mister Patrick. He will be the leader of the exploitation team." The skinny guy who'd been staring Kel down nodded. "And this is Miss Sarah. She'll be assisting Mister Patrick during their part of the mission."

Now Kel did not feel as much curious as he did annoyed. Using an honorific and first names only was a tool that they used frequently when working with host planet troops. He was known as "Mister Kel" on a dozen worlds. Introducing these two people like this was ludicrous. Even RI used cover names to avoid raising attention when trying to conceal identities. This raised a big red flag with him, as he knew it did his teammates.

When the older man did not continue, Braley struck like a fighter landing a cross over a lazy guard. "And what is the mission of the exploitation team?"

Nice timing, Captain, Kel thought. *It was the perfect opening.*

The older man shook his head. "You don't need to know at this time."

Blocked.

"Details will be revealed to you as needed to support their mission and at the discretion of Mister Patrick."

The colonel's jaw was clenched.

The old man doesn't like this, either.

"I see," Braley said. "Well, as we work together to prepare for the mission, I trust Mister Patrick will have more to tell us so we can better achieve the mission goals."

Braley's cool, Kel thought. *This isn't the time to battle with the civilians.*

Braley would wait to speak to the command group later. The colonel's jaw muscles rippled.

The captain's gonna have receptive ears to gripe to.

"Excellent, Captain." The older man swiped his greasy hair back over his brow. "Colonel, we have a few more items to discuss with your staff before we depart."

The colonel stood. "Of course. Team Three, perhaps you would like time with your new element before you begin the planning process. Gentlemen?" He indicated the door.

"Well," Braley started after the door sealed, "Mister Patrick and Miss Sarah, was it? I've got a few questions and I'd appreciate your complete candor. We're about to undertake what is potentially the most dangerous mission of our careers. Our orders are to take you with us. My inclination is to tell the command group that your addition jeopardizes mission success and to recommend a command review before I do anything else. Unless you can change my mind."

Mister Patrick laughed and made an odd tic with his body. "Nice try, Captain. That's not going to happen. I don't work for you nor do I answer to you. Understanding that early will save you a lot of grief and maybe transportation to a prison planet."

Kel felt his face flush. *Did that twitchy little goofball just threaten the captain?*

"Now, now, Mister Patrick," Braley said, the picture of serene calm. "Let's not get off on the wrong foot. My meaning is simply this: my team and I cannot perform miracles. We can't simply wish you both into a state of competency that would allow your participation in this mission, your superiors' desires notwithstanding."

"They're your superiors, too, I might remind you, Captain," the man said with a sneer. Kel had already developed an intense dislike of the man, and it was growing with every one of the childish retorts. The young woman stared at a spot on the table in front of her.

"Yes. Of course. But if we're going to work together to succeed in this endeavor, here's what my team and I need to know. Do either of you have any military background or training?"

Sarah shook her head vigorously. "No."

Patrick smirked. "My background is quite sufficient."

It was a non-answer.

"Okay. How about orbital freefall training? If I find you don't want to answer me directly about that essential matter, we can solve the issue by taking you into orbit to have you demonstrate those skills to the satisfaction of our jumpmaster immediately."

Kel glowed warmly at the thought of tossing the man off a Talon and watching him drop to the surface of Area Doxy, flailing and tumbling out of control.

The man frowned. "No. No, I am not trained in orbital freefall. We were told that we could be infiltrated with you by other means."

He was a petulant child. Kel knew the type.

"Yes. That is correct. Even so, a tandem jump takes training for the passenger. Given the urgency to launch this mission, time to train you both may not exist."

The man kibitzed with Braley on every item for another ten minutes. The woman would shake her head in the negative to every one of Braley's questions regarding proficiency with weapons or advanced physical training. The man smirked and answered every query with, "My background is sufficient."

"Do either of you have any armor?"

They already knew the answer to that question. Only the Legion had armor, and neither of these civilians had the air of Legion about them. To that, even the man shook his head in the negative.

Braley looked to Bigg and exhaled loudly. "Well, Top. That's a place to start. Let's get Joe up here to escort these two to the sustainment cell for an armor fitting."

He shot a wink at his team. It would take hours for an armor fitting. Hours that Braley and the team would spend bringing their concerns to the one man who might be able to help them.

Colonel Hartenstein.

13

"So, how'd it go with the colonel?" Sims asked when the team was back together in the module. They gathered around the table buried in reams of new documents from the intel and planning cells.

Braley seemed subdued. "I'll give you the gist of our conversation. I told him that from our viewpoint, the mission would be jeopardized by the participation of our two assigned civilians. He agreed. After listening to our concerns, he went on to let me down as easily as he could. No dice. They'll be accompanying us. His hands are tied. Apparently, he already tried to fight that battle on our behalf."

Sims frowned. "What do you make of that?"

"I know who these people are, or at least who they represent," Bigg answered.

"They're Republic Intel, right?" Poul queried.

"No. I don't think so."

"Who are they then, Bigg?" Braley queried. "I recognized some of the suits. Some of them we've seen before. They are most definitely RI."

Bigg waited a moment as he chose his words. "I'm not sure. They just don't seem like a regular part of RI as we'd call it. I'm pretty sure this is something coming straight from the House of Reason."

Kel searched his memory. He vaguely recalled Bigg mentioning something about other no-name agencies on the Republic's payroll that he'd had dealings with in the past. "Like who? And why haven't I heard of them?"

Bigg shrugged. "How many people have heard of Dark Ops—even within the Legion? There are other organizations that have functions protecting the interests of the Republic that no one knows exist. These guys might not be from an organization with a name we know, but I'm telling you they're from some agency that exists outside of RI that has a direct pipeline to the House of Reason. This whole 'exploitation team' thing has me bothered."

"Well, I didn't tell you the last thing the colonel laid on me," Braley said softly.

Everyone leaned forward as their captain lowered his voice even further.

"He said that the accomplishment of the mission was an absolute, and that he'd respect our judgement and support our actions to ensure mission success."

Trying to read between the lines, Poul blurted, "Does that mean the colonel just approved us to smoke-check these losers if we think they're compromising the mission?"

Bigg sighed. "For an operator, that's the most crass and blunt thing I've ever heard. Do you really think that's how the colonel intends for us to handle the problem? Just kill them?"

Sims guffawed, but Poul didn't look deterred. "No, Top, of course not. That's just the first thing that came to mind."

Kel had to admit the thought had crossed his mind too. Now he knew that he wasn't alone.

"All right, let's keep it together, guys," Bigg said. "First things first. Poul, we can spare you for now. After our twin problems get back from getting a taxpayer-funded set of DO armor, I want you and Crane to devote one hundred percent of your attention to getting an assessment of those two. We know they won't have a clue about the armor. They won't be getting a full package with all the bucket-tech, but they need to get familiarized pronto. Then I want you to get a read on any actual weapon operator experience Mister Patrick has. I'm thinking that Miss Sarah needs at least a personal defense weapon. We'll consider your recommendations for arming them after that.

"Finish up your request for the specials and get the captain's auth, then get those two out for some range time. The rest of us will continue sorting through this additional intel and get our preliminary op-order going."

Braley nodded. "By the end of today we need to make the call of whether a freefall insert is still an option or if we have to look at the risk of a stealth ship landing. Kel, you're the tandem trainer. What's your estimation of taking two never-jumped civvies on this drop? Can we get them trained in time if that's the only option?"

Kel considered. "We don't have time to do a live-drop with them. My best recommendation will be run them through a holo-simulation. They really don't have to do much but stay still and not throw off our stability. What do you think, Sims?" The big leej would be the other jumpmaster taking a civilian down to the moon's surface with them.

"I'd agree. The holo simulation will give them the basics. If we do a live practice and they get goofy, they'll never be better for a second run, which in their case would be the actual infil. Less chance of us getting hurt, I think."

"Worst-case scenario, we drug them at drop time," Kel said. "I have some short-acting sleepers that would make them pretty cooperative for a jump if need be. The sims runs will let me assess their coping mechanisms during a real jump."

"Great," Poul muttered. "The most difficult mission we've ever had and we're going to drop with two tranqed civvies who can't shoot."

That night the team assembled again around the table. They'd cleared away the document stacks and Joe was joining them for the evening meal. He'd arranged several courses from the main dining facility. They usually ate well when on home base, but when in isolation, the mess made extra efforts to make gourmet meals for a team in the ISOFAC. Joe was proving to be an excellent liaison evidenced by the choices he'd made for their menu.

"So, what did you conclude about our two guests?" Braley asked between bites.

"Well, our young lady is a good listener and a quick study on the armor," Poul replied. "We took them over to the obstacle course and let them try the basic course with and without the power augments. It's all pretty intuitive, but I'd say she showed good aptitude. Mister Patrick did all right, but he's so defensive it's tough to teach the guy anything. He's certain he knows it all. That dude's dangerous."

Joe agreed. "We took them to the range for a familiarization. *Mister* Patrick," Joe sniffed, "showed us the same attitude on the range. He's clearly had some training, but he's not as good as he thinks he is. I'm no psych, but the guy's got some kind of meta-cognitive disorder. He has no ability to self-assess. He believes he's mastered something the very first time he's shown it. I have to believe this guy has some redeeming quality to warrant him being on your mission, but he didn't show me that today."

Bigg shook his head. "With some daily training, can they be given weapons?"

Joe looked to Poul, who spoke for them. "The woman, I think she can handle a personal defense weapon. She was able to absorb enough today to be safe employing a hand blaster. A little daily practice and she'll be fine. As for Mister Patrick, if we decide to arm him with a carbine, let's use one of the deconfliction specials and not tell him." They had K-17s modified for issue to indigenous troops that would sense proximity to anyone in Legion armor. The tech package would block the weapon from firing if the muzzle came within about a meter of friendly personnel. It was not common knowledge that the weapons they issued for use to non-Legion troops were limited in that way.

"Oh, that goes without saying," Braley said. "Did you get any information out of them today? Were you able to get any read on who they were or what their backgrounds are?"

"Nope," Poul said. "Neither of us even tried with the man. Sarah was never more than a meter away from Patrick the whole day. Whenever I tried to make small talk with her, she locked up. Patrick kept giving her the evil eye. Maybe he's her handler. She has a good, if not intuitive sense about tech. My read is that she's the brains of the two. She's not an intelligence officer. I'm betting she's an analyst. He's the case officer, or whatever."

That made sense. It was troubling that familiarity with Patrick was not increasing their confidence. Kel had worked with many case officers from RI, as had they all. Most had been competent individuals, some even impressive. Yes, very cliquish and generally dismissive of other's opinions, but after you worked with them awhile, they relaxed and proved professional. Of course, Kel could recall noteworthy exceptions.

"Great," Bigg said. "Keep working them. Continue with the daily sessions and get them as ready as you can. Also keep up the subtle attempts to get more information from them. Get the two separated whenever possible. But I only want you spending mornings on that task. By 1200, I want you both back here to help with prep. I'm looking at being ready to brief back the mission in four days."

Kel thought about it. "Then I should budget some tandem freefall sims time day after tomorrow. They'll be a little more familiar with the armor by then, and Sims and I won't have such a tough task. I get Sarah, by the way."

Sims frowned. "Really, Kel. Isn't that kind of childish? Bigg should decide."

They looked at Bigg expectantly, who sawed away at the pie on his plate.

"You know the rules. Kel called her first."

The next afternoon the colonel paid them a visit in the module. They were all busy writing their portion of the plan. Kel was busy thinking about the medical part of the mission. They would have limited options for dealing with casualties on the covert reconnaissance and no option for early evacuation of a severely injured man. He was budgeting room on one of the DOGRs for a med-analyzer when the colonel made his appearance.

"Gentleman. Don't mean to interrupt, but I wanted you to hear this from me. I just received a denial from the mission operational control for your request for a Mark-Four and the OSP."

"Denied, sir?" Bigg asked, incredulously. "They denied us a nuke package in case we have to make a fighting withdrawal? They denied us an OSP in case we meet heavy resistance or have an urgent tactical target to destroy? Denied? For a Savage planet mission?"

"Who denied it, sir?" Braley asked on behalf of the whole team. Everyone was facing the colonel.

The colonel met Bigg's gaze. "The operational command authority for this mission lies outside of Legion command. The general has not been read into this mission. It is being controlled by the Planetary Security Council."

Other than stating the legal authority for the mission, the warning order had neglected to discuss the chain of command. Normally the command authority for an operation is stated within a warning order. They all noticed its conspicuous absence.

"We're being run by the House of Reason and its spies," Bigg concluded. "Unbelievable."

The colonel looked sympathetic. "I'm not taking their denial at face value. I am continuing my protest and seeking clarification as to why the denial was issued. It could be some simple bureaucratic intermediary who issued the denial. Planning cell and I are still working the problem. I am raising concerns through every pipeline available. I might not be DO commander by the time I'm done. I wanted to let you know, though, that at this time you'll have to plan around those items not being available."

With that said, the colonel left. As the door slid closed, everyone spoke at once.

"Everything about this mission stinks," Poul said.

"Seems if they want to get us killed, they could just poison us right here in the ISOFAC," Sims said. "It'd save a lot of tax dollars."

Bigg looked to Braley. "I have to say, sir, I agree. No way this happens if General Rex was still alive."

Kel remained silent.

Braley, always the calm leader, did his best to assuage their anxiety. "Here's what we can do right now." Everyone listened. "We keep planning. Give ourselves every advantage possible. We do not rely on technology. We rely on ourselves. The colonel knows the seriousness of the situation and came here personally let us know that he is on our side. We have to trust that he has our interests as well as that of the mission at the center of his efforts. We can be confident that this issue isn't closed. Let's get back to work."

Back at his workstation, Kel avoided looking at Poul. He knew that if he glanced in Poul's direction that his friend would use that as a cue to make some comment. He didn't want to trigger the man's habit of speaking out at the wrong time. It didn't work.

"Oh, dear Oba," Poul muttered. "If you ever wanted to drop a meteor on the House or Senate chambers, now would be great."

Sometimes when it rained, it poured. This was one of those times. It was as they rose to gather for a quick PT session that it began. Kel was stirring sugar into his kaff while the rest of the team sipped theirs black. They were planning on a thirty-minute smoke session followed by combatives. Two men would start a match and whoever submitted would fall out and await the loser of the next bout. Then a second match would start alongside the first, and so on. It was rare for the first winner to continue his victories past one or two challengers, losing to a fresher, more rested man. As the men continued pairing off, after twenty minutes, everyone was wasted.

Kel wandered over to where Poul was standing, nursing his own cup of hot kaff. Kel, his back to the room, spoke in hushed tones. "Hey, man. I'm out of sorts about this mission. I'm feeling a little pessimistic even after the captain's pep talk. Feeling like I'm developing a bad attitude. Not sure if anyone else is picking up on that vibe from me. Felt bad about it when we knocked off last night." Kel had gone to sleep with dark thoughts about their situation.

"*You* have a bad attitude?" Poul said a little louder than Kel had hoped. Poul looked around and shrunk his shoulders in response to his own outburst. "I'm positively *livid*," he whispered. "This whole thing stinks." He didn't get a chance to elaborate further.

"Team Three. We need you in the conference room in twenty minutes." Sergeant Major Nail's voice filled the room. "We have a VIP from the Senate here to give us a brief."

"Acknowledged," Bigg replied. "Well, if we have a VIP, I guess we better get silks on. Hurry it up."

Kel took his kaff with him into his sleep chamber to change uniforms. This was turning into a bad start for the day.

"Senate, huh?" Poul whispered to Kel. Seated in the conference room, the team waited for the command group and VIP to arrive. "All the way from Liberinthine. Must've hightailed it here right after they denied our request for the specials. What do you think this is about?"

Kel shrugged. He was formulating a conjecture when the door opened and in walked the colonel and a civilian, the command group trailing behind them. Nail was the last in. The colonel moved up to the podium, the civilian standing just beside him.

"Team Three, I have the pleasure of introducing Mister Accius VanderBlanc, chief of staff to Grand Senator Lucius VanderLoot, Chair of the Senate Planetary Security Council."

.The elegant man took the spot behind the podium. He was dressed in the height of capital-fashion, wearing a shimmering green suit with a neck silk that subtly changed colors as the man shifted. His face was a portrait of moral superiority coupled with a mild distaste for the lower life forms in front of him.

He's a pol, all right, Kel thought.

"Gentleman, I bring you greetings from Liberinthine, the House of Reason, and the Senate which provides representation and stability to the Republic we serve. Grand Senator VanderLoot sends his regards."

Kel suppressed the bile rising in his throat. Whatever Mr. Fancy Suit said next wouldn't be good.

"I have important matters with the Grand Senator back on Liberinthine to attend to, and cannot extend my time here with you, so I will be brief. The mission on which you are about to embark is of utmost importance to the security and safety of the Republic. It is being observed at the highest level. Never in your lives has your performance or professionalism been more important than in your attention to the successful completion of this mission."

The overly dramatic pause fell flat for Kel. The big gust of wind about to follow wouldn't fill his sails.

"This is a No Fail mission. Do your duty to yourselves and the Republic. Do not disappoint us, gentleman. I say again, this is a No Fail mission."

The man leveled them each a scowl, as though he hoped to intimidate the operators into success. That done, he swept out of the room, Nail moving aside to allow his exit. The colonel and the command staff followed, moving to catch the man's heels. When the last of the staff officers departed, Nail's look said it all. Teeth gritted, face contorted. He was empathetic to what Kel and the team felt. He backed out of the room to leave the team alone.

Kel was usually the last to speak. Not now. "No Fail!" Kel spat. Blood pulsed in his ears. "Did baby just learn a new word? Who in karking hell does that guy think he is? No Fail, my ass!"

Sims sat with his head in his hands; Poul flopped back in his chair, looking at the ceiling and mumbling obscene curses. Bigg and Braley studied the ground as they listened to Kel's further protests.

"Where does a pol even hear the term No Fail? It's time for the Legion to hang them all on the Senate building's columns. Past time. Article Nineteen."

No one spoke for the moment. Kel's outburst had captured everyone's current feelings of frustration.

The concept of a No Fail mission came with very specific implications, all of which seemed to be lost on the Senate's popinjay. A No Fail mission meant pretty much what its name said: the mission was of such importance, or the accomplishment of the mission was so critical to the subsequent larger mission, that it could not be allowed to fail. Inherent within that concept was the implication that the support and assets essential to the accomplishment of the mission were provided.

Simply declaring a mission "No Fail" without putting the essential elements in place to support it was ridiculous. You couldn't tell a squad of ten light infantrymen that their mission to assault a position fortified with a hundred heavy blasters was "No Fail." It was an absurd use of the term. This was the situation the team found themselves in.

There were three doctrinal No Fail missions in the Legion's mandate. The first was Joint Denied Entry. The Legion were usually the first troops on the ground in a planetary assault, making a beachhead for Republic Army divisions. The Legion would not fail to provide safe portage for the army by establishing a planetary foothold from which to carry out a large-scale invasion. The second was Spaceport Seizure. Whether a terrestrial space field, an orbital, or deep space station, if the Legion was assigned to capture it, it would happen. There might not be anything usable left of the station, but it would happen. The last No Fail mission for the Legion was High-Value Tactical Call-Out/Kill or Capture. If the Legion was assigned a mission to kill or capture an individual, it could also be assured to happen.

Legion Dark Ops was a covert action force with missions harder to define. They were the only unit tasked with performing strategic-level clandestine missions. While they performed many other types of unique missions, in a sense, all of their missions were No Fail—or had the potential to be. If properly supported. Under the current climate, telling Team Three that their ill-defined mission to a Savage World, with two civilian non-combatants in tow—plus no heavy firepower—was a No-Fail mission, was puerile at best.

"Did that fancy-lad jump all this way just to tell us *that*? He could have sent a holo," Sims said. "I'm with Kel. He was just like a child trying out a new vocabulary word he learned in school today. Ridiculous."

"Sure, but we're the other schoolchildren," Poul said.

"What?" Bigg asked, confused. "I don't get your analogy."

"Or, maybe we're the teacher? Wait, we're the... ah, forget it." Poul slumped back and returned to stare at the ceiling.

"All right, all right. Gents, let's get back on track," Braley said. "We've already burned too much time on useless tasks this morning. No time for PT. Poul, get with Joe and keep on your tasks with the twin civvies." They'd all taken to calling Patrick and Sarah "the twins."

"The rest of us, back to the tank to keep working. Briefback is creeping up on us. I'm telling planning cell that we're sticking with a freefall insertion, and want the Navy liaison ASAP. Then the Navy planners can start working on their approach plots before we sit down tomorrow for the final flight coordination. Kel, consider moving up your tandem training sims with the twins to this afternoon. You're jumpmaster for this drop. You can finish the drop plan with the Navy tomorrow while we have them here."

"Yes, sir," Kel replied. He'd finished up the med support plan and requested all the necessary supplies. He'd already inspected everyone's individual med kits. After working out the specifics of the drop calculations, he had little left to do besides help load the DOGRs and rig equipment. He still needed to load conditions on the Savage moon to calibrate his N-22 for any long-distance shots that might present themselves.

"Braley?" Kel asked before they broke up. "I'm not trying to undermine the mission, but I do have a question."

Braley looked at Kel earnestly. "I have a few, too. What's yours?"

"Why now? I haven't heard a reason behind the urgent impetus for this mission. What's got a fire under everyone's seat to make this happen now? They've known about this place for thirty-plus years and done nothing."

"I think we have a winner. I want to know, too. After the way today's started my feeling is, we may not get to find out."

Kel and Sims stood from their workstations to go relieve Joe and Poul from the burden of training the twins. Their introduction to orbital tandem-freefall would soon commence. In reality, all the two had to do was remain still and arch their backs as they fell, keeping their arms tucked across their chests. Depending on how they did during the simulations, Kel would make the decision whether or not to sedate them for the infiltration jump. The door chimed and in walked the colonel and Nail. It had been a little over three hours since the trauma of the morning meeting with VanderBlanc.

"Gentlemen." The colonel nodded, then looked around the module. "Where's Sergeant Radd?"

"Sir, he and Sergeant Crane have been working with our civilian counterparts to prepare them for the infiltration," Bigg said. It was just like the colonel to care about the individual, noticing that the whole team was not present. Whatever he'd come to tell them, it was important. Just then, Poul and Joe walked into the room. Poul came to a brief position of attention when he saw the colonel. Joe took the hint and stayed outside, closing the door.

"Let's sit. You too, Sergeant Major." Nail took the invitation. After they were all seated, the colonel spoke.

"I had a little one-on-one time with our distinguished visitor before he hurried back to his private yacht. A few important things came out of our time together. Most important is that I got his bioscan on the request for the specials. They're heading out of depot to us as we speak."

That was good news. A MkIV and an OSP were absolutely crucial for this mission. Why the items had been denied in the first place was still a mystery.

"The packages are going to be delivered directly to the *Avenger*. Some of the other depot-level items are on their way to you here."

The frigate that would be ferrying them and their stealth delivery vehicle to the Proteus system were in orbit now. Kel was looking forward to meeting the pilots and crew of the smaller stealth ship that would shuttle them farther in-system. The Navy representatives would be here this afternoon, and tomorrow would be the first opportunity to sit with the crew. The stealth delivery vehicles were fast-attack ships repurposed for delivering kill teams as one of their assigned missions. As a child Kel had not been enamored of spacecraft like some boys, but he had to admit, the stealthed-out fast attack ships were sexy. He would have constructed a holo-model of one to float in his room had one been available back then.

"I have more to tell, but first I wanted to have a discussion with the team." The colonel paused as was his manner when making a point, and leaned forward onto his elbows. "I want to speak openly and freely. Or at least, as openly and freely as you possibly can with me." Everyone smiled. The colonel knew that there was a barrier to true open communications between them. He was a colonel. And a legendary figure. He knew that it was intimidating for a subordinates to speak their mind around him. "I want to know, other than the obvious problems of support by the command authority, what bothers you about this mission?"

Kel and the rest of the team looked to Braley. It would only be proper that their team leader started off. He took the cue. "One thing is the mission statement, sir. We're of course expected to always act on our own accord to accomplish a mission. But in this case, it seems as though we're being asked to determine what the mission actually *is* as we assess conditions on the ground.

"On one hand the planet is identified for possible planetary denial, but other than having the stealth delivery vehicle on-call for us, there's been no mention of a bombardment flotilla out-system to be waiting on-call. Who are we transmitting our collections and assessments to for further analysis and action?"

He was right. They would tight-beam burst communications to their delivery vehicle, but the craft could not send an active transmission out of system from its hiding spot in the nearby asteroid belt without a chance of compromise.

"And I would agree with you. As it stands, there is no mechanism for an immediate evaluation by the mission command authority for planetary denial. It's troubling," the colonel confirmed.

"The other thing, sir, is... why now? It's not clear to us why the mission is being tasked now, and so urgently? Savage planet evaluation is always urgent. The discovery was made by your team decades ago. So, why now?"

The colonel nodded. Kel got the vibe the colonel was silently communicating agreement.

"What else?"

"Lastly, these two civilian straphangers," Braley continued. "*Mister* Patrick has made it clear that he does not feel any obligation to observe my authority and will not discuss any aspect of their role in the mission. That's just ludicrous!"

"Granted," the colonel said. "What's your take on them?"

Bigg gave the team's assessment of the two. They felt strongly that Sarah was a technical analyst and that Patrick had the air of an intelligence operative. Bigg didn't reveal his suspicions about where they hailed from. "Can I ask if you have any insight about the two, sir?"

It was the colonel's turn to chuff. "I got shot down by VanderBlanc. I flat out asked him who the two were and got the most maddening 'You don't need to know at this time' I've ever received."

"They're treasure hunters," Kel blurted out.

"What else could it be?" said Sims. "We don't need them for anything. They're along for the ride to exploit any Savage tech they can find. I can't figure out why they feel the need to be so secretive about it."

The colonel nodded. "That would be my assessment too. My best guess is that the request for a MkIV and an OSP brought a knee-jerk reaction based on their potential destructive capabilities. Once I explained the context in which those items are used, I was able to convince VanderBlanc that we wouldn't use them wantonly. Clearly, the powers that be are concerned about destroying whatever's there."

"Is that why we're involved? Is that why the Navy isn't just carpet-bombing the place?" Poul asked.

The colonel stood. "The redactions of our mission report most specifically removed all of our raw data regarding the Savage activities and the tech we observed. It's always puzzled me. My acumen is that your second question of 'why now' is linked to your third question—why the addition of the civilian experts to your team.

"I'll keep working on those queries, but I'm thinking that only Team Three will be able to find out why, and probably only after it's all said and done. I want you to solve this mystery for me, men. There's a debt that I need your help to repay."

14

"Keep breathing and fix your eyes on a spot on the ground below us. Try not to look at the horizon."

Kel monitored Sarah's vital signs. Her pulse was up in the 120s. Kel's own was 50. Their bucket displays were filled with the holo re-creation of Area Doxy. It was a very good simulation in Kel's opinion. Only knowing that he was still on Victrix prevented him from feeling the stressors of an actual jump. They were in one of the Navy flight simulators. The chamber could vary the gravitational field to create different stresses as pilots would actually experience them.

Sarah was attached to the front of Kel's harness and was doing what they'd shown her. On exit from the dropship he'd had to coach her into a good arch after she initially tensed up, but was doing a fine job now.

"Our fall will be longer over the Proteus moon as it's a low-G mass. The landing will be a little softer too. This won't be bad, though, you'll see. Just be ready to get your legs under you and to trot with me so I don't land on top of you. I'll try for a no-forward motion landing as I flare, but the program may give us some crazy winds on the ground just for fun. Here we go. As you feel that ground rush... there it is... Now!"

Kel flared the huge canopy and they came to a gentle hop onto the ground. Sarah was standing with Kel.

"Nice job! What do you think?" he said as he detached her from his chest.

"I'm kind of thrilled just to be alive, honestly. It was, it was... kind of fun!"

Kel laughed. "I'd say when we get back from our jump onto Four-Three and you're ready to freefall with me, I'll take you up. With a couple of tandem jumps under your belt and some more ground training, you'll be ready for accelerated freefall training. No sweat!"

"That's quite enough, Sergeant," he heard Patrick say through their comms. "Keep on topic with *Miss* Sarah." The projection ceased and revealed the sim room.

"Our turn, *Mister* Patrick," Sims said as he entered the chamber with his civilian charge. "This will be about a twenty-minute run as you saw with Sarah and Kel. As soon as those guys exit the chamber, we'll start the sim program from inside the dropship."

Kel let Sarah exit and secured the chamber door behind them. They watched through the portal. Sims directed Patrick into position for rigging and then went through the preparatory jump commands with him on a real-time basis as they moved toward the imaginary ramp to look down onto the planet below. Kel knew this was his chance.

Kel removed his bucket and placed a raised finger in front of his lips as he gestured Sarah to do the same. She nodded and complied. She brushed her hair behind her and looked up at Kel. He spoke in quiet tones.

"You did a good job in there. I just wanted you to know I think you're very brave. I know how stressful this all must be on you. The entire team and I are going to do everything to protect you the entire time. You can count on that."

After a moment she nodded her head and simply said, "Thank you."

Kel wasn't sure how to press on, but decided he should try. "I'm not trying to put you into a bad position, but it would help us to keep you safe if we knew what you were doing here. You and Patrick, well, this sort of thing clearly isn't in your wheelhouse."

The young woman pursed her lips and nodded. Her eyes dropped back to the floor.

"Okay. Look, we know that you're a techie and that Patrick is here handling you. That much is clear. I just want you to know, if there's ever anything you want to tell us, it'll go no farther. You have to believe our only intention is to make this mission succeed and to bring everyone home. Think about it. Button up, Sarah." Maybe silence would be a good option for now. "Let's watch the rest of their run."

Sarah pulled her bucket back on, then turned to watch out the portal.

Sims was working to control their fall, spinning counterclockwise as Patrick flailed and shrieked.

"It would be more comfortable for you if you'd listen to what I'm saying. Arch. Just arch. Throw your pelvis forward. Relax. Keep your arms crossed over your chest." The man attached to Sims's harness was doing everything but relaxing. "I can't deploy the canopy if we're spinning. All right, I'm going to use the attitude control jets to slow us before I deploy. Try to keep still."

The small jets on Sims's armor fired, the program slowing and controlling their spin until Sims could safely deploy their canopy. Kel watched as the pair drifted under canopy. Sims tried to coach the man as they came to a landing, but Patrick stayed curled into a ball as Sims's feet touched the ground.

Kel turned to Sarah and gave her a thumbs down. She returned his gesture with a nod. The door to the simulator opened and Patrick was the first out.

"We're going to land," the thin man huffed. "Freefall is not a viable option."

Sims followed the man out. "I think we should try again. It's just a matter of getting the hang of it. You were getting close right at the end. Let's give it another try."

"No!" the man said. "Freefall was a tentative method of insertion. A stealth craft landing makes more sense and that's what I'm insisting on."

"A stealth craft isn't invisible," Kel calmly interjected. "It has a greatly reduced signature, but it's still detectable without tactical deception like chaff and air attacks to confuse enemy sensor suites. Freefall is our safest option for infil."

"No. Not happening. My vote outweighs any military decision. We're landing. Come on, Sarah."

The man stormed out of the facility. Joe was waiting for them outside. He watched Patrick storm off, then rolled his eyes and chased after him.

"Pretty bad, huh?" Kel asked Sims.

"Guy was going black. His heart rate was over 160 for a while. You're gonna to have to tranq him," Sims replied.

"With pleasure."

Mister Patrick had taken his protest to Captain Yost and to Colonel Hartenstein immediately on their return from the freefall simulation training. After they both shot him down, he made his usual threats.

"I don't work for either of you. The Legion is subordinate to my authority. Be expecting a communication from your superiors, gentleman," he huffed and stormed out of the module.

They saw the man later that afternoon, cowed and sullen.

"Looks like his bosses told him to put on his big-boy pants and shut up," Sims whispered. They heard no more protests from Mister Patrick the rest of the day.

They gathered in the team's load out bay to sort gear. Poul and Bigg were uncrating the new DOGRs, just arrived from the depot. "Kel, come look at this," Poul asked him.

"Moving," Kel said as he stowed a mini-medcomp. Two huge grav containers sat open on the deck. Inside were coffin-sized cuboids unlike any DOGR Kel had seen before. Their surfaces were faceted and slightly rough, like the surface of a stealth craft. "What's up?"

"Check these out. Is this what the colonel was talking about when he said he had some more special items coming to us from depot? You ever see a dogger like this before?"

Kel ran his hand over the surface of the one in front of him. "Can't say I have. Stealthing 'em is a good idea."

Bigg grunted. "Let's fire them up and run the diagnostics."

"Rog," Poul said. Kel watched as Poul ran his hand over the central panel and waited until the faint green light showed, then placed his hand over the biometric pad for a scan. The DOGR awoke, rising on all eight legs. A small square head on a snake-like extension peered out of the body, and canted toward Poul.

"Greetings, Sergeant Radd. Fitting day for a walk-about, say what? Bertie, you awake?"

The other DOGR turned and responded. "Couldn't agree more, Phillip. 'Bout time we got to work, say what?"

"What the..." Poul began. "Do you mean to tell me..."

"Tell you what, Sergeant?" the DOGR named Phillip replied. "That we're reporting for duty as ordered? Indeed!"

"They sent us full AI doggers instead of just saff-sucks!" Bigg said in surprise. "Cool!"

"AI? That's a bit insulting, Master Sergeant Biggetti, even if it is true," replied Bertie. "The official term for us is Autonomous Combat Multipliers, although we prefer our given names, Bertie and Phillip, if you don't mind."

Kel scratched his head as he pondered the two hulking masses. He watched them as they seemed to stretch their legs, crouching and extending to full height, then performed a series of small jumps in place.

"Time we got to introduce ourselves to the rest of the team, gentleman, if everyone would be so kind as to key their biometrics to us both. If you please?" Kel forgot which one was which.

Poul moved next to Kel. "They sound like those army boys we met from New Cardiff that one time, remember? Those guys had me in stitches. Who the heck programmed these AIs?"

"Braley! Sims!" Bigg yelled across the bay. "Come meet our new friends."

Working with the Navy was a relief. After dealing with resistance and difficulties on all other fronts, the Navy crews were a model of professionalism and cooperation. The pilots of the fast attack vehicle that would take them into the system were especially comforting to meet.

"The *Black Cat* is at your disposal, gentlemen. Ours is yours," Captain John Wurtz told them. "It will be close quarters on board, so I can't offer you much in the way of luxury, but I know you Legion types would be put off if it was too comfortable."

Kel liked the man instantly.

"The *Blackie* can do some amazing things. Whatever it can't do, you don't need done," Lieutenant Vreeland the co-pilot said. She jolted Kel like a stunner charge. He was locked in. Her hair was tied in an ornate bun, matching her dark eyes. Kel darted his own to his link when he realized he'd been staring, hoping he hadn't been caught. Kel thought he saw a smile when she saw his reaction.

"Hey, you see Kel blush when that lieutenant smiled at him?" Poul teased him later. "Yeah, you got busted, hero. Don't worry, I promise you she's used to being stared at. Fit, I'm saying."

"Did I see?" Sims howled. "Dude, don't make our trip out uncomfortable, okay? We need her to fly, preferably not while thinking about how to dump some stalker off her ship. She might vent the rest of us with you."

The day after their briefback, the team, their two civilian straphangers, and new team members Bertie and Phillip—who were very particular about being addressed by their names—were in a Talon flying to meet their ride, the Republic Naval frigate *Avenger*.

Docking with the frigate in its large portside exterior bay was uneventful. As soon as the ramp dropped, the team descended to find a master chief petty officer waiting for them on the flight deck. The dark, barrel-chested man dressed in sharp-creased browns approached them as they descended the ramp.

"Gentleman, I'm Master Chief Tyler-Smith. I'll be your liaison while on the *Avenger*. Whatever you need, whenever you need it, you may comm me directly, and I will solve any issue you might have. May I take you to the team module where you'll be quartered?"

"Master Chief," Bigg replied, extending his gauntleted hand for a gentle shake. "We have palletized equipment that we need to personally control that needs to be loaded onto the *Black Cat*. We also have some items waiting for us from depot to take charge of. We have two members of our team that could be escorted to the module, if you please?"

"Very good. I'll make sure they get there. The *Black Cat*'s crew chief is headed over now. Their ship is in the controlled access section on the starboard side hanger."

Bigg spoke to the twins on L-comm. "Go with the master chief; he'll take you to our quarters and you can get bunked. We'll join you in a couple of hours. Rest of us, let's get to work."

While they waited for the crew chief from their stealth craft to arrive, Kel paused to take in the sights around him. He'd been on many Navy ships before, from the enormous Capital-class cruisers to the sleek Talon dropships and lots in between. The portside hanger was a flurry of activity. The frigate had a detached air wing assigned to it, and flight crews worked on the Shark tactical fighter-bombers in the bay.

Dozens of men and women moved about the huge bay. They zipped around in small grav sleds, towing munitions. It looked like a collision would occur at any second. But the chaos was a carefully orchestrated dance more complex than any musical production. Kel knew that technicians, experts in their field, worked tirelessly in difficult and uncomfortable conditions to do their jobs with supreme efficiency and with pride. Kel had never wanted to be in the Navy, but he had a great appreciation for the job they did.

"Hey, Kel. Look at that swabbie," Sims said. He followed the line of Sims's helmet across the bay. An orange-shirted spacer with a gut so huge his shirt did not cover it, bent over inspecting a rack of proton bombs. The man was covered in grease and grime from hard work. Every time he stood, he had to hike his trousers back up to keep them from falling farther below his buttocks.

"Oh man," Poul said. "The Navy's finest."

Kel ignored what they were saying. It was easy to feel superior to other people when you judged them on outward appearances. Kel grew up being taught to respect the worthiness of all professions. The man they watched was engaged in difficult and dirty work. His military appearance was suitable for the task he was performing. Legion fitness standards were irrelevant to this man's job. Whatever the man was doing, Kel knew that they couldn't perform the same task without extensive training.

There's truly more that I don't know than I do, he marveled to himself. He tried to live a grateful life, appreciating the people around him who demonstrated the vast skills it took to make the galaxy work.

"Hey," Bigg said. "Come here, men. Did I ever tell you guys about the bravest man I ever met?"

Everyone shrugged, even Braley.

"This must've been thirty years ago. I was a young sergeant in Claymore Company, just back from my first successful operation as a squad leader. I was making transit through the Betelgeuse Space Station. I decided to wet my whistle and found a bar. The place was crowded with spacers and civilian tradesmen and I was about to leave when I saw a uniformed man at the bar wave me over. I walked over and took the empty seat next to him, not knowing what to expect.

"My new companion was a Navy chief. He wasn't an impressive guy to the eye of a twenty-year-old legionnaire. He looked like he was about fifty. Turns out he was just over thirty. I have to tell you at first, I didn't want to drink with a spacer. I was hoping to run in to some other leejes. But this guy was very friendly. Asked me what I was drinking, and put me at ease pretty quickly. That chance meeting changed my life."

Kel thought he knew where this was going.

"My story was pretty obvious. I was wearing my combat drop badge with three gold stars—we used to wear them back then—and everyone knew the Legion had just kicked-ass on Lisander Four against the Skree for joining the Savages. Turns out the chief had been in orbit aboard one of the cruisers, I don't remember now which one.

"The chief was the head of an ordnance section. Seemed like a pretty dull job to me, loading bombs on ships, and in a not-so-subtle way, I said the same to my host. To his credit he didn't take offense. He bought me another drink and after a while, when I wasn't so full of myself, I asked him about his job.

"See those proton bombs over there?" Bigg pointed. "In the nose of those bombs is a plasma detonator. He told me how an ordnance tech prepped every one of those bombs by hand. The plasma detonators had to be inspected, a diagnostic completed, and then placed into the nose of each bomb.

"Now it turns out there's a funny thing about those detonators. Sometimes, one will arm itself. Call it the lowest government-bidder phenomenon or what have you, but sometimes those damn things just arm themselves. It could happen anytime they're being handled. If one went off in proximity to a bomb, or after it was loaded into a bomb, the results could be devastating, as you can imagine. If one of those bombs went off, it could destroy the better part of a hanger bay and kill everyone on the deck. At the very least, it would fry to a crisp whoever was holding it.

"I asked my new friend how often something like that happened. He told me, 'Every shift.' I asked what happened when one prematurely armed itself. He said it wasn't very technical. 'You have to get it off the ship at all costs. There are ditch ports for disposal of unstable ordnance. You walk it over there, hoping it doesn't go off, and ditch it into space, then get a new one and go back to work.

"I asked him if they ever went off. 'All the time. Lost two techs last year. This week I had one go off not a second after I'd ditched it. That was a close one.' He said that during the campaign over Lisander Four they'd prepped over five thousand proton bombs on his ship alone. Five thousand. Five thousand plasma detonators that had to be prepped by hand. Every shift, every tech having at least one detonator arm itself prematurely.

"I watched the guy smoke two packs of stim-sticks while we sat together. I only stayed for a couple drinks. He wouldn't let me buy him even one. He bought a metric fifth of whiskey and another two packs of stim-sticks from the bartender before he got up. When he did leave, he shook my hand and told me, 'Thanks for letting me buy you a drink. The Legion did an amazing job and it was an honor to be a small part of what you did,' and left."

Poul and Sims looked at the deck, not saying anything.

"Now, I've thought about that chief a thousand times over the years. On the hardest day of my life, I don't think I've ever done anything as brave as what that guy did on the most average day of his career. If I had to do what he did, I'd probably live on stim-sticks and whiskey, too. All I'm saying, brothers, is that all these people around us," Bigg swept his hand across the flight deck, "all these people have a warrior spirit just like we do. They just show it in different ways." Bigg turned and went to one of the pallets and started checking the manifest on his wrist, leaving the rest of the team to think about his words.

Everyone remained silent for several minutes, reflecting on Bigg's story. The moral of Bigg's story was clear: treat everyone with respect. You never knew how tough someone else's job was. Kel had been moved by Bigg's story. He knew the other guys had as well.

Kel heard a thud and what sounded like choking before the sound cut off in his bucket. Poul lay on the deck, his body convulsing. Kel's heart raced. He was about to pullout his medpack when he saw Sims doubled over, hands on his knees, convulsing as well.

They're in hysterics! Laughing! About what?

Sims was touching the side of his bucket, indicating for Kel to find him on a sub-channel. He did, and was instantly deafened by the sound of the two men howling in laughter.

"What?" Kel asked, confused. "What's so damn funny?"

"I can't... I can't... Oba, please, you tell him, Sims."

Sims kept it up for another few seconds before he took in a deep breath and tried to tell the tale. He was able to, but with many breaks for breaths in between sentences. "Oba! We were feeling pretty ashamed after Bigg's story. We both looked over at the swabbie we'd just mocked so badly."

"Tell him. Tell. Him!" Poul said, out of breath from the effort as he continued to cry and laugh simultaneously.

"The guy had his finger jammed so far up his nose it looked like he was doing brain surgery."

"Bwahahaha!" Poul howled into their ears.

"We saw the guy pull his finger out and, there must have been something big on it, because the guy's eyes shot open when he saw it."

"Go! Go! Go," Poul cackled.

"We watched the guy slyly look left, and then right," Sims said as he pantomimed the man's actions, his own index finger up in the air. "And when he thought no one was looking, *he ate it.*" Both men collapsed again into a heap of laughter.

Sims coughed. "We dropped off the team channel as fast as we could. We didn't want to ruin Bigg's moment."

It was a seven-day jump to just outside the Proteus system, a testament to just how far beyond Galaxy's Edge these Savages—or Savage descendants—had settled. The approach would keep the system star between them and the third moon of the fourth planet, arriving just below the system plane. From there they would transfer to the *Black Cat* for the ride to the Savage moon. It was a long seven days. By the third day tensions were high within the module. There were five bunk rooms, Braley and Bigg taking one; Kel, Sims, and Poul crammed into another; and one each for Sarah and Patrick. No one complained that the twins had each staked out a room for themselves, especially since no one wanted to be in close quarters with Patrick.

The team spent most of a full shift every day with the crew of the *Blackie*, optimizing the space for their gear and the team. Phillip and Bertie were fine with going to sleep until drop time. The dull AI of the MkIV was not able to protest its forced quiescence, and after a diagnostic to make sure it was fully functional, returned to slumber.

The pilots were confident they could make a stealthy jump into the system but that it would be four days of flight from there to reach the moon. They wouldn't be able to travel close to light speed, instead having to maintain a velocity more suitable for any asteroid-like body from the system's Kuiper belt, hoping to disguise their path like that of an ice ball taking an excursion closer to the fourth planet. Those things combined with a zero active emission profile would give them maximum stealth.

Even though everyone was working on prepping the *Blackie*, it still left ample time when the team had to be in the module with Patrick and Sarah. Conflicts started almost immediately. Patrick did not want to participate with the rest of the team in morning physical training in the frigate's small gym, and refused to let Sarah participate without his presence.

"Sorry, Patrick," Braley put his foot down. "This is going to be a physically demanding and stressful mission for you both. Prep doesn't stop until the mission starts. I can't force you to get off your butt and participate, but you will not hamper Sarah from preparing herself physically."

There was nowhere to have a private conversation with the man and Braley was forced to confront him in front of the whole gathering. In Kel's opinion, this was exactly what needed to happen. Maybe some kind of peer pressure would bring the man around.

"That's ridiculous," Patrick retorted. "We'll be in armor with power assist and it's a fractional gravity enviro. We still have the integrity of the mission to think about. I know you guys are trying to manipulate Sarah for information. Don't think I'm not aware. Cutting me out of L-comm to communicate with her is an amateur move. No, you boys go play your muscle-head games. We'll be right here."

"No." Bigg took his turn. "For a guy going into a non-permissive environment, you show little concern for your own skin. Here's what's going to happen. Tomorrow at 0600 you will both be accompanying us to the gym. If we have to drag you, so be it. If you walk on a treadmill at one-quarter gee, so be it. But you will not prevent Sarah from training. Because if you're a liability on the ground, we'll just leave you. But you will not hamper Sarah's ability to be functional and survive."

Patrick scowled and left the common room for his cubicle, leaving Sarah behind.

"Sarah, let's spend a little time on some dry training with your blaster," Poul said. "You're getting pretty smooth on your draw and presentation. I'm thinking that pretty soon you could rate on the Legion qual course if you keep this up."

Sarah gave Poul a reserved smile. "I'll go get my blaster."

Braley turned to the group. "This is getting worse instead of better. I don't know how to appeal to the man's rational self-interest to prepare himself. Any ideas, guys?"

"Anywhere he could take a nice fall and break something?" Poul asked. "You know, nothing life-threatening, but just serious enough that he has to stay behind?"

Everyone looked to Kel.

"He's not going on this mission."

The *Black Cat* filled the cordoned area of the starboard hanger of the *Avenger*. The multi-role fast attack ship was sleek and intimidating in the best of ways. It had the profile of a diving bird with a gentle forward swell that contained the flight deck and four-man crew quarters, and a lengthened rear section that had been converted to open bay space for its current purpose to invisibly shuttle the operators to their destination. They had used every available square centimeter to secure their gear, Phillip and Bertie now active but stacked next to each other on top of other grav containers.

"I've had to squeeze into some cramped pubs to get a pint before, Bertie, but this is ridiculous."

"You've never been in a pub in your life, Phillip. Neither have I," Bertie replied next to him.

"Manner of speaking, mate. Manner of speaking."

Seven acceleration couches were stacked like shelves against the fuselage leaving a small corridor to the kitchen and fresher. The next few days would be strained as the crew worked their magic to pilot a surreptitious course to the moon. The bay was filled with the parachutes and gear, much of it lashed to the curved fuselage. They had full rations in the small passenger kitchen, practically gourmet compared to the minimal weight recon meals they'd take to the surface.

Kel checked Patrick's harness, then Sarah's. Some people dealt with stress by turning inward, some by lashing out at those around them. Patrick was definitely of the latter category. Sarah, the former. She had said very little to anyone even during training. She asked technical questions and accepted suggestions but never volunteered anything, not even engaging in small talk. Kel could tell that she was nervous though, and rightly so in his opinion.

"It will be *really* boring the next few days until we start rigging, then things are going to happen at a fast pace. If you have any discomfort or if there's anything I can do, please say something," Kel said as he finished securing the harness to her recumbent form on the acceleration couch. "Once we jump and set an acceleration, we'll take turns getting out of armor and rotating into the common space for breaks from the couches."

As had been her pattern, she said nothing but nodded. Kel hesitated, but placed his gauntleted hand over hers, trying to comfort her. "You're doing great, Sarah." She nodded again and Kel could see through the clear visor that her eyes were shut tightly.

The crew chief, Darmond, stood at the head of the compartment. "Lady and gentlemen, the captain informs me that we are about to get underway. There will be no stops on our journey, so if you have any special sightseeing requests or dietary needs, feel free to tell someone who cares. Two minutes until departure." She made an exaggerated bow and turned back to the crew compartment.

The crew of the *Blackie* were just their sort of people. They were a tight-knit group with a good sense of humor. To Kel that always implied competence. The chief engineer's mate, Chief Joseph Lopez, reminded him of the grizzled sort of hero from all the best space adventure holovids he'd loved as a kid. He wouldn't have been surprised if the man moved around the ship with some kind of exotic pet clinging to his shoulder like the vids always had. In a way, Kel was disappointed that he didn't.

Kel had worked closely with the two pilots to hammer out the complex insertion plan. First to park the orbital support platform, then to maneuver to jump altitude. All while remaining low signature. It was a version of running errands to the market then the pharmacy, but if someone sees you, you're vaporized. The lieutenant smiled when he braved looking her in the eyes. Now he found himself distracted, picturing the color of her lips at their last meeting. Candy red.

"That pilot made herself up just for you, stud." Now even Bigg was teasing him. Poul and Sims had made it a point of letting the whole team know he was smitten. "You know how I know she's quality? She registers we might not come back, and is busting her hump to save our skin when this is done. But she still takes the time to give a leej something to dream about. Make sure you say something nice to her, Kel. Thank her."

He'd complimented her on her plan to put them in a geostationary position to deploy the OSP. Keeping the tail on a tangent opposite the moon's surface would minimize the decrease in their stealth signature to any sensor aimed their way while the tailgate was down.

He knew that wasn't what Bigg meant.

Kel felt the *Blackie* lift imperceptibly. Once they came out of jump and started their acceleration to reach a constant velocity, the grav decking would remain at half-G and no inertial attenuators would be used. The energy signature of the craft would be reduced to little more than that of background cosmic radiation.

He checked the team's vitals before strapping into his own couch. Sims was already snoring softly. The rest of the team was settling in just as well. Even Sarah's normally high heart rate was only slightly elevated, and lowering as he watched the numbers. Patrick's heart rate showed a stress level higher than what he should be experiencing while lying down.

"Patrick, it'd be a good time to sleep," Kel said to him on a private channel. "If you want a chill tab, there's one in your bucket nipple."

"I'm fine. Watch after yourself."

Kel clicked off and chuckled. *I'm watching out for all of us.* He closed his eyes and thought about tart cherry candy.

15

Patrick crowded with them around a grav container to play tiles. Patrick was a pretty good player. He beat Kel handily every round, and was behaving better than he had since they'd known him. He laughed at some of Sims's and Poul's jokes, and for a short while, it seemed the man was coming around. It didn't last.

Braley and Bigg lay in their couches watching the game. Kel caught the look Braley shot to Bigg, who gave an imperceptible nod. Braley slid out of his couch and pulled up a crate across from Patrick.

"You want to play winner?" Patrick asked.

Braley laid his forearms over the tiles. "Thanks, maybe later. Patrick, I was hoping we could have a talk. We're a day away from rigging. It would be helpful to the mission if we could talk about your purpose for being here and how it's going to impact—"

Patrick made a hiss like inert gas leaking from a coil. "I was expecting this. Sorry, *friends*," his tone souring at that last word, "not going to happen. Just do your job and when I have something I need from you, I'll tell you."

Braley stood, and shrugged. "You can't say I didn't try. I'll let you get back to your game then." Braley gave Kel a wink. Sarah lay on her couch, datapad on her chest. She saw Braley's low-key message. She caught Kel's eye for a moment, then returned to reading.

It started about an hour after they dimmed the cabin lights for the sleep cycle. Waves of distress from the fresher woke Kel. The surges of violent peaks separated by gasping troughs made Kel cringe. He hadn't taken Patrick for a praying man. Kel got to his feet and moved to the fresher door.

"Patrick, it's Kel. You all right?" Only moans issued from behind the door. "Sims, help me get him out."

The door was not secured so Kel did not have to use an override code. The man lay on the floor, pale and shivering.

"Let's get him to the medcomp."

They pulled the man out his fetal position and stood him up, slinging an arm over each of their shoulders. Patrick was gray and covered in sweat; his head slumped toward his chest as they carried him away.

"What's happening?" Sarah asked from her couch. "Is Patrick okay?"

"I don't know," Bigg said. "Kel's checking him now. The medcomp will figure it out. Give it some time."

After a few minutes, Sims returned.

"How is he?" Sarah asked, the most animated they'd ever seen her.

"Kel's working on him now. He's not looking too good, I can tell you that. Hey, someone turn up the air exchangers. It's getting pretty rank in here."

Sarah paced the small corridor while everyone else climbed back on their couches.

"Get some rest, Sarah," Poul said. "I'd trust Kel over any doctor. He's that good. I'm sure Patrick will be fine."

Poul meant well, but his words had no effect. She said nothing as she continued to pace. After a few more minutes, Kel returned to find Sarah waiting.

"How is he? What's wrong?"

Kel shook his head. "It's Mardenberg. He's gotten a severe case of gastroenteritis. The medcomp's treating his nausea and vomiting and replacing his intravascular fluids, but it's going to take several days to get him on his feet. Even with him supine, he's lost so much fluid from both ends that I'm giving him vasopressors just to maintain a decent blood pressure."

"A bacterial infection? That doesn't seem possible," she said. "I thought the nano-immunos were supposed to prevent any random pathogen exposure from producing a disease-state?"

Kel nodded. "True. But Mardenberg is a toxin producer. The nano-immunos will fight even a large bacterial inoculation, but they won't neutralize a big toxin load, and I gave him enough of the toxin to make sure his immunizations wouldn't stand a chance of stopping it."

Sarah's eyes went wide. "You what?" she yelled.

Kel flinched. He'd never heard her make a noise above her usually slight speaking voice.

"The Trexellian two-step!" Phillip exclaimed from his perch. "Nasty."

"Shall I make a cholera cot?" Bertie added.

"Shut it, you two," Bigg scolded.

"I gave him enough Mardenberg toxin to ensure he would get a disabling case of gastroenteritis," Kel explained dispassionately. "At the evening meal I switched the ration he prepared with a tainted one when Poul tripped into him in the kitchen. Patrick will shed the toxin in a few days and the medcomp will get his electrolytes replaced and his fluid status balanced. He won't be getting up for a while, I should think."

"Why would you do that?" the young woman shrieked.

"Because I ordered him to," Braley replied, now standing behind her. Truth be told, Braley had not ordered Kel to do so, nor had he told him how to disable the man. The method and timing had been Kel's decision. He'd prepared for the possibility back on Victrix. Way back when Braley had asked Kel if there was a feasible way to prevent Patrick from deploying with them.

"But, why?"

They were going to have to spell it out for her. It was come to Oba time, and Braley was ready to be her teacher.

"Patrick was a detriment to the mission and was judged by us all to be a danger to himself and the entire team. His refusal to cooperate with the simplest of requests to prepare for the mission as well as his inability to give any guidance as to what his purpose is for being with us mandated his removal."

Sarah stood with mouth agape.

"Now we come to the difficult part, Sarah." Braley motioned for her to sit on the crate. "If you can't convince us in the next few minutes that your participation in this mission is vital, you won't be accompanying us either."

The young woman sat on the edge of the crate, and the team crowded round. She didn't look defiant or emboldened. She looked frightened and weary. Kel felt sorry for her, but he was tired of the games. Braley nodded to Kel. He'd been able to form as much a connection with her as any of them. It was time for a soft touch.

"Sarah," Kel began, being as gentle as he could, "it would help for us to know something. Who are you? What's your background? What qualifies you to be part of this so-called exploitation team?"

She clenched her fists. She was trapped in a cage with barely tamed beasts. "I was told that I could go to prison if I revealed any part of this."

"Sarah, look at me, please."

The woman met Kel's eyes. Hers were windows of strain, fine cracks of red on white.

"Those kind of rules don't apply in these circumstances. Anyone who threatened you like that is working outside of the law. You can't be legally compelled to withhold information that's vital to the accomplishment of this mission, especially when risk to humans is involved. This is a Savage world denial mission." Kel was making this up as he went along, but he thought it sounded pretty good. "We've all worked with spy-handlers. You're not an intelligence agent. You're some kind of analyst. Whatever Patrick told you about confidentiality is not true when it comes to sharing information with us. He's told you that for reasons of his own."

The young woman seemed to consider this, then opened the flood gates.

"My name is Sarah Wittawat. I have multiple doctorates in physics and engineering. My specialty is in the assessment of foreign technology. I work in a lab analyzing recovered technologies for any potential application. My specialty is Savage world tech."

Not even an officer's composure could keep Braley joining the team in their noises of exasperation.

"Wait. That's it? That's the big mystery Patrick was being such a jerk about?" Sims said. "Big deal. That's no secret. Sure, it's been studied. Some of the Savages developed tech out of step with the rest of the galaxy, did weird genetic experiments, cybernetics, all kinds of screwed up stuff. Everyone knows that. None of it was great tech. So what?"

Sarah took a deep breath in and blew it out. "Well, you're wrong about that. Some of it anyway. As the Savages expanded their territory, yes, what came from that was stunted and not very good. But some of what they achieved on those lighthuggers... we can't begin to duplicate. But, that's not all. Some of the tech we have at our—" she struggled for the right word, "—facility—that's been collected for analysis is not Savage. It's alien."

Poul shrugged. "And again, we say—so what? We work with alien races all the time. Their tech is generally terrible. No one has found an alien race with tech more advanced than human-Republic tech. Big deal."

The small woman shook her head. "No. I'm not making myself clear. What I'm talking about is alien tech that belongs to no known galactic race."

Poul guffawed. "What, like the Ancients?"

"I'm not saying that," Sarah said, not at all sounding wounded by the dig. She struck Kel as an expert now speaking in her element. "But there are trace artifacts in the collection that have been studied for generations and still not decoded. What these Savages—Savage descendants, really—have is something more akin to alien than Savage tech. Something unlike anything recovered or observed in the known history of the Savage Wars." Sarah wrapped her arms around herself. "What I'm telling you could get me sent to a prison world."

Kel shook his head, almost amused with what he was hearing if it weren't for the fact that being denied this information could threaten everyone's lives, not to mention mission success. "So let me get this straight. Patrick and whoever sent you here threatened you about revealing some kind of ancient alien tech that these Savages—what?—stumbled into? The whole reason for keeping us in the dark was to prevent us from finding out that you guys are along for the ride to see if you can take it from the Savages? Who cares?"

Poul slapped his forehead with his palm. "Sarah, I've been watching holo-vids about this kind of thing my whole life. I can think of a dozen shows with the same plot. There's even investigative documentaries and conspiracy nuts who talk about the same thing. If that's what you guys are concealing, it ain't a secret."

Sims joined in. "You guys think we already don't know that your people have a near-instantaneous cross-galaxy comm system that's faster than using standard hypercomm? We all know it exists. We've been too many places out on the edge working with your people. We've seen RI get near instant guidance from the core when the rest of us were stuck with hypercomm relay malfunctions. It's no secret, ma'am."

"They're not 'my' people, Sims," Sarah said, sounding defensive for the first time. "I don't even know who Patrick works for. I got picked for this because I've been studying the Proteus Four-Three report for years. I have examples and reports from other Savage and alien tech hauls that I've compared it all to."

"So why didn't Patrick just use a cover story?" Bigg asked her. "He could have said that you were sent with us in order to exploit any Savage tech we find. That would have made for a perfectly acceptable cover story to fit your mission. Why the complete shut down on information? Why have you two been so obstinate about cooperating in any way? That's what doesn't make any sense."

Sarah sighed. "I don't know. Patrick and the men who recruited me told me that's how it has to be. Patrick wouldn't say much, just that it was going to be a significant opportunity. He promised me that I was going to be very well rewarded by the House of Reason if we returned with a big find. I told them I didn't care about any of that. The chance at finding *real* alien tech—advanced beyond what we think of any non-human species as capable of— is what I'm interested in."

Kel shook his head. He was now able to put together the picture together from his suspicions. "Patrick is some pol's idiot nephew or something. He may have an RI background, but he's no super-secret agent. He's connected. That's why he's here."

Braley looked at Kel as he considered this. "You've been around the spiral arms with these types. Do you think this thing is being run by the Senate and not by RI?"

Kel shrugged. "We know RI is involved to some degree, but everything about this has the smell of politics to it. I doubt it's an operation run by some no-name agency. It's an opportunity for a pol to grab some kind of glory. I'd bet on it. I'm trying to not let my bias against the pols taint my assessment, but it has the stench of their kind of scandalous math that never adds up."

Braley spoke to the young scientist. "Patrick, we didn't need or want. You, we've had an intuition might be useful. But you need to tell us why. We're here to evaluate this group of Savages for planetary denial. We don't need you for that."

Sarah looked up at Braley. Now there was a fire in her eyes. "You do need me. If what I think may exist is actually down there, you'll never get off that moon without me."

They rigged Phillip and Bertie and directed them as out of the way as they could get them, then rigged the MkIV. Helping each other rig up for the jump was a task they'd performed together hundreds of times, yet each time Kel thought about the consequences from a second's lack of attention to detail. That he would be sure—always, was a mantra he'd said to himself a million times as a legionnaire. Back on the deck of the *Avenger* the last thing Kel and Sims had done before the final load out was to pull each chute and run a diagnostic over every shroud line and canopy cell before repacking it themselves.

Chief Lopez and the crew chief, Darmond, worked between them as they rigged, lending an extra hand and helping to move the empty containers out of the way. Kel was the jumpmaster and would be the last to rig himself and Sarah. He had to personally inspect each teammate and their attached loads to ensure it was done correctly.

First, they applied the freefall compatible armor upgrades to each other, then parachute containers, while threading belts around the K-17s held against their bodies. Then they stepped into the carrying straps of their rucksacks and balanced the load between their knees. Lastly came attachment of the extra weapons containers. Kel checked each jumper, finishing his inspection sequence by tapping the person on the back of their bucket.

Lopez and Darmond had crewed freefall operations before. They were quick studies and assisted by holding weapons and loads in place as Kel activated the mechanical snap connectors and maglocks to bond the items to the jumper. Without the two aircrew, the process would have taken much longer. Every moment in full gear waiting to jump was a trial of pain even in the reduced gravity of the bay. Kel loosened or adjusted straps as needed to center and secure every jumper's items as much as possible.

Braley was the last in line. As he tapped his team leader on the back of the bucket, he took a moment to look at his team. No matter how many times he'd done this, he was still surprised at how surreal the scene seemed. *Only an insane person would do this.*

Kel rigged Sarah, then himself with the assistance of his Navy associates, now well versed in the process after helping with the rest of the team's preparation, and sidled over to Sims. "Wanna do a pin check?" he said referring to the most critical part of the personal inspection by a jumpmaster—ensuring that the canopy deployment pins had not become damaged during the rigging process. Kel turned to Sims for him to inspect the rear of his parachute container and tapped Kel on the back of the bucket.

"I guess it's okay, but if it's your time, it's your time. Been nice knowing you."

That made Kel laugh.

"Sarah, we'll get you attached to my harness after we deploy the satellite. Just stay put." She gave him a thumbs up from where she stood near the edge of the tailgate. She wouldn't see much but space once they lowered the tailgate and Kel didn't want her to get nervous.

"That guy gives us a second's worth of trouble and he's going out an airlock," Chief Lopez said as Kel nudged his way around to the front of the OSP. "We'll be the only ones who'll ever know, and we'll never talk."

Kel grinned. "I doubt it'll come to that, but thanks."

"Don't worry, I'm an old hand with a medcomp. I'll get him on his feet again. The rest will be his choice."

Lieutenant Vreeland's face came over his bucket screen. "Two minutes to release point." Kel had a visual of the lieutenant. He chided himself for never finding the right time to say something to her. Anything. Sure, she was an officer, but they were in different services.

I'm the king of missed opportunities. If we ever make it back, I'm going to change that about myself, and I'm going to start with her.

He knew it was an idle promise. If they made it back, he'd be gone on another mission in no time.

First, they had to make it back.

Lopez and Darmond dropped the visors on their vac suits.

"Stand by for decompression."

There was nothing noticeable about the change to a vacuum atmosphere in the compartment until a red light appeared by the tailgate ramp.

"Dropping ramp."

The tailgate opened slowly to reveal the blackness of space. The OSP was active and Kel received the confirmation code in his bucket that the unit was ready for deployment.

"Let's nudge her out," he said as the two flight crew members helped him release the locks tethering the large cube. They worked on three sides to ease the mass out of the bay, transferring as little rotational motion into their efforts as possible, and watched as the OSP cleared the end of the ramp and gently floated away.

"Flight. Package is clear," Lopez said over comms.

"Roger. Five minutes to drop point," replied the co-pilot.

"Time to rig, Sarah." Kel turned around and moved to where Sarah waited short of the ramp.

"I'm scared." Her voice was tiny in his ears.

He held her shoulders. "Fear is a normal emotion. But it's not meant to stop you from doing what you have to do. We're all scared. We just know how to keep moving forward one foot at a time. I'm with you the whole way and I won't leave you. Promise."

"I hope not. I don't have my own parachute."

Kel laughed. "That's the spirit. Turn and let's get rigged."

He moved them to the end of the ramp. He had the jump program running in a small window in the lower left field of his visor. The spacecraft descended toward the moon and the surface rolled into view.

The moon was tidally locked, one side fixed in perpetual darkness. The orange glow of volcanoes dotted the surface and he imagined the icy terrain below. The pull of gravity became imperceptibly stronger as they made the slow descent. Somewhere over the horizon was the terminator. Straddling that narrow habitation zone between night and day was the Savage civilization, waiting for them in all its mystery and horror.

"Two minutes," the lieutenant said. "We'll be waiting for your call. Good hunting." With that, Kel's focus became the edge of the ramp. He opened another window showing him a rear view from his bucket. The team, followed by the two DOGRs and the MkIV, crowded close behind him on the ramp's edge.

"One minute," Kel said as he moved them the final centimeter toward the edge of their last safe refuge. "Thirty seconds."

He watched the program's chrono count down and anticipated the last seconds until it ran out.

"Go."

He stepped into the void.

16

Touchdown was a rebirth. The fall, a frozen time of metamorphosis from which new life came. Changing from weightless, amorphous, and free into a thing bound by form, shape, and gravity at its end. Maybe it was a rebirth only because death had been cheated again. Perhaps that's why it was always accompanied by pain.

Kel activated the canopy release and destruction sequence as he released Sarah from the chest harness. He dropped his rucksack, stepped out of it, and reached for the K-17 at his side. He slid out of his harness and was oblivious to its programmed disintegration as it hit the ground.

"Get down," he told Sarah as he dropped, lying prone and placing his carbine in front of him.

The landscape before him was sharp and irregular. No matter how much he'd poured over the holos, he was unprepared for this. Eons-frozen ice packs left remnants of collisions between floes during ancient periods of thaw, captured permanently as jagged formations of ice-covered snow. He'd imagined blowing winds raising snowdrifts. Instead, it was eerily still. Wide shelves of land sat above the icy plain in the distance, the dark gravel reflecting the reddish glow from the nearest volcano.

The weapon container holding his N-22 lay nearby and he dragged it to him by its tether. Using his carbine, he scanned the horizon. Distant volcanoes belched black smoke, and the gas giant Proteus Four dominated the dark sky between patches of clouds.

"Sound off by roster," Bigg said over L-comm.

Braley went first, then everyone responded in turn—"Fit to fight," Sims said.

"In one piece," went Poul next.

"Up," said Kel.

"No complaints," Sarah said.

Like a pro, Kel thought. *What gibberish would Patrick spout were he here?*

He'd almost forgotten about their new teammates.

"Phillip ready."

"Bertie up."

All business now, the AIs made no unnecessary chatter.

"Mark-four, diagnostic," Bigg ordered.

The dull voice of the simple AI responded, "Optimal. Ready."

No one spoke, but remained in their prone position. The team continued scanning for any indication of human activity, and after thirty minutes Bigg broke their silence. "Anyone have anything?"

Everyone responded in the negative.

"Good. Let's get the DOGRs rigged with the heavies and our rucks. What's the read, Kel?"

Kel had been running an environmental survey as he lay in the perimeter. It required no distraction from his ability to provide security over his sector of observation. Once activated, the program ran independently without need for further input from Kel.

"Atmo is breathable. Background radiation is nominal. No toxins detected. High sulfur and CO_2 content, though. Carbon monoxide at detectable but inconsequential levels."

"Rog. I'm sending burst traffic to *Avenger* now."

Looking skyward for a moment, Bigg directed an L-comm nanoburst back to the ship, sending them the message: *Successful infiltration, no resistance.* Without the need to scream down for emergency retrieval, the *Blackie* would proceed to the asteroid belt, awaiting their next transmission. Daily the team would send a coded burst to the ship updating the crew on the team's condition, compressing data into a transmission that lasted less than the time it took a proton to flip.

"Good," Braley replied. "Nice drop, Kel. Right on target. Sims, Poul, start planning the route to the mission support site. Let's try to be moving in ten."

They started their patrol toward the terminator and their first planned MSS. Poul and Sims took the point of their wedge with the rest of them forming the arms of the arrowhead. Sarah and the three robots were positioned in the center of the team's formation.

Kel felt the hunter in him come alive. A warmth grew in his gut he knew could melt the ice under his feet. There was an old adage about walking into harms' way. *Ships are safest in port,* Kel thought, *but that's not what they're made for.* The visage of his deadly teammates caused pride to swell within him. *I'm definitely made for this.*

Kel oriented himself to the new battlespace and the surreal terrain filled him with curiosity and excitement. It was unlike any environment he'd ever found himself in. The volcanoes, the ice, the black rock shores, all made for a dream-like mural, crafted from some mad artist's distorted vision. *What kind of humans could have survived here for a millennium? What are we going to find?* At the end of this journey he knew, there would be Savages.

Poul and Sims spoke sparingly on a sub-channel as they worked together to lead the team on the best possible course through the difficult terrain. As unlikely as it was that they were being observed, they took a circuitous course that followed the lowest elevations and keeping high ground to as many sides of them as possible. *Savage eyes are on you*, his mother's voice said as he buried his small head under the covers.

Where the ancient ice floes met the gravel shores, immense ice shards pierced the sky. They'd debated sending out a drone to help plan the route but decided it was not a risk worth taking. Navigating by map alone was not the best choice for speed, but would help them remain undetected. Instead, they had to backtrack frequently when they came to a dead-ended ice canyon, losing time as they made their way back to find a clear passage forward.

Sarah kept pace with the rest of the team. The gravity was fractional and she carried no extra gear. But Kel knew her physical and psychological preparation had been rushed before their deployment.

"Sarah, are you doing all right?" he said, keeping his focus on the icy footing before him.

"It's amazing, isn't it? To think that there's human life that's survived here for so long."

Well, not 'human,' Kel thought. *We don't know what sort of enemy we're walking toward at all.*

"Yes, it is. Are you feeling well? Your internal temp looks good."

"Yes, Kel. Thanks."

"We'll go for another eight or nine hours if we can. Other than a security halt we won't stop. If you get too exhausted, I'll put you on one of the doggers. Don't be ashamed to say something."

"I'm good to go," she said curtly. Kel heard pride in her voice as she repeated the phrase she'd picked up around the legionnaires. It made him smile.

"Rog. Keep sucking water. Don't dehydrate."

Ten hours passed as they marched north. The patterns of the floes became more predictable as they went, and it had been hours since their guides had led them into a canyon from which they then had to retreat.

"Find us an RON, guys," Braley said over the full team channel.

"Rog," Sims replied.

Their ideal spot for a place to remain overnight would give them cover but also allow them observation in all directions as well as good avenues of escape if they encountered a hostile force. Within an hour, Poul and Sims had a good candidate selected.

A pass between sheets of collided ice led to an ancient beach within a small rocky cove. A short wash led to the plateau above where sentries could watch over the cove in all directions.

"Phillip and Bertie, we're going to pull our rucks off and get you guys pushed out for LPOP. We'll go fifty-percent security and give everyone a few hours of down time before we get moving again," Braley said. "Kel, I want you to take the first rest break. Check on Sarah and then test conditions for breaking seals on our buckets."

As they pulled the last of the rucksacks off the two DOGRs, Poul took Bertie and escorted him into the ice cliffs leading into the rear of their cove.

"Let's get you set up here, Bertie old boy," Poul said, mimicking the sing-song pattern of speech the two robots used. "Keep mum on the voice traffic unless you need us."

"Right you are, sir. I won't say a bloody word. You'll indubitably know it's happening when you hear me work my magic with the heavy."

Sims took Phillip up a sharp draw. Legs folded under him and the heavy blaster just clearing the lip of the plateau, the AI extended his head to the same level. "This place makes me a bit narky. If there's trogs what wants to come out and test us, I'm keen to give 'em the full Monty."

"Uh, you do that," Sims said. "I'm going to post up here with you awhile, Phillip my friend. I'm anxious to take a good look around."

"Likewise,   boss."

Kel found Sarah a small depression with her rucksack and sat next to her. "I'm going to warm a ration and pop my lid. It's minus 10, so I don't plan to take too long to check the air and eat. I go first since I'm the medic. If I notice any problems, everyone else can stick to paste from their bucket nipple."

Braley walked into their small dip in the ground and placed his feet in, sitting on the edge. "I got an eye on you. Go for it, Kel."

If Kel had any acute adverse reaction to breathing the local air, Braley would get his bucket back on him and let the suit flood him with pure oxygen. Kel pulled out a small packet and squeezed the dot on the top seal and waited for it to warm. The food was calorically dense and low residue so their suits would have little solid waste to deal with.

"Here goes." Kel popped his bucket off. Even in the biting cold the sulfur tinge was unmistakable. Kel took a few shallow breaths and began eating quickly and efficiently. He took a couple pulls from another packet containing kaff, warm and black. He would have preferred some sugar, but didn't think much about it. Just as he finished, he could no longer feel his face.

Bucket in place again, Kel spent a few minutes running a self-diagnostic. His blood oxygen saturation was normal, as were the rest of his vitals. He worked to make his tongue function as the last of the chill departed. "The air makes everything taste like it smells. Sulfury. No ill effects from the atmo. Braley, Sarah, dig in. Bigg, all good down here."

"Rog. Button up and get some sleep. I'll wake you guys in a few."

Kel laid his carbine alongside him then put his empty ration containers in his ruck and moved to prop his back and head on his rucksack and watch as Sarah and Braley repeated his actions to sample the local air. Sarah had a pained face as she ate. Braley looked unperturbed as he devoured a ration and a kaff. Like most of them, kaff did nothing to deter them from sleeping when the time came. Soon their buckets were in place.

"All good, Sarah?" Kel asked.

"Blech. Like you said. Sulfury."

"Take a dental rinse from your bucket. It'll help. Get comfy and get some sleep. We'll be moving before you know it."

Kel closed his eyes.

A minute later, Bigg's voice filled his bucket. "Ready for a shift? Come take my spot, Kel."

"Moving," he replied.

Has it really been three hours?

Sarah sat up as well. Kel pinged her over comm. "Stay here, Sarah, and soak up some more sleep." Braley was already standing and moving toward their six to Poul and Bertie's position.

"I can pull a watch, too."

Kel smiled to himself. "We might take you up on that later. We have another ten hours or more on foot. You'll help us best by being able to keep up the rest of the day. Okay?"

She nodded and lay back on her ruck. Kel was impressed with her level of motivation. So far, he had not been wrong about his assessment. Highly intelligent people were also adaptable. She was adapting rapidly to the demands of their environment.

Kel climbed up the wash to where Phillip crouched. Bigg lay prone to one side of the DOGR, Sims on the other. Kel brought his N-22 and now crawled on hands and knees forward to lay beside Bigg. "Thought I'd get some long-range eyes out there. See anything?"

"I can see the terminator ahead," Sims said. "Might be my imagination but the sky is much brighter in that direction."

Bigg agreed. "We're on the right course. If we hit where we think we're going, we'll be overlooking the main settlement. We should be able to see the top of Mons Alpha in another twenty klicks." They named the huge artificial mountain Mons Alpha. All overhead plots showed that as being the hub for all the high-speed avenues of approach. The suburbs radiating out from the mass came close to a series of canyons and plateaus from which they hoped to make their clandestine mission support site. It should take them another thirty kilometers to reach, about ten more hours of patrolling, if they encountered nothing to slow them down. So far, they seemed to have arrived unobserved. Or at least, unmet.

"Get going, you guys. Phillip and I have the watch, right-o?" Kel said, trying some of the New Cardiff vernacular.

"Indeed we do, good sir. Not spoiling for a fight, but wouldn't mind, say what?"

On the move again and after several hours, they left the bizarre terrain of the ice floes behind. Moving into an expanse of low flat-top hills separated by shallow valleys, they kept the same circuitous pattern, avoiding cresting any high ground and maintaining routes through the lowest possible terrain. In a few places it was prudent to activate their mimetic camouflage and move slowly, one at a time, through exposed passes. To observation by the naked eye, the crypsis was impressive. They were truly invisible. Even with visual augmentation in the infrared and ultraviolet electromagnetic bands, there was little to see. With rapid movement the concealing effect was lessened. At a slow, controlled stalk even the upright human form was difficult to detect.

The sky became noticeably brighter as they moved north. They took a security halt and formed a small perimeter in one of the valleys while Bigg and Braley made their way to higher ground for a visual reconnaissance, or what they preferred to call a "sneak and peek." What the term lacked in formality it made up for in accuracy. After a half hour, the two returned and sat in the middle of the circle.

"We can see Mons Alpha in the distance," Bigg said. "I collected some topo of the route. Sending."

At a distance of only a meter the L-comm emission would be no detriment to their concealment. Kel magnified the images. A window popped up in Kel's visor. The mapping program updated and the glowing lines of their proposed path jogged to the horizon like a trail left by glow bugs.

"I think we're going to find a site for our hide pretty easily," Braley said. "And a route that'll keep us below the tip of that Savage mountain top. Once we're dug in, we can get sensors out and risk a fly-over by a nano-drone for a passive-only collection." Recording visuals and not transmitting them for simultaneous live view would render most efforts to detect the miniscule drone impotent.

"Sarah," Braley continued, looking at the diminutive scientist in her armor. "That's where your work is going to begin. We're going to need help with analysis. No more loafing like the rest of us grunts. It'll be time to use that brain."

The young woman flashed them a thumbs up from where she lay next to Kel.

"Copy."

Someone's getting the hang of this.

"Okay boys, start digging." The team lay in a small crevasse, the mesa above them overlooking the valley of the Savage city and the hulking mass that was Mons Alpha.

Kel wanted to see the black pyramid rising from the valley floor with his own eyes.

Bigg directed the two AIs as they dug into the mesa. Kel and Poul pulled the N-22s out from their cases and prepared for their stalk across the mesa plateau above. Sarah watched them intently as they each pulled out a large net that they draped over the rifles. Kel made the universal sign for her to wait here, holding his palm up flat for her to see. She nodded in receipt.

Kel and Poul stepped around where the two DOGRs were digging into the canyon wall, piling a respectable mound of dirt behind them. By the time he and Sims returned from planting sensors, the hide should be near completion.

He started his ascent, his rifle glued to the front of his chest by the mag-lock. Just before cresting the plateau, he triple checked that his mimetic camo was working. He detached his rifle and activated the net over it. He pushed the rifle ahead of him at a slow, unhurried pace and followed it over in the same sloth-like manner. Now the stalk began. Flattening his profile from head to feet, he cranked his head to turn his eyes forward to plot the course, choosing a clump of vegetation as his first way point.

It was fifty meters to the forward edge of the plateau. Small patches of dry vegetation dotted the surface along his planned route. Moving only a few centimeters at a time, they pulled themselves by flexed fingers and pushed off flattened feet, one smooth push-pull after another. Even a dedicated observer whose attention was trained on the mesa would have difficulty detecting their movement. Movement was the first target indicator. Taking time to move was the key.

It wasn't long before he felt the familiar cramp in his right butt cheek as he crawled. He'd taken enough regen tabs to heal every molecule of collagen in his body and done all the recommended therapy. Nonetheless, every time he had to stalk on his belly and push off with his right leg, the stabbing sensation was there. He'd finally seen a doctor about his complaint. The answer was plain. There simply wasn't a cure for all pains. His reward would be lying in the comfort of the hide later, in any position save on his stomach. It wouldn't be a luxury apartment, but Kel would find little to complain about. This time, he didn't have to dig the hole. That alone sold him on having the Autonomous Combat Multipliers with them permanently. Better than that, Phillip and Bertie had turned out to be entertaining company. He was betting that they had many more talents to share.

The drifting of his mind, tuned to automatic, stopped. They arrived. He pushed his rifle in front of him, making sure the netting was still in place, and rotated it up as he activated the repulsor pod and raised his head and chest to rest behind it. Precise as a robotic surgical arm, moving at the speed of sloth.

The change in position was welcome. His pain vanished. Settling behind the rifle, he scanned through its powerful digital optic. Starting at a low magnification he slowly shifted the scoped rifle as far left and right as he could. Between the two of them, they could observe anything almost 180 degrees to their combined front for as far as they could see. And if they could see it, they could kill it.

To his front lay the Savage city. Kel programmed a chrono countdown for two hours. At the end of that time, they would each take turns placing sensors on the face of the plateau while the other watched, then reverse to make the slow return. The molecular thin wire they would trail from their heels would connect the sensors to their datalinks, broadcasting an undetectable signal. Then the waiting would begin.

Almost five hours later, Kel slid off the mesa and down the slope. He took a moment to lay on his back as Poul slid gracefully to a halt beside him.

"I never want to be on my belly again," Poul groaned. Kel was too tired to answer and likewise groaned back, parroting the noise.

Phillip and Bertie worked on the canyon floor, spreading the excavation tailings along the canyon passage. Bigg and Sims stood looking at the entrance to their hide. It was barely a meter-and-a-half tall and just as wide. They were positioning a phased array camo net over the hole. The nano-tubule weave became rigid when in place and would resist the movement of even a strong wind.

"Whaddaya think, master sniper?" Sims asked him.

Joints popping, Kel rose and inspected the entrance. He crabbed from one side to the other, checking it without spectral augment, then adding different wavelengths, looking for any obvious indicator that a tunnel mouth existed in that spot. He knew where to look so it was hard to be objective. Not perfect, but not bad.

"It'll do."

Braley walked backward towards them, a spool of micro-wire in one hand, a small branch topped with a gray brushy growth in the other. As he retreated towards the entrance, he used the branch to dust the surface of the dirt, removing distinct human and robot tracks. It did not completely remove the evidence of activity, but concealed how many beings had left sign in the pass.

"Let's get in," Bigg said, holding the camo net to one side. "After you gents. I'll clean up behind us."

Kel took the cue and entered, crawling into the portal and through the narrow tunnel on hands and knees. Dim light filled the space ahead and within a dozen meters Kel was able to stand in their new home. It was impressively large, a ten-by-six-meter space. The MkIV and their rucksacks along with the other weapons and containers sat against the walls. Sarah sprawled in a corner, leaning against her rucksack. Kel saw his own ruck and plopped down beside her, laid his N-22 by his K-17, and stretched back. Right now, the borrow was as good as a suite at the Galaxia.

Bigg was last in, crawling over the DOGRs lying in the tunnel passage. "We're covered. Let's get the sensor packages up and running." Everyone took out a datapad. Bigg set up the control node and after a few minutes, reclined with the rest of them against his own rucksack, feet poking into the center.

"Okay. I'm up. Everyone, check their feed."

Kel checked his pad. The sensors he and Poul placed transmitted a wide panoramic image from the front of the mesa to overlook the city beyond the flat plain. He manipulated the image over a section that showed some of the nearest structures and magnified it. The resolution was excellent and Kel panned around to test the system.

"Nice job, everyone," Bigg said. "Great job, Phillip and Bertie. So far, I gotta say, this is my all-time favorite hide. Very roomy. Don't let it go to your heads."

"With a little more time, we could put in a guest room or two," Phillip said.

"A den might be a welcome addition," said Bertie.

"Very nice. Link yourselves into the feed to help us with the watch. Sarah—" she watched him attentively. She should be exhausted after walking for twenty out of the last thirty hours, "—now is when your expertise comes into play. We're looking for activity and patterns of movement. Any context you can provide to what we're seeing will be helpful. Any tech you spot, try to classify it."

"On it," she replied. If she was fatigued, she kept it to herself.

Bigg pointed at her. "But don't burn out. We'll be taking watches. It's hard to stay sharp in these conditions. Take breaks whenever you like, but I want you available when one of us sees something of interest to analyze it live. Good?"

"Good," she replied, again without further commentary. Kel was trying to picture what this part of the mission would've been like had Patrick made the trip with them. He shuddered to imagine.

"Kel and Poul, you two knock off first. Get chow and some Z-time. I'll get us a rotation going, but we need at least two of us in addition to Phillip and Bertie watching the feeds at all times. Boys," Bigg said to the two AIs, "anything you see that we miss, bring it to the attention of whoever's on watch until we tell you differently, got it?"

"Sure thing, boss," Phillip responded.

"We've got our eyes peeled for dodgy trogs, boss," said Bertie.

"See that you do."

"If we get compromised," Braley said, "we'll make a fighting retreat back along our route to a position where we can call up the OSP. Otherwise, we'll move to the best position of advantage from where to mount a defense."

Everyone responded in the affirmative. Kel checked to make sure his ruck was sealed and that his weapons were close by. If they had to move, he'd be ready. He wasn't hungry and decided to rack out right away. He thought about taking a metabolic scrub tab to remove some of the ache in his muscles, but decided to hold off. If they were in the hide for any amount of time, their effects would be more appreciated the longer he was cramped up in the small space.

Three days later, he was taking a tab every eight hours. For the first time in his life he felt toxic, claustrophobic, and anxious. Poul had stopped joking yesterday. Sims quit all communication save clipped grunts, and even they were rare. Collectively, they'd observed no activity of any kind on the sensors. It was dead as crops after die-back. Nothing hinting at Savages or any life at all had appeared.

Kel began to wonder. *Is anyone even out there?*

17

Suffering produces endurance. Endurance produces character. Character produces hope.

Sitting in the hide was an exercise in suffering that had produced only perplexity, boredom, and despair.

Some Dark Ops missions required exertions of a super-human nature. When coupled with the inevitable sleep deprivation that accompanied combat operations, the stress was taxing in every conceivable way, stretching nerves taut as wire. This was different. As different as electrocution was from hypothermia.

Kel hated strategic reconnaissance. One special form of that mission was the Stay-Behind. It involved what they were doing now—sitting in a deep dark hole. For that particular mission the goal was to hide in just such a place, concealed and dormant, while waiting for an advancing enemy force to roll over. Then at the appropriate time, leave the hidden location to appear in what was now occupied territory and commence to wreak havoc throughout the enemy's rear areas. He'd never performed a true Stay-Behind mission, but had trained it many times. It was dreadfully dull.

For a mission that had begun with great apprehension of the danger they would face, this one had turned into a bad joke. There was little to do except watch and wait. So far, they'd done plenty of both with little reward. The sensor feeds revealed nothing.

The tasteless, plain rations they consumed removed even the small reward that was normally provided by the daily meal. As he popped his bucket to consume one, he reminded himself that it could be worse. Whether the rumors were true or not, their belief in one particular story made it as good as fact in their minds.

The Legion once experimented with appetite suppressants for the purpose of reducing the amount of sustainment rations needed for these missions. A team had been issued the appetite suppressants for testing and sent into a hide. After a week the results were analyzed. The team had consumed less than half of the ration allotment compared to that of a normal mission. Their physical performance post-hide experience was unchanged. The test was initially thought a success. Two weeks later, the team experienced a side effect from the drugs; everyone's teeth fell out.

Kel took the last bite from the ration pouch before putting his bucket on and swishing dental wash through his teeth. *No, it could be worse.*

It was a mantra he chanted a hundred times a day. *It could be worse.* It echoed in his every thought, so often that now he heard it swimming in his bucket. A school of little silver fish, looping around him in a circular fishbowl, never to leave. *It could be worse*, the fishes sang as they made their endless race track. *It could be worse.*

He broke the cycle when he realized he'd been wrong. *This* was the worst.

At seventy-six hours into their entombment, Bigg and Braley woke everyone for a team meeting.

"All right, gang," Braley started. "We have a decision to make. Let's start by reviewing what we know so far and if there's any dissent, I want to hear it. That includes you two," he said jutting his chin toward the bots. "None of us has registered any activity on the visual or EM bands, agreed?"

"It's dead out there." Kel had images from his last three days of watch burned into his mind. He could see them with his eyes closed. Nothing changed from hour to hour, day after day. A still life less interesting than a bowl of fruit. The huge black mound rose from the center of the city. Under magnification, he'd scanned every one of the blocks composing it. Other than the monotonous angles of the various cubes and rectangles making up the irregular mountain, it was featureless.

The surrounding block-like buildings were even more banal and dreary. Where windows existed, they were blank, dark mirrors. From this vantage they could see two linear cuts on the surface they'd supposed were roads leading off to other cities. Nothing stirred.

The only source of animation was from the top of a volcano on the far horizon. During daylight, smoke bled from its mouth in tiny streams. At darkness it glowed a dull, angry red. A predictable but welcome change in the scenery. The animation sucked them all into a trance like a campfire.

"Sarah, any conclusions to share?"

Sarah nodded. "What we have is an absence of evidence, not evidence of absence. I can't make any definitive conclusions, but it's a significant juxtaposition from the on-the-ground report by Legion Reconnaissance. Parties of laborers and those directing their activities were noted by all the observers as proliferate. There should be a large population commensurate with the size of the infrastructure we've observed.

"I've considered other factors that might explain the quiescence we've seen. I can't find any evidence of recent environmental disruption to explain why the population seems to have vacated."

Kel thought about what Sarah had told them after confronting her on the *Blackie*. The evidence pointed to the Savages working toward some great project when Colonel Hartenstein was last here. Mons Alpha seemed the logical result of that effort. Kel grunted. "So, we've got a decades-old report of a Savage presence confirmed by a firsthand observer, the colonel, a man we trust. The report is redacted, buried, and all participants in that reconnaissance essentially silenced."

Everyone remained quiet as Kel pieced together the bits of information that led to them being here.

"And here we are. No Savages, no explanation as to where they went. Did they abandon this one city? Do we need to move south and search another? Are they underground? Did they leave for another planet? Something was going on here, and the Republic has stewed over it for thirty years. I'm ready to find out."

"Damn right," Poul said.

"Let's make it happen," Sims agreed.

"Bigg?" Braley said as an open-ended query.

"Before we go take a look, any objections to launching a drone? I can send one out for passive collection on a route over the center of the settlement then return for a data dump. At least for a first look. If we get nothing, I think sending it back out for a live-feed and some directed observation would be smart before we go exploring."

Kel couldn't think of a reason not to. "Seems the safest bet."

Phillip sounded off. "We've run the spectrum on a frequency down to the microsecond. No emissions from any source. Still as a statue out there, gents."

"Anyone else?" Braley asked. None dissented. "All right. Let's be in a condition to move out. We'll send a quiet package out over the city and see what it brings us. Let's do it."

"Be right back." Bigg grabbed a fist-sized drone and crawled over the DOGRs to the entrance.

It took about an hour, but when Bigg returned, he looked cheery. "Drone's back. Pads out. Let's look at this together." Bigg had sent the drone on a path through the canyons then well up to higher altitude and out over the frozen city.

They had an improved look at the roads. The linear constructs were in all appearance dry canals several meters deep, but otherwise featureless. The empty paths between buildings were devoid of clues about the culture that housed the missing. The basic symbology associated with beings living in close proximity was absent. No centers for congregation or activities, no decorations or signs. Even Repub military bases had more character.

The stabbing pain between Kel's shoulder blades disappeared for the first time in days as the drone moved to the object of their curiosity. The mountain. The mass looked much as it had from their reconstructed map views. The varied cuboids gave it a sharp, irregular outline that reminded him of a child's stacking of blocks. Only instead of being endearing or cute, the black geometry sucked away light and hope.

The lid of the treasure chest was about to be opened. The drone passed over the peak to show the face hidden from them these last long days. In his boredom Kel had taken to imagining on the other side would be a large patio with umbrellas and tables, waitstaff serving gourmet delights to relaxing Savages. No such luck. It was a mirror of the portrait he could draw from memory.

Watching thirty minutes of the drone's recorded flight on his pad, nothing Kel saw changed his assessment. Besides the change of perspective to an overhead view, they knew as little as before. Kel looked up from his pad as the drone reversed course through the canyons and back to the hide.

"Anything of note to anyone?" Bigg asked.

"Drive it back out, Bigg," Poul said. "Time to be a little bolder, team daddy. Go live and let's buzz whatever merits a closer look. Don't know what else to recommend."

"Can we get out of the hide to do it?" Sims asked. "If the drone stirs up a nest of hornets, we might as well be in a position to fight or flee for our lives. I don't know about anyone else, but I'd like to limber up beforehand."

Braley looked at Bigg. "I don't have a good argument against."

Bigg nodded. "Agreed. First let's buddy up to empty waste reservoirs, then we'll get out into the canyon. I'm ready to get some blood moving in my muscles, too."

Kel stood and moved over to Sarah. "One more time, buddy." He handed her a fresh waste pouch to swap for him. The waste-consuming nanites would be about expended since the last change and a new one due regardless. Sarah had become adept at the intricacies of prolonged armor wear.

Sarah groaned. "I have brothers. A lot of my friends growing up had to share rooms with their siblings. I always had my own room. If we ever get home, I'm going to thank my parents. No offense, but I never want to live this close to another soul again."

The three robots stood on the canyon floor. They'd loaded the heavy blasters and rucks onto Phillip and Bertie again. Kel had his K-17 slung on his back and his sniper rifle riding high on his chest. If the drone activity did engender some response from the city, Kel's plan was to get up on the mesa and delay any Savage advance. He was looking forward to it. On pure particle beam setting, he could punch through ten centimeters of reactive armor with the N-22. He defied the Savages to produce any tech to defeat that.

"Here we go," Bigg said.

Kel watched the feed in his bucket. They were no longer worried about a tight-coded transmission on the L-comm band revealing their location. Shunning active transmissions was a sound tactic. Now the strict precaution seemed unnecessary, like tiptoeing through the backdoor into an empty house. Did it really accomplish anything?

The drone again zipped from the canyon's mouth over the plain to the city beyond. Bigg slowed the drone near the transition from desert to duracrete and from a height of twenty meters drove between the first two structures. The flat roofs were crowded with solar collectors. Bigg hovered the drone over a building to peer inside a window.

It was a bare room, devoid of any sign of habitation past or present.

"No one's home," Poul said.

"Looks like no one's ever been home. Or if they were, they moved out and took the kids and all the furniture with them," Sims added.

"Let's keep going." Bigg swung the drone over the building and past more flat-roofed buildings. "I'll just randomly drop down and take a peek every so often. Nothing stands out as different or interesting. Let's look in here." He peered in several windows at different heights. Empty rooms with walls bare of art, motif, or clues thwarted their curiosity.

"This is disappointing. I thought we were going to bring the hate to some Savages," Sims said. "Instead we're housing inspectors condemning abandoned properties." It was the most words he'd uttered in days.

"Hmmm," was all Kel could muster.

"What?" Poul asked. "Think the Savages are staying hidden, waiting to ambush us when we least expect it?"

"I'd settle for that," Sims said. "Shame to go home with full charge packs."

They continued the remote exploration. The more he saw, the more Kel relaxed. *Maybe they picked up and left for better digs?* He leaned against the canyon wall to ease the load on his feet. It had been so long since he'd stood for more than a few minutes at a time that his feet ached, even in the low gravity. *If no one's home, at least we can take a walk around and get our bodies moving.*

"Dive toward that canal-road thingy," Braley said as the drone cruised over the rooftops and the linear structure came into view.

"At your service," Bigg replied. Everyone's stress level was lowering, Kel thought. The switch for everyone's personality flipped on and powered up as brains were waking post-dormancy in the hide, the fog of the dungeon lifting as he'd hoped. It wouldn't be necessary to administer mood elevating agents to the team.

As Kel surmised, the "road" was sunken and while it could have been a means for vehicular transit, the most obvious form was that of a canal, now dry. Kel's early interpretation seemed correct. "They had a canal system for moving water from the glacial side to the bright side of the planet. Doesn't seem like diabolical Savage tech to me. It's basic infrastructure."

"Where's all the crazy Savage stuff?" Poul asked. "You know, the sacrificial altars? The human slaughter pens? The cybernetic zombies? What I'm seeing looks like an abandoned settlement and a nice one too, by the looks of it. Well, a little drab in the décor department. I'll give them a break on that one, given they were stranded on a desolate moon barely capable of sustaining life."

Sarah was the first to see it. "What's that? Between those buildings. Can you move over to that courtyard just on the other side of the canal? Yes, that one. Doesn't that look like one of the external locks on a lighthugger?" A curved cone sat on its base, distinct from the plain, utilitarian square and right-angle buildings surrounding it.

"I've never seen a lighthugger," Sims replied.

"I've looked at thousands, probably tens of thousands, of the surviving images. That's either inspired by one or one itself. Fascinating."

"It's an external lock you say?" Bigg asked as he drove the drone around the structure. "It's not very big. Not big enough for anything other than personnel."

"Well, doesn't that look like an access to you?" she asked.

The drone hovered. A recess sunken into a coaming protected the feature, shaped as only a passage for humans would be shaped.

"They're underground. That's the only thing that makes sense. Knew it." Sarah pocketed her pad. "Seems like we have a destination."

They patrolled cautiously out of the canyon and across the ever flattening plain toward the city. Bigg kept the drone above them in a stationary orbit. Their unblinking eye in the sky. They all had a window open showing the down-looking view between them and their destination. As they neared the first ring of buildings, Poul and Sims slowed as the team automatically spread out.

"At the duracrete pad, I'll take Poul and Sims and we'll bound to that first line of buildings," Braley said. "Bertie, you're with us."

Kel swapped the N-22 to his back and brought up the carbine. He checked the under-barrel launcher to make sure he had an ener-grenade loaded as he moved.

"Moving." Bertie joined them at a trot like some tank-animal hybrid, the barrel of the heavy blaster on its back dampened to a smooth ride. The short muzzle turreted as the bot chose potential targets on the move. Multitasking at its finest.

Kel and Bigg lay prone with Phillip standing between them, the blaster on his back pivoting like his twin's as he selected potential sources of danger for ballistic remedy. A vaccine, ready to stamp out disease. Sarah lay down behind Kel.

The bounding element stopped at the entrance to the complex. On the left Sims posted up on the corner; Poul hugged behind his partner. On the right Bertie crouched at the building's corner, Braley peering over him.

"Set," Braley said over L-comm.

"Moving," Bigg replied. "Let's go."

Kel sprang to his feet. "Sarah, stay behind Phillip." They trotted ahead, following the same path their teammates had taken across the hundred-meter bound. Only empty windows watched their progress as they moved into position behind their teammates. Kel looked back to see Phillip trotting behind and keeping a pace that Sarah could follow, the MkIV alongside her. In a few seconds the three were at the building.

"It'd be good time to pop into some of these buildings for a firsthand eval," Bigg said.

"Agreed," Braley replied. "Block right, move left." He stepped out behind Bertie and into the open space. Bertie moved forward and posted himself to their right, scanning the other buildings across the courtyard. Braley turned to follow Poul and Sims as they moved around to the left, weapons raised as the rest followed.

Kel pushed farther to the right and away from the front the building to increase his visual angle as he searched along the building's front. "Halfway down the side there's an entrance," he confirmed. "Phillip, stay out and cover long."

Poul and Sims moved to the recessed entrance, Kel close behind. As he moved forward Sims took his non-firing hand off his weapon and reached toward the closed portal. Before he got close, the portal slid open.

Sims snapped his weapon up as Kel closed the last two steps to be on-line with his teammates.

The three gazed into the space ahead. Interior lights grew in intensity, illuminating the entryway to reveal another set of doors beyond the short antechamber. Poul initiated the movement through the threshold, Sims and Kel flowing in with him. They moved to the next set of doors which likewise slid open to reveal a large empty room. Muzzles moved efficiently and sectors of fire collapsed to meet in the middle. Yellow tinted illumination expanded at their presence, revealing only floors, ceilings, and walls.

"Come in," Kel told Braley and Bigg. They would be paused at the entryway, awaiting the sound of gunfire or a verbal indication that they were needed inside.

Kel relaxed slightly when the two men entered, Sarah behind them. "Nothing to see here, it seems. Shall we make a cursory search?"

Phillip blocked the entryway with his massive body, his thin neck pivoting as he scanned.

"You three take left, Bigg and I'll go right. If you find stairs, sound off," Braley said.

They spent ten minutes flowing through the different rooms. Portals responded automatically to their presence. Lights functioned in each new space, revealing nothing about who had been here. The successive higher floors were just as empty. They gathered back at the main entryway.

"Seems like we could spend an eternity searching all these buildings," Bigg said. "I doubt we're going to find anything useful."

Braley nodded. "Agreed. Sarah, what do you make of this?"

"It's interesting that everything is functional. The solar collectors are still producing energy. The building's vacated, but in good repair. I'd like to inspect the rooftop and any power conduits to get more hints about their tech, but it only seems remarkable for its mediocrity. Besides that, I'd say it doesn't strike me as being abandoned for any obvious cause, just unoccupied."

Kel had the same impression.

"Make for the canal viaduct and the cone?" Braley offered. Kel had no objection; neither did the others. "Let's move out. I'll bound us when we have any significant danger areas to cross. Poul, Sims—keep the lead."

As they pushed out of the entryway and back into the courtyard, Kel again took his position in the wedge. He walked slowly, ready to challenge all the windows and buildings that lay to his side of the formation. The vacant city was more unsettling than finding it full of mongoloids armed with razortooth halberds.

I know we're going to find something. But when?

Only one bridge spanned the canal near their route to the portal. As they neared the overpass, Kel and Bigg moved forward with the two DOGRs and sprinted to the near side.

"I'm going across. Come on, Phillip," Bigg said as he trotted across the arched bridge.

"Set. Bring them up, Braley," Bigg said from the far side. Kel and Bertie remained in place as their teammates hurried across.

"Set, Kel," Braley told him.

"Moving. Let's go, Bertie," he said. As he moved, Kel peered over the bridge to the canal bed. There was no wall or railing along the sides to impede his view. As they reached the far side where Bigg and Phillip still watched, Kel paused. Ahead, the rest of the group were each on a knee, facing outward. "Bigg, let's wait up. I want to check something about these canals."

"What?" Bigg asked.

"Just a quick inspection."

"Go."

Kel lowered himself into the canal, dropping the last meter onto its bed. The edges of the canal were dished, not square. "There's a field coming from the center of the canal bed. It's magnetic. I can feel it. It's not strong, but it's there." He took a mouthful of bucket water, knelt, and removed his helmet. He spat the water on the ground and watched the path of the water. The pool ran together and formed a trail along the center of the bed, following a slope downhill and away from him.

"Kel, let's go," Bigg prompted him.

"Moving." He took a short run to fuel his jump, gaining height as he leapt to reach the edge and easily vaulted himself over to stand beside Sarah who had been curiously observing him.

"Why'd you do that?" she asked.

"Testing a theory. The canal's an aqueduct, all right. It's built with a slope leading away from the city to the outskirts. But there's a magnetic field underneath it. That's got to be a maglev field for transport. Likely the canal is dual purpose."

"That's great, professor. Can we go?" Poul said. "I've got the peak of the dome in sight ahead."

"Lead off then, Poul," Braley replied. "Phillip, Bertie, take a flank each." The two AIs silently moved. Kel wondered what the private banter between the AIs sounded like. Was it as quirky and peculiar as their Standard?

After a few blocks they posted up between the last buildings this side of the courtyard. It was the only courtyard formed in a circle; everything else in the city was built in a grid. Everything about this site drew attention like a floral shirt at a wedding. It was the singular exception to the architectural code the builders had apparently allowed. In its center, the tall domed structure sat. A narrow portal on its smooth surface beckoned like a friendly face at a party full of strangers.

"Sims, you and I'll breach," Bigg said. "Everyone else, get eyes out. Move." They eased forward, weapons pointed in all directions in the form of a strange spiny animal, some sea creature guarded by its quills. At the portal, Kel faced out and furmed a tight exterior perimeter as the rest joined him to protect Bigg and Sims as they evaluated the entry.

"This one ain't springing open in welcome. I'm searching for an access panel. You see one?" Sims asked Bigg.

"Negative on my side. No hinges. It pushes or slides," Bigg said as he verbalized the first of properties a breacher considered as they contemplated destruction.

"Gentlemen," Phillip interrupted, "I'm detecting a microwave EM band emission directed at us from the portal. Low output. We're being scanned."

Is that a sign of life, or an automated function? Kel wondered, his trigger finger ready to tap the safety.

"Decision time, sir. Breach it or beat feet?" Big asked.

"Breach it," Braley returned without hesitation. "Get us out of this open danger area."

"Torch," Bigg said without missing a beat. Purple light flared and the plasma cutter hissed as it sunk into the door.

"Stuff's thick," Braley said.

"Not making too much progress, I'd say," Sims replied.

"Bertie, bring my ruck," Bigg requested.

The AI trotted closer and backed up, presenting its right side. "Cutting tape in the left pouch, boss," Bertie said.

"Thanks, got it." Bigg worked fast. "Stand by. Ignition."

A bright flash and then metal ground on metal.

"Positive breach. Wait one," Bigg said. "Braley, come take a look."

Kel wanted to turn back and look to satisfy his curiosity, but didn't. Because, violence occurred in the span of a blaster bolt. He pictured a Savage horde springing forth from spider holes in the courtyard. To give up your sector of responsibility was to fail. The most crucial moment in a life of duty, lost. Honor, forever scarred. He would stay on his watch until his eyes burned and his arms shook. Until his heart stopped and his body withered. It was a vow carved in his heart with the ferocious intensity of their plasma torches.

"Gonna be tight. Phillip, look at this. Can you guys get down this?"

"That's a tight radius," Philip said. "We'll need to divvy out the rucks to be thin enough, but we can keep the blasters on top. We'll make it."

"Good," Braley replied. "Listen up, team. What we've got is a tight spiral staircase leading down. Bigg, launch another drone. Let's see if we can get some idea what's below. Stay on your sectors, guys."

A new drone feed popped up in Kel's bucket, the drone speeding down the stairs.

"Ten meters," Bigg read as it descended. "Twenty meters. Thirty meters. Forty. Fifty. Still going." He paused his count. "A hundred fifty meters. Two hundred. Three hundred. There. It's paused. There's a landing and another portal. What's the call, sir?"

Braley pondered a microsecond. "I say let's take it. I'll stay back with Bertie and cover our rear. Take them down, Top."

Bigg scoffed. "How about Bertie and I stay back? I'll weld this portal back in place when you call us down."

Braley didn't argue. "Rog. Phillip, take the lead, then me, Sims, and Poul. Sarah, you come down after the MkIV. Kel, bring up the rear. Let's grab rucks and move."

Kel was last to pick up his ruck. The MkIV, its rear legs crouching to shift its weight rearward as it descended, disappeared from his view down the spiral. Sarah hesitated to follow the MkIV down and turned to look at him.

"Right behind you, Sarah," he reassured. She nodded, then held onto the outer hand rail with both hands as she started to take a single step down, one at a time. Kel turned to Bigg. "Holler if you need me."

"Afraid you'll miss some glory, boss?" Bertie asked. "We've got this."

Bigg chuckled. "You heard the man, Kel."

He followed Sarah down. Below he could see the infrared illuminators from someone's bucket, probably Braley's, lighting the way.

Tramp, tramp, tramp went their boots on the stairs, the tick, tick, tick of their feet making a tin symphony to let the world below know they were coming.

Minutes passed.

"We're getting closer," Braley commed. "Bigg, let's not get too spread out. If it's all quiet up there, might as well button up and follow."

"Rog. Sending a SITREP to the *Blackie*. Might be the last for a while." After another minute, Bigg said, "Moving."

Kel checked the counter. They were one hundred and fifty meters below the surface. It shouldn't be much farther. The exterior drone feed faded out and the window in his bucket closed after losing the transmission completely.

"This one's actioned from the other side, too," he heard Sims say. "Ready to cut it, sir?"

"Set the strip but let's wait to light it until Bigg's closer. Where you at, Top?"

"One hundred meters. Give us a few."

Kel felt the vibrations from the stairs as Bertie's mass approached from behind. They were moving at a pace much faster than Braley's lead had been. Soon the AI's head poked around the tight spiral.

"Last man," Bigg said as he caught sight of Kel. Kel was halted at Sarah's back, the tail end of the MkIV just in front of her. He could not see the landing below. "Braley, we're behind you. Breach when ready."

"Gentlemen, there's another of the same EM band emissions on us," Philip informed them. "We're in a sensor field."

"Hit it," Braley said.

A bright light flashed. Kel squeezed his eyes shut, and heard the metal thud below him. A dim light spilled into the crowded landing.

"Whoa. That's a big one," Poul whispered.

Their file began to move and Kel nudged Sarah aside to push around her. He couldn't move past the MkIV, but looking over it as they descended, he saw what awaited on the other side of the landing.

He didn't know what he expected.

It wasn't this.

18

"Would you look at that. Amazing," Poul exclaimed.

At the landing Kel was able to push around the MkIV and through the portal to where his three teammates and Phillip waited on a large deck. A gaping smooth-walled cavern extended into the distance. A faint blue light filled the space from the ceiling fifty meters above. Another fifty meters below, the vast cavern was filled with water, a placid cistern, two hundred meters wide and extending away from them around a gentle curve and out of sight a kilometer or more ahead.

"This isn't a natural formation. This was tunneled. Look how uniform the walls are," Sarah said.

She was correct. The cavern was carved into a symmetric arch over the body of water, perfect in its dimensions. Kel looked about. The deck they stood on sat equidistant from the walls on either side. A catwalk led from the deck to both sides, hugging the walls at mid-level around the curving cavern.

"The temp's quite a bit warmer, almost twenty," Kel read off. "Atmo's good. Cleaner than topside."

"Left or right?" Poul asked.

"Left," Sims said. "Stay on the convex side."

"Agreed," Braley said. "Phillip, up front between Sims and Poul."

The catwalk was a full five meters wide and had a thin railing at its edge. *That's a very human feature to have in-*

cluded, Kel thought, and fell in behind Sims. Braley had already occupied the outermost spot nearest the railing. Braley would have a look at anything ahead before Kel, much to his dislike. Being part of a team meant you weren't always first in the fight. Knowing that but maintaining aggressiveness while waiting for your moment to get to work was how you stayed in DO. It wasn't a place for spotlight legionnaires who only shined when the light was on them. It's how it was supposed to be everywhere in the Legion.

"Where does it project on the map?" Braley asked.

In a moment Bigg replied, "Looks like it's heading toward Mons Alpha." Kel saw the three-dimensional overlay on his visor. "I'm sending the nano ahead."

Kel diverted some attention to the drone feed as he went, grateful he was no longer blind to what lay ahead. As fascinating as it was to discover the huge cavern, Kel disliked their position. This was a terrible place from which to fight if they encountered resistance. An escape back up the spiral staircase would be difficult, like fighting from a cage while opponents with long sticks poked you through the bars. Ahead lay either nothing... or everything. They kept their pace slow as they moved cautiously along the interior radius of the cavern. They remained silent as their feet scuffed the floor. Minutes crept, their anticipation building.

"Look at that," Bigg said. "Hold."

Kel turned his attention to the drone feed and enlarged it in his visor. The drone hovered at catwalk-height a half-kilometer ahead of them. Just above water level multiple smaller caverns branched off at even intervals at right angles into the curved walls. The drone lowered and Bigg drove it to sit in front of the nearest tunnel.

A smaller similarly arched but straight tunnel was illuminated in a brighter yellow spectrum. Row after row of long containers of planted vegetation sat in neat lines as far as he could see. Kel saw movement and tensed.

Small treaded robots rolled along the floor.

"This isn't all for nothing. There's someone here," Poul said.

"Contact," Phillip said. The blaster on his back discharged as he said it. "Target down."

"What do you have?" Sims said, surprised. "I didn't see it."

Poul responded, his face behind his raised weapon. "Got a guy on the ground ahead exposed just a sliver past the far curve. Man, that was fast, Phillip."

"One-o-seven meters ahead on our side. Individual biped. Humanoid on a small conveyance. I made a snap decision based on the rules of engagement, Captain. I didn't see an obvious weapon and stunned him. Hope it was the right choice, sir."

"We're in it now," Braley said serenely. The wait was over. "Move to contact."

Kel itched to raise his weapon. He was still in the second file behind Sims, aching to move farther right for the angle around the radius of the curve. The pace picked up as they rolled ahead, their momentum building.

"He's still on the ground. Not moving. I got him," Sims said.

Poul and Phillip continued to push ahead. Kel and Braley paused to look at the body that Sims was covering with his blaster. On the ground next to the being lay some kind of repulsor bike.

"Cover," Sims said.

"Hands," Kel answered reflexively as the only one without a shot ahead, and removed a restraint from his armor. He pushed the being's arms to its side before throwing the restraint on its abdomen. The enerchains unfurled and wrapped around the midriff, making several snaking coils around the body and upper extremities.

Their captive was human, or at least humanoid. Like the Savages in the colonel's description, this creature had a bare bulbous cranium and elongated limbs to match its torso. It was thin and frail underneath its loose, pale clothing. Kel placed a vital sign tape on its chest. The card showed the Savage was stunned but alive.

"Captain, its vitals are stable, but its brain's still scrambled, probably for a while."

Sarah knelt by his side, staring at the Savage. Kel moved to put another restraint below its knees, then took out a flexible airway and placed it in the creature's nasal passage. He hoped it would be long enough to reach past the thing's tongue as he placed a seal over its mouth to make sure it would be silent if it awoke suddenly. He'd done all he could to prevent the creature from asphyxiating with its mouth now sealed.

Braley and Bigg stood face to face. "Bigg, we have to get out of here and find somewhere to strongpoint. What's the move?"

"This goes on for another kilometer. There're passages ahead at the end of the cavern. We should get off this catwalk."

"Agreed. Do we take the prisoner with us?"

"Don't see movement ahead. Yet." Bigg looked down to Kel. "Rig a travois and let's take him. We might get some information."

Kel dropped his ruck and pulled out a small bundle. He rolled the Savage toward him on to its side, and laid the bundle on the ground behind it. He stroked the top of it and waited for it to unroll itself and widen. Kel rolled the body back, and the litter underneath enveloped the body in a drab green cocoon. "Mark-four, to me."

The dull bot trudged forward. Kel lifted the head of the litter and attached it behind the MkIV. "Ready to move."

"Double-time," Braley said, their heavy trots pounding the catwalk to bounce off the curving canyon walls, a noise even a blind Savage would know to fear. It was the sound of the stampede. The sound you ran away from before being trampled to death.

Kel expected to make contact again at any moment. They were compromised. They'd come to poke the bear. Now the bear had growled. Then again, this wasn't much of a bear. It was a scrawny humanoid on a hover bike. Nothing to take back to the cave to show the tribe with pride. Why had only a single Savage been sent to evaluate the intrusion? Why hadn't a platoon of Savage marines swarmed them, like in so many of the stories? Was there a chance the Savage dragging behind on the travois had been on his routine? That the encounter was a chance one? They couldn't gamble on it. They had to improve their tactical situation.

"Move left," Braley said.

The catwalk ended at the terminus of the cavern on another large deck and two wide passages leading off it left and right.

"Bigg, cover us with some APs," Braley said.

"Already on it."

Their column slowed and flowed into the left passage, a straight corridor. At its head Kel assisted Bigg to place palm-sized cards on the walls facing the deck. The M3 anti-personnel mines would spray thousands of needle-like projectiles when detonated. The first mine went from gray to the same dull brown as the sandstone around it, the next adapting a moment behind, deadly chameleons.

"We're good," Bigg said and jogged past Kel.

The column was paused at the first portal they'd come to. The portal had slid open in response and his teammates spent the longest of agonizing microseconds evaluating the room from outside the threshold. The critical time spent, like a speeder at a traffic drone revving repulsors and waiting the release, Sims and Poul moved in decisively. Braley peered into the room, then pushed across the threshold and turned to direct his weapon down the corridor.

"We're clear," Sims said from within. "We found our strongpoint."

Kel moved up behind Sarah and gave her a gentle nudge. "Get in." She followed the MkIV towing the travois. "You too, Phillip and Bertie. Inside," Kel prompted, the AIs prancing in like trained horses as he said so.

Behind them, Bigg was facing in the direction they'd just come from.

"Take two off me," Kel said to Bigg, offering his back where two M3 AP mines sat in his ruck, in the same outer pocket they all carried them in. Kel felt Bigg pull out the mines as he turned back down the passage. Two more of the mines turned brown on either side of the portal facing into the corridor.

He followed Bigg back in and the portal closed. Kel pulled his own torch off his waist and tacked a bead of weld across the center seam of the sliding doors. The ten-meter square room held benches and instrumentation against the walls. Short cubes that were neither chairs nor couches sat in the space. Panels blinked multicolored lights.

The drone had taken up a station near the corridor's head, having attached itself to a spot on the wall. They had an external view of the deck and the entrance to the corridor down which they had fled.

"Hey, somebody's awake," Sarah said. Kel moved to where she stood behind the MkIV. On the travois the Savage's eyes were open and darted back and forth, its head confined by the litter wrapped around its body as both protection and restraint. Kel checked the vital signs monitor. He wasn't sure what constituted normal for the being, but they were all close to human norms. The creature struggled and mumbled, its mouth taped shut. It coughed and strained. Kel realized the cause of the extra torment and pull the airway out of the thing's nose to drop it on the ground. The being's distress eased as it met Kel's helmeted gaze.

"Guys, our companion is conscious."

Braley moved to look down on their captive. "Doesn't look like much of a threat. Does he need further medical aid, Kel?"

"Not that I can tell."

"Leave him restrained. Sarah, I'm ready for some answers," he said to the diminutive armored figure. "Time to earn your pay. See if you can get him talking and give the translator something to work with. Oh, let's let him see that we're human."

"Ready to try?" Kel asked Sarah. "Let's pop our lids."

Kel went first. He set his bucket down on one of the benches and turned to the wide-eyed Savage. "I'm going to take this tape off your mouth," he said and reached toward the thing's face, certain that the being would not understand the words but hoping his manner would communicate his absence of harmful intent.

The Savage closed its eyes tightly in reaction to Kel's advance and as the tape came off, sucked in a huge breath. Sarah moved to the other side and knelt to be on eye-level with the creature. Its pale face pinked as it sucked in more air. It looked at Sarah, then at Kel, and made a long unintelligible utterance. Somehow, though Kel couldn't understand the words, they did not seem entirely unfamiliar. The sounds were soft and full of sibilance.

Sarah spoke and the creature listened attentively. She made the universal child-like attempts at communication—pointing to herself, then to Kel as she used the word "human" to describe them both, and then gave their names. She gestured to the Savage, inviting it to speak. It uttered more speech.

Sarah looked up at Kel. "I should have something soon."

Kel put his bucket back on and moved to where the team was gathered in their loose circle. The drone feed showed no activity outside. So far, the bloodthirsty hordes hadn't taken offense at their breaking and entering. A rapid-fire conversation was underway.

"... I agree, but that's not the issue right now," Poul was saying. "We're here."

"It is the issue, man," Sims said. "If someone came busting into my home shooting up the place, I'd react pretty sternly. So, what's next? Do we continue and provoke these people into violence so we can pull out and say, 'Bomb 'em, they're kelhorned Savages,' or do we just get out and report what we've seen so far?"

Kel had clearly entered the conversation at a critical point.

"Bigg?" Braley prompted.

"We all know the answer. We have our mission. We press on. We don't get to make policy on whether a Savage culture is good or bad. We've been told to evaluate this place for extinction versus isolation. The decision-makers need all the information we can give them. I'm certain we don't have that yet. But it's clear that they aren't a bunch of mud-hut building barbarians. They have advanced tech. The proscription against Savage worlds was made so that the galaxy doesn't fight another thousand-year war for survival against these aberrancies."

"Kel?" Braley asked.

"Uh, I kinda of came in on the middle of this. What's the question?"

"There's no question," Sims said. "I was just bringing up that as we try to figure out the next move, that so far, I'm not seeing something that looks like an existential threat to the galaxy. This whole mission rubs me the wrong way. Why didn't they send diplomats to make contact? Why didn't they just dust this place thirty years ago? None of it adds up and the longer we're here, the more I wonder if it is worth any of our lives to answer those questions."

Silence fell over the group.

"Hey. I'm sorry," Sims continued. "You know I'm just talking here. I'm ready to KTF like always. But I know I can't be the only one thinking these things."

"No, Sims, you aren't the only one. I agree, this is a mess." Braley sighed. "But it doesn't matter now. I am bringing us out of this one together and in one piece. And if it takes us having to kill everybody on this moon to get you all home, then so be it. We didn't set the parameters of this mission. It was given to us. Everyone, keep doing your job and I promise you, whatever happens, if in the aftermath someone reads this differently and wants to hang us, the responsibility is mine."

"You know it's not that, sir," Sims continued. "None of us is ever going to point fingers or second-guess a combat decision. Look, forget I said anything. Let's get on with the mission, good?"

"Hey, guys," Sarah said. "I think the translator's got enough of a lexicon built to communicate with. Come meet Drassar."

Poul and Sims guarded the welded-shut entrance with Phillip and Bertie. The rest of them stood around the Savage captive, still restrained on the incline of the travois. Sarah's bucket was off and she held her datapad in front of her, allowing it to translate as she questioned the Savage.

Braley pointed to get her attention. "Ask it where the population is. We want to know why the surface is empty."

Sarah nodded and rephrased the questions through her pad. After a moment the pad uttered speech that Kel thought sounded similar to the Savage's. Drassar made no immediate response, then spoke.

"*Interrogative*—who wants to know?" The translator programs inserted approximations and reconstructions when it did not have a fluency established with a new language. In this case, the question seemed like a reasonable translation.

"We seek those separated from our race when they left Earth," Braley answered. "Your ancestors settled this moon. There is a great city above. Where is everybody?"

Sarah made several attempts back and forth to clarify the question.

"We are the *People.*"

"Why is there no one on the surface?"

"Unnecessary. We live in perfection. We seek *evolvement,*" the device again substituted its best approximation, but the meaning had been missed. The translator gave other approximations. "*Awakening. Conjunction.*" It wasn't helping.

"Are there more of the 'People' here underground?"

"I am not alone."

"How many?"

The Savage said nothing.

"Let me try a different tack," Braley said. "Years ago, my people visited this world and saw hundreds of your people here on the surface, working and building."

The creature registered comprehension in a human way as its eyes widened. "*Interrogative—*you saw the *stupids?* The great work finished. The *inferiors* ceased. No need."

Kel puzzled. "Could he be saying the labor force was... exterminated? Like, no longer necessary once they finished the 'great work.' That's what I heard him say." Kel remembered the part of the report about the laborers being treated harshly or executed. Or disappeared.

"Drassar," Braley continued. "Explain the 'great work.'"

"You must not be here. Leave now."

"Heads up. We got company," Poul interrupted.

Kel saw it, too. Moving across the deck and into the corridor toward them were dozens of Savages dressed like Drassar. In the center of their mob, a red-robed figure.

"Now!" Braley yelled.

There was no lag in the noise and vibration as the feed shared the instantaneous destruction just meters away on the landing. Bodies turned to red mist and what remained fell like stringless marionettes. Part of the mob had made it into the corridor; they were stunned as they looked back in the direction of the deck, holding their ears, stunned into inaction.

"Whatever they've got in their hands doesn't look like a welcome gift," Sims said as he took his torch and cut through the spot-welds in a single pass with a purple jet of flame. Kel joined Poul, guns up as the portals slid open Kel worked the trigger as he glided out like a skater on a frozen pond. Without hesitation they fired. The decision to kill had been made for them. Their shots hammered the Savages in percussive staccato pulses of light and ember, the surprise of their ferocity another unexpected intrusion. In a world where these Savages were the masters, violent death dispelled all illusions of grandeur.

"Time to go," Bigg said. "We're fighting our way out of here. Weapons free. Leave the captive."

Kel kept his attention ahead, looking past the bodies filling the corridor floor ahead. "Grab those mines," Poul said.

Kel felt them being returned to his rucksack. "Which way?"

"Back the way we came," Braley said. "Let's move."

Kel and Poul took the lead. As they stepped over the bodies, he surveyed the weapons in their hands. They did not look unfamiliar. Places for two hands to grip, a mechanism for firing, sighting device on top. He was satisfied. Nothing too otherworldly looking.

In the open deck above the cavern, bloodied bodies ripped to shreds by the M3s littered the ground.

"We up back there?" Kel asked Poul.

"I'm last man," Sims said.

"What'd we do with the Savage?" Kel asked.

Sims grunted. "I just released the litter from the robot and left him on the floor restrained. Is that what you wanted me to do, Bigg?"

"Yeah. Best of only bad options."

Braley moved forward into Kel's peripheral. "There's one of those red guys the colonel told us to look out for." Kel glanced down at the shredded bundle wrapped in scarlet. "Seems some things haven't changed from the report. The red guys still seem to be running things."

"Braley," Bigg said. "I'm launching a swarm. Time to find a way out of here."

"Do it," Braley responded.

The micro drones passed above them and fanned out. Bigg had initiated the emergency mapping program. The drones would autonomously spread throughout the structure, coordinating between each other to rapidly explore all avenues of travel and create a three-dimensional representation of the spaces as they went.

Kel started to assess possible routes. To his left across the deck was another passage like the one they now stood in. It led off at an oblique angle and turned out of sight. He braced his arm and weapon against the corner and looked slightly over his optic. His index finger touched the face of the trigger. A stroke of his thumb and he would fire, followed immediately by launching an ener-grenade down the passage.

"Got it," Bigg said. "Fastest way out looks like the other corridor. There's a ramp, leads up to surface level. Right under Mons Alpha. I'm switching some of the drones to sentinel now." In a moment they would have a visual feed of the route ahead.

Braley and Bigg conferred on a sub-channel as Kel kept watch.

Poul didn't distract him. "Hey man, we took these Savages by surprise. We can roll right through any of them waiting for us. We can't give them time to get their act together. We got this."

Kel grunted agreement. Maintaining their violence of action and momentum would be what would keep them in the dominant position. It was time to keep the pressure on, to burn like a fire storm of certain death, rendering cinders out of anything in their path. The time for subtlety was over.

"Map coming up," Braley said. "Phillip, move up with Kel and Poul. We're taking this route." The mapping program popped up in Kel's bucket. "Time to go."

They flowed across the deck to the next corridor.

"No movement ahead. Continue," Bigg said, monitoring the sentinel feed from the center of their train as they moved forward. There was the danger of having too much information projected on their visors that could distract. The HUD, useful as it was, could be a lethal distraction. You could lose awareness as the eye and brain focused on a remote image in favor of the visual cues right in front of you. Kel and Poul's job was to keep the way ahead safe. Kel killed everything but the icon, the arrow projected in his bucket to guide their way, a supernatural guide. What

Bigg did now was practically unearthly. He used more than mere technology to chart their course. He used his hunter's instinct. His voice carried the power of the almighty for them as the keeper of the all-seeing eyes.

"Keep the route," the voice said. Bigg, if not a god himself, was at least an emissary.

He continued to feed them information as they traveled, giving them the synthesis of the drone feeds. The portals they passed remained closed, and they had no time to clear them. Right now, traveling was their primary task. Any threat from an opening would have to be dealt with as it appeared. So far, that hadn't happened. Kel wondered if the occupants were locked down within, trying to avoid the intruders, or waiting instead to ambush them. If so, they wouldn't live long enough to feel regret. Not the anticipation of the kill. Not the thrill of the ultimate victory. That belonged to them, not the Savages.

As if the Savages felt anything a human could.

The corridor widened and ascended to a ramp, then a landing, then took a turn back toward them and up.

"It's clear to the top. Just roll through," Bigg said.

Poul and Kel did just that, Phillip keeping perfect pace with them. They popped together around a corner, weapons at the front, leading the force of their tsunami up, and up, and up, projecting power like a rising flow of magma, ready to burst and flow over whatever lay at the top of the endless switchbacks.

Bigg kept up the verbal guidance as they continued up one ramp after another. "We're near ground elevation," Bigg said, giving welcome news that the end of their visit to the Savage under world was close at hand. The sick alien sky would be comfort. The stealth Talon could pierce it like a vibroblade through butter when called to retrieve them. "One more landing ahead." He thought they'd never reach the end of the inclines, the muscles of his legs punishing him for being immobile too long, a reminder of human frailty but one he had long trained to ignore. "Large open area ahead. Post there for a visual."

Kel hugged the corner of the last landing, weapon aimed up the ramp. Poul faded behind the DOGR for cover as the three of them held the way ahead.

"You take a look, Poul," Kel said, telling his partner that he could divert his attention to the image in his bucket while Kel stayed focused ahead.

"What is that?" Poul said, puzzled. "Your turn, Kel. Tell me what you see."

Kel clicked and brought up the drone image. Bigg had been silent as to what lay ahead. Kel couldn't describe it either. The top of the ramp ahead opened to a massive chamber. It was the inside of Muns Alpha. The mountain was not a solid structure, but a shell. Rising from the floor of the chamber, filling the interior up to the peak, sat a construct unlike anything Kel had ever seen.

"No idea. Don't see any movement on the ground, though."

"I know what it is," Sarah said excitedly. "That's why we're here."

19

"What is it?" Braley asked.

No one had a reply. Kel was impatient and wanted to start moving. The object at the center of their attention filled him with dread. Concentric rings stacked on top of each other in successively smaller diameters, glowing and pulsing upward toward the peak. His skin prickled with electricity even through his insulated armor. Arcs of energy bounced up the rings. He could not see the top.

"What do you mean, 'that's why we're here'?" Braley directed back to Sarah. "Are you telling us this psychotic gizmo is the jackpot? If you know what it is, spill it. Fast."

"I think, maybe, it's," she stammered, frustrated in her failure to produce a clear result, then recovered. "I told you we study tech recovered from other Savage worlds. Some of it has incredible destructive potential. Some of it we think is even alien tech, it's so fantastic."

"Sarah," Kel echoed. "Get to the point. What is it?"

"We theorized for years over what would explain what that recon team saw here. It's some kind of energy or matter-transfer tech. A scalar resonance concentrator or a geogravitic power converter, something along those lines I bet. It's all stuff that violates every law of physics and thermodynamics and shouldn't exist, but here it is. This is what's behind the Savage 'magic' Colonel Hartenstein's team observed. What they saw on their recon hinted that the tech actually existed. This was the 'great work.' They completed it."

"So, what's it do?" Bigg asked.

Sarah spoke hurriedly. "Change the phase of matter from one state to another maybe, collecting and storing the differential energy that results from the shift to other states. The concept has been theorized lots. No one has ever made it work, though. The Savages the colonel encountered here had some kind of working version of the tech, just smaller scale. The red guys making folks disappear? That's always been my theory behind it. But it would take a massive collector and concentrator. Well, here it is. But as to how the energy could be controlled and directed? Not a clue."

Kel had a theory, too. They were in danger. He couldn't hold his tongue any longer. "Bigg, Braley, we need to move."

"What's the way out, Bigg?" Braley asked.

"Still looking. Hmmm. There's several of these large alcoves on the ground level. I can't think of another purpose except as a location for portals. They're close enough to the exterior that even if there isn't an exit there, I can make one." Kel imagined one of Bigg's breaching charges bringing the whole mountain down on them.

"Mark the nearest and let's make our way to it. On you," Braley said.

The icon in Kel's HUD shifted in a new direction, as did his resolve. *I'm leading us out of here and away from that... thing.*

"Nothing moving," Bigg said as they continued up the ramp, continuing to be their spiritual intermediary between the ground and their all-seeing eyes.

Kel searched the expanse beyond the top of the incline. It was for Savages he searched. Pale ones. Crimson
ones. Ones he had not yet given names. And it would be
death he brought to them. But the pulsing mountain drew
him in, stole his attention, filled him with wonder and awe.
The dancing arcs rode invisible paths upward, disappearing out of view at the peak. It attracted and repelled him
in its magnificence and dreadfulness, capturing him like
when as a child he saw his first rainbow shredder in a
shallow lagoon. Their alluring beauty hid their venom. It
was something new, amazing, and unusual while deep
within, he knew he should fear it.

"The power this concentrates must be tremendous,"
Sarah said. "Unbelievable."

"Let's do it," Poul said as he pushed around Phillip.
"I'm ready to leave."

"On me," Kel said as he stepped off.

Kel continued forward and right. The circular path
around the huge pulsing mass was a hundred meters
wide from the machine to the exterior shell of the mountain. To reach the first alcove was three hundred meters
at least. He wanted to run, but fought the impulse. Speed
killed. What was most important now was to not blunder,
to not run blindly into any hidden threats. They were the
hunters, not the hunted. As they came closer to their proposed exit, he saw it.

Movement.

His head snapped up as he unconsciously drove his
weapon to his plane of sight.

A humanoid shape.

Kel fired.

"Contact. Red Savage, my twelve, fifty meters eleva-tion." Kel increased the magnification to look closer. He saw the red figure drop like a bag of duracrete.

Another blaster bolt fired from behind him.

"Red figure. Ten o'clock. Same elevation," Braley said. Now they were paused, guns fanned out in all directions searching the walls above them for targets.

"No! Don't stand still! *Move!*" Sarah yelled.

As Kel stepped off to follow the suggestion, to his right he saw a red-robed hand extend from behind a wall. Kel drove left as he fired. He felt something behind him. A change. A coldness. He couldn't name it. He ignored it as he continued to move laterally, gaining a greater angle on the red figure, firing all the while. Behind him full-powered blaster bursts hurtled outward in a barrage of destruction, hail raining back from the heights as they demolished the faceted walls above.

Sarah's voice wailed in his bucket. "We've got to keep moving. They'll target us if we're still. Keep moving!"

"Moving!" Kel ran for a nearby alcove. Sarah's ad-vice was sound, whatever her reasoning. Moving out of the large open area was a must. Poul was with him. He turned momentarily to see Phillip behind him, trotting as his heavy blaster aimed up at the sloped walls, firing in a random pattern. Kel dashed into the alcove, cleared the space, and brought his weapon up. Close behind him was the rest of the team. Sarah ran beside Bertie whose blaster continued to pepper the space above them. Sims followed her.

"Where's the Mark-four?" Bigg asked. "What the...? Mark-four. Diagnostic."

The mechanical voice did not answer.

The bot remained where Kel had first made contact with the red Savages. Paralyzed like a stone monument. Bigg continued to challenge it. Kel checked through his optic. There were no damaging marks of a blaster or...

"It's covered in frost. It's frozen in place."

That blast of cold I felt. It was meant for me! he realized.

"Where's the way out?" Braley asked. "Bigg, get us out."

"On it."

Kel stepped back into the alcove. "Phillip, switch with me. Keep their head down. Bring the heat."

The AI responded with action, a blaster bolt streaking toward the sloped walls every few seconds. Bertie did the same from the opposite wall.

"Try not to hit the... big glowing thing," Kel added.

"Consider it done, boss," Bertie replied.

Kel searched the walls around him for sign of any portal or control panel. His teammates did the same.

"Map tells me this is an exterior wall." Bigg pointed to their rear. "Poul, help me."

Bertie and Phillip delivered suppressive fire while Braley and Sims stood by them, carbines up, searching for targets.

Kel activated the datalink on his forearm and a holoprojection materialized. Kel entered the drone network to view the reverse slope above them. With the new perspective, he could see the first red figure he'd shot directly above their current position. The slumped body was not moving. A limp arm hung over the narrow balcony. Behind, a slit opening in the wall revealed itself. From this angle he could see them now. At intervals along the sloping wall were a ring of similar slender portals and narrow balconies.

He panned around, searching for motion. The cascading lights reflecting off the machine made finding targets difficult. After a quick scan and seeing no red figures, Kel sent a drone to another splayed red body on a balcony they'd all but turned to rubble. As the drone neared, Kel could see through the access to what lay beyond. *Now I've got you! Red demons in your little Savage nests.*

Kel drove into the threshold revealing the crimson-robed Savages' inner sanctum. A concourse curved around the interior shell. Panels of blinking lights lined the walls and islands of instrumentation sat evenly spaced down the curving hall.

"Ready to light it," Bigg said. "But we need distance. This is going to be a big shot. It's shaped, but there's going to be a lot of spall. We need to get behind cover. I can't guarantee the overpressure might not damage the... thing," Bigg said, pointing to the glowing mountain outside.

Kel looked out at the red-robed body on the floor between them and where the MkIV sat crippled. "Watch it. Coming through," he said as he made his way between the DOGRs. "I'm making a dash for where our friend came from," he said, pointing toward the wall behind the body. "There's some kind of cover over there. Wait till I clear it. Moving."

Kel dashed past Bertie and Phillip, and raced toward the body, picking a spot on the wall where the Savage's feet pointed. Where was that door? He found it. The concealed entrance sat pocketed behind the exterior wall. A ramp led upward and he halted his run at the entrance.

"Got it. Come to me. Best cover we're going to find."

Kel stood outside the entrance as Braley led the pack toward him, his right arm cradling his carbine, his left arm around Sarah as he shielded her with his body as he ran. The rest of the team and the DOGRs followed, still launching destruction in a ring above them. The last into cover, Bigg yelled, "Burning!"

Kel posted at the hidden entrance with the DOGRs covering the team's passage and continued to watch as the charge blew. The blast threw debris into the chamber, followed by rays of light. "Positive breach," Bigg yelled at his side. "Let's move."

"Wait," Braley said. "Everybody, listen to Sarah. What she's saying makes sense." Kel had been aware of the conversation the two had been having but couldn't follow it. The pulses of blaster fire from Phillip and Bertie continued in the background, falling debris sporadically crashing down to shatter on the floor.

"We have to find the control center or we won't make it," Sarah said. "They're using some kind of scalar resonance to generate power, but they're using the effect in a very controlled manner here in the mountain, focused like a point weapon and not spread over a huge area."

"So, they're trying to hit us one at a time?" Poul asked.

Sarah clenched her fists as she spoke, struggling to explain clearly. "I don't think they can use the power against us in a large spread or with a high output without damaging something here in the mountain. And, they have to aim it. If we run outside into the open, they can target a large area. The energy potential of this thing is massive. It's beyond massive. It's colossal. If they can predict our path, we'll never outrun them. They can probably fry or freeze a square kilometer at will."

"How?" Braley asked.

"We made guesses using the most far-out theories we could come up with. It's possible they've found a way to manipulate matter by changing entropy directly. They either increase entropy to the point of vaporizing matter into nothing... or they lower the entropy of a mass to absolute zero, like they did to the Mark-four."

Entropy? Kel thought. "Braley, what's she mean? You're the only one on the team with a degree."

Braley sighed. "Kel, my degree's in history and moral philosophy. I took the bare minimums in science. You know more than I do."

Kel thought he understood Sarah's meaning. "Drag that body in here." He pointed at the crimson-robed corpse just outside.

Bigg was closest and sprung into motion, hesitating only long enough to grab the legs and drag it backward into the small landing. The rest of the team crowded up the inclined plane behind them.

Kel activated his blade and with a blue glow cut off the garment in one smooth motion. The undergarments fell away to reveal the ashen skin.

"What are you doing? We don't have time for this," Bigg said.

"Look." Kel lifted the dead Savage's arm. The others could see it as well. A fine mesh of wires and circuitry ran along the skin of the upper limbs, leading to a lattice work covering the thing's chest in a vest. "It's some kind of instrumentation. A control mechanism. It's how they aim, I'm betting. It's not telekinetic or magic. If they have to aim it, then moving is our best bet. They already missed me. If they can't catch us standing still, they can't fry us. Or freeze us. Or whatever."

"That's what I've been *saying*," Sarah replied. "That's how they aim the effect at small targets. But to harvest energy, massive amounts of energy, they'd do it over large areas. They can probably pull energy out of the volcanoes, off glaciers, anything. It's geogravitics. They've discovered how to make it work."

Kel still didn't understand, but he knew what needed to be done. "We can't destroy this thing while we're in here and live, and we can't get out of here to destroy it—they'll wipe us out crossing open ground. There's a concourse on the level above us. I'm betting that's where this access leads." He pointed up the ramp. "Can we disable their fire direction center? Sarah, if you see the controls, can you make sense of them?"

"I don't know. But we've got to try."

"I've got signal again," Braley said. "Bigg, Poul. Get outside. Link with the OSP. Start selecting targets. Get as close as you can to Mons Alpha without raining rods directly on top of us. That should interrupt a little more of the Savages' decision-making process."

The two men nodded.

"Get a burst to the *Blackie* and get them on station for a hot extract. The rest of us, assault forward. Don't let one of those bastards raise a hand."

Poul looked to Bigg. "Ready to run for it, Top?"

Out the portal they ran, like only two dark operators ready to KTF can.

"Let's go," Kel told Sims, and they moved up the ramp. Three switchback ramps led up to the concourse. They raced upward and slowed at the last. Kel and Sims each tossed a stunner around their corners and waited for the charge to dissipate before popping around. Braley stepped between them to briefly look in each direction.

"Fight left."

Kel faced left down the curving corridor. In a heartbeat Braley and Sims were on line with him.

Braley commanded, "Bertie, rear guard. Phillip, protect Sarah. Move."

They pushed ahead. After a few steps, Sims said, "Hold," and fired a stunner from his grenade launcher. It bounced off the concavity of the outside wall and traveled out of sight before discharging its purple cascade.

Moving forward, they passed columns and islands covered with pulsing lights. Every dozen meters, a bank of similar instruments covering the walls on both sides gave way to blank, black wall again. A blaster bolt from the rear sizzled the air.

"Movement behind us," said Bertie. "Two individuals. Both down."

Continuing on, Braley asked, "Sarah, anything useful?"

"No. This equipment looks like repetitive intermediary stuff, I'm not saying it's not critical. We don't find anything else, if we break all this, it's bound to do some harm. But I'd feel better if we found something that looked like a central control." Kel liked her analysis. He was more than ready to break all the Savages' stuff with a temper tantrum of tungsten rods and proton explosives.

"Braley," Bigg's voice came over L-comm, "OSP run commencing. Stand by."

Kel's heartbeat quickened and a new energy filled his chest. *Let's see how you like our tech, Savages!*

"Got a danger area ahead," Sims said. "Opening on my side. Hold."

Sims launched another stunner. Kel couldn't see it from his side of the concourse, but the grenade impacted somewhere beyond.

"Sent it through the archway," Sims reported. "I'll send another one down the hall past it as we move up."

They continued to move and Kel now saw the arched entrance ahead on their right. Sims launched another stunner down the concourse. *Jackpot.* The unmistakable sound of a stunned body dropping like a wet towel came from ahead, more gratifying than ice on a hot day.

"Take the room," Braley said as they rolled forward with him.

Kel kept his attention down the corridor on the red-clad body on the floor farther down the hall, the victim of Sims's last stunner. He shot the downed Savage with three quick successive blasts from his carbine.

"Stunner out," Braley said, tossing, pausing, letting the flash fade. Kel's right shoulder touched Braley's back. As he felt the loss of contact when Braley moved, he followed. It was a circular room with a high, faceted ceiling. The room was filled with more of the flashing instrumentation.

"Bertie to your six, boss," the DOGR said from behind Kel.

"Keep it up, Bertie. You and Phillip watch the hall."

"Got it, boss."

"Kel, need you here," Braley said.

Kel felt a distant 'crump' through his armor. After a moment, another.

"Sounds like the OSP is bringing the rain. What do you make of him?" Sims asked, pointing at the ghostly pale figure at his feet. A restraint was already around the Savage's waist, Sims trained his carbine on the being's head. Kel gave the same treatment with his blade he'd given the corpse, the red robe falling away to his cut. The glow turned deeper blue as he sliced through the intricate gold and silver wire mesh around the chest and the arms, leaving the half-naked Savage lying in a bed of tangled wires.

"That should have him defanged," Kel said as he took out another restraint and dropped it over the calves, watching it wrap several times around the legs and tighten.

"Captain," Bigg's voice came to them from outside Mons Alpha, "our ride will be in orbit in thirty minutes, awaiting our beacon."

"Rog," Braley said. "Sarah, it's now or never, otherwise we're just going to break everything we see."

Sarah stood at one of the freestanding consoles working feverishly with her datapad, several holos running at eye level. "I think this is significant. I could spend a year studying this, maybe the rest of my life. Some of it seems to make sense; some of it, it's beyond me." She turned. "Can we ask him some questions?" She nodded at the trussed Savage.

"Kel?" Braley asked.

He looked down at the Savage. He could administer the neural activator. He had no idea if it would work, or if the Savage would die from the shock. But he already knew the answer. It didn't matter. "On it." He pulled his ruck off, reached for his med kit, and soon had the Savage resting up against a flat column. "Here goes." He pushed the hypo into the creature's jugular and waited. At first, the body remained limp. Then instantly, the thing tensed, gasped, and fought the restraints, its eyes wide open.

"We got a live one here," Kel said. "Brain's still scrambled, but he's conscious. He's all yours."

Kel stepped back as Braley and Sarah moved closer. Sims remained at the Savage's side, his carbine still pointed at the thing's head. While the team gathered round, Kel surveyed the curved room and the workstation where Sarah had been. A recess in the console's polygonal surface stood out. Just wide enough for a body. He approached. A model of the moon materialized, suspended over the central console. Holos from Sarah's datapad floated beneath, somehow insignificant, crude, and incomplete in comparison. Children's finger paintings hanging in a gallery of masters.

It's not a projection. It's a physical model. Kel reached out to touch the large floating globe. It was firm and unyielding. Not a holo. Reproduced in relief were the cities and terrain in dazzling clarity. He traced his finger over one of the volcanoes. There was no dimension to it. The surface was smooth, the detail perfect. Almost sensing his volition Kel effortlessly spun the sphere until he found Mons Alpha. The image was clearer than a drone. Advancing up the canals from the south were the Savage multitude.

"We've got company coming from the other settlements," Kel said.

"He's trying to speak," Sarah interrupted. She dropped to both knees, eye level with the Savage, her bucket removed, her blinking wrist link held high. At first, the Savage recoiled. Like a dog threatened by a stranger thrusting himself close, eagerness suppressing fear. It was a certain way to get bit. "Who are you?"

The translation issued. The Savage's red capillary painted eyes opened wide, the grogginess in them gone. Its face conveyed rage, eyes narrowed to slits, cruel blue lips mocking them in sneer, scorn building. Its contempt reached critical pressure and the harsh hissing vocabulary burst forth like steam, then stopped. After a short lag, the translator spoke.

"Who we are is perfection. Who you are is corruption. We knew the day would come, and here you are, as foretold. You did not disappear into the void of the universe. You survived and have followed us. I always doubted. I was wrong. Foul creatures!"

An icy chill traveled down Kel's spine as the Savage cursed them.

"Captain. We got trouble," Poul's voice came over their comms. "Someone called in reinforcements. High-speed vehicular movement in our direction along both of the canal highways. Still at a distance of twenty kilometers. OSP will start interdiction momentarily."

Braley replied, "Copy. Keep us advised." He turned from the interrogation scene. "Sounds like we've got the attention of the rest of the population. Time to move."

"Wait!" Sarah said. "We have to get more out of him."

Braley reached down for her. "Too late. Time to go."

Sarah resisted. "*Wait!*" She turned to the Savage. "Don't let your magnificence die with you. Let me carry it to the galaxy."

Its face twisted into a silent laugh. "We suffered and overcame and built the greatest civilization to ever exist. No imperfection exists among us. It took generations, and now, only in my lifetime, was the great work completed. Only to be destroyed by the savages we left behind us." It shot a glare at Kel. "The galaxy knows irony too well."

"Sarah. Now," Kel said as he and Braley lifted her to her feet. She pulled her arms away and ran to the station beneath the globe. "I can get it all without his help. This is why we're here. I need some time!"

"OSP has destroyed the transports, sir," Poul said. "They're halted ten kilometers from the city. We have massive foot traffic approaching behind them, though. OSP's fifty percent depleted."

"Braley," Bigg interrupted. "We've leveled everything up here except Mons Alpha. I'll leave us some rods for that if you can get out of there in time, otherwise I have to spend them on the hordes coming this way. Your call."

"We're moving now, Bigg. Look for us coming out the breach point. Kel," Braley said pointing at Sarah, "grab her and let's go. Back the way we came."

Sarah stood frantically driving cursors and commands across the holos. "Now Sarah, or I'm going to carry you out."

"It's not enough. It's not enough!" She shook her head in disgust. Picking up her datapad, she hissed through her teeth, resigned. "But it's what I've got." She put her bucket on. "I'm ready. Believe me, I'm not staying here a moment longer, either. Let's go!"

"Ready to move," Kel said to them all. Sims and Braley stood to either side of the DOGRs, looking out into the passage. The Savage behind them sputtered incomprehensibly, yelling some last curse at their backs. "What's he saying?"

"'Disorder receives you.'"

Kel frowned. "Huh?"

Sarah grunted. "Beats me. I hope I have the rest of my life to figure it out."

They ran. Slowing only as Kel and Sims alternated launching stunners to bounce off the radiused wall and past the infinite curve—just in case. They found the ramp and kept the same pace as they negotiated the switchbacks down again to the pulsing, throbbing gargantuan construct. In the same spot stood the MkIV, frozen where he'd seen it last.

"Mark-four. Diagnostic," Kel said.

The bot held its repose.

"Block left, move right," Braley said.

Kel remained on the left side, posted up until the rest of the team made it to the exit. "On us," Braley called. He dashed to the hope of daylight, Bertie behind him providing rear guard. They stood in the rubble of the beautifully wrecked wall, bathed in light not warm, not yellow, but tinged red with the illness of the Savage moon.

"Coming out. Bigg, where you at?" Braley said.

"Just outside. We have eyes on the entrance. We'll meet you."

"Stand by for shot," Braley said. "Get ready to run."

Kel didn't have to be told twice. He was as eager to burst from Mons Alpha as a drowning man to break the surface of the water, lungs burning to take in the breath that meant another moment of life. Their last act before leaving the control room was to pull the remaining plasma charges out of the DOGRs and place them at every cardinal point in the circular room. So many that it was overkill. Kel's favorite quality. Sarah thought the room was the control node they'd sought; if they were lucky, the only one. Denying it to the Savages was their best chance for escape. But would it start some chain reaction to turn them and the whole mountain into a smoking hole?

"*Run.*"

Kel pushed Sarah ahead of him as they broke into a mad sprint. Bigg and Poul waved them forward from outside a cluster of buildings, some of the last still standing after the barrage of the OSP.

"Where's the explosion?" he asked as they ran. Had he missed the cataclysm? "Did it blow?"

"Yeah. Monitor shows the shot completed," Braley said. "We're still here."

Stating the obvious was a small comfort. They reached their waiting teammates. Sims was the first to turn around. "Still standing back there," he said referring to Mons Alpha. "There's smoke rising from the far side. We were way deep in that thing. Maybe that's from our shot. Who cares? I say, make it rain."

"Poul, take us out," Braley said. "Phillip, up front. Gents, get the OSP targeting Mons Alpha, but hold the steel rain until we're farther out. Hustle."

Kel stayed to the rear with Bertie's heavy blaster turreted rearward. The shortest route through to the edge of the city and the plains beyond took them across the canal. There was no viaduct nearby. It would slow them down.

"Bigg, make it rain already," Sims pleaded.

"We far enough away?" Braley asked.

"Who knows?" Sarah responded. "I think we shut down the control center. Maybe there's no urgency to hit it. I don't know what will happen," she said, panting for breath, "if a hyper-accelerated rod penetrates the shell and hits the device... the whole moon might crack."

"Let's wait," Bigg replied. "We'll be across the canal soon."

Dodging through one block of empty buildings after another, the canal finally came into view. They crossed at a spot close to one of the OSP strikes. The huge crater left no doubt. The canal would never carry anything again. Bigg and Poul were first to leap down and turned to reach for Sarah as she lowered herself over the edge. Kel looked behind them.

"Make way," Phillip said. "Don't want to hurt anyone."

"Heads up, lady and gentlemen," added Bertie. The two bots backed up from the edge of the canal before accelerating in a short run to leap together, landing nearly in the middle of the canal. With a single bound they were up and over to the other side, clearing the wide distance effortlessly.

"Whoa!" Poul said. "That was slick."

"It's amazing how light a fella feels when not weighed down by everyone's kit," Phillip said.

"Far side security set," Bertie confirmed. "Waiting on you folks."

Kel was the last. He tried to emulate the DOGRs' example and took a few steps back before breaking into a run and leaping. Even in the reduced gravity, the impact was accentuated by a loud pop from his knees. He grunted. *Someday soon I'll have to stop treating my body like a machine.* Sims and Poul waited at the far side with their arms on each other's shoulders to act as a step. Kel took a hop, briefly contacted their interlocked arms with his feet, and pushed off to reach the top of the canal's rim. He grabbed Poul's outstretched hand, hoisting his teammate to him. Poul turned to do the same for Sims.

Braley, Bigg, and Sarah stood waiting. "Let's move," Braley said. "Poul, back up front with Phillip."

No sooner had that been said than Bigg interrupted. "More vehicles coming. Sleds. They're running along the side of the canal." Bigg pointed down the canal to their left. "Other side of Mons Alpha looks like I've got vehicles and dismounts on overland routes out of the canals, too. They've gotta take a zig-zag path, but if they make it to the plains they can run us down."

Kel looked down the canal, and increased the magnification. Somewhere at the far edge of the horizon, the air above stirred.

He brought up the feed from Bigg's eye in the sky. Small dark rectangles and masses of gray specks kept moving toward them from both directions.

"Fire mission," Bigg said. "Poul, help me with the target feed."

"Rog," Poul replied. A holo opened before Poul as he manipulated cursors over the live topo from the drone.

"Sending," Bigg said.

Flash. Bodies hurtled in the air. An expanding foam pillow cloud of dirt propelled, then enveloped the flying Savages in its cushion as they disappeared in the maelstrom. The funnel clouds rising on the horizon of the destroyed city mesmerized him, his awe further augmented by the simultaneous spectacle of the strikes in his HUD. Three rods followed the first, walking down the line of the advancing horde. It was surreal to watch the strikes from above, the impacts of the deadly hail and its cataclysm, followed by the delay of the bass echo welling from the kinetic pounding just beyond view. Thunder. Rolling from the ocean hidden behind the skyscrapers. For the moment he experienced life from a celestial vantage, marveling how clear the events were when seen from this supernatural perspective. He wanted it to be like this always. To see his life from all angles.

Kel turned his attention to the other feed where similar strikes created havoc on the masses detouring Mons Alpha. Their pursuers halted and dispersed, moving in every direction except forward. They'd broken the charge.

"I'm saving what she's got left for the mountain. Time to hoof it," Bigg said.

"Best pace to the rally point," Braley said. "I've got a channel open to the *Blackie*. She should be in range any minute."

They ran. After a few minutes, Kel saw Sarah slow. "Hold up, Bertie. Take Sarah piggyback." Kel did not wait for a response from their scientist. He scooped her up off her feet. Bertie trotted over. Kel plopped her on Bertie's back in front of the blaster mount. "Go," he said as he anachronistically slapped the DOGR's rump. Kel resumed his run.

The plain ahead gave rise to the same mesas they'd been on previously, the cursor driving them toward a canyon. Phillip and Poul were the first to reach the canyon mouth and slowed to a trot as they entered. The rest of the team passed through, Bertie and Sarah lagging behind.

Bertie pulled to a stop and Sarah slid off his back.

"Thanks, Bertie," she gasped.

"A pleasure to serve, miss." Bertie did an about-face and scanned behind them. "Nice day for a jog... Contact. Aerial. Five hundred meters." Bertie's blaster fired.

Kel strained to see anything in the skies behind them. "What do you have?"

"Drone. EM emission positive for Savage." Bertie fired again. "It's evading. I'm on it." Bertie leaped away out of the canyon and back toward the plain.

"Braley, we have a drone chasing us. Bertie's on it. Says it's Savage."

Bigg spoke. "I've got the *Blackie* on L-comm. They're suborbital and taking a nap of the earth approach from the dark side. Five minutes. We have to move. Strike for our LZ. Now."

Kel watched the plain for sign of Bertie. The AI was out of sight, but blaster fire rose into the air from a small depression revealing his location. "Bertie, let's go." Another bolt fired skyward. A tiny puff and flash of detonation appeared in the sky above. Bertie pranced lightly and triumphantly out of the bowl.

"Got him, boss. Bit erratic there for a min—"

The desert plain in front of Kel boiled and ignited. Mirage lifted off the surface and a cloud of red filled the air. Kel threw himself backward into the canyon. His skin cooked and he howled. He frantically shuffled to crab-walk away, until his arms and legs collapsed. Just as quickly, the white pain was gone. He blacked out.

Kel found himself on his back, his skin wet in his armor. Voices filled his bucket. Incomprehensible. Then, arms reached down, lifting him to his feet.

"Kel, what happened?" He could hear again. It was Sims.

"They're on us."

20

"What happened?" Bigg shouted.

Kel stumbled with Sims to the waiting team. "They're on us. The Savages. They've got our grid. Bertie brought their drone down, but not fast enough. Bertie, do you hear me?"

"Bert's bought it, boss," Phillip said. "He delayed the brutes, but he's gone. Time we get cracking if we don't want the same."

"We can't wait," Braley said. "Hit the mountain."

Kel's skin burned. He ignored the sting as he urged the annihilation of the mountain. He felt a kinship with the ancient barbarians of Earth. They feared what they didn't understand. What they didn't understand, they hated. And what they hated, they destroyed. He hated the giant glowing device and its secrets he would never comprehend. Understanding didn't matter.

He only wanted it dead.

The mountain remained. Resolute and defiant.

"Bigg, rain hell on it," Sims begged. "If it cracks the moon, it doesn't matter now."

"I'm sending!" Bigg shot back. "Nothing's happening."

"Is it the Savages?" Poul asked. "I'm trying, too. I get a confirmation, it's..."

"It's not the Savages," Bigg said. "See?"

Kel checked the link. An error light blinked.

"No!" Poul exclaimed. "Mechanical failure? You gotta be kiddin' me."

"Move out," Braley yelled. "Beacons on, everyone. Poul, get us to that LZ."

Sarah sank to the ground like a beast of burden that had carried its last load before refusing to rise again. "Sarah!" he yelled. This was no time to quit. "Sarah, we've got to move. Get up," Kel said with exasperation as he bent to jerk her to her feet.

"Don't you see?" She looked up at Kel. "They can fry or freeze everything around us. They've got our location close enough. They're probably powering up for another strike now. They send another drone or just choose a wide grid around where the ship lands, and that's it. Cinder or icicle, take your pick. We can't bring the *Blackie* to us. It's not fair to them."

Travelers were inspired by new vistas and the hope to see turquoise waters lick a distant shore. Legionnaires were inspired by duty and the hope to see their honor made material through action. Even with one's head removed, a warrior should be able to do one more useful thing before dying. Sarah was right. Bringing the Talon in would be a bonfire in the night, marking the Savages' next strike for them as efficiently as if they bounced them a grid.

Poul froze his move to lead them to the LZ. "We can't bring the bird in."

Sarah's assessment was true. So, it was time for them to do that last useful thing.

Everyone looked to Braley. Some things needed no discussion. "Blackbird," he said, "this is Able Phantom. Wave off, do not approach—"

Kel's bucket buzzed.

"Diagnostic complete. Status optimal." It was the MkIV! Kel had been the last to challenge it. It made its presence known like a corpse risen at a wake.

"Braley! The Mark-four's up and functional! I just got an interrogation response. Blow it!"

Without hesitation Braley called, "Blackbird, ground yourself. Nuclear explosion inbound. Say again, ground yourself immediately. *Bigg, do it!*"

Bigg spoke with purpose. "Mark-four. Authentication for release. Immediate deployment. Cosmic-seven-eight-three-Quasar. Initiate!"

Kel pushed Sarah down and lay on top of her. He brought his arms over his bucket as the world around him came apart. For a moment he touched the violent sun. Through eyelids squeezed shut, the flash overwhelmed his retina. Then, darkness again. The pressure wave advanced, then receded. His sight returned. He rolled off Sarah and lay next to her as he listened to the chatter over the team channel. Bigg's voice was first.

"Everyone okay?"

"Two Mark-fours," Poul said, rolling to his back. "Two nukes in as many months. That's gotta be a record. We're going to be legends."

Sims sighed. "First we've got live to tell the tale. Good here, Bigg."

"We're not even ten klicks away. What kind of dose are we receiving?" Braley asked.

Kel sat up. "Give me a minute, checking now." He brought up the detector readout in his bucket. "We should be good, but we don't want to hang around here forever. Did everyone's rad-gel deploy in their armor?"

"Oh! Uh, yeah," Poul said. "Rad-gel. Forgot about that. Thought I was wet for a different reason."

"Able Phantom, Able Phantom, this is Blackbird. Do you copy?"

Braley responded for them. "We've got you, Blackbird. We're still here."

"Good to hear. We're grounded thirty clicks out from your last location. We're having trouble reading your beacons. Are we cleared to approach for retrieval?" L-comm was shielded from EMP. The sideband they used for communication with their aviation support wasn't as protected. That meant the ship's electronics would also have difficulty reading their personal identifiers.

"Roger, Blackbird. Look for our phased transponder. LZ is cold. No hostiles anticipated at this time, how copy?"

"Good copy. Going airborne now. Will identify marker. ETA five minutes."

"Roger." Braley broke transmission with the aviators. "Let's get up on this mesa and drop the strobe. Our ride will be here soon."

Poul led. "This way. Everyone ready to move? Sarah, it's a shallow grade from this side to up top. Your last hump."

Sarah chuckled. "Thanks, Poul. I'll make it. Wouldn't want to miss the view we're going to have."

Cresting the mesa, Kel looked back at the city. Debris filled the air and the massive nuclear cloud hung in place, the mushroom a shock of white against the backdrop of swirling colors of the planetary body they circled. Debris rained down around them and plinked off their armor.

"Strobe out," Poul said. The fist-sized beacon pulsed a multi-band light and a microwave transmission, a visible guide with tight-beam signal that focused its direction after challenge by the searcher.

Standing beside Kel, Sims pointed at the cloud, now settling lower. "I'd say that ought to do it. I reckon that brought us some breathing room."

Kel zoomed in to see what was left of the city. Through the haze the Savage-built mountain was gone.

"Why'd the Mark-Four come back up after all this time?" Sims asked.

"I thought about that. Everything's rated for deep space use," Kel said.

Sarah joined in. "The Savage device raised the entropy around the robot to freeze it, but absolute zero's a theoretical. Deep space is only a few degrees above that. The sudden temperature differential must have just temporarily overcome the operating parameters for its solid state brain. With enough time, the temp increased and it came back online. Your Mark-Four must not have the liquid core processor of a smart AI like Phillip and Bertie. That kind of flash freeze would've damaged a cellular processor just like biologic tissue. Had they been hit, it would've been lights out for good."

"Incoming," Poul said.

The sleek stealth ship approached.

"Able Phantom, we identify your beacon. Touchdown in one minute." Captain Wurtz's voice was comforting. Kel pictured the co-pilot, Lieutenant Vreeland. Did she paint her lips for him today? He hadn't thought about her in days. Would he feel the curious longing for her again once on board, now that his existential ponderings were finished? His thoughts were interrupted by the sound of the crew chief.

"We're going to have you enter by the port-aft jump door," came Chief Darmond's voice. "I have a decon area sealed off over the tailgate ramp. Anyone need immediate medical attention?"

Kel answered. "Negative, Blackbird. We can all stay sealed in decon."

"Roger. Just grab some deck. When we're in orbit, we'll do several cycles of scrub and vent until you're clean. Then we'll open up the pax compartment."

"Understand all. Standing by," Kel replied. "The crew chief's sealed off part of the bay for decon from any residual radioactive material before we can move into the rest of the ship. Don't pop buckets until I tell you it's safe." He was saying it mainly for Sarah's benefit. The team all knew the routine.

"Here she comes now," Bigg said.

The stealth ship suddenly appeared, a massive presence from a few meters above the ground, then made a slow turn in hover to touch down on the mesa. The rear door opened and a set of short stairs extended.

"Hustle." Bigg jogged to the aircraft and motioned the team past him and up into the blackbird.

Kel turned to see Phillip trotting in last position. "Up you go, Phillip. Right behind you."

"Thank you, kind sir," Phillip replied as he took a single hop to clear the ground and land inside the ship. Bigg tapped Kel on the shoulder to send him through.

"Last man. Flight, we're all accounted for," Bigg said.

"Roger," Lieutenant Vreeland said. "Hug deck, guys. Going orbital. Hang on."

The crew had enabled the full counter inertial field for their escape. Even so, gravity pushed into them with the force of a giant kneeling on their chests. Phillip sat silent, his eight legs tucked underneath.

"Phillip," Kel said gently.

The large square head turned.

"Here, boss. Wot's up?"

"Phillip," Kel hesitated. "I'm sorry about Bertie." While the two DOGR bots were artificial intellects, Kel wasn't sure what to expect. He'd had limited contact with AIs who had their level of freedom before. He'd come to think of both DOGRs as being sentient and very much a part of the team. Bertie was a lost comrade. "Bertie saved us all by tracking down and destroying that Savage drone. He kept them from getting a better bead on our location. He saved all our lives, I'm certain of it."

"You bet, boss. He did a smashing job. He'll be sorry he missed the last, though. Having that Mark-four go off was jolly satisfying. I'll fill him in later."

Kel frowned and canted his head in puzzlement. "You'll tell him... later?"

The AI made a chortle. "Oh, sorry. You probably don't know. I've got Bertie with me right here," the AI jutted its chin toward its back in a very human-like gesture. "We're in constant communication. Always having a chat, you know? We keep a real-time backup of each other. No worries. When I get back to depot, they'll put his base personality into a new colloid matrix core and I'll top off the rest. He'll have to take my viewpoint on everything that happened after he bit the dust, but he won't mind. No sir, don't you worry, ole Bertie will be back on the job in no time."

Poul chuckled. "Phillip, that's great. I'm glad to hear it. I'd like you guys to stick around. You're real members of the team."

"Thank you kindly, boss. We're pretty fond of you lot, too. Bertie and I was just talking 'bout how much we'd like to cobber around with you gents some more."

"Hey, Phillip?" Sims asked. "If you download to each other, what would've happened if you'd gotten the magic bullet back there, too?"

Phillip paused. "Oh. Well. 'Spose it's best not to think about things like that, boss. When it's your time, it's your time, and all that. No sense getting spun up about things you can't control."

After three cycles of decontamination and venting, Kel checked every surface of the compartmentalized space around them. "Chief Darmond, we're clear. Zero residual detected."

"Roger," she said. "Retracting bulkhead now."

The barrier retracted away into the ceiling to reveal the cramped passenger bay where Chief Darmond and Lieutenant Vreeland waited by the forward hatch. Kel popped his lid and stepped aside to make room for the rest of the team to spread out into the bay. Lieutenant Vreeland's beautiful face was marred by a grimace.

"Wow. Get a little sun there, Kel?" Poul said.

"What?" he said as he turned to his teammate.

"Your face is bright red, man. Your radiation immuno wear off?"

Kel touched his face. It had felt like he'd been on fire when the Savages' last strike hit. Sarah moved to look at him. "You're burned. That energy discharge would've fried you had you been any closer to its epicenter." Being flash cooked was not a feeling Kel would forget.

Poul plopped into a jump seat along the fuselage. The bay was much more spacious than it had been on in their way into the system full of their gear. "I need a break."

"Don't get too comfortable. We're on our way to rendezvous with the *Lord Nelson*," the co-pilot said. Kel knew the *Nelson* was an Ohio-class heavy cruiser. The biggest.

"Why is there a heavy cruiser here?" Braley asked.

The aviator smiled. "They don't tell me much, but I think it's safe to say that not long after we departed for Proteus, this mission got some extra attention. After your last sitrep we were tight-beamed by the *Avenger.* This mission's been placed under the control of the Republic Forces with Fleet Admiral Sobieski in command. There's a heavy battle group in system with the *Nelson* as the admiral's flagship. The admiral is awaiting your arrival."

Kel looked back at the rest of the team. Poul grunted. "That's great. So *now* they're going to land an expeditionary assault force? Could have saved us the trouble."

"*You.*"

Patrick was being escorted through the hatch by Chief Lopez. "Look who just got out of the Medcomp," the Navy chief said. "He insisted on seeing you." Patrick tore himself away from Chief Lopez's steadying grip.

"You'll wish that you'd died on that moon. Life on a prison planet isn't half the punishment you deserve," the man said, swaying, his thinning red hair standing out against his blanched skin.

"Been saving that speech up for us, buddy?" Sims said with a short chuckle.

"Sarah," he snarled, pointing at the scientist. "Remove yourself from the vicinity of these criminals immediately. You are detained as well until I debrief you to determine your complicity and whether you've breached security for this mission."

Kel was about to speak when Sarah stepped past him.

"Know what, Patrick? I don't think anyone cares about your imaginary authority."

The sickly man flushed red with rage as he shoved a finger in her face. "You know what I can do to—"

Sarah's fist rocketed toward Patrick's mouth, catching him in the jaw. His head snapped back. Blood went flinging into the air with a pearly white tooth. An exclamation point of scarlet and white.

Poul shouted, "No, Sarah! Not in armor! You'll kill him!"

It was too late. Patrick crumpled onto the deck.

Kel pushed around Sarah to see Patrick in a heap, his back against the forward bulkhead. Chief Lopez was already kneeling beside the injured man. Kel reached for Patrick's head to examine it but was cut off by the chief.

"He's fine. That mouth will stay shut for a while. Guess who's going right back into the medcomp? One of you guys want to give me a hand?"

"I didn't see a thing," Lieutenant Vreeland said as she did an about-face to leave the compartment.

"I've got him, Chief," Poul offered. "Lead the way."

Kel heard a snicker. It was Bigg. Braley stood with his lips pursed, suppressing his thoughts.

"*That* goes on the top ten list of the greatest things I have ever witnessed. Simply stellar." Sims patted Sarah on the back.

"We're all lucky you didn't kill him," Kel said. "Striking a naked opponent in armor usually results in serious injury or death."

The woman shrugged. "I was a little out of control, but I had enough sense to have the power augment off. I think I've heard about all I ever want to hear from *Mister* Patrick."

Twenty minutes after docking with the *Nelson* they still sat in the landing bay as the decontamination of the *Blackie*'s hull continued. "We're clean," Captain Wurtz's voice came over the comm. "Disembarking will commence in a moment. Not sure what our next ride will be, back with the *Avenger* or another cruiser, so I wanted to take the opportunity before you special operators all disappear into thin air. I speak for the whole crew when I say it was an honor to have you on our ship. It was our pleasure to serve."

"The honor was ours, Captain," Braley said into the compartment. "You have our admiration and our thanks. Let's do it again soon, just not real soon."

Kel heard the feminine laugh of their co-pilot join the captain's through the comm. "Roger that."

"Hey, buckets on," Bigg said. "Incoming."

Kel put his lid on to catch the voice over L-comm. He knew whose it was immediately.

Sergeant Major Nail continued, "... so look out. There're some big wigs waiting. Don't be surprised."

"Nail's here," Poul said on the team channel. "When'd he show up?"

"Reckon we'll find out," Sims said. The tailgate lowered slowly; the light and noise of Navy life filled the bay.

"All right," Bigg said. "Let's be on our best behavior. It's great to be alive and everything, but there's still plenty of opportunity for us to end up in cuffs. Let Braley do all the talking."

"Rog," Kel said in unison with the others. As they strode off, Kel turned to look back at the ship. Lieutenant Vreeland stood in the bay. She waved to Kel. Kel raised a hand in response.

"What's the matter, hero? Miss your moment?" Sims asked with a laugh from Kel's side.

"You're a killer, man. What would you do with a girlfriend anyway?" Poul stood by his other side and pulled Kel back into their formation and started walking again. "You never got the nerve to chat her up, huh?"

"Nah," Kel deflected. "It wasn't like that."

"That's okay, brother." Sims said. "Better luck next time."

Kel continued. "No. I mean it. It wasn't that I didn't have the opportunity. I just didn't know that I wanted to. Not really. Before we dropped, I thought about what life might be like if it was, you know, different. If I had someone like her. But what if... that drop was the last, you know? Even when I told myself I was going to let her know I was interested, another part of me resisted. How would that be fair to her? Doing what we do. Anyway, it's done now. I'm just ready to get on with it. You know, time for us to get spun up again."

"That's the Kel I know and love," Sims said. "Not an hour since we nuked a city and already thinking about his next opportunity to KTF."

"I used to think about it," Poul added as they walked. "About what life would be like if I wasn't doing this. And about the brothers we've lost. And could it be one of us next. Now it just seems like it happens to other guys. Not us. Not Team Three."

Bigg broke into their private channel. "Heads up, Three. Eyes forward."

By the flight operations center was a reception committee. Nail was easy to pick out in his all-black armor, his bucket on. Next to him stood Colonel Hartenstein, his bucket under his arm. Next to him stood another Legion figure in armor, his bucket also off. Kel got a closer look. It was Legion Commander General Steiner, and next to him a short woman wearing the rank of a full admiral. Admiral Sobieski, Kel assumed.

Big wigs twelve o'clock!

High backed chairs rimmed the conference table of the admiral's ready room, the dark grain of the exotic wood standing out against the light leather seats. Natural elements giving the room a hint of luxury appropriate for a fleet commander. Behind the admiral's desk a view screen was currently fixed on the naval battle group, the tiny Savage moon caught in the multi-colored albedo of the gas giant behind it. Sarah was answering questions on her assessment of the Savage culture.

"No, Admiral. There's no question as to the heredity of the culture on that moon. It fits all known Savage culture descriptions. The last Savage we interviewed confirmed it to my satisfaction. Moreover, the tech we witnessed unquestionably represents a threat until it can be further studied. If any of it's recoverable, that is."

"Your acquisition, Doctor?" General Steiner asked from her left. "Will it be enough to test the validity of that hypothesis?"

It's a little more than a hypothetical threat, General, Kel thought, miffed. *Nearly killed us all.*

Sarah shrugged. "I believe the Section will be spending years trying to answer that question."

'The Section'? Kel wondered. *Sarah admitted she works on evaluating unknown tech. Was that the name of her secret research facility, 'The Section'? Who runs it?*

"Captain, anything further to add?" Admiral Sobieski asked. Braley sat nearest the head of the table by the flag officers. Everyone's buckets sat on the table in front of them. There would be no private L-comm chatter during the meeting.

"No, ma'am. We concur. Proteus Four-Three is a Savage planet with threat-level tech."

Admiral Sobieski addressed Team Three. "There will be a thorough investigation. For right now, the threat has been established to our satisfaction. I hold the authority and while your consensus is important to me, the decision is mine alone." Kel though he saw a nod of approval from Colonel Hartenstein.

"Are there any dissenting opinions based on what we've heard?" No one spoke. The stern woman looked to the rear admiral by her side. "I'm authorizing the strike. The order is given. Please see that it is carried out."

The man stood. "Yes, Admiral." And turned to leave the room.

Admiral Sobieski rose and the table took the cue to do the same. She gestured toward the wall viewer. "Has anyone ever witnessed a crustbuster?" Kel joined the rest of the team to stand in front of the huge viewer. It looked very much like an actual window. Admiral Sobieski's height did not diminish her gravitas. He and the other operators lined up to gaze over the diminutive officer's head. Kel turned and pulled the hesitant Sarah forward into their formation.

"One minute, Admiral," the voice came over the ready room's comm.

The admiral continued. "The Savage Wars raged for a millennium. Humanity was nearly extinguished by the twisted aberrancy that was the Savage legacy."

The lead battle cruiser of the formation launched a missile. The projectile covered the distance to the moon in the blink of an eye, leaving a blue trail in Kel's retina for only a moment. The view magnified to show the moon.

The missile struck the dark surface. Kel wasn't sure what to expect. A huge jet of ice and gas shot into the atmosphere, the blast radiating outward from the impact in a growing cloud. It kept expanding into a circle, spreading without pause with the force of a boulder rolling downhill, gaining momentum as it went. The effect rolled across the surface, engulfing the moon's dark face and crossing the terminator into light. Behind the effect starting back at the missile's impact the next wave began. The surface billowed and lifted, traveling in a second unrelenting wave out across the moon. Now the entire globe seemed to oscillate. His eyes must still be strained from the Savage attack, because the impossible happened. The moon shook. Then collapsed. The moon shrank, condensing, diminishing, until after another moment, it stilled. The moon compressed to half its former size. The blank sphere floated in space. The glow from the volcanoes was gone.

"The Savage Wars have been over for some time." The admiral turned away from the viewer to look back at the team. Her eyes stopped at Kel. "Let's all hope these were the last of them still out there."

They sat with their guests in the cramped lounge of the Legion module. The *Avenger* was on course to Victrix. His mind strayed during the conversation to which he was currently a listener, not a participant. Kel had seen the *Blackie* in the port flight bay. He reexamined his deliberations about the raven haired lieutenant and reversed himself yet again. It's like Bigg said, what could it hurt? She was in a dangerous profession herself. Maybe in the next few days he would get that chance to keep the small promise he'd made to himself.

He thought about the other woman he'd come to know better.

Sarah had departed with the *Nelson*. The whole team met to wish her a safe journey on their last morning together. Poul had been the first to try to hug her goodbye. Her discomfort was so obvious that Kel did not attempt the same and instead when it was his turn, took her hand in his.

"You're a strong and capable person, Sarah. I'm proud to have had you with us. You were right. We did need you."

She smiled and met his eyes. "Thank you, Kel. Thanks, all of you. I'll never forget what you did for me, too."

Kel wondered if he would ever see her again or if she would become like so many people in his life—a presence he would always feel, a face he would never see again. Now he looked around the room. The momentary sadness of a new friend's departure left him. He was with his brothers. There was nowhere else he wanted to be. No one else he wanted to be with.

Kel snapped out of his reverie as the colonel continued.

"I don't know that we'll ever have full accountability of how this operation came to be, but I'm confident that we've done what we could to shut down the aegis of its proponents."

"Sir, how did you know?" Bigg asked.

"That it was an illegal operation? I didn't, but I had a strong suspicion."

"The colonel never took any of this on faith," Nail said. "He used his back channel to General Steiner. We were on the first FTL to Legion HQ right after the brief-back. The general heard him out and agreed that it didn't make sense. A few conference calls later, the full House of Reason and Senate called a crisis and authorized the Navy battle group to intervene with its full authority."

"Sir," Braley asked. "Didn't you take quite a chance? If the general had disagreed, had called you on compromising a covert mission..."

The colonel put up his hand. "We all talk about prison planets too much. I've only ever known one individual to get that sentence, and it was deserved. I know you, Captain Yost, as I know all of you. None of you would hesitate to do the right thing, regardless of the consequences. I couldn't be your commander unless I was willing to do the same."

Kel considered the colonel's example. He felt humbled, but mainly glad. It wasn't just doing an end-run around the civilian command authority to question the validity of the mission that they were all grateful for. If they had been forced to go on the Savage mission without the OSP and the MkIV, they would not be alive. They were alive because their commander fought for them. He did not hesitate to do the right thing, to believe what the men on the ground told him.

"What's going to happen to Patrick?" Poul asked. They'd watched him be led away in enerchains by Justice Directorate agents from Liberinthine.

The colonel sighed. "We can hope that he gets justice." Kel kept his doubts to himself.

"What do you think happened, sir?" Sims asked. "What was the sequence of events?"

"I guess that depends on how far back you want to go." The colonel remained silent for another moment. "I have my theory, but this goes no farther, Three. Agreed?"

Kel thought that went without saying but replied with the rest of the team in the affirmative.

"What we saw on Proteus Three decades ago sparked the interest of some faction or entity controlled by the Senate and House of Reason. We saw the Savages building a massive project—the black mountain. Someone made a decision to let the Savages finish their 'great work,' and to keep the knowledge of the Proteus moon classified.

"Three decades later, that entity decided it was time to return to evaluate whether that tech had come to fruition or not, and sent you in to help exploit and recover it. To what end and by whom, I don't know. This 'Section' that the young scientist works for examining Savage and supposedly ancient alien tech—it has to be some black entity under the Senate or RI."

Kel knew the colonel must be correct. Other forces more secret than Dark Ops were in play. It was just like the admiral's statement about the Savage Wars. How she'd met Kel's eyes for dramatic effect. It was theater. Political expediency. Just as there would always be the potential of more Savages somewhere in the dark, there would always be buried secrets in the Republic.

"It doesn't seem that the Planetary Security Council or the House of Reason as a whole knew of this mission. The general and I were met with incredulity that seemed genuine on the part of Senator VanderLoot."

Kel wondered how anyone could accurately evaluate the sincerity of a pol. How does one judge the intention of a resting snake?

"That VanderBlanc character who showed up from the Grand Senator's office, claiming command authority for this operation on behalf of the Senate? I don't know if he's a rogue actor or is truly acting on behalf of the Grand Senator. What I do know is that he couldn't be running this thing alone. This whole operation was executed as part of a conspiracy that has obviously existed for decades.

"Whether any subsequent investigation truly wants to discover that or not, my guess is they'll simply hang Patrick out to dry for it like a patsy. I suppose we'll just have to wait and see."

It seemed like a reasonable theory.

Sims shook his head. "Sir, I'm still not sure why we were there or what we accomplished." Kel looked over at his friend sitting cross-legged on the floor. Sims was normally stoic, the definition of a true believer. It had struck Kel as being out of character for Sims to have voiced doubts about the mission earlier. That he was doing so now in front of the colonel amazed him.

The colonel smiled. "Welcome to Dark Ops, Sergeant Sims."

Everyone laughed.

"No, Sergeant," the colonel said. "I apologize. I wasn't trying to be glib with you. What we experienced was a flaw in our system of oversight for covert activities. The command authority that governs Dark Ops is at times nebulous.

"We know there are other black activities run by the Republic. General Rex's last mission was an effort to prevent Dark Ops from becoming one of the same—that doesn't leave this room. DO is Legion... but we aren't the only ones out there. We don't know precisely who the others are or what their function is, but this seems to be evidence that they may be operating outside of oversight—illegally. Fully deniable. Of course, the House of Reason has almost unlimited power to determine what's legal and what constitutes an authorized activity, so...

"To answer your question, Sergeant Sims, for me it's simple. What I think you accomplished was this—you held fealty to the Legion, and to those who came before you. You did what I could not; you finished the mission on Proteus. You ended the Savage threat from ever leaving that moon. And you've given me peace."

EPILOGUE

Breaks were conundrums to Kel. A puzzle he inherited. His father hated their annual vacations. His mother fretted how after the second day of the family outing, her husband became restless and irritable rather than relaxed and at greater ease, shedding his responsibilities for what was a very short time out of the year. His father always said how much he needed the break. But there he was, barely into their vacation, and already acting as though he didn't want to be there. The contrariness of it all made Kel uneasy as a child. Now he could relate.

Being back on Victrix was hardly a vacation, but it was a break. One he told himself he needed after the last few months of sustained operations. They worked in the team room. There was equipment to be accounted for and replaced, training to be refreshed, rest to be taken. Sleeping in his own quarters every night was a welcome change, but only for the quiet. The apartment wasn't a home, he was so rarely there.

The administrative work was crushing. They had to complete the debrief of the mission on Cassell and answer hundreds of interrogatories from multiple agencies about the Mercian Underground and their subsequent penetration into South Andalusia. It seemed every few days their reports and interviews simply sparked a logarithmic explosion of further questions. It was exhausting.

Soon he felt as he knew his father had. He knew his father loved them, but he was a man always torn between worlds. The world of the self and the world of duty. Was he that way because he'd been a legionnaire? Had he been a legionnaire because he was that way? It was time for Kel to get back to his real life. What he did now was a necessary part of that. But his calling was to be... *out there.*

One bright spot was the news that Phillip and Bertie would be reassigned out of depot to Dark Ops. Three's recommendation to include the Autonomous Combat Multipliers on Dark Ops missions was met with resounding acceptance. They all hoped the pair would be assigned to Team Three permanently. Poul had started to do a pretty good imitation of the AIs' accent. Kel admitted that his own needed work.

One morning after a team workout, Kel entered the team room. He was looking forward to a day of no interviews or reports to write. He had the morning planned to update everyone's medical records and nano-immunizations. If he could get that accomplished, he could look forward to spending the next several days with Poul on the sniper range without distraction. He was already thinking about his gear layout when his link buzzed. It was from Bigg.

Kel. We need you in the Command Group.

Kel groaned. "I'll be back, guys," he said to Sims and Poul, busy at work in their own gear cages.

"Let me guess," Poul said. "Ops cell needs you. Got a solo mission brief for you. Nice having you with the team for the last few months, Kel."

"Nah," he said dismissively. "I don't have a clue what it's about, but it's probably not that. Bigg's calling me to the command group."

"Well, you heard the colonel," Sims said. "Prison planets are apparently not a significant threat. Whatever it is, don't worry."

"Thanks. I won't."

Kel made his way outside to cross the quadrangle to the command group building. He bounced up the stairs and through the double doors to find Braley and Bigg with Sergeant Major Nail in the foyer outside the colonel's office. The adjutant moved to the colonel's open door to knock briskly on the jamb.

"Send them in," came the gravelly voice. Nail stepped to the side and gestured for the three of them to enter. He followed and closed the door behind them. The colonel rose from his desk. Kel came to attention with his teammates.

"Please, gentlemen, be at ease. Sergeant Turner, won't you come have a seat? Gentlemen?"

What's this about? Kel didn't feel as though bad news was coming, but was curious about the circumstances. The other men all had subtle smiles. Clearly, this wasn't something to be concerned about. Kel sat in the offered chair as the colonel joined him, the other men sinking into the couch.

The colonel looked at Kel. "Sergeant Turner, your performance in Dark Ops has not escaped attention. This is an organization that demands the highest level of competence and proficiency. You've met that standard and exceeded it. In fact, there have been several incidents where your direct participation has been recognized as the sole determinant to mission success."

Oh no! Kel thought. *They're going to award me some kind of medal.* The colonel must have seen the dread on Kel's face.

"I'll come to the point. I'm offering you a direct commission to first lieutenant and the chance to eventually command a kill team. You've been recommended by your team leadership for higher levels of responsibility and authority on numerous occasions. This step is a natural progression for you that will be to the benefit of both the Legion and Dark Ops."

Kel was stunned. He looked to the men across from him. Braley beamed and nodded his encouragement. Nail gave him a thumbs up.

"I can't think of anyone more deserving, Kel," Bigg said.

Kel felt a lump in his throat. "Sir. Yes, sir. I'll do my best to follow your example and the example of the men in this room. Thank you, sir."

Kel stood as the colonel rose and felt the strong grip take his, hands slapping his back as his comrades joined in. "Very good, Lieutenant. There will be some admin necessities and I have some bars for you. We'll take care of that later. For now, finish up what you need to with the team."

The team! "Sir, does a promotion mean I have to leave Three?"

Nail said, "There's some things to work out, Lieutenant."

Lieutenant! he thought. *I'll never get used to that.*

"You'll also be buying for everyone at the Century Club tonight." Nail reminded him of the obligation that came with promotion. "But for right now, Team Three doesn't have to worry about much."

"Three is on a mandatory ninety-day refit," the colonel explained. "Unless the Republic goes to war, Team Three is on block leave starting next week. All of you, finish up critical tasks and then get lost. Lieutenant Turner, we'll have your promotion ceremony tomorrow. My adjutant will bounce you details. Thank you, gentlemen."

Kel came to attention, then followed the others out of the office. He closed the door behind him and walked out of the foyer into the main hall, trying to maintain his balance. He felt dizzy. *Did that just happen?*

Bigg and Braley waited for him to join them in the bright sunlight. As they walked across the quad, Kel remembered the other news they'd received. "Where're you going to go for three months, Kel?" Braley asked,

Kel thought. "I don't know. Maybe I'll just stay around here."

"Stay here? Are you crazy?" Bigg smacked him playfully on the back of the head.

"I have to do that while I still can," Bigg laughed. "No. You will absolutely get off Victrix for somewhere else."

But where? Kel had no desire to go back to Pthalo. His parents were dead and he had no other relatives. "I don't know. The only time I've taken leave in the five years I've been in DO is when my parents died. I don't know what to do or where to go."

Braley put his hand on Kel's shoulder as they walked. "It's okay, Kel. You'll figure it out."

As they walked up the stairs, Kel had an inspiration. The brief excitement was quickly replaced by trepidation. *Will they even remember me?*

Kel's grav container followed behind him as he moved across the concourse of Orion Station to the commercial

shipping port. His heart raced as he crossed the red line of the loading area and looked to the berths to find the gangway of the *Callie's Dream*. A small crowd stood at its entrance. His pace hastened as he found himself weaving through the traffic of passing sleds, straining to keep the sight of the Yomiuri family while not getting run over. He saw a break and quickened his pace. As he got closer, he could make out everyone's faces.

Caroline and Jim Yomiuri stood at the center of the group. Their son, Ochio, looking older and filled out. Their chief engineer, Yoshi, and his plump wife, Auntie Meiko—the *Callie*'s cook and wellspring of morale—stood among them. Her face broke into a wide smile as their eyes met, her arms crossing to hug herself. He recognized the other adults crowded around, the children nestled in between. In the back he saw Tara, half hiding behind the family, her face veiled by her hair.

Kel ran to Auntie Meiko's open arms and gave her a big hug. The women all came forward to hug him, the men slapping his shoulders and laughing. Everyone spoke at once, greeting him with welcomes and hellos.

He paused lastly in front of Caroline and Jim, shook the captain's hand and got a hug from Caroline. While he gave her a big squeeze, something swept over him. Its unfamiliarity shocked him. His chin quivered and tears blurred his vision. He saw images of the young urban guerilla Rolf's head snap forward as he was executed. He saw Pieter blasted off the combat grav sled in front of him. The nuclear cloud grew over the spaceport. His heart raced as he remembered running for his life out of the Savage city. So many other images came to him, overwhelming him.

"Kel, what is it, honey?" Caroline asked with concern as she studied his face. "Are you all right? Are you in trouble? Are you hurt?"

The questions made his tears fall harder. He was embarrassed. The last time he'd shed tears, his best friend had been killed. He ran his sleeve across his eyes.

"I'm fine, really. I'm—" he sucked in a breath. He tried to form the words, but wasn't sure himself why his elation had turned to such deep sadness. Kel had been in combat many times. The stress was nothing new to him. He'd been excited to the point of being overwhelmed at the prospect of seeing the Yomiuris. *Why am I crying?* The answer evaded him like a dream vanished with morning's first light. "I'm just so happy to see you." He took a few breaths and tried to collect himself. "I'm... I'm just so sorry."

Caroline looked at him, puzzled. "What do you have to be sorry about, dear?"

He blurted out. "I'm sorry I've been out of touch for this long." Kel thought about the family often and with longing. It was rare when he'd had the opportunity to send them a message to wish them well and could never include any details about himself. In the last year he had not sent them a single note. His regret burned.

"Oh, don't worry, Kel." Her own eyes shone with tears. "We were so happy to get your message. We've wondered about how you've been for so long."

This only made the sobs well up. He swallowed them down and stammered, "I... I was just afraid that you'd all forgotten me." His embarrassment grew with his revelation. It was as much a surprise to him to realize he had felt that way.

The captain put his hand on Kel's shoulder. His voice broke. "We could never forget you, Kel. Everything you did for us. You're a member of our family. We know how hard things are for you, what your life must be like. It's okay."

Kel tried to calm himself. His embarrassment grew as more tears fell down his face.

"Sweetheart," Caroline said as she took his face in her hands, "we could never forget you. We love you."

Kel wiped his face again. Caroline hugged him again, and everyone drew close. He felt Auntie Meiko rub his back and the children hug his legs.

"You're safe now, Kel," Auntie Meiko said as she also touched his face. "You're home."

From the shadows of the cargo bay across from the berth, a silent gray figure watched as the crowd pushed the legionnaire up the gangway and through the airlock. The nondescript man faded into the passing dock workers.

The subject displays all the personality traits and behaviors associated with other types of high-risk takers.

The man sat on the bed of the hotel room, typing on the holo keyboard.

Observing the subject in a variety of situations, he maintains his hypervigilance, though well-concealed and subdued, as part of his tradecraft and bearing at all times. This is as much a professional necessity as it is a sign of stress.

The subject's exposure to constant physical danger and proximity to situations with the potential for sudden violence has not resulted in any indication of instability. His continued demonstration of advanced problem-solving ability and his adaptation to cope with his changing environment is superior, and has not degraded despite the cu-mulative stressors he has experienced.

What is clear is that like many of the type, he has reached an age where his need to experience spiritual growth and further develop his human-ity has been realized, and is causing him inter-nal conflict. The bond that he has formed with an adoptive surrogate family has given the subject an outlet for his need to develop more completely as an emotional being.

This potential weakness can be exploited.

Based on my observations, my recommendation is to leverage this relationship. The need to insert an operative to forge an exploitable weakness does not appear to be a necessary allocation of assets. The avenue for disruption and control is already present to a high degree of certainty.

They sat with Kel at the center of the group, filling the wardroom. Kel had a child on each knee, bouncing them as he listened to everyone tell stories about the chil-dren and their accomplishments. Auntie Meiko pushed a warm kaff mug into his hand and stood behind him as she rubbed his back again. Jim's brother Tan was telling a story about the confusion of a merchant to whom they had delivered not the ten pallets of Meridian olives he was expecting, but a hundred.

"He finally resigned himself to the fact that the error was his. The look on his face when he said, 'I guess we'll be figuring out how to sell olives to koobs,' was priceless!"

Kel took in the room. Everyone smiled and laughed as Auntie Meiko brought out trays of sandwiches and snacks. Something suddenly struck Kel. It was a distant memory, one recovered from the empty bin of his mental files.

As a child, his mother always sang as she worked in the kitchen of their small home on Pthalo. Kel had learned to tune her out as he read or played, waiting for his father to return home from work. Now, the song she most often sang came into his consciousness, just as if she were with them in the next room.

"Oh sorrow, be banished,
Joy sent from above!
A family's the blessing
Sent to us in love.
A father and mother
And children are found
To make a home happy,
In endless abound."

Laughter filled the galley. Tara sat across from him, her hair now brushed away from her face as she watched Kel, smiling brightly whenever he looked her way.

Sorrow be banished, indeed!

A smile spread across his face as he realized the truth.

I'm home!

KEL'S RULES FOR SUCCESS

1. All skillsets are important. Mastering your body and weapons is the most important.

2. Learn to recognize threats early by identifying the elements of intent, means, and opportunity. Some of them are cultural or species-specific. Study your opponent's culture.

3. Intent can be difficult to establish with alien species. Presence of a weapon and using it, however, is universal.

4. Verbal noncompliance is the most important pre-assaultive behavior. If the suspect is not following your commands, be ready for violence.

5. In all situations train to place the sights where they need to be and manipulate the trigger without moving the sights. Once you can do that, then learn to do *everything else*. Then come back to shooting. Because when it's time to shoot, that's all you should be doing. Shooting. When the time comes, the only thing that matters is putting shots where they need to go.

6. The mechanical offset of your aiming system is real. Know it and when you must apply it.

7. Medical skills are a warrior skillset. Everyone is a medic. You are the most important medical provider, especially if it's you who becomes injured.

8. Don't be a leader who yells. It's entertaining in a holo-vid but doesn't work in the real world.

9. Treat others as you want to be treated. When leading, try to be the type of leader you would want to follow. When following, try to show the leader the respect and cooperation you would hope to receive if you were the leader. You must know how to do both in the Legion.

10. Teach your subordinates what you wish you would've known at their stage.

11. If someone interrupts you three times in a conversation, stop talking to them. They are incapable of receiving information. Don't waste your time and theirs.

12. You can only have a rational conversation with a rational being.

13. Safety is the most important factor in all training.

14. Never make a drop without your primary weapons attached directly to your body or armor. Weapon containers frequently don't arrive the same place you do.

15. Of all marksmanship fundamentals, follow-through and calling your shot are the most important. They are the keys to progressing to the next level of performance.

16. Be your own best critic. Never accept praise that you've done a good job if you know you've done a bad one. Never accept criticism that you've done a bad job if you know you've done a good one.

17. If a commander insists you follow a bad plan, make your case for a better one. Give a concrete alternative that still accomplishes the intent of the mission. If you cannot change the plan, accomplish the mission in the best way you can to ensure safety of the team. If you succeed, you'll at least be alive to ask forgiveness.

18. No capability is disabling. Learn everything you can. "We'll never need to know that" is a weak excuse for failing to learn all you can when the opportunity presents.

19. Every job is important, and every person's profession is valuable. Appreciate competence in others.

20. Train your body daily wherever you are, however you can. Relying on a specific place or piece of equipment to train only leads to excuses not to train.

21. Weapons skills are a path to self-development.

22. Discipline is worthwhile for its own sake.

23. Take a day off once in a while.

24. The best way to be dangerous is to be superiorly fit.

25. Tolerate no behavior that sacrifices safety.

26. Speed by itself is not a valid tactic, technique, or procedure.

27. Sometimes the job is to put yourself in a position where you may die.

28. Don't take yourself too seriously. Try to find the humor in any situation. If it's not the appropriate time to share with anyone else, save it for later. The worst situations often create the funniest moments in life.

29. Think of the welfare of others first.

30. Always ask yourself what the right thing to do is. Then do it.

31. Overkill is underrated.

32. Anyone worth shooting once, is worth shooting twice.

33. The weapon-mounted white light is not an aiming device. It's an accessory sun. Use your sights.

34. It is acceptable to look to different role models for different attributes to emulate. Some excel at one thing above all others. No one excels at all things.

35. Take the most difficult technique and make it your favorite. Don't waste too much time practicing what you are already good at.

36. It is better to practice as many skills as you can for ten minutes each day, rather than one skill an hour weekly.

37. Action beats reaction.

38. Always keep your gear and weapons ready. Don't let your head hit the pillow without first ensuring your gear is maintained and serviceable and that your

weapons are in a ready state. Always assume your next call-out will be five minutes after you fall asleep.

39. Much training can be done by mental rehearsal. The mind doesn't know the difference between a repetition imagined well and a repetition performed. It is another way to build experience. However, the task must be pictured correctly or you build useless experience, even detrimental habits.

40. You must shoot regularly to be good.

41. You do not have to shoot massive quantities of blaster bolts each session to be good. Set a standard for yourself and meet it each session, then move on to something else. The Legion needs you competent in many things.

42. Always plan for a fail-safe breach. If you can't get in, you can't accomplish your mission.

43. Your job is to go in harm's way. There is no need to be anxious. If you aligned jump coils every day, would you be anxious using an autospanner? If your job was harvesting vat-grown protein, would you be anxious filtering off product? Anxiety is a form of fear. The basis of most fear is that you will not be able to perform when called upon. Train until everything you do is subconscious and routine. Make your performance accessible on demand.

44. Know how to recognize the situation when it is appropriate to ask the most vital question: *If not us, then who? If not now, then when?*

45. Time spent in rehearsal before a hit is time well spent. Continue to practice breachpoint procedures, basic shape negotiation with and without a partner, procedures in the room, up until the last minute. At the staging area draw on the duracrete with a holopen to create rooms and shapes. Don't sit waiting for the signal to assault. Continue your preparation.

46. When training, your first shot can be as good as your hundredth shot. The idea that you have to warm up to shoot well is a trick your mind plays on you. Train yourself to make every shot count from the first and don't accept mediocrity.

47. Practice doesn't make perfect. It makes permanent. Perfect practice makes perfect.

48. So-called *Big-Boy Rules* are nothing but an excuse for poor planning or preparation. Injuries in training or on an op resulting from poor planning and unnecessary risk-taking is unacceptable.

49. A big part of physical conditioning is learning how to deal with pain. Someone who quits when they feel pain is a detriment to the team. That is why the selection process to become a legionnaire is the way it is. It has been this way throughout the history of elite units.

50. Holo-vids that show the hero fighting hand-to-hand with multiple alien villains, falling off high structures only to leap up and run to the next fight, shooting with amazing accuracy without using his holo-sight or bucket—are all fantasy.

51. I've seen individuals much tougher than me get taken out of the fight by a twisted ankle or broken leg. It happens.

52. I've seen individuals I've thought were not as tough as me fight while incredibly injured.

53. Dehydration will degrade anyone's ability to process information. Their physical abilities deteriorate soon thereafter. Make yourself drink even when you don't feel thirsty.

54. Hand-to-hand training helps build aggression, but it is proficiency with weapons systems that lets us dominate the fight.

55. The bad guy has a say in when the fight is over.

56. Just because you shot at them, doesn't mean you hit them; just because you hit them, doesn't mean you hurt them; just because you hurt them, doesn't mean you killed them; just because you killed them, doesn't mean they're dead *right now*. The dead ones can kill you.

57. If the head is separated from the body, you can consider them dead. Except for Reptasaurians. They can still kill you, for a little while anyways.

58. Hot chow is good for morale.

59. When dealing with I-squared and guerilla forces, violations of discipline must sometimes be dealt with harshly. It is important that their own leaders enforce this discipline.

60. Aliens have alien minds. Do not forget that. Ever.

61. If mission success necessitates you must arrive at the objective with all personnel and equipment, infiltrate by walking there. It's the surest way to arrive with the entire force. Orbital freefall is sexy. It's not always the best way to get there.

62. Always have a backup.

63. The essence of marksmanship is that the target is you. When your mind is unfocused, the target is fuzzy. Your arms shake. The sights move. Looking at the target hoping that the shots will appear where you wish them to be does nothing to achieve the outcome you desire. Focus your mind to perform the fundamentals correctly; that will give you the results you desire. Only focusing on the steps of correct performance—not on the outcome desired—will lead to success. Thinking about the outcome means you're not thinking about the act you need to perform. Perform the act correctly. Let the outcome take care of itself.

64. Learn one thing well, and you can learn anything. What one man can do, another can. Desire is the most important determinant. Few people are truly born with natural ability.

65. Look for the similarities, not the differences when learning something new. If you can teach yourself to identify the underlying principles of how even one thing is done correctly and efficiently, you can learn virtually anything.

66. When using weapon systems with chemically-pro-pelled projectiles of less than about 12 mm in diam-eter, you must place your hits where they will do the most damage. That means making the threat bleed out rapidly or ruining their brain, wherever that may be. Knowing your enemy's anatomy is vital. Simply shooting at the center of mass is unlikely to cause rapid incapacitation in most beings. Humans have been known to remain deadly and in the fight even after being shot multiple times, even in highly vital areas. Blasters make the task much easier, but have their own limitations. Don't be attached to one type of weapon system.

67. Which weapon is best? What output in Joules or beam dispersion is optimal to produce incapacitation of a threat? I've always maintained that I prefer not to be shot in any part of my body with any type of weapon. Learn to use what you have and use it well. They can all be deadly in the right hands.

68. Be an observer of your environment as a predator would. Do it at all times.

69. Most good things in life wait on the other side of fear.

70. Fear is a natural emotion. It exists for a purpose, but that purpose is not to prevent you from doing what you need to do.

71. There are requirements and there are capabilities. When it comes to gear and weapons, not one item is best for all applications. We determine what is "best" depending on the requirements for the mission and the capabilities of the item. What we use in a particu-

lar instance may not be "best" for you in another context of use. Just because you've heard a rumor that
Dark Ops uses it, doesn't mean it's better than something you use.

72. Read daily.

73. Be mindful of your responsibility to develop others
and try to be generous with your time to teach others.
They'll be generous to teach you when you can learn
from them.

74. No one likes a know-it-all. Know when to shut up.

75. I can find an exception to every one of my rules.

ABOUT THE AUTHORS

DOC SPEARS is a veteran of the United States Army.

JASON ANSPACH & NICK COLE are the co-creators of Galaxy's edge. You can find out more about them and Galaxy's Edge by visiting www.GalaxysEdge.us or by joining the Galaxy's Edge Fan Club on Facebook.

Explore over 30+ Galaxy's Edge books and counting from the minds of Jason Anspach, Nick Cole, Doc Spears, Jonathan Yanez, Karen Traviss, and more.

HISTORY OF THE GALAXY

1ST ERA BOOKS

THE FALL OF EARTH

1ST ERA SUMMARY

The West has been devastated by epidemics, bio-terrorism, war, and famine. Asia has shut its borders to keep the threats at bay, and some with power and influence have already abandoned Earth. Now an escape route a century in the making – the Nomad mission – finally offers hope to a small town and a secret research centre hidden in a rural American backwater. Shrouded in lies and concealed even from the research centre's staff, Nomad is about to fulfil its long-dead founder's vision of preserving the best of humanity to forge a new future

2ND ERA SUMMARY

They were the Savages. Raiders from our distant past. Elites who left Earth to create tailor-made utopias aboard the massive lighthuggers that crawled through the darkness between the stars. But the people they left behind on a dying planet didn't perish in the dystopian nightmare the Savages had themselves created: they thrived, discovering faster-than-light technology and using it to colonize the galaxy ahead of the Savages, forming fantastic new civilizations that surpassed the wildest dreams of Old Earth.

HISTORY OF THE GALAXY

3RD ERA BOOKS
RISE OF THE REPUBLIC

3RD ERA SUMMARY

The Savage Wars are over but the struggle for power continues. Backed by the might of the Legion, the Republic seeks to establish a dominion of peace and prosperity amid a galaxy still reeling from over a millennia of war. Brushfire conflicts erupt across the edge as vicious warlords and craven demagogues seek to carve out their own kingdoms in the vacuum left by the defeated Savages. But the greatest threat to peace may be those in the House of Reason and Republic Senate seeking to reshape the galaxy in their own image.

4TH ERA SUMMARY

As the Legion fights wars on several fronts, the Republic that dispatches them to the edge of the galaxy also actively seeks to undermine them as political ambitions prove more important than lives. Tired and jaded legionnaires suffer the consequences of government appointed officers and their ruinous leadership. The fighting is never enough and soon a rebellion breaks out among the Mid-Core planets, consuming more souls and treasure. A far greater threat to the Republic hegemony comes from the shadowy edges of the galaxy as a man determined to become an emperor emerges from a long and secretive absence. It will take the sacrifice of the Legion to maintain freedom in a galaxy gone mad.

HISTORY OF THE GALAXY

5TH ERA SUMMARY

An empire defeated and with it the rot of corruption scoured from the Republic. Fighting a revolution to restore the order promised at the founding of the Republic was the easy part. Now the newly rebuilt Legion must deal with factions no less treacherous than the House of Reason while preparing itself for war against a foe no one could have imagined.

HONOR ROLL

We would like to give our most sincere thanks and recognition to those who supported the creation of *Galaxy's Edge: No Fail* by supporting us at GalaxysEdge.us.

Jordan Brann	Tommy Cutler
Ernest Brant	David Danz
Geoff Brisco	Alister Davidson
Raymond Brooks	Peter Davies
James Brown	Walter Davila
Jeremy Bruzdzinski	Ivy Davis
Marion Buehring	Nathan Davis
Matthew Buzek	Ron Deage
Daniel Cadwell	Tod Delaricheliere
Charles Calvey	Ryan Denniston
Van Cammack	Anerio Deorma
Chris Campbell	Douglas Deuel
Zachary Cantwell	Isaac Diamond
Brian Cave	Christopher DiNote
Shawn Cavitt	Matthew Dippel
Kris (Joryl) Chambers	Ellis Dobbins
David Chor	Gerald Donovan
Tyrone Chow	Ray Duck
Jonathan Clews	Cami Dutton
Beau Clifton	Virgil Dwyer
Alex Collins-Gauweiler	William Ely
Jerry Conard	Stephane Escrig
Michael Conn	Steven Feily
James Connolly	Meagan Ference
James Conyers	Adolfo Fernandez
Jonathan Copley	Ashley Finnigan
Robert Cosler	Kath Flohrs
Ryan Coulston	Jeremiah Flores
Andrew Craig	Steve Forrester
Adam Craig	Skyla Forster
Phil Culpepper	Timothy Foster
Ben Curcio	Bryant Fox
Thomas Cutler	Mark Franceschini

Elizabeth Gafford	Kyle Hetzer
David Gaither	Korrey Heyder
Christopher Gallo	Aaron Holden
Richard Gallo	Clint Holmes
Kyle Gannon	Charles Hood
Michael Gardner	Joshua Hopkins
Nick Gerlach	Tyson Hopkins
John Giorgis	Ian House
Johnny Glazebrooks	Ken Houseal
Justin Godfrey	Nathan Housley
Luis Gomez	Jeff Howard
Justin Gottwaltz	Nicholas Howser
Gordon Green	Kristie Hudson
Shawn Greene	Mike Hull
Erica Grenada	Donald Humpal
Preston Groogan	Bradley Huntoon
Brandon Handy	Wendy Jacobson
Erik Hansen	Paul Jarman
Greg Hanson	James Jeffers
Ian Harper	Tedman Jess
Jason Harris	Eric Jett
Jordan Harris	James Johnson
Revan Harris	Randolph Johnson
Matthew Hartmann	Scott Johnson
Adam Hartswick	Tyler Jones
Ronald Haulman	Paul Jones
Joshua Hayes	John Josendale
Adam Hazen	Wyatt Justice
Richard Heard	Ron Karroll
Colin Heavens	Cody Keaton
Jason Henderson	Noah Kelly
Jason Henderson	Jacob Kelly
Jonathan Herbst	Caleb Kenner

Daniel Kimm
Zachary Kinsman
Rhet Klaahsen
Jesse Klein
William Knapp
Marc Knapp
Travis Knight
Ethan Koska
Evan Kowalski
Byl Kravetz
Brian Lambert
Clay Lambert
Jeremy Lambert
Andrew Langler
Dave Lawrence
Alexander Le
Paul Lizer
Richard Long
Oliver Longchamps
Joseph Lopez
Kyle Lorenzi
Charles Lower
Steven Ludtke
Brooke Lyons
John M
Richard Maier
Ryan Mallet
Chris Malone
Brian Mansur
Robert Marchi
Jacob Margheim
Deven Marincovich
Cory Marko

Lucas Martin
Pawel Martin
Trevor Martin
Phillip Martinez
Joshua Martinez
Tao Mason
Ashley Mateo
Mark Maurice
Simon Mayeski
Kyle McCarley
Quinn McCusker
Alan McDonald
Caleb McDonald
Hans McIlveen
Rachel McIntosh
Jason McMarrow
Joshua McMaster
Colin McPherson
Christopher Menkhaus
Jim Mern
Robert Mertz
Pete Micale
Mike Mieszcak
Ted Milker
Jacob Montagne
Mitchell Moore
Matteo Morelli
William Morris
Alex Morstadt
Nicholas Mukanos
Vinesh Narayan
Bennett Nickels
Trevor Nielsen

Andrew Niesent	Brian Robinson
Sean Noble	Daniel Robitaille
Otto Noda	Paul Roder
Brett Noll-Emmick	Chris Rollini
Greg Nugent	Thomas Roman
Christina Nymeyer	Joyce Roth
Timothy O'Connor	Andrew Ruiz
Grant Odom	David Sanford
Colin O'neill	Chris Sapero
Ryan O'neill	Jaysn Schaener
Tyler Ornelas	Landon Schaule
James Owens	Shayne Schettler
David Parker	Andrew Schmidt
Eric Pastorek	Brian Schmidt
Zac Petersen	Kurt Schneider
Corey Pfleiger	William Schweisthal
Dupres Pina	Anthony Scimeca
Pete Plum	Preston Scott
Paul Polanski	Aaron Seaman
Matthew Pommerening	Phillip Seek
Nathan Poplawski	Christopher Shaw
Jeremiah Popp	Charles Sheehan
Chancey Porter	Wendell Shelton
Brian Potts	Brett Shilton
Chris Pourteau	Vernetta Shipley
Chris Prats	Glenn Shotton
Joshua Purvis	Joshua Sipin
Max Quezada	Christopher Slater
T.J. Recio	Scott Sloan
Jacob Reynolds	Daniel Smith
Eric Ritenour	Michael Smith
Walt Robillard	Sharroll Smith
Joshua Robinson	Michael Smith

Tyler Smith
Alexander Snyder
John Spears
Thomas Spencer
Peter Spitzer
Dustin Sprick
Graham Stanton
Paul Starck
Ethan Step
Seaver Sterling
Maggie Stewart-Grant
John Stockley
Rob Strachan
William Strickler
Shayla Striffler
Kevin Summers
Ernest Sumner
Carol Szpara
Travis TadeWaldt
Daniel Tanner
Lawrence Tate
Tim Taylor
Robert Taylor
Justin Taylor
Daniel Thomas
Steven Thompson
Chris Thompson
William Joseph Thorpe
Beverly Tierney
Kayla Todd
Matthew Townsend
Jameson Trauger

Cole Trueblood
Scott Tucker
Eric Turnbull
Brandon Turton
Dylan Tuxhorn
Jalen Underwood
Paul Van Dop
Paden VanBuskirk
Patrick Varrassi
Daniel Vatamaniuck
Jose Vazquez
Josiah Velazquez
Anthony Wagnon
Humberto Waldheim
Christopher Walker
David Wall
Justin Wang
Andrew Ward
Scot Washam
John Watson
Ben Wheeler
Jack Williams
Scott Winters
Samuel Wolfe
Jason Wright
John Wurtz
Ethan Yerigan
Phillip Zaragoza
Brandt Zeeh
Nathan Zoss